Having thoroughly enjoyed the first two books in this series, *Beauty Unveiled* and *Glory Revealed*, I was more than excited to hear that Paula would be completing the trilogy with **Grace Extended.** I was then deeply honored to be given the opportunity to get a first look at the anxiously awaited manuscript. Oh my—it did not disappoint!

Though it may sound strange, I have to say, **Grace Extended**—in my opinion—is more painting than book. Vibrant strokes of beauty, pain, loss, and betrayal kiss the gently muted hues of love, forgiveness, and ultimately, redemption, creating something so real you want to reach out and touch the virtual landscape. Paula's skillful mastery of word and (seemingly endless) knowledge of period, language, histories, and human nuance, add depth, texture, and breath to the page, making you read a little faster than intended, so great is your need to see what happens next.

From beginning to end, I found myself drawn deeply into her expert brush work, and in the end felt I had been left with something quite breathtaking. I genuinely wanted to stand back, hands clasped behind my back and quietly ponder—as one might in the Louvre when spending time with a work they love and are reluctant to leave.

When I closed the book and stepped away, my final thought was—Monet's *Water Lilies*…in word. Simply lovely.

I cannot wait to see her next work.

Barbie Loflin
author of *I Wish Someone Had Told Me*

Mrs. Parker has done it again. **Grace Extended** is the crown jewel of the *Sisters of Lazarus* series. In her masterful style, she brings color to the greatest story ever told, transporting the reader into the very midst of the lives of its characters. Its intrigue is transcendent and transformative, not only inspiring but motivating. A *Must Read*!

Donna Williams
Vice-President, EPIC Ministries, Inc.

Fully capturing the tension and drama of the early church, *Grace Extended* is an explosive read that I could not put down! From tears through moments of worship, Paula K. Parker's **Grace Extended** led me on a true journey of faith, and inspires me to cling even closer to Christ. Set against the backdrop of the Roman oppression of occupied Jerusalem, the reader follows the history of the early Christian Church through the lives of the characters so vividly portrayed.

Mary's journey of unanswered questions to difficult life events as she learns to lay her complete trust in Jesus when all she has is faith is just one facet of **Grace Extended.** The reader also follows the stories of other characters found in the book of Acts, and from the previous two books in the series.

Deep, moving, inspiring, and masterful!

Tracy H.Sugg
Sculptor, Fine Art Bronze & Monuments
Sculpture that Reflects a Touch of the Infinite

Paula Parker has transformed the characters of the Bible during Jesus' life and after his crucifixion, into real people with vibrant relationships. I have found a deeper appreciation and awareness for how very complicated and alive these people and their situations really were. Accurate historical information combined with creative storytelling makes **Grace Extended** a must read.

Francine Locke
Producer, ElFilm Productions,

In today's modern world value and self-esteem issue abound. It's as if a cruel joke has been played on humankind whereby the traits that are really valuable have been diminished and the outward, temporal things have been inflated beyond measure. As I read *Sisters of Lazarus: Beauty Unveiled* I saw this reality in a new way. I traded my 'I'm not worth much' tag for 'I'm extremely valuable to God.'

This book is captivating—I couldn't put it down—and brings to life that which is most important."

Monica Schmelter
General Manager, WHTN-TV

In *Sisters of Lazarus*, Paula K. Parker pens a riveting story of love, longing and faith. Parker's novels bear the profoundly satisfying mark of her gift as a playwright. She combines masterful storytelling with well-crafted dialogue. The result is a cast of Biblical characters fresh and human and real.

Through the eyes of Lazarus, Mary, and Martha the reader eagerly connects with three siblings from a normal, dysfunctional family. Gone are the dusty, unapproachable characters of Sunday school. Set in Bethany, 2,000 years ago, Parker breaks the time barrier with her brilliant use of cultural detail. The veil lifts, and we are brought face to face with flesh and blood people who jump off the pages and into our 21st century world. We resonate with their struggles, dreams, delights, disappointments, and the unpredictable ways God continually touches the human heart. Thank you Paula for giving powerful new voice to another ageless story."

Bonnie Keen
Dove Award winning recording artist

Paula K. Parker captivates her readers with an intimate look at a miraculous and timeless story of true beauty. *Sisters of Lazarus* not only gives a unique perspective on what it must have been like to walk with Jesus and bask in His love, but the Bible comes alive giving the reader a new appreciation for the story of Mary, Martha, and Lazarus—unveiling a beautiful story that has never been told!"

Holly McClure
Producer, film critic

Paula K. Parker offers an artistic tale of intersecting lives, fractured self-worth, hearts held prisoner to their legalistic perspectives, and in the middle of it all is Jesus. Though she tells a story set centuries ago, it is no different from our stories today. And she offers us the same hope. The hope that Jesus is in the middle of our 'stuff' too."

Denise Hildreth Jones
Author of *Reclaiming Your Heart*

GRACE EXTENDED

GRACE EXTENDED

Sisters of *Lazarus*
Book Three

PAULA K. PARKER

WordCrafts Press

And we know that in all things God works for the good of those who love him, who have been called according to his purpose.

Romans 8:28

Once, there was a young girl whose father died, and she was mistreated by her step-mother and two step-sisters.

Once, there was a young boy who believed the lies of a wicked queen and betrayed his brother, two sisters, and their friends.

Once, there were three men who refused to worship an idol and were thrown into a fire.

Once, there was a man who was sick and his sisters sent for their friend, who had the power to heal. But the friend didn't come, and the brother died.

Once, there was a man who was wrongfully crucified.

In each of these cases, we put a period at the end of the sentence. However, our punctuation is wrong. God uses a semi-colon and finishes the story, for His glory!

Whatever is going on in your life, remember;

> *—but God…*

Jill Windham
Lead Pastor, Movement Church

Forgiveness is the fragrance
a flower leaves upon the heel that crushes it.

PART ONE

Chapter 1

7 Sivan 3793

*T*he world mocked Abel.

As a child, Sivan was his favorite month. The early spring, with its soft winds, lured him out of doors to run in grass a shade of green that went beyond description, amidst flowers opening their blossoms in a rainbow of colors. When he grew into a man, he still enjoyed the signs that winter had passed, and life had returned to the earth.

But now, the wind carried the putrid stench of foul decay. His sandals slipped over sharp stones as he descended the steep ravine into the Valley of Hinnom. Even the trees that grew around the upper edge were misshapen and skeletal. Instead of mounds of soft grass and flowers, wherever he looked, Abel saw mountains of burning trash sending up smoke that hovered as a pale shroud, blocking all signs of life.

The Valley of Hinnom twisted around the western and southern walls of Jerusalem. Channels under the city carried rainwater, trash, human waste, and debris to empty into the valley. To keep the channels from clogging up, Governor Pontius Pilate arranged for slaves to catch the slop in buckets and dump it into mounds, where other slaves would burn it. Wild dogs, feral cats, and unclean carrion eaters—crows and rats—roamed over the mounds, sniffing, digging, and fighting to find food.

Other people scuttled around the valley, trying to get to each mound before the slave carrying the burning torch arrived, screaming and waving at the animals, in hopes of finding discarded clothing or food. Some of the people were poor, but others were from the cluster of caves that pocked the edge of the valley. They had been driven out of Jerusalem to live there, alone and separate. Not because of anything they had done, but because of what they were.

Lepers.

On the far side, near the caves, stood a man. Arms crossed, chin lifted, he glared at the valley—and the people—as if it were his kingdom. Joktan ben Philemon; Abel's father.

Without forethought, Abel grasped the sides of his garments to shake off the dust and lifted a hand to smooth his beard and adjust his head covering. Even in this valley of death and decay, his father would berate him for the slightest speck of dirt on his garments. He smoothed the cloth covering the basket he carried and began picking his way across the valley.

He kept his eyes focused on where he stepped; there was no need to speak to slaves or the poor—they were beneath him. He wove wide paths to avoid the lepers with skin the color of maggots and covered with open wounds; on some, the disease had progressed, and they were missing parts of their feet, hands, ears, or noses. He stopped when he came to a line of stones laid across the ground and waited.

"You are late!" The voice was gravelly, the words slurred. "You have to be at the Temple soon. The sacrifice waits for no man."

Taking a deep breath, Abel softly expelled it as he lifted his head to look at his father. A short time ago, it was common to hear people comment he was a younger version of his father. Now, no one would say that.

Joktan ben Philemon was shorter than his son, but Abel knew he was standing on his toes to give the appearance of added height. His white tunic and black robe hung loosely, evidence of him having lost weight. His head was covered, but the patches that were left of his beard were whiter than his skin. Joktan reached up to scratch an oozing, ulcerous spot on his cheek, pulling away a swollen lump of fetid flesh the size of a tetradrachm.

Abel swallowed hard to keep from vomiting. From what he had observed, his father felt no pain from the leprous spots; as such he often injured himself unknowingly.

Joktan saw his son's reaction and grinned. He examined the rotting mass clinging to his fingers and lifted his hand to fling it at his son.

"Aaaiiieee!" Abel jumped to avoid being hit. It landed beyond his feet. A rat scurried to pick it up and run away.

Joktan clasped his sides, laughing. "Abel, you have the stomach of a woman! I was not aiming to hit you; you have to remain ceremonially clean today. Enough!" He wiped the drool from his mouth. "I am hungry. What did you bring?"

Abel set the basket beyond the line of rocks and stepped back. The Law given to Moses stated that a person with leprosy must wear torn cloths, let his hair be unkempt, cover the lower part of his face and cry out, "Unclean!" to keep other people from coming too close. The Traditions of the Elders took it further and stated that a leper could not come within four cubits of an Israelite.

Joktan saw no reason why he would have to leave the Valley of Hinnom. He was not going to beg. "Why should I, when my family will bring me what I need?" As such, his garments remained whole and his face, with its rotting flesh, uncovered. To uphold the Traditions of the Elders, he laid a line of rocks exactly four cubits from the entrance to his cave. This would prevent Abel from coming too close and thereby becoming unclean.

Not that Father cares about my being clean so I may enter the Temple to worship. Abel thought, watching his father ripping apart the bread and cheese to shove into his mouth and washing the food down with a swig from the wineskin. *He needs me clean so I can approach Rabbi Caiaphas and Rabbi Annas.*

Every day, Abel brought food, clothing, whatever his father needed. While Joktan ate—which was difficult to watch, as the leprosy had spread to his mouth, causing him to bite off parts of his lips and tongue—he would riddle Abel with questions and instructions.

"Tell your mother the bread is hard again. *Racha!* Foolish, worthless woman! She cannot prepare even the simplest food."

"Yes, Father."

"This tunic had a spot. Tell your sister she is *racha* just like her mother. If she does not change, no one will ever wish to marry her." He cocked an eye at his son. "Do not let any man come sniffing around her. She will not have my permission to marry until I am healed."

"Yes, Father."

Joktan kept quizzing his son about his mother and sister, charging him with judgements and instructions. Abel's answer was always, "Yes, Father."

Joktan's interrogation turned to his son. His studies. "What does Rabbi Gamaliel say? I will not tolerate less than perfection."

"Yes, Father. I am studying hard. Rabbi Gamaliel was kind enough to praise my work."

Joktan grunted. "What about this man who also studies with Gamaliel? The one called Saul?"

"Saul Paulus. Paulus is his family's name."

"Using a Roman name," Joktan spat, "and not honoring his father with the traditional *ben* or *bar* before his father's name. What else do you know about him?"

"I know little," Abel suppressed a sigh, "as he speaks little of his family. I know he was born in Tarsus in Cilicia, which makes him a Jew *and* a Roman citizen. The time we are together at the Temple, he only focuses on studying the Holy Scriptures, the Law Yahweh gave to Moses, and the Traditions of the Elders."

After the fall of Israel as a sovereign kingdom, the Pharisees and teachers were concerned the Law would become diluted, merging with beliefs of the pagan nations who ruled over them. As a result, the Pharisees and teachers expanded their interpretation of the Law to regulate every aspect of Jewish life. These interpretations— known as 'The Traditions of the Elders'—were considered by the Pharisees and teachers to be as binding as the Law itself.

As soon as he spoke about Saul's devotion to his studies, Abel knew what his father's response would be. *You would do well to have such focus.*

"You would do well to have such focus." Joktan glared. "Why are you smiling?"

"Ah… I… uh… I'm thinking about the day you will be healed,"

the lie slid off Abel's lips, "and will be able to return to your duties at the Temple."

Joktan's lips split, bleeding as he grinned. "I look forward to that day as well." A frown creased his brow. "But, as long as you are lazy, that day will never come. What information do you have to present to Rabbi Caiaphas and Rabbi Annas? Have you discovered who stole the body of the Nazarene? Do you know where his followers hid it?"

"I have not discovered those things."

"*Racha!* You are a fool like your mother and sister! Have you watched these followers of the Nazarene, as I instructed you?"

"Yes, Father."

"Where do they go?"

"They go to the Temple. To the marketplace. To each other's houses."

"What do they do in those houses?"

Abel blinked in surprise. "How would I learn that, Father? They do not extend the hospitality of their homes to me."

"You can ask their servants."

"Why would they tell me anything?"

"A few coins loosen many a lip."

Abel gaped at his father. "You want me to pay servants to betray the people they work for?"

Joktan shrugged. "It worked for Judas." He nodded his head toward the right. "It happened over there."

"What?"

"Where Judas *hanged* himself. Do you see that tree?" He pointed. "The one there on that southern slope, just before the Hinnom joins the Kidron Valley?"

Abel nodded.

"That is where Judas did it. Everyone," he spread his arms wide, encompassing the people wandering over the burning mounds of trash, "talks about it They tell the same story Rabbi Caiaphas' servant Malchus told. Judas threw a rope over that tree, tied it around his neck, and *stepped* off the edge of the ravine." He harrumphed. "It did not kill him right away. He writhed and squirmed, his body swinging back and forth. Then the tree branch broke and he fell," he pointed, "on those sharp rocks at the base of the ravine. His body burst open. The dogs ate well that day." Joktan grinned. "Those who saw it happen said that, before he jumped, Judas cried out, 'I betrayed innocent blood.'"

"That is the same thing he said that day," Abel swallowed, "when the Nazarene died." He remembered. He had been there. He had been up the one to speak with Judas, his childhood friend, about the teacher from Nazarene.

Judas ben Shimon was the son of a wealthy banker in Jerusalem. When he was ten, Judas went with his mother and sister to visit family in Galilee. During their absence, his father was accused of stealing from a Roman client. His wealth could not save him. He was arrested, tried, and found guilty before a mock court, and crucified. No one heard anything more about his family until last year, when Judas showed up in Bethany. Calling himself Judas *Iscariot*—after the town in Kerioth where he and his mother and sister had fled to avoid the Romans—he was a follower of the teacher from Nazareth, Jesus ben Joseph. Abel later learned that Judas was more than a disciple; he was also *Sicarii*; a secret group of zealots who plotted to subvert and overthrow the authority of Rome.

The High Priest, Rabbi Caiaphas, Rabbi Annas—Caiaphas' father-in-law—along with other Temple leaders, were concerned with the growing popularity of the Nazarene teacher. Abel remembered how proud he felt when his father volunteered him to watch Jesus ben Joseph and find a way to arrange a meeting between him and the Temple leaders.

Days before the week of Passover, Abel had seen Jesus and his twelve disciples go to the house of his cousin Martha and her husband, Simon. Later that evening, he had seen Judas leave. He followed Judas and convinced him to speak with the Temple leaders. During that meeting, the High Priest had offered the disciple thirty pieces of silver to arrange a meeting with Jesus. Several days later, Abel had learned that Rabbi Caiaphas and Rabbi Annas did not want to talk to Jesus. They wanted to kill him.

On the night of Passover, Abel and his father had gone with

Judas and a detachment of Temple Guards out of the Water Gate, through the Kidron Valley, to the garden in the Mount of Olives, a place where—Judas explained—the Nazarene would often go to pray. Jesus had been arrested and endured a night of multiple trials before the Jewish leaders, the Roman Governor Pontius Pilate, and even the Tetrarch Herod Antipas.

During one of the times Pilate was examining the Nazarene, Abel and his father—along with other Temple leaders—had been walking in the tunnel leading from the Antonia Fortress to the Holy Temple. Rabbi Nicodemus ben Melech and his son Michael had stopped the High Priest and accused the Temple leaders of violating their Law in their treatment of Jesus.

The High Priest had waved away Rabbi Nicodemus' accusations.

"Jesus ben Joseph condemned himself when he pronounced himself the son of Yahweh," the High Priest had said. "Pilate and Herod are merely the means to his death."

"Death?!" The word, coming from behind them, echoed in the tunnel.

They turned. Judas stood a short distance from them; the light from the torch cast bizarre shadows on his face.

Judas rushed toward the priests, but Caiaphas' servant Malchus jumped in-between the disciple and the High Priest, arms spread wide.

"Death?" the disciple choked on the word. He looked from Caiaphas to Annas. "You told me you only wanted to speak with the Teacher. You cannot do this! I cannot do this! Jesus ben Joseph is innocent!" He reached into the girdle at his waist and drew out a leather bag. It clinked as he extended it to Caiaphas. "Here! Take back your blood money. I have sinned! I have betrayed innocent blood!"

The High Priest glanced at the bag in Judas' hand. "What is your sin to us?" he asked. "That is your responsibility."

He turned and gestured to his father-in-law to precede him into the Temple.

"Aiiiieeeee!" Judas screamed as he lifted the bag to throw it at Caiaphas.

Chaos erupted in the tunnel. Shouts echoed against the stone walls. Abel remembered everyone ducking, throwing their arms over their heads, or jumping back against the tunnel's wall. The bag missed the High Priest and hit one of the marble columns. The cord around the neck of the bag loosened as it fell. Coins skittered across the Temple floor.

Screaming curses at the priests and at himself, Judas had turned and ran out of the tunnel.

Later, they learned from Malchus that the Nazarene's disciple had hanged himself. Abel frowned, remembering Rabbi Caiaphas suggesting since *he* was unclean—having gone into the Roman praetorium—he could see to Judas' burial. The Temple leaders had given him the thirty pieces of silver to buy the potter's field as a burial ground for strangers.

He had used some of the coins to hire two Gentiles to bury the body, but he did not know it was *there*, Abel turned to look, *on that tree,* that Judas had died. *I did not want to know that,* Abel thought. He shook his head, trying to clear the image of Judas hanging on that tree, falling, his body bursting open. There was a lot about that day that he wanted to forget.

"Abel!"

He tore his eyes away from the tree and looked at his father.

"Offer coins to the servants of *that man's* followers."

"Father, the only ones I know who followed him—who are wealthy enough to have servants—are Rabbi Nicodemus and Rabbi Joseph bar Neriah from Arimathea."

Rage tightened Joktan's skin, causing several pustules to burst open. "*Racha!* You fool!" Abel had to step back to avoid his father's spittle. "Today is Pentecost, the Feast of First Fruits! It has been over fifty days since Yahweh smote me with leprosy for allowing the followers of *that man* to live! Once they are *all* dead, Yahweh will heal me." Reaching down, Joktan picked up the basket and threw it at the nearest mound of burning trash. The fire flared as it consumed the basket and cloth. "May all of the people who follow *that man* burn in the fires of Gehenna." He looked at Abel. "Now *go!*"

Abel turned to leave but jerked back as a pack of wild dogs ran past him to leap on a nearby mound, growling and fighting, snatching at something on the ground, ripping whatever it was they had found. *It is a dead animal,* he thought. *A bird. Or rat.*

"One less Roman *pig*," Joktan retorted. When he saw the unspoken question on Abel's face, he grinned, and not pleasantly. "I saw the soldier bring it this morning. A woman was following him, screaming and squawking about, *'Her baby.'*"

Abel's eyes widened as he gaped at his father.

"The other lepers explained it to me," Joktan shrugged. "If a Roman woman gives birth to a child that is sickly, deformed—or *worse, a girl*—it is taken outside of the city and left on a trash heap."

One of the dogs ran past; Abel saw a small arm in its mouth.

As I said," Joktan smiled, his lips and tongue bleeding, "one less Roman pig."

As his father clutched his sides laughing, Abel bent over and vomited.

Chapter 2

*M*ary woke to threads of sunlight tickling her eyes. Looking toward the windows on the eastern wall, she saw light peeking through the shutters to slant across her bed chamber.

Our bed chamber, she smiled, turning to look around the room that had been hers and Michael's since the day, over seven weeks ago, when he came to take her home as his bride.

It had been an ordinary day—*if you could call any of the days following the resurrection of the Lord Jesus to be ordinary.* She and Abigail had been helping Martha pack their belongings. Even though their Uncle Joktan was no longer a threat to them, the High Priest was watching the Lord Jesus' followers, spreading lies that some of them had stolen His body, which would have been a crime against the Roman Empire. Simon and Lazarus thought it best if they left the area for a while. Once Abigail gave birth, Lazarus planned to take his wife and child to Cyprus, while Simon and Martha were going to Gaul. Rabbi Joseph ben Neriah of Arimathea, a member of the Sanhedrin and Rabbi Nicodemus' friend, had asked to journey with them.

Mary was supposed to go with Simon and Martha. Even though she did not want to leave her newly betrothed husband, Michael had told her, *"I understand that you must go with your brother or sister. But I wanted you to know, before you left, that you were* betrothed to me. *No matter where you go, no matter where you are, I will find you. Be waiting for me, for this I vow: I will come for you."*

That day Martha, claiming pregnancy-related fatigue, had suggested they bathe and lie down to rest. Mary was sleeping in her bed chamber when Martha—along with her friends Ruth and Leah—had rushed in to announce *Michael was coming for her.* It took her several moments to realize that *it was her wedding day.*

The next several hours were a lovely dream. Mary felt like a queen in the beautiful garments that her mother and sister had both worn for their own weddings. Michael, dressed like a king, arrived to escort her to his father's house. There, amidst their family and friends, blessings were spoken, and the wedding feast began. Amidst the laughter and blessings, a voice spoke. *"I wish to speak of the bride."*

Mary had recognized that rich, well-modulated voice and turned to see the Lord Jesus walking toward them. A gasp had ripped around the room at His sudden appearance and all grew quiet to hear what He had to say.

He had looked at Michael. *"You are a blessed man, Michael ben Nicodemus. Yahweh has given you a beautiful bride; but her beauty goes beyond face and form."* He turned to smile at her. *"Mary is gentle and kind. She loves Yahweh and seeks to use that love to serve others. This is the beauty I speak of and this beauty is eternal."*

"Thank you, Teacher," Michael had said and grinned at her. *"I agree with you."*

As the room erupted into laughter, the Lord Jesus had stepped closer to her and Michael. *"May Yahweh bless you with many years of joy in each other and in your children."*

Her eyes filled with tears. She had thanked Him for coming to their wedding feast, adding, *"I hope someday to attend your wedding."*

"I promise you, Mary," He had smiled, *"you will."*

As the guests gathered around the Teacher, Mary had heard Michael whisper her name. Looking she saw him standing, with a hand extended to her.

"Come away with me, my Beloved."

She realized, by reciting the love poem of King Solomon, Michael was indicating it was time to consummate their marriage. Her heart still raced as she remembered taking his hand and looking into his face, whispering the Beloved's response, *"I belong to my Lover, and his desire is for me."*

Drawing her hand through his arm, he had led her to *this* chamber. She looked around the room; *our bed chamber.*

The room was larger than her bed chamber in the home of her

childhood. Although unlit, lamp stands placed around the room gave off the scent of perfumed oil. The walls were covered in tapestries of flowers and pomegranates made by Michael's mother and by her own mother. *May their memories be blessed.* Along one wall there were several carved chests for holding their clothing and a wash table with a bowl and pitcher and a small stack of folded linen towels. Near the wash table was her dressing table—Michael had arranged for that to be brought from her old bed chamber—where she kept combs, ribbons for her hair, bottles of perfume, her jewelry box—and a mirror. The polished metal was in a bronze frame and stand that allowed the mirror to be tilted. This was a wedding gift from Martha and Lazarus and was similar to one she had given her sister.

The table held another wedding gift from her siblings; her alabastron. Carved from white alabaster, it was about the length of her hand, flaring from a long, delicate neck into a wider base. Sealed inside the alabastron had been a pint of pure spikenard. The warm musky perfumed oil was so treasured that a pint of it was worth more than 300 denarii.

It had been part of her dowry, to be saved for her wedding; yet she had poured the oil over the head and feet of the Lord Jesus. While it shocked all present, the Lord Jesus had said that what she had done was, "beautiful."

She did not see her alabastron again, until the night of her marriage to Michael. That was when she learned her brother and sister had refilled the alabastron and arranged to have it brought here, to their bed chamber. The alabastron was empty, but she kept it as a remembrance of love.

Next to their bed—a thick pallet on a wooden frame—was a small table with two cups and an *amphora* filled with water.

On a table near the window was a large urn filled with flowers. She smiled. That was Michael's doing. He knew she loved flowers and, since the night of their wedding, he had seen to it that the urn was always filled with flowers. *I do not know what he will do during the winter months.* But, knowing her husband, he would figure out something.

My husband. The thought washed over her like the sunlight. *Thank you, Yahweh, for blessing me with a husband who loves You and loves me.* She rolled on her side to look at Michael.

The linen coverings on their bed draped a body that was tall and muscular. Dark lashes lay on chiseled cheeks. She reached over to twist a black curl around her finger, causing a hair to brush his nose. She let go of the hair, pulling her hand back when Michael shook his head, snorted, and rubbed his nose before throwing an arm above his head.

A moment later, he opened his mouth and puffed out a soft snore.

Mary bit back a laugh and put a hand beneath his jaw to gently close his mouth. Her hand was still on his jaw when Michael startled and opened his eyes. She shifted her hand to his cheek as he turned his head to look at her.

He smiled. "Good morning, my Beloved."

"Good morning, my Lover."

"What a beautiful sight to wake up to." Reaching up, he took her hand and carried it to his lips.

"Ahh…thank you, my husband." She scooted over to lay her head in the hollow of his shoulder. "I never tire of waking up next to you. I wish we could stay here all day."

He stroked her back. "Why can we not?"

She sighed. "Because we have commitments."

"Let us ignore those commitments." He leaned down to kiss her.

"We cannot. Today is Pentecost, the Feast of Ingathering. You and your father have responsibilities at the Temple. I promised I would oversee the food for the followers in the upper room of the warehouse. Those people have been praying all night; by now, they will be hungry."

"Let them pray that Yahweh will send manna from Heaven." He leaned in for another lingering kiss.

"Michael." She pushed him gently away. "You know we cannot."

"As you wish." Michael flopped onto his back, blowing out his cheeks. "Although I do not understand why, since Pentecost is a day of rest from ordinary labor, a couple newly married cannot be alone to," he smiled at her, "*rest.* Perhaps I should ask Rabbi Gamaliel this question."

Color bloomed in Mary's cheeks. "Michael, you would not."

"I will not, but it does not seem right." Pursing his lips, he slanted a glance at her.

"Michael ben Nicodemus," she laughed, "you are pouting like a young child."

He lifted his eyebrows. "Is it working?"

Mary laughed. "No, my Lover; it is not." She rolled over and stood. "Besides taking food to those praying," she crossed to the wash table and poured water into the bowl, "we have guests. Ruth and I must oversee the meal Elisheba and the other servants prepared last night. This will give the servants a day of rest, so they might celebrate the feast day." She paused to wash her face. Lifting a towel, she turned toward Michael while patting her skin dry. "You and your father are taking Ruth and me to the warehouse before going with the other men to the Temple for the sacrifice; is that right?"

"Yes."

"Then we had better hurry." She set the towel aside and crossed to open a chest and selected a cream-colored tunic and moss-green girdle and head cloth. "As my father and grandfather—may their memories be blessed—used to say, 'The sacrifice waits for no man.'"

Chapter 3

*L*eaving Michael dressing in their bed chamber, Mary walked through several corridors, down the stairs, and through another corridor—*Will I ever get used to living in a such a large house? At least I no longer get lost in it*—before turning into the dining room.

The size of the room would allow for a great number of people to partake of a meal without feeling confined. In the center, four low tables with thick cushions placed on the floor beneath them, formed a rectangle to allow the diners to see each other. Limestone tables against each wall held platters covered with linen cloths and amphorae beading with condensation.

A young servant girl was moving around the room, filling tall lamps with oil. She turned and bowed her head when Mary entered.

"Good morning—Jemima, is it not?" Mary asked.

The young girl lifted her head, almond eyes crinkling as she smiled. Tendrils of ebony hair escaped the head cloth to curl around her face. "Good morning, Mistress. Yes, my name is Jemima; Jemima bat Eder. It is kind of you to remember."

"It is a blessing I remember," Mary returned the girl's smile. "There are so many servants in my husband's house. I am determined to learn all of their names." She looked around. "Has my sister-in-law come down for breakfast?"

"Your sister-in-law is here now."

Mary turned to see Ruth crossing the tiled floor.

Dressed in a soft yellow linen tunic, Mary's close friend—and now her sister-in-law—was petite, with delicate features, full red lips, and almond shaped eyes. Beneath a wheat-colored head cloth, Ruth's thick braid fell straight to her waist.

"Good morning, Mary. Good morning, Jemima."

Jemima bowed her head. "Good morning, mistress." The servant bowed her head to Ruth and moved away to continue filling the lamps.

"What shall we do first?" Ruth asked.

Mary smiled at her sister-in-law's gentle reminder that, as wife to Michael, *she* was now mistress of this household. "We need to make certain there is sufficient food for breakfast. Jemima? Would you please ask Elisheba if she has a moment to speak with us?"

"Yes, mistress. At once." She bowed her head and left the room.

Ruth followed Mary as they crossed to the limestone tables to lift the cloths covering the platters. "Bread," Mary said. "Cheese. Dates. Grapes."

Ruth peered into the amphorae. "With milk and water to drink. This is more than Father eats for breakfast. He generally prefers just bread and milk."

"I know," Mary furrowed her brow, "but with guests in the house—"

Ruth nodded. "You are correct. That does make a difference to him." She smiled. "He will appreciate you wanting to honor our guests."

"Good morning, mistresses."

Mary and Ruth turned as Elisheba bat Penuel entered the room.

Tucking wisps of grey hair back into her head covering, the servant's simple, sand-colored tunic shifted over broad hips as she walked towards them. Elisheba had seen more than fifty summers; she was twelve when she had come to this house as a handmaiden to Hannah bat Mattaniah, Rabbi Nicodemus' new bride. She was present for the birth of each of Hannah's children, caring for the mother and infant with a dedication born of love. When Hannah died giving birth to Ruth, Elisheba cared for Rabbi Nicodemus and his motherless children with the same firm but loving hand she used to oversee the house.

Michael told Mary his father had repeatedly offered the faithful servant a pension, so she could retire, but she would not hear of it. "Mistress Hannah brought me here. I would not dishonor her memory by abandoning her children." It did not matter that Mistress Hannah's children were old enough to care for themselves.

So Elisheba stayed, overseeing the house—and family—of her beloved Mistress Hannah. When Michael brought Mary home as his bride, Elisheba saw in her another motherless child to love.

Returning her greeting, Mary said, "Thank you for making this wonderful breakfast. I know our guests will be pleased."

"You are kind to speak thus, mistress," Elisheba smiled, "but I would not want guests of this house to think we did not feed them well. As my grandmother—may her memory be blessed—always said, 'The goose bends its head while walking, but its eyes wander about.'"

Mary bit her tongue to keep from smiling. Elisheba sprinkled her conversation with things that her grandmother had said. That the quotes had nothing to do with the topic at hand meant nothing to the elderly woman.

"Yes, well," she glanced at Ruth, who was smiling and nodding at Elisheba, "I am sure you are right. Now, about the food for those who are praying at my brother and Simon's warehouse. Is there anything Ruth and I can do to help? We will be leaving with the men once breakfast is finished."

"Mistress Mary," Elisheba pursed her lips, "leave the cooking and cleaning to the servants. You will soon have *other* responsibilities." She raised her eyebrows, nodding toward Mary's abdomen.

Mary felt her cheeks redden. From the first week of their marriage, Elisheba made it clear what she believed Mary's *responsibility* to be: bearing Michael's children.

Elisheba opened her mouth, but the sound of voices in the corridor forestalled her.

"Rabbi Nicodemus, I am truly confused." Mary recognized the voice of Peter bar Jonah, the fisherman who had left his boat and nets to follow the Lord Jesus. She breathed a sigh of relief. Whatever Elisheba might say to her in private—or before other women—save for Michael, the older servant would never embarrass her in front of any man.

"As I was saying, the food you requested is ready. When you wish to leave, I will have it sent to the carriage," the older woman said as Nicodemus and Michael escorted a dozen men—including Peter and the rest of the Twelve—into the dining room. She turned to bow her head to the men. "Good morning, Rabbi Nicodemus. Good morning, sirs. The meal is ready." She indicated the side tables. "As my grandmother—may her memory be blessed—used to say, 'A full belly and warm feet brings contentment to all men.'" Nodding her head once more, Elisheba left the room.

Mary suppressed a smile, noting the startled glances between their guests. Michael crossed to take her hand. Grinning, he lowered his voice, "Elisheba is in her element this morning."

"She is indeed," she whispered.

"She is always thus when we have guests." Michael said. "The more guests, the more things her grandmother had to say. Be prepared for an increase in her grandmother's wisdom, Beloved. I am certain she looks upon those who are praying at the warehouse as guests of this house."

Mary choked, but contented herself with a speaking glance at her husband before turning to greet her father-in-law.

There was nothing about her father-in-law's attire—white linen tunic, with a black robe and head covering—which suggested that not only was Nicodemus ben Melech one of the seventy members of the Sanhedrin, the highest religious council of the Jewish people, he was also one of the wealthiest men in the land. If Nicodemus' daughters looked like their mother, it was obvious from the rabbi's curly hair and beard—now more white than black—from which parent Michael got his looks.

"Ah, my beautiful daughters," Nicodemus embraced her and Ruth. "You know our Lord Jesus' closest disciples, Peter bar Jonah and Matthew bar Alpheus," he indicated the two disciples with a quiet smile. Nicodemus brought forward the tall man standing next to Matthew. "And I believe you know Matthias bar Esdras, who was chosen to replace…" he drew a quiet breath, "Judas Iscariot. I believe you also know Stephen ben Chariton," he indicated a man with dark hair and a ready smile, "one of our Jewish brothers from Greece who is also a believer in the Lord Jesus, and Joseph bar Achaicus," an older man with grey hair and a twinkle in his eyes, "who is from Cyprus." Father Nicodemus gestured to the young man at Peter's side. "Joseph is a relative of a young man I believe you know, John Mark ben Gershom."

"Good morning to you all," Mary smiled as she added the blessing of a host to a guest, "Peace be upon you."

"Good morning," the men added the guest's response. "And on you, peace."

"Father," Ruth said, "of course we know John Mark. His family's house is several streets over." She turned to the young man. "How is your mother doing? I understand she was not feeling well."

A few years older than Ruth and herself, John Mark was short, giving him the appearance of a child next to the men in the room. Dressed in a white tunic over a deep blue robe, he was slight of frame, with deep brown, wavy hair and dark eyes. He was the only son of Mary bat Simon. When John Mark's father died, his near kinsman, Joseph bar Achaicus, moved from Cyprus to Jerusalem, to help his mother raise the boy. Mary, Joseph, and John Mark were followers of the Lord Jesus.

"How kind you are to ask after Mother." A bashful smile lit John Mark's face. "She is better after spending time near the lake in Capernaum. Which reminds me," he turned toward Mary, "she asked me to tell you, 'Mazel tov.' We are sorry we were not in Jerusalem when your wedding took place. May Yahweh bless you with many years of joy." He looked at Michael. "You are a blessed man to have such a beautiful wife."

"Thank you, John Mark," Michael smiled at her. "I agree with you. My wife is beautiful, and I am blessed.

Two years ago, Mary would have preened to have men speak thus of her beauty. Now, when she thought of her appearance, she discounted it, mentally listing her features as Elisheba would list the food supply in the kitchen. *Shorter than Martha. Womanly curves. Thick wavy hair. Delicate features. Almond-shaped eyes.* Combined, she knew she had a physical beauty, but that was no longer important to her, except—she smiled at her husband—*when Michael looks at me.*

"You are both kind," Mary responded, "but what is beauty? Our Lord Jesus—may His name be blessed—spoke to me of Abraham's wife Sarah. He said she was beautiful, not because she had a face or form many men desired. She was beautiful because she was gentle and kind. She was beautiful because she loved and obeyed Yahweh and used that love to serve others.

"Like Mother Hannah bat Mattaniah, my husband's mother—may her memory be blessed." She smiled at Father Nicodemus. "Her names mean "grace" and "gift of Yahweh." I did not know her, as she died giving birth to Ruth, but from what my father-in-law tells me, she extended grace and love to everyone. *That* is how I wish to be remembered."

"Wisdom *and* beauty," Michael lifted her hand to kiss it, smiling into her eyes. "My wife is *a rare find.*"

Mary recognized the memory Michael referenced. It was the Passover after they had first met the Lord Jesus. She and Martha were serving the meal to their guests when she overheard Uncle Joktan talking to Rabbi Nicodemus. He was condemning the Teacher because He had healed a lame man, telling him his sins were forgiven. Michael had noticed her frown and had commented, *"You do not understand why your uncle focuses on what Jesus ben Joseph said and ignores the fact that a paralyzed man can now walk."*

She had nodded. *"Are not miracles from Yahweh? As my mother—may her memory be blessed—used to say, 'Two men look at the same bush; one man sees the thorns and calls it a weed, while the other man sees the flower and calls it a rose.'"*

Michael had smiled at her that night as he was smiling at her now. *"Wisdom and beauty—a rare find."*

Looking back, she realized *that* was the first moment she felt drawn to Michael. She shared a lingering smile with her husband, until a throat clearing brought her back to the present.

"My son," Nicodemus stroked his beard, "if you are finished smiling at your wife, I think our guests would like their breakfast."

Mary flushed while Michael grinned. Slanting a frown at her husband, she hurried over to help Ruth with the meal.

One thing she loved about her father-in-law was how he escorted each guest to their place at the table. No matter who they were—or their station in life—his grace and kindness made each feel their location at the meal was that of an honored guest.

Once everyone was seated and the food placed on the tables, she and Ruth sat as Father Nicodemus spoke the blessing over the meal.

"Blessed are You, Lord our God, Ruler of the universe, Who brings forth bread from the earth. Blessed are You, Lord our God, Ruler of the universe, Who creates the fruit of the tree. Blessed are You, Lord our God, Ruler of the universe, at Whose word all came to be. Amen."

The conversation over the table was lively and varied: the delicious food, comments Mary knew Elisheba would be pleased to hear. The crowds in town for Pentecost; while not as busy as Passover, Jerusalem would swell with Jewish people from around the Roman world. Those praying in the upper room of Lazarus and Simon's warehouse. John Mark's idea.

Indicating the young man, Father Nicodemus told Mary and Ruth, "This young man has a desire to write down the story of our Lord's life and ministry. It is a remarkable plan."

"You are kind, Rabbi Nicodemus," John Mark said. "I think it will help us not to forget what the Lord Jesus said and did while He was among us."

"It will help me spread the message of the Lord Jesus—may His name be blessed—when I go back to visit my family," Stephen said.

"And who will write this story?" Peter said. "I am not skilled at writing. It confuses me."

"I will write it," the young man said. "All you need to do is tell me what you remember, and I will write it down."

"Speaking of confusion," Rabbi Nicodemus turned to Peter, "During our earlier conversation, you mentioned being confused. Would you please explain?

The big fisherman dropped his bread and dusted his hands. "Rabbi Nicodemus, on the day the Lord Jesus—may His name be blessed—ascended, He told us to wait for the Holy Spirit to come. However, before the time of His...*arrest*," Peter swallowed hard, "He often spoke of a *comforter,* or a *counselor.* He said this person would be with us, to...guide us...and teach us." Peter turned to the other disciples with a questioning look. "Is that what you remember?"

The men nodded.

"I recall Him saying it was for our *good* that He would go away," John ben Zebedee said. "That unless He went away, this *counselor* would not come. And once the counselor came, he would convict the world of guilt."

Peter gestured towards John, "That is what I recall. Rabbi Nicodemus," He turned to the elderly rabbi, "what I am confused about is *who* is this *comforter*? Is he a person," he spread his arms wide, "as we are? If he is, how will we know that he is the one whom the Lord Jesus meant? And if the comforter is this *Holy Spirit*, what does that mean? Will we be able to see him? Will he appear to us, like the angels appeared to Mary Magdala at the Lord's tomb?"

Peter shook his head. "When the Lord Jesus was with us, none of us really knew *Who* He was. We thought He was the Messiah, but I—we—realize now we did not understand what that meant. I do not want this *comforter*, this *counselor*, to come and we not know him. Sir, I am not a scholar. I am a fisherman." He looked at Nicodemus, "What should we do?"

Mary's father-in-law lowered his brows as he stroked his beard. "Peter bar Jonah, you might not be a scholar, but you," he indicated the other disciples, "all of you, did something none of the Teachers in the Temple have done. You walked with the Lord Jesus daily for three years. That speaks much of your knowledge. As to your concern, on the day the Lord Jesus ascended, I recall you asking Him that same question: 'What should we do?'"

"I did."

"What was His answer?"

Peter looked at the other disciples and back at his host. "As I said; He told us to wait. To not leave Jerusalem but *wait* for the gift His Father promised."

Rabbi Nicodemus smiled. "Then my advice is to obey what the Lord Jesus said. *Wait.* You are welcome to stay here as our guests, however long is needed." He wiped his mouth with the edge of a linen napkin.

"In the meantime, I suggest we help Ruth and Mary take the food to those praying at Lazarus and Simon's warehouse." He stood.

"Afterwards, we men can go on to the Temple for the celebration of First Fruits. But we must hurry. Remember; the sacrifice waits for no man."

Chapter 4

$\mathcal{A}$bel crouched in the shadow of an old sycamore fig tree. The crowds walking toward the Temple would hide the sight of a single man, but he wanted to make sure he was not seen by any of the people coming and going from the building that belonged to his cousin Lazarus.

To obey the Law Yahweh gave Moses that the Passover meal should be eaten within the walls of Jerusalem, Lazarus' father, Abel's uncle Jacob—*I refuse to bless his memory*—had purchased a building in the Upper City, near the Xystus Market, the Temple, and the palace of King Herod.

Built of cut stone, the front room was large enough to host a meal for many people. During the year, his uncle—and later his cousin, Lazarus—used this building as a place of business. However, several days before Passover, their family would move into it as a temporary home in order to celebrate the holy day.

There was no such law concerning living within the walls of Jerusalem for the Feast of First Fruits. Since Abel had been watching those who followed the Nazarene, he noted there appeared to be many people coming and going to that building.

Abel had been inside that building many times. Abel's father—who had always been careful with his coin—did not spend money to host meals. Instead, his father assumed, as near kinsman to Lazarus and his sisters, it was his due for them to extend the hospitality of their Jerusalem home to celebrate Passover. Looking back, however, Abel never considered any of those meals as a *celebration*.

That stemmed from the hatred his father had for what the building represented. Joktan frequently railed about how his younger brother Jacob had decided not to follow in the honored footsteps of their ancestors and become a priest. Instead, he had joined relatives who owned several caravans. Jacob showed skill in buying and selling and eventually became a full partner.

Abel remembered the countless times his father had sworn he would never forgive his brother for the betrayal to their heritage. It did not matter to Joktan that Jacob's skill increased his relatives'—as well as his parents'—coffers. Nor did it matter to him that Jacob married the daughter of a Temple leader and had three children; Martha, Lazarus, and Mary.

The true source of Joktan's bitterness stemmed from the fact that no matter how he had tried—studying hard, obeying the Law to its smallest letter—it was obvious to Joktan their father loved Jacob more. Joktan denounced the wealth his brother accumulated, as well as everything his wealth bought. As far as Joktan was concerned, his brother's money had stolen his father's approval from him.

When Jacob was dying, Joktan had gone to visit his brother. He came home to inform Abel that he and Jacob had agreed Abel would marry his youngest cousin, Mary.

Abel drew his lips into a thin line. He had been proud when his father had told him of his impending betrothal to Mary. A wealthy wife was what every man wanted; that Mary was beautiful as the gold on the Temple walls was a secondary consideration. Not only would they have wealth and the power money could purchase, most important, Joktan said, they would finally prove that Abel's grandfather had been wrong in allowing Jacob to become a merchant.

But that was before last year, Abel snorted like a bull. It all began when his childhood friend, Judas *Iscariot* had shown up in Bethany as a disciple of Jesus ben Joseph.

Lazarus had invited the Nazarene and his twelve disciples to celebrate Passover with them. During the meal, Mary had shocked Abel with her shameful behavior by speaking with men who were not relatives. When he had chastised her for this, stating that when she became his wife more would be expected of her, she informed him they would never marry. She shamed him further by announcing in front of all present, "*...before I marry you, I will marry Michael ben Nicodemus, or Judas Iscariot, or even Jesus ben*

Joseph!" Over a year later, Mary's words still circled in his brain like vultures over a corpse.

Joktan was furious at Mary's inappropriate behavior, but Abel noted his father blamed *him* for the loss of Mary's dowry. Months later, when Martha and Mary *announced* Lazarus was dead, Joktan once again stated the money would come to him through a marriage between Abel and Mary. When Lazarus *pretended* to be resurrected—which his father asserted was an obvious ploy to make it appear that Jesus ben Joseph performed a miracle—once again Mary and her dowry were lost.

Abel straightened up, stretching his back, and jumped back when he saw his cousin Martha and her husband Simon bar Hiram walk up the street and enter the warehouse. The swell of Martha's belly through her robe announced her pregnancy to all. *Even Martha— whom all believed too plain to ever win a husband—is married and with child.*

A moment later, a carriage pulled up and out jumped Michael ben Nicodemus. Turning, the young man helped Rabbi Nicodemus and two women step out; his sister Ruth and *his wife* Mary. A second carriage pulled up after them, with a number of men.

Abel plopped down on the ground. He wanted to spit as if he had tasted a morsel of week-old fish. *Mary! Married to Michael ben Nicodemus.* Michael did not need a wealthy wife; his family was one of the wealthiest and most powerful in Jerusalem. And Martha married Simon, who had been a leper. *It's an abomination that he who had been a leper should have wealth and a wife.*

He did not remember the names of the other men with Michael and Mary, but he recognized them as being followers of *that man.* He had seen most of them at his cousins' house. He had seen them in the garden on the Mount of Olives when he and his father had accompanied Judas Iscariot and the Temple Guards to arrest Jesus ben Joseph. Abel grinned as he recalled those *loyal disciples* abandoning their friend and running off into the night.

Abel turned around and peered. The group was laughing and talking, as they lifted baskets out of the carriages. Suddenly, the scene changed to a countenance ravaged with pain, hair matted beneath a crown of thorns, the face covered with blood, dark eyes gazing into his soul.

With a groan that rose from deep within, Abel slipped to the ground. *Not again. Please Yahweh, not again!*

Abel was back on that barren, rocky hill of Golgotha, the Place of the Skull. His father had left him to stand watch. The soldiers were drinking and tossing dice. The Nazarene's family and followers were weeping beneath the cross.

"Father."

All had turned to look as Jesus ben Joseph spoke.

The Nazarene's face was lifted toward the sky. He had groaned, pressing on his nailed feet and pulling on his arms—nails through his wrists—to lift himself up high enough to fill his lungs. "Father," he had rasped, "forgive each of these people." He had pulled up again. "They do not know," another breath, "what they are doing."

Jesus had slumped down with a moan. He was still for a moment, his chest barely rising; then he had opened his eyes and looked directly at Abel.

Even now, Abel could still see that man's gaze. He could not identify what he saw in the *Nazarene's* eyes. It was not hatred, nor was it condemnation. Abel knew from his own father what hatred and condemnation looked like. He saw pain and sadness, but there was something more. Something he had never before experienced. Whatever it was, he could not bear what he saw in Jesus' gaze; Abel had lowered his eyes and turned away.

Since that day, over seven weeks later, the gaze of the Nazarene still haunted him. Abel was certain it was his punishment from Yahweh for not tracking down *that man's* disciples.

Able put his hands on his head and squeezed, as if it would remove all memories of that day, of that look. *Once all the Nazarene's followers are dealt with, Yahweh will forgive me, heal my father, and these nightmares will go away.*

Chapter 5

"Martha, your honey and date cakes are delicious as always," Rabbi Nicodemus smiled.

"Rabbi Nicodemus, you are kind as always," Martha extended the basket of cakes. "Have another."

Nicodemus reached in to select one and, as she began to lower the basket, grabbed another.

"Father," Michael laughed, "you just finished breakfast. If you continue eating those cakes, Elisheba will have to enlarge your clothing."

"You hush, Michael ben Nicodemus," Martha grinned at her brother-in-law. "If a respected member of the Sanhedrin wishes to honor me by eating my date cakes, who are you to question it?"

"Listen to her, Son," Nicodemus said around the cake in his mouth. He swallowed. "Martha, I would ask you give Elisheba your recipe, but I do not know whether she would take that as an insult."

"We would not wish to insult her. You will have to come to Simon and my house for supper, and I'll make extra cakes."

"I await that invitation with much joy! Simon bar Hiram," he said to the man standing next to Martha, "with a beautiful wife who is an amazing cook, you are a blessed man indeed."

"I agree with you, Rabbi," Simon patted his own stomach. "Although you and I both might have to have our clothing enlarged."

"Come, let us join our friends upstairs before we eat all your wife's cakes."

As the men ascended the stairs, Mary crossed to the table filled with covered baskets of food, amphorae of water, and cups. "It looks as if I will have to ask Elisheba to double the amount of food we bring," Mary moved several empty baskets from a side table. "Does anyone know how many people are in the upper room today?"

Martha put the basket of date cakes on another table. "I think someone said over one hundred, although with people coming and going, I do not know how they can keep up with their number."

When Jesus told Peter and the rest of those on the Mount of Olives to, *"Wait,"* He had added, *"Do not leave Jerusalem."* Rabbi Nicodemus—and those believers who had homes in Jerusalem—welcomed those who did not, which included all the Eleven.

Not knowing what to do while they waited for the *comforter*, several days after Jesus' ascension, Peter and the other disciples showed up at Lazarus and Simon's warehouse. Lazarus relayed the story later that night, when he and Abigail were having supper with the family at Rabbi Nicodemus' home.

"Peter asked permission to use our upper room as a place for them to be together and pray. They explained it was the room where they had celebrated the last Passover with the Lord Jesus, may His name be blessed. Of course, we said 'Yes.' They are in the upper room, praying even now."

At first it was the Eleven—along with Jesus' mother, His aunt, and Mary Magdala—who gathered to pray. A few days later, other followers of the Lord Jesus heard about it and asked to join them. Soon, the upper room was filled throughout the day, and all the watches of the night, with people praying and sharing remembrances of what the Lord Jesus had done and said. During one of these times of prayer, the disciples, led by Peter, selected Matthias bar Esdras to replace Judas Iscariot as one of the Twelve.

Shortly after the believers began gathering, Martha had told Mary and Abigail she planned to bake bread to take to those people. "The warehouse belongs to our family," she said. "That makes them our guests."

Mary and Abigail offered to do the same. Elisheba, always interested in feeding anyone associated with the family of her beloved Mistress Hannah, put the servant girls to work, preparing bread and cheese to take to those praying.

"There," Mary set the last basket on the table. "I hope it is enough. Let us join our husbands in prayer before the men go to the Temple."

Both floors of the building had a main room and several smaller rooms. The central room on the upper floor was smaller than its counterpart downstairs. The room itself had no decorations, only lampstands placed between the latticed windows.

Not that decorations would make any difference. The central room, as well as the smaller side rooms, were packed with people. Some were kneeling, others standing, and some sitting, their voices filling the air with a hum as they prayed.

"Do you see our husbands?" Mary whispered, scanning the room, "Wait, there they are; by the window, with Lazarus and Abigail."

"Praise Yahweh, a spot by the window," Martha whispered, lifting her tunic away from her body with a little shake. "The room is already stuffy. I cannot remember Sivan being so hot before."

"You have never been pregnant before."

"You speak truth."

They waited as Peter led the believers in the *Shemah*: "Hear O Israel, the LORD is our God, the LORD is one!" After speaking the first line of the *Shemah*, Mary repeated the second line silently, as every Jewish child had been taught: *Blessed be the name of His glorious kingdom for ever and ever.*

In the silence after the prayer, she and Martha stepped quietly to where Michael and Simon stood with Rabbi Nicodemus, Lazarus, Abigail, and Ruth. She smiled a greeting at Rabbi Joseph bar Neriah, who stood near her father-in-law. Mary glanced out of the window—which faced the street—and noticed a man standing behind the old sycamore fig tree across the street. She frowned. Normally someone standing beneath the shade of a tree would not be unusual, but the poor man was clasping his head as if in pain.

She started to draw Michael's attention to the man, but Peter began the prayer the Lord Jesus had taught them. She closed her eyes and joined in:

Our Father, Who art in heaven,
hallowed be Your Name,
Your kingdom come,
Your will be done,
on earth as it is in heaven.
Give us this day our daily bread.

And forgive us our trespasses,
  as we forgive those
  who trespass against us.
  And lead us not into temptation,
  but deliver us from evil.
  For Thine is the kingdom,
  and the power, and the glory,
  for ever and ever.

The room resonated with the "Amen," and the voices grew quiet.

Mary loved this prayer, but it brought up many questions. She was beginning to understand the impact of the Lord Jesus' death. She still wept when she thought of that day on Golgotha, that He was to be the sacrifice for her—for everyone's—trespasses. But He was the Son of Yahweh; He had strength beyond hers. *How do I forgive others as He forgave me?*

Then there was the *kingdom.* Mary had been raised to believe the kingdom would be restored when the Messiah came, drove out the Romans, and returned Israel to the glory it had known under King David. Now, with the revelation that the Lord Jesus was the Messiah, but not as everyone expected, she had begun to wonder what else she had misunderstood. Not just about Yahweh's kingdom, but *everything* she had been taught. The problem was, no matter who she asked—even her beloved father-in-law or the esteemed Rabbi Joseph—no one could answer her questions.

Maybe this counselor *the Lord Jesus spoke of will have the answers.* Drawing a deep breath, she prayed, *Lord Jesus, I want to do what You commanded. I want to be the godly wife to Michael that King Solomon wrote about. I want to be as You described Sarah. I want to be the gentle, kind, and loving woman You spoke of during our wedding feast. On that last day—on the Mount of Olives—You said You would be with us always, but I do not understand what that means. How can You be with us when You are gone? I have so many questions, and no one has the answers.*

Mary heard a gentle breeze but did not feel its brush on her cheek. She heard another gust whistle around the room but did not feel its touch. She frowned when she heard a third blast that sounded as if a giant was trying to yank the shutters off the window.

Then she heard a gasp rippling from those around her. Looking up to see if someone was hurt, her eyes widened, her jaw dropped.

The sound of the wind was whipping around the room, yet not a single head cloth nor garment of clothing was disturbed. What caused the gasping, and drew every eye, was the massive flame in the center of the room above their heads. It flickered and danced, sending showers of red and yellow into the air.

Suddenly the flame *divided*—that was the only way Mary could describe it—into countless smaller flames. Mesmerized, she watched the flames floating toward each person in the room, to hover over their heads.

She sensed the flame dancing over her own head, saw its illumination around her. She felt the flame's warmth but not, as she would expect, from above. The warmth began in her chest and radiated outwards, from her stomach to her legs; from her arms to her fingertips, from her neck to her head. As the warmth rose, Mary felt a bubble forming in her throat. When the bubble reached her mouth, she opened her lips.

"Θα τραγουδήσω στον Κύριο, γιατί είναι πολύ έντιμος. Το άλογο και ο αναβάτης του έχουν πετάξει στη θάλασσα."

She had heard Greek spoken by Stephen ben Chariton and by other Greeks in the marketplace, but she did not know it. Nevertheless, she knew she was speaking the praise of Moses after Yahweh parted the Red Sea. "*I will sing to the LORD, for He is highly exalted. The horse and its rider He has hurled into the sea.*"

"*Vineam de Aegypto eiecisti gentes et plantasti eam,*" Martha spoke the language of the Romans—a language neither she nor Martha knew—yet Mary understood what her sister said. "*You brought a vine out of Egypt; you drove out the nations and planted it.*"

People around the room were speaking languages Mary had heard in the marketplace but could not identify; yet she understood them as they spoke praises from the Holy Scriptures.

"*You laid the earth's foundation!*" Michael called out, "*You marked off its dimensions! You stretched a measuring line across it and laid its cornerstone, while the morning stars sang together and the angels shouted for joy!"*

"*Who among the gods is like You, O LORD? Who is like You—majestic in holiness, awesome in glory, working wonders?*" from Rabbi Nicodemus

"*Give thanks to the LORD, call on His name,*" Lazarus cried. "*Make known among the nations what He has done. Sing to Him, sing praise to Him; tell of all His wonderful acts. Glory in His holy name; let the hearts of those who seek the LORD rejoice!*"

Abigail sang, "*Like Your name, O God, Your praise reaches to the ends of the earth; Your right hand is filled with righteousness.*"

"*You were in the blazing furnace with Your servants: Shadrach, Meshach, and Abednego,*" Rabbi Joseph shouted. "*When they came forth, all saw that the fire had not harmed their bodies, nor was a hair of their heads singed; their robes were not scorched, and there was no smell of fire on them. Because they trusted in You and were willing to give up their lives rather than serve or worship any god but You.*"

The unseen wind blew the flames; they pulsed and shimmered around the room, illuminating it as though they were standing under the midday sun. Mary felt each pulse from the flames as if they were coursing through her veins. The voices of the people raised in praise of Yahweh sounded to Mary like that of a mighty waterfall.

Chapter 6

$\mathcal{T}$he Nazarene's face faded from before Abel's eyes.

Grabbing hold of the trunk of the sycamore fig tree, he pulled himself upright. He glanced at the sun. It was time to go to the Temple.

The Feast of First Fruits was the second of the three great feasts and concluded the cycle of time that began at Passover. According to the Law Yahweh gave to Moses, it was to be a holy convocation, a day where no one worked. All the males in Israel were to appear before the Lord at the Temple. There would be the ceremony of the loaves, the worshippers would offer personal gifts of first fruits, followed by a recital of thanksgiving for Yahweh's past deliverances of Israel. A day of celebration in Yahweh's goodness.

Abel frowned. *Not that* my family *has anything to celebrate.* But he joined the throng of people walking to the Temple. His father would question him as to the details of the ceremony and would know if he had not attended.

The crowds thickened as he reached the edge of the Xystus Market. Due to the season—with its milder weather—there were as many people, often more, in Jerusalem for this feast as there were for Passover. Abel sighed. He had intended to get to the Temple early, to try to speak with Rabbi Caiaphas. His father demanded Abel report to the High Priest frequently, even if he had learned nothing more regarding who took the Nazarene's body and where they had hidden it.

The crowds moved, and he finally reached Solomon's Porch.

Even oppressed as he felt, Abel never ceased to be amazed at the sight of the Holy Temple of Yahweh. Originally built by King Solomon, according to the instructions Yahweh gave to King David,

the Temple had stood for over 350 years until King Nebuchadnez-
zar of Babylon destroyed, pillaged, and burned it. The pagan king
had carried all its treasures—as well as the people of Judah—to
Babylon. The Temple was rebuilt under the supervision of the priest
and scribe Ezra, and even later under Nehemiah—who had been
appointed by the Persian King to be Governor over Jerusalem—
although it did not have the grandeur of the original Temple.

About fifty years ago, Herod—the man who had been appointed
by the Roman Senate to be king over Israel—restored the Temple.
It took almost twenty years to complete the restoration. He dou-
bled the size of the Temple, making it broader and taller than the
original. Rising eleven stories, it was covered on all sides with
massive plates of gold; gleaming in the sunlight, it could be seen
from miles away. One of King Herod's additions was a series of
cloisters or colonnades, with tall marbled columns supporting a
cedar roof, which encircled the Temple. The spot on the eastern wall,
where Abel stood, was called Solomon's Porch, so named because it
contained remnants from the Temple built by King Solomon that
had been brought back after the captivity in Babylon.

He was about to go through the colonnade, when the sound of
voices caught his attention.

Looking behind him, he saw people running toward the Upper
City. Floating back on the wind were cries;

"Fire!"

"Get buckets! Get water!"

"Where?"

"The warehouse of Lazarus ben Jacob and Simon bar Hiram!"

A fire! Without thought for the sanctity of the Holy Temple,
Abel began pushing and shoving his way through the crowd.

He saw several men moving to the side of the crowd and stopping to *gird their loins*. Abel copied them; bending forward, he
reached through his legs to grasp the hem of the backside of his
tunic. Straightening, he gathered the material above his knees, tied
it, and tucked it into his girdle. This action allowed him to move
unencumbered by his garments.

He ran down the street, passing men and women carrying

containers, pots, amphorae filled with water from homes, from the Gihon Springs, from wherever they could find water. Putting out a fire was not simply an act of kindness; a fire in one building could easily spread to another.

A crowd had gathered by the time he arrived at his cousin's warehouse, men banging on the door, calling out, asking the location of the fire, and whether anyone was injured.

Abel moved to the shade of the sycamore fig tree. Through the opened window on the upper floor of the warehouse, he caught a glimpse of what appeared to be flames and heard garbled voices calling out. He held his breath. He had seen dozens of people arriving at the warehouse earlier that morning, many he knew to be followers of the Nazarene. He felt a swell of excitement, of hope. It would be wondrous indeed if a stray spark from a nearby kitchen would burn down the warehouse, killing all within, and resolve his problems. *Perhaps Yahweh is punishing my cousins and all those who followed* that man!

The door to the warehouse opened; the Nazarene's followers spilled into the street. Abel squinted, trying to see signs of singed clothing or hair, blackened skin. But there was none of that. Instead of terrified, the people were jumping up and down, laughing, clapping their hands. They were all talking at once, some shouting, some even singing.

Several men from the crowd ran inside, carrying their containers of water. Others in the crowd listened to the Nazarene's followers, frowning. One man pointed at Peter. "You are speaking Egyptian."

"I am from Greece," another man pointed toward Mary, "and she is speaking the language of my people."

"That woman is speaking the language of Rome," a woman indicated Martha.

"How can that be?" another man asked. "I am from Cappadocia. These people are Galileans. How do they know my language?"

Others in the crowd took up the question, indicating they were from Parthia, Mesopotamia, Cappadocia, Pamphylia, Libya, or other regions of the world. In each case, the people claimed to have heard the followers of Jesus ben Joseph speaking in their own language.

One of the men who had run inside came back to the door. "There is no fire." He waved his hands, dismissing the followers of the Nazarene. "They are just drunk."

Abel saw the one called Peter bar Jonah step forward. He lifted his hands. "My brother Jews—and all of you who live here in Jerusalem. Please listen! I will explain." Extending his arms wide to those who had come out of the house with him, he said, "These men are not drunk." He nodded toward the sun. "It is only the third hour of the morning. No," his voice echoed through the street, "you are all witnesses to what was spoken of by the prophet Joel, when he said:

"*In the last days, Yahweh says, I will pour out My Spirit on all people. Your sons and daughters will prophesy, your young men will see visions, your old men will dream dreams. Even on My servants, both men and women, I will pour out My Spirit in those days, and they will prophecy.*'"

Peter took a breath, "The prophet also said, '*I will show wonders in the heaven above and signs on the earth below, blood and fire and billows of smoke. The sun will be turned to darkness and the moon to blood before the great and glorious day of the Lord. And everyone who calls on the name of the Lord will be saved.*'

"My brothers, listen. Jesus bar Joseph from Nazareth was a man approved by God by many miracles, signs, and wonders. Many of you *saw* these things Jesus did.

"He was handed over—by you, the Jews—but," Peter jabbed a finger skyward, "this was Yahweh's set purpose and intent. But you," he lowered his finger to point at the crowd, "with the help of wicked men, put Him to death by crucifying Him." He met Abel's eyes. "You did it."

Abel stared at Peter as one would a cobra. Then, the disciple's face faded from his view to be replaced with a face covered in blood beneath a crown made of thorns, eyes filled with pain. Staring into his soul.

"Aaiiiieeeee! Noooo!" Abel grasped his head, turned, and ran away, screaming, "Noooo! Stooop! Leave me alone. Leave. Me. Alone!"

Chapter 7

"Three thousand! Can you believe it?" John Mark laughed, clapping his hands. "Three thousand people believed on the Lord Jesus—may His name be blessed—*in one afternoon*. And the wind and flames dancing…that must have been the Comforter the Lord Jesus spoke of. It was *amazing!*" He saw the tray of food Jemima extended to him. "Ohhh…are these Elisheba's oat cakes?"

The dining room of Nicodemus' home was filled with people, eating, talking about the morning, rejoicing at the increase of those who believed in the Lord Jesus. Several clapped Peter on the back, congratulating him for delivering his *first sermon*.

"Imagine my brother preaching!" Andrew had laughed.

"I thought he spoke well," Mary said. "Do you not agree, Ruth?"

"I do indeed." Ruth stepped closer. "Mary, your cousin, Abel," she dropped her voice. "I saw him…"

Mary's smile faded. "I did as well, when we came out of the warehouse. I had *hoped…*" she tried to find the right words, "the power of the Comforter, the Holy Spirit, was so strong…I was *certain* he would hear Peter's words and be drawn to the Lord Jesus, may His name be blessed."

The crowd gathered outside the warehouse that morning had been so intent on Peter's words that besides herself, only Martha, Michael, Lazarus—and now Ruth—appeared to have noticed Abel running away.

After breathing a prayer for her cousin, Mary had turned her attention back to Peter. She had heard the words from the prophet Joel before, but—as with most prophecy—they had confused her. Yet, listening to Peter, she realized that she—that everyone—had *seen* the prophecy from Joel fulfilled.

The blood. The Lord Jesus lost so much blood from the floggings and—Mary swallowed—on the cross.

The Fire. She herself had seen the flames dancing over the heads of everyone in the upper room.

The sun turning to darkness. She had been on Golgotha when sun had gone dark for three hours while the Lord Jesus hung on that cross.

The moon turning to blood. Mary remembered the evening after the Lord Jesus died, she saw the moon, red as the darkest wine.

After pointing out how the prophecy had been fulfilled on the day the Lord Jesus died, Peter went on to say, "But, Yahweh raised Him from the dead, freeing Him from the agony of death, because it was impossible for death to keep its hold on Him."

After speaking of different passages from the Holy Scriptures and how they had been fulfilled in the Lord Jesus, Peter proclaimed Yahweh had raised the Lord Jesus to life and that His followers were a witness to that fact.

"Exalted to the right hand of God, the Lord Jesus has received from the Father the promised Holy Spirit and has poured out what you now see and hear. For King David did not ascend to heaven, and yet he said, *'The Lord said to my Lord: Sit at My right hand until I make your enemies a footstool for your feet.'*

"Therefore," Peter's voice echoed, "let all Israel be assured of this: God has made this Jesus, whom you crucified, both Lord and Christ."

The crowd had been silent, listening as the big fisherman had spoken. As his last words floated away on the breeze, a man in the front of the crowd stepped forward.

"Brother, your words cut me to the heart." He looked at those standing near him. Many in the crowd nodded agreement. He turned back to Peter. "What should we do?"

Peter smiled. "Repent and be baptized, every one of you, in the name of the Lord Jesus, for the forgiveness of your sins. Then you will receive the gift of the Holy Spirit. This promise is for you and your children. It is also for all those who are far away—it is for *anyone* whom the Lord our God will call."

Chapter 8

*A*bel ran until he reached the Temple. Stopping, he bent over, hands on knees, gasping in breath. Each beat of his racing heart echoed; *I must see the High Priest. I must see the High Priest.*

"Are you alright? Is something amiss?"

Abel glanced at the man sitting on the ground. His legs and feet—where they protruded from his ragged clothing—were twisted and deformed. As far back as Abel could remember, this cripple sat in that same spot every day, a basket in front of him, begging for alms. *He is cripple, yet he asks if I am alright.*

With a huff, Abel straightened, smoothing his garments and head coverings. "I am fine."

"That is good." The cripple picked up his basket and shook it. "Alms for a poor cripple?"

Abel ignored him and walked into the Holy Temple. He passed through Solomon's Porch colonnade, through the East Gate, the Court of Women, up fifteen steps to the Gate of Nicanor where parents would dedicate their newborn children to Yahweh, and through the Court of Israel, where only Jewish men were allowed. After crossing the marbled floor to the Court of the Priests, he turned to walk through a long-arched doorway into the Holy Place.

Measuring forty cubits long and twenty cubits wide, the walls were lined with cedar on which were carved palm trees, flowers, and cherubim. In this room was placed the altar of incense, the seven-branched candelabrum, and the table of shewbread. In the center of The Holy Place was the Veil of the Temple, which prevented men from carelessly entering the heart of the Temple, the Holy of Holies, where resided the holy presence of Yahweh. Made of fine linen and blue, purple, and scarlet yarn with figures of cherubim embroidered onto it, the Veil stretched the height and width of the room and was thick as a man's hand.

In the center of the Veil, running from top to bottom, were fine mending stitches.

Abel recalled *that* afternoon, when he had come to the Temple to report the Nazarene was dead. The table of the shewbread, the altar of incense, and the candelabrum were overturned from the earthquake that had rocked the city. But what shocked him was the jagged rip, running from the top of the Veil of the Temple through to the floor.

When Abel asked what had happened, his father voice had trembled. *"I…do not know. It was the* earthquake. *"*

"The earthquake *caused* that?" Abel had asked.

His father had nodded. *"I was in the Holy Place, with Rabbi Caiaphas and Rabbi Annas. At the ninth hour, just as we offered the perpetual sacrifice, the earthquake started. The tremors knocked over the menorah and the table for the shewbread. That table is heavy; it is made of pure marble. As we were trying to lift them, we heard a terrible rending sound. The pillars supporting the Veil of the Temple were still standing, but in the middle of the upper edge of the Veil there was a…* tear. *As we watched…it ripped from the top to the bottom."*

Standing in front of the Veil was Rabbi Caiaphas. The High Priest was talking with two men, one who was Rabbi Gamaliel ben Simon. Shorter than most men, the renowned teacher had heavy white brows and beard, a hawk-like nose, and dark, piercing eyes. One of the oldest teachers in the Temple, age had not dimmed his mind. He knew more of the Holy Scriptures than even the High Priest.

Abel was one who claimed the honor of studying under Rabbi Gamaliel. As did Michael ben Nicodemus and, Abel frowned, as did the other man standing with the teacher and the High Priest; Saul Paulus.

A man of moderate size, what hair Saul had was black as was the one eyebrow that spanned his deep-set eyes and long, hooked nose. Younger than Abel, Saul's restraint added years to his bearing and countenance. He was without humor; since the day Saul arrived at the Temple, Abel had never seen him smile. His conversation never wavered from the Holy Scriptures, the Traditions of the Elders, and condemning those who did not precisely follow their precepts.

Saul had left Jerusalem shortly after the day of the Nazarene's crucifixion to go his family's home in Tarsus. Abel had hoped he would not return. It was difficult to report to his father that this fellow was better in their studies.

Abel hesitated—he would rather not speak in front of Saul Paulus—but Rabbi Caiaphas saw him and gestured for him to approach. He straightened his head covering, smoothed his garments, and crossed the floor to where stood the most powerful man of the Jewish people.

"Greetings, Abel ben Joktan," the High Priest said and added the extra greeting for the Festival, "Peace on you. Time of gladness."

Abel bowed his head. "And on you peace, Rabbi Caiaphas, Rabbi Gamaliel," he slanted a glance at the third man, "Saul Paulus," before adding the proper response, "Festivals and seasons of joy."

"Greetings, Abel ben Joktan. Festivals and seasons of joy." Saul's face did not reflect the joy in his response.

Rabbi Gamaliel's smile alone was welcoming. "Greetings, Abel ben Joktan. Festivals and seasons of joy, indeed. A beautiful morning to celebrate Yahweh's provision in the harvest."

"Yes, yes," Rabbi Caiaphas brushed aside the second most sacred holiday. "What have you to report today, Abel ben Joktan? Have you discovered which of the Nazarene's followers broke the Roman seal and stole his body? Do you know where they have hidden it?"

Who stole the Nazarene's body? Where did they hide it? The High Priest asked those same two questions each time Abel brought a report, as if the suggestion of those actions had not come from himself.

On the third day following the crucifixion of Jesus ben Joseph, Rabbi Caiaphas had called Abel and his father to the Temple. They had met the High Priest in the Court of Gentiles, along with Rabbi Annas—Caiaphas' father-in-law—and Marcus Lucius, the soldier who had been with the detachment of soldiers overseeing the three crucifixions on Golgotha. It was this same soldier who had laughed as he won the Game of the Kings, who had rejoiced as he broke the knees of the two brigands, who had rushed to thrust a spear into the side of Jesus ben Joseph. He had been assigned to lead the detachment of soldiers to guard the Nazarene's tomb.

That morning in the Temple, the soldier had been wide-eyed and trembling as he had reported that *two angels* had descended and touched the massive stone that sealed the tomb, triggering an earthquake. When he and the other soldiers awoke—for they had fainted in fear—the tomb was empty.

To cover the soldiers' *miraculous* story, Rabbi Caiaphas had paid them to say they had fallen asleep and the Nazarene's followers had stolen the body.

From the questions the High Priest daily put to Abel—clear and without hesitation—it appeared he believed the story he had made up and not the original report of the soldiers.

What else could it be? Abel thought. *Angels opening the tomb?* He shook his head. *No.*

All of that flashed through his mind in the time it took to glance at Rabbi Gamaliel and Saul. He did not want them to be witness to his disgrace. There was nothing for it; the High Priest was waiting. Abel lowered his gaze. "I have not, Rabbi Caiaphas."

"Why have you not discovered these people?" Saul demanded, as if he—like Rabbi Caiaphas and Rabbi Gamaliel—had authority to question him. "It has been seven weeks since the Nazarene was crucified."

Abel's chin shot up, his gaze kindling at the other man. "I grew up in Jerusalem, Saul Paulus; these people know me. They know my father and I were not followers of Jesus of Nazareth. They will not willingly come forward to confess to crimes against Rome."

Saul snorted and turned to the High Priest. "Let me find these people who defy the law, Rabbi Caiaphas. I assure you," he glanced at Abel, "*I* will not take seven weeks to find them. Indeed, there is a man who attends the Synagogue of Freedmen with me I believe to be one of this man's followers."

"Who is he?" The High Priest asked.

"Stephen ben Chariton. He is a Jew from Greece. I have already begun challenging statements he makes in the synagogue."

Abel held his breath as Rabbi Caiaphas' eyes swung between

Saul and himself. He would *not* beg to be allowed to continue his hunt. *But, how will I explain to Father that the High Priest gave this fellow the task that was originally mine?* he thought. *The task that would see Father healed and my own nightmares removed?*

It was the teacher who decided the matter.

"Saul Paulus, you have been gone from Jerusalem for nearly seven weeks," Rabbi Gamaliel said. "You cannot catch up on your studies if you are searching for this man's body and for those who took it from the tomb."

Saul's lips thinned. Abel could see the muscles in the man's throat work before he nodded his head.

"You are correct, Rabbi Gamaliel," Saul said before directing a superior gaze towards Abel. "*My studies* are important."

Abel ignored Saul and turned back to the High Priest. "I do have something to report about the Nazarene's followers." He relayed the story of what had happened moments ago outside the warehouse.

The High Priest jumped on it like a leopard on a goat. He questioned Abel at length, having him repeat certain sections of his story again, before finally saying, "So, the Nazarene's followers are growing in number. And spreading more lies. Yet more things to add to the list of problems caused by this man. Abel ben Joktan, I give you leave from your studies with Rabbi Gamaliel—"

"What?" Abel interrupted. "Sir, my father will insist I continue."

"Abel ben Joktan," Gamaliel placed a hand on Abel's shoulder. "I honor your father's dedication to your study of the Holy Scriptures. With your father's," he paused, "*situation,* there is no need to upset him further by relaying information that would distress him. And," he lifted a hand to silence Saul's gasp at the teacher's suggestion of lying, "should anyone ask about you, I will tell them I am satisfied with your studies. Which," he looked at Saul, "I am."

The High Priest waved away Gamaliel's concern over Joktan's *fatherly* dedication. "Abel ben Joktan cannot study in the Temple and hunt down these people and the location of the Nazarene's body. *That is most important!* Apparently, the death of Jesus ben Joseph was not enough. We need to do something before the lies of his followers infect more people."

Chapter 9

"Mary Magdala, you must take another oat cake," Mary indicated the tray Jemima held. "They are freshly made."

"Thank you," the older woman selected a cake and took a bite. "Mmmm…these are delicious. I would love to have the recipe for these."

Mary smiled. "I will see that it is written down for you."

Michael grinned as he watched his wife. He knew these oat cakes were her special recipe, yet she refused to draw attention to herself.

"Your wife is lovely and gracious," Matthew said. The older disciple had a quiet smile.

Michael beamed. *My wife!* "She is indeed."

He, along with Matthew, Peter, and John Mark, were watching the crowd fill the reception room.

Since the day of First Fruits, the word about the Lord Jesus had spread. Not only did those believers who had gathered to pray in the warehouse's upper room share the message of the Lord Jesus, but the people in the street who had believed after witnessing the miracle of languages shared the story with their friends and family.

The new believers wanted to learn more about the Lord Jesus from those who had known Him. While Peter and the rest of the Twelve were happy to oblige, they realized there was not a place big enough for all the believers to gather. As a solution, many believers opened their homes as gathering places for people to come hear the Twelve. The gatherings varied from home to home, but they all included worship in prayer and song, a teaching by one of the Apostles or one who had been close to the Lord Jesus—such as His mother—and the *anamnesis*. This was the name many gave to the remembrance meal, the one the Lord Jesus shared with His disciples on the night He was arrested.

On this day, John and James were at the home of Lazarus and Abigail, while Philip and Thomas spoke to the believers gathered at Simon and Martha's home. When Nicodemus learned they would have the honor of Peter and Matthew speaking in their home, he decided to use the reception hall.

Used for formal gatherings—or when the size of the crowd was too large for the private family courtyards—the walls of the long room were of white stucco. Near the top, and between the tall marble columns that supported the ceiling, was a broad key pattern that was repeated in the gold and yellow mosaic of the floor.

Mary had told Michael she had arranged for food. He watched as she moved among their guests, encouraging each to try some of the food Elisheba and the servant girls had set out on the side tables.

"Mary bat Jacob is indeed the godly woman King Solomon wrote about in his proverb." Peter said.

"Yes. Yes, she is." Michael felt his heart swell at the praise given his wife.

"One day I hope to have such a wife," John Mark said, his gaze moving to rest on Ruth, who was also mingling among the people in the hall. He startled when Peter snickered and quickly added, "If the Lord Jesus wills it."

Peter burst out laughing. Matthew smiled.

"I know how you feel," Michael clapped the young man's back. "As King Solomon wrote, *He who finds a wife finds what is good and receives the favor of Yahweh.*"

"Perhaps Yahweh is waiting for you to finish writing Peter's memories of the Lord Jesus," Matthew said.

"As long as *I* do not have to write them," Peter lifted his hands in a sign of surrender. "Else, no one would ever understand the story of our Lord Jesus—may His name be blessed—and the message of the His sacrifice."

"All you have to do is talk," John Mark patted a bag he carried. "I have brought ink, stylus, and some parchment. I am ready to write whatever you feel the Lord Jesus wants you to say."

"John Mark, I have arranged for a table to be brought for you to write upon," Michael said. "Peter, if you are ready, I will let Father know." He crossed to where his father was talking with Rabbi Joseph.

After listening to his son, Nicodemus clapped his hands to get his guests' attention. "Thank you all for coming to my humble home. I am honored to see so many friends and—" he smiled, "people I hope one day to call *my friends*."

Michael smiled. A gentle and humble man, his father never allowed his affluence nor prestige to temper the way he treated people. He regarded all people—no matter what their standing—as his equal.

"Although our Lord Jesus—may His name be blessed—taught us not to be concerned with food, I know He would approve of my thanking my *daughters*," he directed a smile at Ruth and Mary, "for arranging today's meal."

The people in the room echoed Nicodemus' thanks. Mary and Ruth smiled and nodded in response.

"Now, if you will be so kind as to sit, Peter bar Jonah will speak to us about the Lord Jesus."

Michael crossed the room to sit near the wall with Mary and Ruth. Once the crowd was settled, his father gestured to the disciple.

Peter nodded his thanks to his host before turning to face the crowd. Taller than most men, his hair and beard had more gray than black. His arms bulged with muscles under a simple beige tunic, even though it had been three years since he left his boats behind to follow the Lord Jesus.

After leading the group in the prayer the Lord Jesus had taught them, Peter said, "Rabbi Nicodemus, I wish to thank you—and all the others—who are opening their homes for the followers of our Lord Jesus—may His name be blessed.

"In order that those who are new believers in the Lord Jesus, I—along with the other disciples—have been asked to share what we remember of the years we walked with Him. John Mark ben Gershom," he nodded to the young man, "feels called to write down my words, so that the story of the Lord Jesus can be shared with others."

The big fisherman paused, filling his lungs. "I remember the first time I saw Him.

"I am sure you have all heard of John ben Zechariah, he who was called *the Baptizer.*"

Heads nodded around the room. A little over three years ago, a young man showed up in the Judean countryside, announcing he had been called to prepare the way for the coming Kingdom of Yahweh and urging people to repent of their sins and be baptized in the Jordan River.

"My brother Andrew had become one of the Baptizers' disciples; not me." He gave a self-deprecating smile. "We were fishermen; my days were spent either in fishing, sorting fish, selling fish, or mending our boats and nets. I did not have time to sit and listen to a man preach, even if he was considered by some to be a *prophet.*

"One evening I was on the shore of the Lake of Galilee, mending nets. Andrew—who had been gone all day—came running up. 'We have found the *Messiah,*' he said. He wanted me to meet this man.

"I had finished my work for the day, and was curious about someone who might restore Israel to the glory of King David's reign, so I went with Andrew.

"When I first saw the Lord Jesus, nothing about His appearance suggested a military leader. He was about thirty years old at that time, shorter than me. He was strong, as He had been trained as a carpenter.

"After Andrew introduced us, Jesus ben Joseph smiled at me. There was something in his gaze," Peter grew pensive, "as if he could see *into* me," He placed a hand on his chest, "into my *soul.*"

"Then He said, 'Come and follow Me. I will make you fishers of men.'"

"I do not know what happened. I did not know how to explain it to my wife." Peter grew silent, as if reliving that moment three years earlier. "But there was *something* about Him. Something that drew me, something that made me believe everything He said." His gaze refocused, and he looked at the people sitting in front of him. He smiled and shrugged. "I left it all. I arranged for the care of my wife, but I left our boats. Our nets. My home. I left it and followed Him.

"In the next few days, I heard the Lord Jesus teach, I saw Him drive an evil spirit out of a man. My wife's mother was sick with a fever. The Lord Jesus went to my house and took her hand. She was healed."

Michael heard people murmuring in response to the Lord Jesus' miracles.

Michael felt Mary slip her hand into his and squeeze. He knew she was thinking about the Lord Jesus healing Simon of his leprosy. Raising Lazarus from the dead. Healing Martha's heart and her own hurt.

Peter continued talking about some of the memories he had of the years walking with the Lord Jesus. His teachings on the love of Yahweh. His parables of the sower, the lampstand, the mustard seed. Calming a storm.

Then the big fisherman turned to the events of the last Passover. Jesus entering Jerusalem to the acclaim of the people. People chuckled when he told the story of Jesus turning over the tables of the moneychangers in the Temple and condemning the High Priest and other Temple leaders. *Caiaphas and Annas have never cared for the people*, Michael thought, *and it is obvious these people do not care for them.*

The laughter stilled when Peter spoke of the Lord Jesus' arrest.

The trials. The floggings. The crown made from thorns.

His crucifixion.

The sun going dark.

His death.

The earthquake.

His burial.

The blood moon.

Peter paused to take a sip of water. Then he continued with the morning Mary Magdala had arrived, exclaiming she had seen the Lord Jesus alive, and how they had not believed her, nor the other two men who claimed to have seen Him.

The Lord Jesus appearing to the Twelve. "He rebuked us for not believing Mary and the others," Peter said. "He showed us His hands and feet, which still had the wounds from the nails, and His side, which had the wound from the Roman soldier's spear."

"What did you do?" The question came from Michael's young nephew, David. The toddler was sitting in his father's lap.

Peter grinned at the child. "We believed." He shrugged when the crowd burst out in laughter. "With the Lord Jesus standing in front of us, what else could we do?

"Then the Lord Jesus commanded us, "Go into all of the world and preach this gospel—this good news—to everyone. Whoever believes and is baptized will be saved, but—" he paused before continuing, "whoever does not believe will be condemned.

""These will be the signs that will accompany those who believe. In My name they will drive out demons—"'

An "*Oooohhh*" rose from the crowd.

""They will speak in new languages."'

Many in the crowd nodded. They had been witnesses of that miracle.

""They will pick up snakes with their hands; and when they drink deadly poison, it will not hurt them."'

Michael notice no one cheered. *I would not wish to test this promise.*

""They will place their hands on sick people and they will get well."'

While Peter's voice was still echoing around the room, people in the crowd surged up.

"I want to know this Man."

"Please. My daughter is sick. Would you pray for her?"

"My brother has a demon. Please help him."

"I believe. I want to follow the Lord Jesus."

Chapter 10

8 Tishri 3793, Bethany Marketplace

"Mistress Martha," Ethan the beekeeper protested, pushing wisps of grey hair out of his eyes, "I assure you. This is the best honey my bees have made this year. Here," he gestured to the table holding an open crock of honey and a basket of bread pieces, "please taste this and give me your opinion. Your honey and date cakes are considered the best in Bethany. Indeed, I have not eaten any as delicious since my Sarah died—may her memory be blessed."

Martha picked up a piece of bread, dipped it in the crock, and took a bite. "Hmmm. I think…" she wrinkled her brow as she chewed, "this might be the *best honey I've ever tasted.*" she finished in a rush.

"I agree with my sister." Mary smiled at the elderly man. "I have found none like it, even in the Xystus Marketplace. I will take four crocks. My father-in-law also loves my sister's cakes and I want to surprise him with some for the feast following the Day of Atonement."

"Thank you, Mistress Martha, Mistress Mary," Ethan bowed his head. "It is an honor to know Rabbi Nicodemus will eat cakes made from my honey."

After a quick barter—Mary might love his honey, but she would not offend the elderly man by refusing to haggle—she gave the beekeeper her coin. While he placed the wrapped crocks in the basket Jemima was carrying, she and Martha moved into the crowd swarming the Bethany Marketplace.

"Whew, I know Tishri is early autumn," Martha grasped the front of her cream-colored robe, pulling it away from her belly, "but this month feels especially hot."

"It is hot, but perhaps you feel especially so because you are approaching the last part of your pregnancy."

"You speak truth. But it might not be so hot if this marketplace was not so crowded." She grinned at her sister. "I appreciate it must feel small compared to the Xystus Marketplace in Jerusalem."

"I know the Xystus is larger," Mary said, "but I prefer this one." She lifted her blue robe, sidestepping a man leading a camel. "When I was a young child, I told Father—may his memory be blessed—that this marketplace reminded me of a hive of Ethan's bees."

Due to the little town lying two miles from Jerusalem, the marketplace in Bethany was a popular place for people traveling to and from the center of the Jewish world. Among local residents who combined their purchases with news or gossip, the streets of the marketplace were filled with travelers from other countries, priests in their somber garments, and Roman soldiers in their red tunics with armor and weapons. Beyond booths for foodstuffs and household items, there were also stalls for horses, camels, and donkeys; cages of chickens, pigeons and doves; and pens of sheep or goats. Children ran among the booths, often chasing cats, dogs, and occasionally chickens, through the streets. The human voices in various dialects or languages mixing with the sounds of animals clucking, barking, whinnying, bleating, screeching, or braying gave life to the marketplace.

"Do you think your preference for this marketplace is because of its link to your childhood?" Martha asked.

Mary considered this. "Possibly. I often came here with Father whenever he was home from his travels." She glanced at her sister. "I am aware this marketplace might have bad memories for you. Because of Daniel ben Ezra."

"No," Martha stopped to inspect some grapes. "Not any longer. I was fifteen when young Daniel mistook my blemished skin for leprosy. I love grapes. Did I tell you I saw him several weeks ago?"

"Then we will have some grapes with our meal." Mary selected several bunches of the fruit for purchase and handed them to her sister. "You saw Daniel? He must be a grown man."

"He is nearly twenty now." Martha smiled. "He told me the

memory of that day still embarrassed him, and he apologized for any hurt it might have caused me."

"What did you say?"

"I forgave him," Martha shrugged, "as I know the Lord Jesus—may His name be blessed—would want. Daniel was but a frightened young child at that time." She placed a hand on her swelling abdomen. "I would not hold that against a child." She looked at Mary. "Speaking of hurts, what about Mother? I imagine her words hurt you as much—or more—than little Daniel's words hurt me."

Mary took a deep breath. "I have forgiven her, as the Lord Jesus—may His name be blessed—would want, although I cannot say I understand why she said those things to me."

"I do not have an answer," Martha said. "Perhaps she felt her inability to teach you to cook or run a household reflected poorly on her."

"I tried to learn." Mary felt a lump form in her chest. "I wanted her to be pleased with me."

"I know you did," Martha laid a hand on Mary's forearm. "I think, in her own way, Mother was pleased with you."

"But she only commented on my looks. I believed what she told me—that it was a good thing I was pretty, else no man would want to marry me—until the day the Lord Jesus told me she was wrong.

"*He* said I was worth so much more. He said beauty of form or face—or even skills—are not where our true value lies. He said my true value lay in the fact that I was created by Yahweh and He loves me. That knowledge," Mary filled her lungs, "*freed* me. It changed me. That is why I poured the spikenard from my alabastron onto His feet; to thank Him. I want to do what I can to help other people know they are *worth so much more.*

"So, yes, I have forgiven Mother *as the Lord Jesus would want.*" She smiled. "Martha, does it still seem strange to think of the Lord Jesus as the *Son of Yahweh*? To be praying to someone who ate at our table and spent nights as a guest in our home?"

"It does, indeed." Martha grinned. "I confess I struggle not to boast that the *Messiah* favored my honey and date cakes."

The sisters burst out laughing.

"That *is* something to boast about," Mary said. "But I confess, it has been a challenge to change from thinking of the wrath and judgement of Yahweh—as Uncle Joktan always used as a threat—to the love and forgiveness of Yahweh, as the Lord Jesus taught."

"Poor Uncle Joktan. He knew nothing of compassion or grace."

"He did not."

"Martha, sometimes when I am praying—or even going about my day—I can almost hear the Lord Jesus' voice again, responding to my prayers." She glanced at her sister. "Have you experienced that?"

Martha nodded. "I have. I have wondered whether I was just remembering what He taught, but sometimes the…*voice*…speaks of things I never heard Him say. Not that the words have ever gone against what He taught," she added in a rush.

"Do you think this is the Holy Spirit—the Comforter—Who came on the Festival of First Fruits?"

"Possibly. As long as what the voice says agrees with what the Lord Jesus taught, I will listen to it." She put a hand on Mary's arm. "I must stop at Abrim's spice booth. My supply of cinnamon and coriander is low."

"Elisheba asked me to buy some cumin and saffron."

After the sisters made their purchases, Mary handed her two bags to Jemima. "This is all of my purchases for the day. Take these things to the carriage and ask Daniel to carry them back to Elisheba. Tell him to return for us at my sister's house at the ninth hour." She gave directions to Martha's house.

"Yes, mistress," the servant girl nodded her head. "I will meet you there soon."

Mary and Martha watched Jemima wind her way through the crowd.

"A loving and rich husband, servants, beautiful clothes, a driver and carriage, living in a palatial home," Martha said. "You have the life many women dream of. To speak truth; you have the life *you* dreamed of."

"I do indeed, although that was my desire *before* the Lord Jesus came into our lives. Now I desire to be like Sarah, like the woman King Solomon wrote about.

"I confess I grow tired of being waited on all the time. I would like to cook or even clean." She slanted a wry smile at Martha. "I know. I know. Cleaning can be fatiguing. But I truly have little to do. Each day I wake up; have meals with my husband and the family or any guests we might have. I speak to Elisheba about those meals and any household decisions. I spend the rest of my days shopping with Ruth, overseeing the garden that belonged to my mother-in-law, or reading scrolls. But that is all. When you invited me to make honey and date cakes today, I struggled to conceal how excited I was. I need something to do with my time."

"Well, you have shown you have the skills to be mistress of a large house." She nodded at the receding figure of Mary's servant. "You have a loyal servant in Jemima."

"She is a sweet girl. I have discovered she is skilled with a needle. You would be pleased. Here, let me carry your basket."

She and Martha continued walking down the streets of the marketplace. "Jemima also shows skill in dressing my hair. I have talked with Michael, Father Nicodemus, and Elisheba about letting her become my personal maid."

"Oh ho! A personal maid," Martha gently teased, "for someone who does not want her value to be found in her *beauty*."

Mary paused to look at a basket hanging at the front of Timeus' booth. "I need Jemima for more than garments and hair." She added nonchalantly, "You yourself know how fatiguing it is when you are new with child."

"What!" Martha grabbed Mary's arm and swung her around to face her.

"Shhhhh…." Mary looked to see if anyone had overheard. Timeus was on the far side of the booth, haggling with Lamech, the innkeeper, over the price of baskets. She turned back to her sister and smiled. "I do not know for certain."

Martha dropped her voice. "How long has it been since you had your monthly flow?"

"About six weeks, although my monthly flows were never regular like yours. It might be nothing."

"You are right," Martha nodded. "It is still too early to know for sure. If you are truly with child, you will give birth in…" she paused to count the months on her fingers, "sometime in Iyar or Sivan. Your child and Abigail's and my children will all be born within a year." She grinned. "What did Michael say?"

"I have not told him yet. In fact, I have told no one besides you. I want to wait until I am certain."

"That is wise. But, let me be the first to wish you *mazel tov*. You will be a wonderful mother."

Chapter 11

Abel stayed hidden behind the corner of the booth of the sandal maker, watching his cousins until they were out of sight.

He had followed Mary all that morning after he left his father in the Valley of Hinnom. Since he had been commissioned by Rabbi Caiaphas to find the body of the Nazarene—it was easier to think of it as a *commissioning* rather than his education being considered unimportant—Abel spent hours each day watching the warehouse belonging to Lazarus and Simon, or switching to watch the house of Rabbi Nicodemus. Most of what he saw were people coming and going, greeting each other—his mouth pulled down in distaste—in "the name of the Lord Jesus."

There was nothing for Abel to do but sit, watch, and think; and his thoughts made for foul company.

It irked him that, whenever he met with Rabbi Caiaphas, he had nothing to report on the conspiracy surrounding the Nazarene's body. It irritated him how frequently Saul Paulus happened to be in the company of the High Priest for these reports. Looking at the Jew from Tarsus, Abel had to force his lips into a smile until he thought his face would crack.

There was one benefit from these past weeks. Abel had become quite adept at twisting the truth. His father still believed he was studying with Rabbi Gamaliel and he was pleased with the praise reported from the teacher. Abel snorted, wordlessly celebrating the strange sense of freedom this skill wrought.

Yet, even that did not satisfy his father.

"Racha! You must find the Nazarene's body and those who hid it," his father had snarled an hour before. "Once we rid the earth of these sinners, Yahweh will heal me."

When Abel saw Mary and another girl—*a servant, from her clothing and demeanor*—exit Rabbi Nicodemus' house, climb into a carriage and be driven away, Abel ran to a nearby pistachio tree, where he had tied his horse. Within minutes, he was following the carriage.

The road was busy with people coming and going from Jerusalem, but Abel was still careful to stay hidden in the crowd to prevent his cousin from seeing him. When they came to Bethany, he was not surprised to see the carriage stop at the marketplace, nor was he surprised to see Martha waiting for her sister. *What better place for conspirators to meet than in a crowd?*

The stall of the local blacksmith was near the entry to the marketplace. Keeping an eye on his cousin, who was being helped out of the carriage by her driver, Abel arranged for his horse to be fed and watered. Soon, he was following Mary, Martha, and the servant girl as they walked through the marketplace.

As the women left each booth, he would stop at it and purchase something, casually talking to the merchant, hoping they might say something to reveal them as part of the Nazarene conspiracy. Thus far, today—as other days—had yielded nothing.

When he saw his cousin send the servant girl away, he chewed his lip, deliberating. After a moment he gave a nod—*Although I do not wish to speak to her, I cannot pass the opportunity she might give me information.* Under other circumstances, he would never speak to a female who was not his relative or betrothed. But his father had suggested he get information from the servants; how else could he do that if he did not talk to them?

Abel waited until his cousins were out of sight before sliding into the crowd to follow the girl.

He saw her walk to the carriage that belonged to Rabbi Nicodemus and speak to the driver as she handed him the basket. As the man drove off, she turned and walked back into the marketplace. Abel followed her until she stopped on the edge of a small crowd gathered to watch a trained monkey.

The animal, wearing a small turban on its head and a tether around its neck, chattered and danced to the flute played by its owner who sat nearby. Then, taking off its turban, the monkey bowed, snatching the coins the people tossed at its feet. Scurrying to its owner, the animal handed him the coins in exchange for a date to eat.

Mary's servant appeared focused on the monkey and did not notice when Abel moved to stand next to her. He watched her reach into the folds of her girdle, draw out a coin, and extend it to the monkey. She went into peals of laughter when the animal ran over, took the coin, and doffed its turban to her, chattering as it bowed its head.

"What a smart animal you are!" she cooed.

Abel extracted a coin from his girdle and handed it to the monkey. The animal bowed and chattered as it took his coin.

"He is a talented animal, is he not?" Abel asked.

The girl smiled at him.

Abel startled as, for a heartbeat, he saw the face of the Nazarene. *No!* He grimaced. *Not here!* He forced a smile when he saw a flicker of alarm on the girl's face.

"It must take work to train an animal," he said.

She nodded slowly, caution in her gaze.

The crowd dispersed. The flute player whistled, extending his hand toward the monkey. The animal scrambled up its master's arm, chattering as the man walked up the street.

"Poor thing," Abel sighed. "His life cannot be easy."

"Why do you say that, sir?" the girl asked. "He appears to love his master, and his master loves him."

"Ah, but that is just it. The monkey has a *master*. He *belongs* to someone else. He is not free to do as he wishes. It is the same for all slaves," Abel paused and added off-handedly, "and servants."

The girl's almond eyes widened. "What do you mean?" There was an edge to her voice.

He gestured to where the monkey was dancing for a new group of people. "The monkey dances. He bows and scrapes. Afterwards, he gathers the coin from those he entertained. But he does not keep the money. He gives it to *his master* in exchange for a piece of fruit.

"Those who are slaves—*and servants*—are like that monkey. *They* wake before it is dawn, *they* prepare the meal and—once their *masters* have eaten—*they* get to eat whatever crumbs are left. *They* do everything, while their masters do nothing. Yet, when it comes to being paid, *they* get little…or nothing. The only value slaves and servants have to their *masters*—or *mistresses*—is what it costs to replace them."

"My mistress is not that way," the girl blurted.

"Ah; you are a slave."

"I am *not* a slave," the girl lifted her chin. "I serve Mistress Mary bat Jacob, who is the wife of Michael ben Nicodemus and daughter-in-law to Rabbi Nicodemus ben Melech."

"Ah…. Rabbi Nicodemus ben Melech," Abel spread his hands wide. "Who has not heard of the one of the wealthiest men in Israel. I am certain he has many servants."

"He does, and he is kind to each of them."

"Does the family of Rabbi Nicodemus treat their servants as kin? Do the servants eat with the family? Do the servants have comfortable bed chambers and," he looked at her simple robe, "beautiful clothes?"

"Well," she floundered, "no."

I have trapped her! "So, you are nothing more to him than a servant." Abel tried to exude sympathy. "If Rabbi Nicodemus were to dismiss you, what would happen? You would go back to the home of your parents?"

The girl's eyes dropped. "My parents are dead." Her tone was flat.

"I am sorry; may your memories grant you peace. So, you have nowhere to go. Do you have money? You work for a wealthy man." He glanced pointedly at the monkey. "You have saved many denarii?"

"No. I—I have not worked very long for Rabbi Nicodemus."

"So, if you were to be dismissed, you would have no place to go, and no way to earn any money?"

"No." The girl's expression reminded Abel of a wounded fawn.

He pushed harder. "I know a way you could earn enough money that you would never need work for Rabbi Nicodemus or anyone ever again."

"How?"

Tread carefully, Abel. "There are men—powerful men—who

believe Rabbi Nicodemus *knows* a secret. These men are willing to pay anyone who helps them discover this secret."

Her eyes thinned. "What *secret*?"

"The names of the criminals who stole the body of the Nazarene teacher, Jesus ben Joseph, and where they hid it."

"What?!" Her eyes widened. "No one *stole* the body of The Lord Jesus—may His name be blessed—because He is not dead. He is *alive*!"

The Lord *Jesus? Is she also a follower?* "Who told you that?"

"Mistress Mary. She told me all about the Lord Jesus." The passion in her voice grew with each word. "How He came to teach everyone about the love of Yahweh. How He loves me. How He died for my sins, for the sins of all mankind, but He rose again. That I am worth so much more." She lifted her chin. "That I have *value* because I am created by Yahweh. And He. Loves. Me." Her gaze blazed with each word. Then her tone softened, as did her eyes. "He died for you too, sir. He loves you."

The girl's face faded before his eyes, and Abel found himself staring at a face covered with blood dripping from a crown of thorns. Onyx eyes filled with pain gazing into his eyes. Into his mind. The lips, cracked and bleeding, opened.

"No." Abel shook his head. "No, no, no, no! *Leave me alone!*" Turning, he ran, stumbling into people, knocking over merchandise, screaming as he ran out of the marketplace, "Leave. Me. Alone!"

Chapter 12

$\mathcal{M}$artha removed the last circle of dough from the hot stone. "There. I think we have made enough date and honey cakes to feed everyone in Bethany *and* Jerusalem." She dusted her hands, rose up on her knees, and tried to stand. And could not. She tried again. And could not.

Mary bit her lip, not wanting to embarrass her sister by drawing attention to her plight. Finally, Martha sighed and looked at her.

"Mary. Jemima. Would you help me?"

"Yes, of course."

Mary and the servant moved behind Martha, placing their hands under her arms to steady her as she stood.

"Ugh!" Martha put a hand on her back as she straightened. "Whew. Thank you. I am thankful to Yahweh for this child—and will love him, or her, with every beat of my heart—but there are times when I feel like a cow." She patted her robe to remove the flour dust.

"You do not look like a cow," Mary laughed.

"You look beautiful, Mistress Martha," Jemima added.

"Thank you. You are both kind." Martha took a huge breath. Expelled it. "Alright. Now that we have toiled to make these delicious cakes, we should at least taste the results of our work. As Mother—may her memory be blessed—used to say, 'Let the farmer be the first to eat from his harvest.'"

"If Elisheba were here, I can only imagine what her proverb on the fruits of our labor would be." Mary grinned. "It would probably have *nothing* to do with farming." She was surprised by Jemima's sudden laughter.

The servant girl covered her mouth, blushing. "Forgive me, mistress. I did not mean to insult Elisheba bat Penuel."

"There is no need to apologize, Jemima. To speak truth, I have to restrain myself from laughing at her proverbs. She has a good heart, but there are days when talking to her reminds me of the time Yahweh mixed the language of those at the tower of Babel."

Jemima pinched her lips as her eyes grew wide. Then the three women dissolved into laughter.

Martha was the first to recover. "We should not laugh at her," she wiped her eyes with the edge of her headcloth.

"We should not," Mary nodded solemnly. She twinkled at Jemima, "But, I cannot help it," and erupted into laughter again.

"Jemima, while your mistress is enjoying herself, would you please help me pour the milk?"

"Yes, Mistress Martha."

Chuckling, Mary crossed the floor and got a tray from the worktable. She carried it back to the table near the fire pit, to place some of the cooled cakes on it.

The women left the cooking area, walked down the hall, up the staircase, and into the room set aside for family and special guests. Pomegranates and flowers were painted on three walls while the outside wall had three large windows with shutters opened to allow in cooling breezes. Tall lamps stood in each corner; even unlit, the fragrance from their oil perfumed the air. Several low tables with thick cushions were placed around the room. Martha crossed to the table near the window and set the mugs down. Jemima placed the pitcher of milk near it.

Mary helped her sister sit on a pillow near the wall and handed her a smaller pillow to tuck behind her back before sitting next to her.

Jemima stood near the table, hands folded in front of her.

"Join us, Jemima," Martha said.

The servant looked at Mary. "I…cannot. Elisheba bat Penuel would be displeased to learn I sat at table with my mistress."

"Then we shall not tell Elisheba. Come," Mary patted the tabletop, "you may join us."

The girl's eyes widened. "Thank you, mistress!" The girl sat gingerly on one of the pillows, as if fearful of crushing its deep-feather softness. She accepted a cup of milk from Martha but refused to take a cake until Martha and Mary had each selected one. She did not join in the conversation but sat quietly eating her cake while Mary and Martha chatted.

"Father Nicodemus told us Mary bat Eli is coming to Jerusalem with Mary Magdala. We are preparing a feast in their honor. Will you and Simon please join us? We will be asking many of the Lord Jesus' followers to come as well. Leah bat Samuel and her husband Azariah bar Cleopas are also coming."

"Leah! I haven't seen her since their wedding. I hope they are doing well," Martha said. "As to your invitation, I will speak with Simon, but I am certain he will be happy to accept. I enjoyed the afternoon we spent with Mary bat Eli when she was here before…" her tone faded as her eyes lost their focus. She stared into the distance, her eyes filling with tears.

Mary blinked away the sheen of tears that gathered in her own eyes. The afternoon Martha referenced had been but days before the Lord Jesus' arrest. The knowledge He had risen and ascended into Heaven did not diminish the painful memories of the last Passover week.

"Yes. Well," Martha exhaled a deep breath and wiped the edge of her eyes. "I would like to see her again. She told me about when the Lord Jesus was born. Being with child myself," she slanted a quick glance at Jemima before smiling at Mary, "I enjoy hearing birthing stories from other women. It helps me prepare."

"I would like to hear that story," Mary reached for another cake. "That night after the Lord Jesus died, when I found her in Mother Hannah's garden—may her memory be blessed—Mary bat Eli told me about the time an angel appeared to her and announced she would bear the Son of Yahweh."

"What?" Jemima's mouth fell open in shock. "An angel? She must have been terrified. Oh…" Color washed over her face. "Forgive me, mistress."

Mary smiled. "There is no need to apologize. To speak truth, I was shocked. She told me when she was but fourteen years of age, an angel had appeared to her and told her she would bear the Messiah, the Son of Yahweh, and they would name Him *Jesus*."

"Mistress, do you think she will tell that story again? I would like to hear it."

"I would like to hear it as well," Martha added.

"I will ask her," Mary said. "I believe there are many who would like to hear that story. Martha, have you heard John Mark ben Gershom wishes to write down Peter bar Jonah's memories of the Lord Jesus?"

Martha nodded. "Simon told me that. I think it is a good idea."

"I agree and so do other people. Michael told me Matthew bar Alpheus wishes to write down *his* memories of the Lord Jesus and mentioned wishing to speak to Mary bat Eli about the Lord Jesus' birth."

"I am glad she is coming at this time. Rabbi Joseph bar Neriah met with Simon yesterday. He apologized for his business taking longer to complete than the two months he had originally expected. He told Simon it might be several more months until he will be ready to accompany us to Gaul."

"Simon still believes it is necessary for you to leave?"

Martha nodded. "He does. He and Lazarus wish to expand their business to other areas of the Roman Empire. This is one reason we agree that it is important to write down the memories of the Lord Jesus' life. He commanded us to be His witnesses to the ends of the earth." She laughed. "I cannot think of the ends of the earth being further away than Gaul."

"I cannot either." Mary drew a deep breath. "Well, perhaps Rabbi Joseph's delay means you will be here when it is time for your child to be born. I would like to see my new nephew or niece while he or she is still a babe."

"That would be a blessing for me as well. I confess I prefer to give birth here in my own home," Martha took a sip of milk. "But I also look forward to seeing some of the places Simon and Lazarus have visited."

"It will also allow you to fulfill the Lord Jesus' wish. What was it He said?" Mary crinkled her brow. "'You will be My witnesses in Jerusalem…'"

"'…in Judea and Samaria and to the ends of the earth,'" Martha finished.

Mary sighed. "I do not see I will be able to do more than be

His witness here in Bethany and Jerusalem. Now that Michael has completed his studies with Rabbi Gamaliel, he will soon become a priest in the Temple. Father Nicodemus hopes one day he will become a member of the Sanhedrin."

"It would be a blessing to have followers of the Lord Jesus as part of the Sanhedrin. That is certainly a way of spreading the message of the Lord Jesus."

"I agree," Mary sighed, "but I do not know how *I* can be His witness to 'the end of the earth,' if I never leave Jerusalem."

"Perhaps the Lord Jesus wants us to be witnesses *wherever* we are," Martha said. "Starting with those closest to us. Family, those in our homes," she nodded toward Jemima.

"But everyone in our family—and in my husband's household—already believe in the Lord Jesus."

"Not everyone."

Mary understood the message in her sister's gaze. "You mean Aunt Naomi and our cousin Rebeca."

"And our cousin Abel."

"You are right," Mary sighed. "And our cousin Abel. Although I do not think he would be willing to *talk* to us, much less *listen* to anything we had to say about the Lord Jesus."

"Possibly, but I do not think the Lord Jesus would consider that a reason *not* to try to tell him."

"You speak truth." Mary let out a long breath. "I will pray for an opportunity to be His witness in my little portion of the earth. It is a blessing that being a follower of the Lord Jesus is easier *now* than in the days leading up to His crucifixion. Speaking of Him will not bring harm to us or those we love."

"Mistress?"

"Yes, Jemima?"

"I meant to tell you about something that happened in the marketplace." The servant related about being approached by the strange man. "I did not know what to think of it. At first, he angered me, suggesting the followers of the Lord Jesus—may His name be blessed—were criminals. Then I realized I only wanted to tell that man how the Lord Jesus loved him and died for him."

"You did the right thing, Jemima," Mary said. "I will have you repeat this incident to Father Nicodemus and Rabbi Joseph. I am certain they will know what this means and what to do."

Chapter 13

By the time he arrived home, Abel's heart still pounded as if he had been chased by Beelzebub. He led his horse to its stable and removed the saddle and bridle. After quickly grooming it, he checked the water and opened a barrel to scoop some grain into the animal's feeding trough. He frowned, noting the diminished level of grain in the barrel.

Joktan had trained his son to be careful with money. However, with having to provide extra clothing, food, and supplies for his father—as well as maintain their own household—the coins in the family's strong box were dwindling.

Walking up the path to this house, Abel touched his fingers to the *mezuzah*—the box on the doorposts that contained portions of sacred scriptures—and entered his family's home.

As eldest son, this house had come to Joktan upon the death of his own father. Abel had grown up listening to his father relate how his brother Jacob had brought back many furnishings and decorations from the lands he visited on his journeys. Rather than live among items from *pagan* lands, Joktan boasted he had sold them all within a week of his father's death. As he never invited guests to his home, it did not matter to Joktan that it left his house looking sparse and poor.

Made of thick cut stone, the house's outer walls reflected the wealthy homes of those in Jerusalem's Upper City; but that is where the resemblance ended. The front room stretched the width of the house, yet the only furnishing in it was a plain, low dining table with thin pillows beneath. Two unadorned lamp stands stood at either end of the room, filled with the cheapest oil available in the marketplace. The only color in the room were the red and blue tiles on the floor; Joktan refused to buy rugs to cover them nor did he wish to pay laborers to remove them. All the rooms in the house reflected Joktan's boastful indifference.

Abel walked through the front room, down the hall, and into the cooking area at the back of the house, where he found his mother and sister preparing the evening meal.

Naomi bat Simeon was the daughter of a man who, before his death, had been a member of the Sanhedrin; Abel had long ago determined *that* relationship was the only reason his father had chosen her as wife. Everything about his mother was diminutive, from her height to her deep-set eyes and small, pinched lips. Abel had no idea what her hair looked like; not once in his life had he ever seen her without a head covering.

His sister Rebeca was a mirror image of their mother, save for the hooked nose she inherited from their father.

Both women were dressed in simple, cream tunics and brown robes. The carefully sewn patches on their garments further reflected Joktan's indifference to his family.

Naomi was at the worktable, putting slivers of cheese and withered dates onto a serving tray, while Rebeca knelt at the fire, watching six pieces of bread bake on a hot stone.

"Good evening, Mother. Rebeca." He did not add the traditional 'Peace be upon you,' greeting. *There is no peace in the household of Joktan ben Philemon.*

The two women startled and jumped up, hunching their shoulders and wringing their hands.

"Uh…good evening, Son," his mother's mother attempt at a smile looked awkward.

Rebeca did not smile; she stared at the floor as she whispered a greeting. Both women stood silent, eyes slanting fearfully between him and the hall beyond him.

Something flared in Abel's chest. He was not sure what to name it, but it angered him to see his mother and sister behaving as if expecting his father to walk through the door. *Stop it! He's gone! He is a* leper *and, he will* never *return. No.* Shame washed over Abel. He hunched his shoulders. *Forgive me, Yahweh for thinking thus of my father. Once the Nazarene's followers are dealt with, You will forgive Father and heal him.*

He tried again. "Sister, how was your day?"

Rebeca's eyes widened, and she glanced at her mother before answering. "It was good. We found some dates at the marketplace." Something washed over her face and she quickly added, "They were in the basket Othniel, the fruit merchant, sets aside for the poor."

Abel dug his nails into his fists. *My mother and sister are scrounging for food, just like the wretches digging in the trash heaps in Hinnom.* He took a slow breath, calming himself before speaking. "That was thoughtful of you." He paused before adding, "Thank you."

The women gaped at him.

Chagrined, Abel realized they had never heard a kind word from his father and few from himself. *I will have to do better*, giving them a thin smile. Nodding toward the tray of food, he asked. "Is supper ready? I am famished."

His mother and sister rushed about, apologizing for wasting his time with 'foolish talk.' Soon, they were sitting at the table, waiting while he offered up thanks to Yahweh for their blessings. While Rebeca poured three cups of water, his mother put four of the pieces of bread on his plate, plus most of the cheese and dates.

"Mother, you and Rebeca should take more food."

"We are not hungry," his mother glanced at Rebeca, "We ate while you were gone."

"Are you certain? There is…*plenty*…here."

"No," both mother and sister rushed to reassure him. "Please, eat." Naomi picked up her bread and—nodding at Rebeca—took a bite.

It did not take long for the women to finish their meager meal. After dusting the crumbs from their fingers, they folded their hands and watched Abel.

Their silence was deafening.

Abel tried again. "I have never eaten bread that tasted this good."

Again, it appeared Rebeca did not know how to interpret his comment. "Thank you. I used *less* flour in it."

"Son, did you see your father today?" his mother asked.

The bread felt like a lump in his throat. He choked and took a drink of water. "I did," he rasped. "He sends his…*best…*wishes."

Mother and daughter mirrored their shock. His mother recovered first.

"He did?"

Abel nodded. "He did." *I wonder whether Yahweh will forgive a lie spoken to avoid hurting my mother and sister. Probably not.*

"Maybe we should go and see him," she said.

"No!" Abel stumbled over his words, "I mean, he would not wish you to be…*saddened…*to see him in those surroundings."

"How kind he is," his mother's eyes brightened with tears. "I will have to make something special to show him we miss him as well. Perhaps some *meat.* What do you think, Son? It should cost no more than one or two *mites.*" She clasped her hands. "I promise to be careful with the money."

A few mites? He thought of their dwindling coffers. *Soon mites will be all we have left.* Abel was not sure what to do. They had already gone through the monies from the priest's portion—the monies paid to priests from the Temple treasure—that was owed to his father. The only thing they had of value was his horse and the land that had been part of his family's inheritance after they returned with the prophet Nehemiah from the exile in Babylon. His family never visited the land to work it in-between Joktan's times to serve in the Temple—he felt farming was beneath his dignity—yet he would never give up the land.

Father would rather Mother, Rebeca, and I starve than sell that land. And yet, here was his mother—doing without food so her son could have more—wanting to do something for a man who cared nothing for her.

He pulled the purse from his girdle and extracted two mites. Handing them to his mother, he said, "Be careful. While Father is…*away…*we must be cautious with our coins."

"I will." His mother handled the mites as if they were precious jewels, before tucking them into her girdle. "Son, if you are concerned about monies, you should ask your father. He will know what to do."

Chapter 14

*D*aniel arrived for Mary and Jemima as the sun was sliding down the western sky. Their conversation on the drive back to Jerusalem was light; the delicious honey and date cakes—which they offered to Daniel—the hot afternoon temperatures; how packed the streets of Jerusalem were.

When they arrived home, Daniel helped Mary down from the carriage.

"Thank you, Daniel." Although mistress of the house, she made it a point to be polite to all their servants. Daniel's frame—big and burly—reminded Mary of how Goliath must have been; his countenance, however, was gentle as a young child. She turned to her maid. "Jemima, I am going to tend the flowers in my mother-in-law's garden. After you carry the basket of cakes to the cooking area, please lay out fresh clothes for me. I want to bathe when I am finished."

Walking up the stone path that led to the arched entryway of the house, she greeted the servant who opened the door.

Although she had grown up in a wealthy family, the house that belonged to Father Nicodemus—*my home now,* she smiled—made the home of her childhood seem poorer by comparison. Intricate mosaics in gold, green, and red tiled the long floor of the main corridor. Along the walls, marble tables trimmed in an egg and lotus flower pattern and rosettes held vases filled with bouquets of fragrant flowers.

Passing several courtyards, public reception rooms, and ceremonial *mikvahs,* she walked upstairs, past several rooms to a small courtyard near the family quarters. This room held the flower garden created by Mother Hannah.

Mary's own mother had loved flowers and had planted a garden at their Capernaum home solely for flowers. Michael told her when his mother learned of her friend's flower garden, she had arranged for this room to be her own indoor garden. As children, Mary and Ruth had played here, imaging the tall ferns to be the jungles of Africa. Shortly after she and Michael married, she took over the care of the plants in this room.

The room was positioned on the east side of the house to shield it from the afternoon sun. The floor and walls were of white marble; Mary had learned Mother Hannah had declared the flowers and plants provided adequate decoration. She agreed. The only furnishings were a few low tables with thick pillows beneath. In the center of the room was an ornamental pool with water lilies, and around the room were pots of tall ferns, dove's tail, jasmine, and lilies that Mother Hannah had planted. To honor the memory of her own mother, Mary had added pots of flowers from her mother's Capernaum garden: henna, Rose of Sharon, lavender, rue, and purple globe thistles. Beneath the long window on the east side were large pots filled with rose bushes. These beauties were part of Michael's wedding gift to her. There were also a few of her own favorite flowers she was trying to cultivate, including a jacinth. The fragrance of its tall spires of clustered purple-blue blossoms was as sweet as a rose. Right now, the flower was but a seed hidden in the pot of soil, but she had hopes of seeing it bloom.

Just like our babe, she smiled, placing a hand on her stomach.

Mary crossed to a small chest behind the ferns and removed a large apron to wrap around her linen garment and a knife for pruning. She breathed in the flowers' fragrance as she moved among the plants, pausing to check for signs of new growth; sticking a finger into the soil to determine if one needed watering; removing spent blossoms; pruning old or diseased leaves. Working in the garden soothed her and tending the flowers that had belonged to Mother Hannah gave Mary a connection to the woman who had birthed her husband.

It was also a connection to the Lord Jesus. It was in their garden in Capernaum last summer that He had spoken to her about her value. Much had happened to their family prior to that summer. Lazarus was betrothed to Abigail, but most importantly, the Lord Jesus had healed Simon of leprosy and it appeared he and Martha would resume their betrothal. Everyone in their family was happy.

Except Mary.

Lazarus had found her weeping in their mother's garden. She had confessed to him their mother had been disappointed because Mary could not learn the basics of cooking or housekeeping. Mary told him their mother had told her it was a good thing she was beautiful and wealthy, otherwise she would never find a husband.

"Your mother was wrong," The Lord Jesus had startled them. *"Beauty of face or form—or skills—are not of value."* He had indicated their mother's lush garden. *"Look at these flowers. They are beautiful, but they will soon die and then where will their value be?*

"You, Mary bat Jacob, are worth so much more than these flowers. You have value because you are created by Yahweh and He loves you.

"What is true beauty? It is written in the Holy Scriptures that Abraham's wife Sarah was beautiful. She had a face and form that many men desired, but that was not what made her beautiful. Sarah was beautiful because she was gentle and kind. She was beautiful because she loved and obeyed Yahweh and used that love to serve others.

"If you seek to love and obey Yahweh above everything else in your life," the Lord Jesus had said, *"if you love others as yourself, that will show in your actions and in your countenance. You will be beautiful; and that beauty will never fade."*

His words had washed over her, pouring a healing balm into her wounded heart. From that day, Mary's concern over her appearance was gone.

That was why she had wanted to give her alabastron to the Lord Jesus. Filled with pure spikenard—worth more than most people earned in a year—it was a gift from her parents to be used to anoint her husband's feet on their marriage night. It was the only thing of value that belonged to her, but that did not matter. She had wanted to give it to the Lord Jesus to help Him spread the word of Yahweh's love to other women—to other people.

"Like Rebeca and Naomi."

Mary's pulse quickened at that voice, rich and well-modulated, and without thought, she looked around, certain she would see Him. However, save for herself, the garden room was empty.

Shaking her head. *I am thinking I hear His voice because I spoke of Him to Martha.* She crossed to one of the tables to pick up a basket. Walking through the garden, she cut blossoms to fill vases for the family's private courtyard.

"Rebeca and Naomi need to know."

Mary stopped, her heart throbbing. There was no need to turn; she recognized the same feeling that had washed over her in the upper room of Lazarus and Simon's warehouse. There was no light from a flame dancing over her head this time, but she felt warmth radiating throughout her body. She filled her lungs and asked, "Lord, is this You?"

"*Yes.*" She could hear the laughter, the joy, in His voice. "*It is I.*" Then the laughter changed. "*You must tell Rebeca and Naomi about being loved by Yahweh, just as I told you. They need to know.*"

"But Lord, they will not listen to me. They are fearful of doing anything that might displease my uncle or my cousin."

"*Mary; is anything too hard for My Father? For Me? Trust in Him with all your heart and do not try to lean on your own understanding. He will direct you.*"

Chapter 15

"*R*acha! Fool!" Spittle flew from Joktan's lips. His words were garbled, due to the leprosy consuming more of his mouth and tongue. "What do you mean you *still* have not found those who stole the Nazarene's body? It has been fourteen weeks since *that man* was crucified. How can you have not discovered *anything*? It is as if you do not *wish* for Yahweh to heal me!"

Abel stepped back from the fury of his father's attack. The heat of his gaze surpassed the fires burning in the valley around them.

Clenching his fists, Abel forced himself to look at the ground. Although he controlled his expression, his thoughts screamed at the man standing in front of him. *Yes, Father! I do wish that Yahweh would never heal you! I wish you would die in the Valley of Hinnom!* Taking a deep breath, he said, "No, sir. I do not wish that."

"Then why you have *failed?*"

"Father, I have done all you commanded. I have watched the houses of the Nazarene's followers. I have followed them. I even spoke to one of their servants."

Joktan jumped on that. "What did this person tell you?"

The memory came unbidden. *"He died for you too, sir. He loves you."* Abel shook his head. "Nothing…of value."

I have value *because I am created by Yahweh and He. Loves. Me.*" Abel squeezed his eyes shut.

"Look at me, you worthless fool!"

Abel opened his eyes.

His father's clothes hung on a frame that appeared bereft of muscle and fat. His skin was ashy and mottled, with deep holes pocking his bald scalp—he no longer wore a head covering—down to the grizzled remnant of beard.

"I will give you only a few weeks more. Then I will *accuse you before the elders.*"

"What?! Accuse me before the elders?"

"You heard me. My tongue is not yet gone." Blood drooled out of his father's mouth.

"Now, begone," he waved Abel off as one would a swarm of flies. "Stop. Before you go, give me your coin pouch."

"What?" Abel's hand went instinctively to the folds of his girdle. "My coin pouch? Do you need to purchase something," he looked around at the mounds of burning trash, "here?"

His father snorted. "You fool! In the Valley of Hinnom, coins have no value. I need them to pay my scribe."

Abel shook his head. *I mis-heard him.* "Did you say, your…?"

"Scribe. Yes, I did." Joktan turned to call over his shoulder. "Itamar! Come here!"

A moment later, a man came out of the cave beyond Joktan. Tall, with dark curls and beard framing his face, he was thin, as all were in the Valley of Hinnom. He hobbled, using a thick cudgel as a walking stick. Behind him followed a boy—a younger version of the man—carrying a box.

They stopped at another line of rocks behind Joktan.

"Yes, Rabbi Joktan?" the man bowed his head. The boy imitated the man.

Abel's father pointed to him. "This is my son, Abel." He pointed to the other man. "Abel, this is Itamar bar Reuben. That is his son, Aran."

Abel nodded toward the crippled man. "Peace on you, Itamar bar Reuben, Aran bar Itamar."

The man and boy returned Abel's greeting and crossed to a large rock to sit. The boy opened the box and began taking out what appeared to be implements of writing.

"Itamar was a scribe in the household of a wealthy man. Then he was struck with a disease, causing his foot and hand to wither. Unable to write as clear or as fast as his employer demanded, he was cast off. Not wishing to beg, he and his son came here, to scrounge among the mountains of trash, to hunt for things to sell. Now," Joktan lifted his chin, "he works for me."

Abel lowered his voice. "Father, I do not understand. Why do you need a *scribe*? If his hand is withered, how can he write?"

"Do you think I spend my days digging through the trash as those *unclean dogs*?" Joktan raised his eyebrows in slow motion, a gesture that managed to be sarcastic, arrogant, and dismissive all at once, "I have important thoughts I need written. Thoughts I can send to Rabbi Caiaphas. I also need to inform the High Priest I have made certain you stay the prescribed distance from me, so you can remain ceremonially clean. Itamar can still write, just slower and with less skill. I care not for either." He held out his hand. "Give me your coin pouch."

Abel slipped his fingers into the folds of his girdle and drew out his pouch. He tossed it at his father's feet.

Joktan picked it up. Loosening the strings, he poured the coins into his hand. "This is enough for now. Bring more when next you come."

"Father," he hissed, "we cannot afford a scribe. Our coffers grow lighter having to provide extra supplies for you."

"*Fool*! Are you mishandling my money? Or are your fool mother and sister wasting coins?"

"No! I am not, and neither are Mother and Rebeca. We work hard to make what coins we have be sufficient for your needs and for ours." "You can save money by eating less." He directed a look at Abel's stomach, "When you see Rabbi Caiaphas, ask him to give you my priestly portion early. Tell him you need it to continue your work in looking for the criminals who stole the Nazarene's body."

Abel gaped at his father. "You want me to *lie* to the High Priest?"

"Yes!" Joktan screamed. Bending, he scooped up a rock to throw at Abel, spewing out curses. "Lie. Steal. *Kill*! Do whatever it takes to find those people who are responsible for my being cursed by Yahweh!"

Chapter 16

Nicodemus' home

"While we were living in Egypt, one morning, my Joseph—may his memory be blessed—told me an angel of Yahweh had appeared to him in a dream the previous night," Mary bat Eli paused to take a sip of water. "The angel told Joseph to take Jesus and me and go back to Israel. He said that those who wanted to… *kill*," her voice caught on the word, "the Child were dead."

The Lord Jesus' mother was a petite woman, with thick black hair heavily salted with gray. It was evident to all where the Lord Jesus had inherited His gentle smile and dark eyes.

Michael reached under the table to take Mary's hand. *One day you will bear our child.* His wife smiled, squeezing his hand, before turning back to listen to Mary bat Eli.

He looked at those seated around the table, as well as those standing around the dining room, listening to the Lord Jesus' mother. Mary had asked his father to allow as many of their servants who wished to hear their guest speak to be present in the room. Michael noticed the servant girl Jemima by the door, listening slack-jawed to the story of the Lord Jesus' birth. Even Elisheba was stunned into a rare silence.

Mary bat Eli smiled at those present. "You can imagine the joy that filled our hearts at the thought of returning to *Israel*. We packed our things and started the journey home."

"Yet, as I understand it," Rabbi Joseph bar Neriah said, "you did not return to Bethlehem, where the Lord Jesus—may His name be blessed—had been born. May I ask why? Would it not have been wise for Him to be raised near the Temple?"

"Others have asked me the same question, Rabbi Joseph," Mary bat Eli said. "My answer is simple. We were warned *not* to come back here."

"Warned?"

She nodded. "As we traveled back, we learned what news we could, including the fact that Herod's son Archelaus was ruling Judea."

A murmur spread through the listeners. All present knew Archelaus and the incident of the Roman eagle.

Archelaus' father, King Herod—he who had been named *Great* by Caesar Octavian—had placed a golden eagle over the entrance of the Temple. When the eagle was discovered chopped down, two teachers of the Law and forty young men were arrested for the act and burnt to death.

Herod died soon thereafter and Archelaus claimed the status of his father's heir, pending the approval of Caesar Augustus. Archelaus announced he would punish those who had ordered the death of the faithful Jews. However, he delayed pursuing the murderers.

A large crowd of Jewish people gathered in the Temple area, offering sacrifices and loudly mourning the death of the forty-two men. They also called for others to join them.

Archelaus, who was feasting with friends, sent a general and a tribune with a cohort of soldiers to reason with these people. Those in the Temple did not listen to the Romans; instead, they stoned the soldiers and returned to their sacrifices.

In response, Archelaus ordered the entire army garrisoned at the Antonia Fortress to go to the Temple. The soldiers killed all present; the reports were of three thousand slain. Following that, Archelaus announced the cancellation of the Passover feast.

It was hoped Caesar Augustus would condemn Archelaus' acts. However, it was soon apparent there would be no retribution for the deaths of these people. Upon hearing the report, Augustus approved of Archelaus' actions, pronounced him as Herod's heir, and gave him the title of Ethnarch.

"If the news of Archelaus' reigning as king was not sufficient, while on our journey, Joseph had another dream from Yahweh, warning us not to come here. We chose instead to go to Galilee, to my hometown of Nazareth."

The Lord Jesus' mother smiled at Martha. "As I told my young friend, Nazareth might be a small, humble village, but those living there have a noble heritage. All in my village were taught that when the people of Israel returned from exile in Babylon, the ancestors of King David settled in the area that would become Nazareth. Most of those living there today are descendants of King David.

"We were also taught that the prophet Isaiah said the *Messiah* would be the *netzer*—the branch—of Jesse, King David's father. That is where our village derived its name. Because of that prophecy, all the women of child-bearing age believed anyone of us could give birth to the *Messiah*.

"When the angel Gabriel appeared to me and announced that I had found favor with Yahweh and would bear His Son, and He would sit on David's throne, I knew what he meant." She closed her eyes and smiled, laying a hand on her stomach, "I would be the mother of the *Messiah*."

Chapter 17

*T*hose in the dining room sat silent, pondering the story related by the Lord Jesus' mother.

Finally, Father Nicodemus stood, thanking Mary bat Eli for her story and inviting the guests to partake of the food and drink on the side tables.

Mary caught Ruth's eye and nodded, before turning to Michael. "I must see to our guests."

"Always the gracious hostess." He raised her hand to his lips. "Ah my wife; you are worth far more than rubies." Then he lowered his voice, "How beautiful you are, my darling! Oh, how beautiful. Your eyes are doves."

She smiled, recognizing the quote from King Solomon's love poem, which Michael knew word for word. She whispered her response, "How handsome you are, my Lover! Oh, how charming!"

Easing her hand from his grasp, she turned to their guests who were standing and stretching, moving to the side tables filled with platters of bread, bowls of dates, cheese, and olives and amphorae filled with water or wine.

She refrained from taking anything. Her stomach had been tender most of the day. She smiled. *Are you making your presence known, my little one? A little longer and I will tell your father.*

Instead, she moved among their guests, greeting them, encouraging them to partake of more food and drink, listening as they laughed and talked about Mary bat Eli's story.

Mary could appreciate the crowd's astonishment. Even knowing *Who* the Lord Jesus was, the story told by His mother sounded *surreal.* The angel's announcement. Their journey to Bethlehem. His birth in a stable. The large star appearing overhead. The angelic host singing of His birth. The visit by shepherds and later the magi. Their flight to Egypt and their return to Israel.

She recalled the night after—she blinked back tears—His crucifixion, when she had been in Mother Hannah's garden. She had heard someone coming and had stepped behind the shelter of one of the large ferns, wanting to grieve in silence. Then Mary bat Eli had come in, unaware she was not alone. Mary remembered overhearing the other woman break down in grief, sobbing and screaming, "*Why? He was my Son! You gave Him to me! Why did You let Jesus die?*"

Mary had stepped out of her hiding place and crossed the garden to embrace the older woman, comforting her as one would an infant. She had encouraged her, "Tell me more about Jesus."

The Lord Jesus' mother had clutched Mary's robe, digging her face further into her shoulder and poured out more memories of His life.

The stories were sweet; the stories were painful. Mary remembered that moment when she caught her breath, her eyes widening, when the grieving mother's stories changed from moments of His life and childhood to the story she had just shared.

I had thought her grief had driven her from sanity. But it was all *true.* She turned to look at her father-in-law and Rabbi Joseph, who were talking with Peter bar Jonah. *I had gone to them for counsel that night. They listened to me, but they did not assume I had mis-heard her or that grief had affected the Lord's mother.*

She smiled, recalling Rabbi Joseph reference something the prophet Isaiah had said, "'*Yahweh Himself will give you a sign: The virgin will be with child and will give birth to a Son, and will call him Immanuel.*'"

Mary had later asked Michael what 'Immanuel' meant.

"God with us."

Mary's smile broadened, her heart filling with sunlight. *He was. Yahweh, in the form of His Son, had been among them. Speaking with us. Laughing with us. Staying at our homes. Reminding us we were* worth so much more. *That we were loved by Yahweh.*

She breathed deeply, nodding. If indeed the Lord Jesus had

spoken to her, she needed to obey Him. But, to go to her uncle's house—to speak with her aunt and cousins—she must be *certain* she had *heard* the Lord speak.

Going to one of the side tables, she lifted a tray of Martha's honey and date cakes. She crossed the room to where her father-in-law stood with the rabbi from Arimathea, Stephen ben Chariton, and Peter bar Jonah.

"To think, Joseph, we have lived to see the fulfillment of prophecy. We have seen the *Messiah*. Beyond that; He was our friend."

"You speak truth, my friend." Rabbi Joseph clapped a hand on Father Nicodemus' back. "Ah, here is your daughter-in-law. What a blessed man you are, to have such a family."

"Thank you, Rabbi Joseph. Here," she extended the tray, "I know you and Peter bar Jonah like my sister's cakes as much as Father Nicodemus."

"Thank you, Mary." He took one and bit into it. "They are delicious."

"They are indeed," Peter said, choosing a couple.

"Stephen ben Chariton, you should try these," her father-in-law said. "I do not think you will find any as delicious in all of Greece."

The Hellenistic believer selected a cake and bit into it. "Hmmm… You are correct, Rabbi Nicodemus. I have never tasted anything as good as these cakes."

"Thank you," she smiled. "When you return to your home, I will see that you have some for the trip."

"I thank you," Stephen replied, "but I have decided to make my home in Jerusalem for now. There are many Greek-speaking Jews here in the city, including those who attend the Synagogue of the Freedmen." He lowered his brows. "Even though we are both Jews and Roman citizens, I am aware many Temple leaders look upon us as lower than proselytes. Not you, of course," he bowed his head to Mary's father-in-law and Rabbi Joseph. "You both have been most welcoming. However, many in my synagogue feel slighted. As such, they are *overly* careful in following the Law and the Traditions of the Elders. I believe the Lord Jesus wishes me to stay here and share His story with them."

"If anyone can do that," Rabbi Joseph clapped a hand on Stephen's shoulder, "it is you. I have heard you are a careful and persuasive speaker. I have also heard that you perform many miraculous signs

"You are kind, Rabbi Joseph. I am humbled that the Holy Spirit has chosen to use me for the glory of the Lord Jesus, may His Name be blessed."

"If you will excuse me," Peter said, "John Mark is waving at me. He is probably wanting to write down more of my memories of the Lord Jesus, may His name be blessed." He grinned as he grabbed another cake before crossing the room to where the young man stood.

"If you will excuse me, I would like to listen to Peter's stories," Stephen also took another cake before followed the disciple.

Mary glanced around to confirm their guests were being served, before turning back to the two Teachers of the Law. "Father Nicodemus, Rabbi Joseph, may I ask a question?"

Nicodemus smiled. "Certainly, my daughter."

"I heard what I *believe* to have been the Lord Jesus—may His name be blessed—speaking to me."

The older men's eyes lit up.

"Truly, my daughter? That is amazing."

"Can you tell us what happened, what you *think* He said?" Rabbi Joseph asked.

She briefly related the incident in the garden, leaving out the detail of visiting her aunt and cousins. What she thought the Lord Jesus asked her to do was not as important as the fact she thought He had spoken to her. "As I recall," she crinkled her brow, "He said, '...*is anything too hard for My Father? For Me? Trust in Him with all your heart and do not try to lean on your own understanding. He will direct you.*'"

With furrowed brows, the two elders folded their arms and stroked their beards.

"'*Is anything too hard for the LORD,*'" Rabbi Joseph said, "is what the LORD said when Sarah laughed at the announcement that she would bear a child in her old age."

"True, my friend," said Father Nicodemus. "It was also what

the LORD said to Jeremiah during the time the Babylonians laid siege to Jerusalem. Despite everything foretold of the downfall of the city, the LORD told the prophet to buy a field from a relative."

"You are correct, my friend. And the last part, *"Trust in Him with all your heart and do not try to lean on your own understanding,"* comes from the Proverbs of King Solomon.

"That is right," Rabbi Joseph nodded. "All of those instances speak of Yahweh able to do something that required great faith on the part of the person."

"I agree with you, my friend."

The two men turned to look at Mary, examining her as one would an item Lazarus discovered on one of his journeys.

She looked from her father-in-law to his friend. "Do you think I heard the Lord Jesus speak?"

Rabbi Joseph looked at Father Nicodemus, who nodded. "We do."

"Well," she thrust her hands wide, "What should I do?" Her eyes widened at the manner she addressed them. Color washing her face, she dropped her hands and eyes. "I—I am sorry. I should not have spoken thus. Please forgive me."

"My daughter, forgive us." Her father-in-law took her hands. "You asked for our advice and we treated it as a puzzle to be solved. Yes, we do think you heard the Lord Jesus—may His name be blessed—speak. What should you do?" he glanced at his friend, who nodded. "We think you should do whatever it was He told you to do."

Chapter 18

10 Tishri, 3794, Day of Atonement

The sun was standing molten overhead when Michael arrived home.

He had but a short time before he must return to the Temple to help with his father's priestly duties associated with the Day of Atonement.

Known as *Shabbat Shabbaton,* "a Sabbath of Sabbaths," the Day of Atonement was for the Jewish people the holiest day of the year. It was on this date that the High Priest would present blood sacrifices for himself and for the people of Israel, to avert Yahweh's wrath for the people's sins during the past year. It was also to remind them that other sacrifices would never fully atone for sin.

Beside the fasting, washings, and other preparations required by the Law, Michael's father had a personal tradition of spending the days leading up to each holy day studying the Holy Scripture. After the previous Passover, his father and Rabbi Joseph had begun a discussion on the different aspects of the Law that they felt had been fulfilled with the Lord Jesus' death and resurrection.

During one of the respites from their priestly duties that morning, his father had told his friend he had been writing down his thoughts on this subject.

"I would like to read your thoughts, my friend," Rabbi Joseph had said.

"I would be honored to have you read them," his father had replied. "Perhaps after our duties here are completed, you would accompany us to my home."

"Ah, my friend, I am sorry, but I have commitments elsewhere. Perhaps another time."

Michael had jumped into the conversation. "Father, my responsibilities are completed for now. I would be happy to go back to the house and retrieve your scroll. Then Rabbi Joseph could read it at his leisure."

"What a thoughtful suggestion, my son. Thank you."

As Michael had turned to walk away, his father had added, "Please give my greetings to your lovely wife."

Michael grinned. *Father might be old, but little escapes his eyes. I will take any opportunity to see my wife.*

Touching his fingers to the *mezuzah,* he entered the house. After greeting the servant who tended the door, he wandered through the house, looking for Mary. He found her talking with Elisheba outside one of the *mikvahs,* the baths used for ceremonial cleansing.

He smiled. Even dressed in a simple tunic of yellow linen, with a cream girdle and matching head covering over her thick braid, Mary looked as beautiful as a queen. The towels laid across her arm should have warned him; it was not until he was closer that he heard the elderly servant's comment to his wife.

"Do not worry, mistress. I will see that the baths are stocked with fresh towels." Seeing Michael approach, the servant bowed her head. "Sir, I was telling the mistress she need not worry about re-stocking the baths, as she did in the home of her youth."

Uh oh. Michael thought, noting the frustration on Mary's face. From their private conversations, he knew Mary realized it was not Elisheba's intent to demean her family or childhood. However, that did not diminish the frown on her face, nor the shortness in her greeting.

"Michael, I did not expect you home now."

He explained the reason for his return, adding, "Would you walk with me to Father's bed chamber? I have but a few minutes before I must return to the Temple."

"Yes, of course." Turning, she extended the towels to Elisheba. "Please see these towels are placed in the *mikvah* near the family's bed chambers. These towels were made by my mother and I wish to use them to honor her memory."

Before the elderly servant could say anything else, Mary slipped her hand through Michael's arm and walked away.

He lowered his voice, "That was well done, my wife."

"Shhh," she said. "Wait."

They walked the length of the corridor in silence. When they turned the corner that led down the corridor to his father's bed chamber, she said, "I realize you are going to tell me Elisheba has been running this house since the death of your mother—may her memory be blessed—and she means well. But, Michael, *I* am mistress of this house now. I do not wish to discard the traditions of my family; I wish to blend them with traditions of your family."

"I understand, Mary. I think your response was exactly to that point." He reached up to touch the lines forming between her brows. "But surely, *mikvahs* and towels are not responsible for this look."

"No," the creases in Mary's forehead deepened. "They are not." She sighed. "Actually, the towels were nothing really. Elisheba had just told me something that *disturbed* me.

"She had gone to the market the other day, in preparation for the feast after the fasting for The Day of Atonement ends. She had come to find me, to tell me something had happened at the marketplace."

"What could possibly happen at the marketplace to cause you to be disturbed?"

"She was buying some dates from Othniel when she saw my Aunt Naomi and my cousin Rebeca. They were picking fruit out of the basket he sets aside for the poor."

"What? Elisheba was *accusing* your aunt and cousin of *stealing* food set aside for the poor?"

"No, no, no," Mary shook her head. "Elisheba said they were talking with Othniel when she arrived at the booth. From what she heard, they were thanking him," tears pooled in her eyes, "because *they could not afford to pay for the fruit.* Michael; my aunt and cousins are *poor.*"

"Oh, Mary."

"I have not given thought to them because of the things my uncle said and did during the Lord Jesus' trial and," the muscles in her throat worked, "crucifixion. I know my uncle was driven from the city because of his leprosy and I confess, I thought he deserved it. However, I have not thought about how that would affect my aunt and cousins. What have you noticed about my cousin Abel?"

"I have not seen your cousin in some time. He has not been with Saul Paulus and me during our time with Rabbi Gamaliel." He shrugged. "I confess, I was happy to not have to face him, remembering as you say, what he and your uncle did to the Lord Jesus, may His name be blessed. But it does appear strange he would not be at the Temple studying. He and Saul Paulus always arrived early, sometimes even before Rabbi Gamaliel. Abel seemed determined to learn all Rabbi Gamaliel taught."

"It is difficult to imagine Abel not finishing his studies," Mary said. "After what he considered my father's betrayal of the faith, my uncle was always determined my cousin follow in his footsteps and become a priest.

"That is of no matter," her hand sliced through the air. "Whatever my uncle and Abel have done, whatever Abel is doing now, I cannot allow my family to take food for the poor, especially as we have more than enough.

"Michael, at the last gathering of believers, do you remember Matthew bar Alpheus telling us about the Lord Jesus teaching on giving to those in need? He said we were to do so in secret, not for praise of man. You and I have seen how the believers are sharing with each other; surely, we are to share with others as well.

"I do not wish to be rewarded for helping my family. I wish to help them because I am certain it is what the Lord Jesus—may His name be blessed—would want us to do." She looked at him, an unspoken question stamping the lines of her face.

His heart swelled at Mary's compassion. "Yes, my wife," he pulled her to his chest. "You are correct. The Lord Jesus would want us to help your family."

Chapter 19

The day felt like it was dying. The sky, grey as a lifeless corpse, was wrapped in a shroud of heavy clouds. The wind moaned as it whipped around the corners of buildings. A cold rain, unusual for the month of Heshvan, was trickling like tears down Abel's face. He pulled his robe closer around his body, as if he could draw some warmth from the soggy linen.

Stepping into yet another puddle—there was no way to avoid them—he turned down the street leading toward the Temple. *Hopefully I can find a spot near the braziers.*

The crowd grew as he approached the Temple. Faithful Jews would not let a sodden afternoon keep them from attending the *Tamid*, the perpetual sacrifice. Offered twice each day, at the third hour and again at the ninth hour, the people gathered to pray while a male lamb—without blemish—was sacrificed, along with offerings of wine and flour, for the sins of the people.

It was the three men at the head of the crowd—and not the burnt offering—that drew Abel's steps. One was Michael ben Nicodemus; the other two he recognized as disciples of the Nazarene. One Abel remembered as Peter bar Jonah and the other man he thought was called John ben Zebedee. If he remembered correctly, this man was a relative of Jesus ben Joseph. *Who better than kin for hiding the truth about* that *man?*

Michael and the Nazarene's disciples were nearing the Beautiful Gate. Made of dazzling brass from Corinth, with rich ornamentations and double doors so massive it took twenty men to open or close them, it formed the main entrance to the eastern side of the Temple.

"Alms!" Abel glanced in the direction of the voice. It was the same crippled beggar who, on the Festival of First Fruits had asked if he were alright and begged for alms. He was sitting next to the gate, shaking a basket. "Alms for a poor cripple!"

Abel saw Peter bar Jonah reach a hand to halt his companions' steps and turned toward the beggar.

"Look at us!" the disciple said.

The beggar lifted his gaze and his basket to the man.

But the Nazarene's disciple did not reach for a coin in his girdle. Instead he closed his eyes for a moment before crouching until he was on a level with the beggar. "I have neither silver nor gold," Peter bar Jonah told the cripple, "but what I do have I give to you. In the name of the Lord Jesus of Nazareth, *He* who is the Messiah, *walk*."

A gasp rippled through the crowd at the disciple's words.

Fury raged in Abel's chest. *No one condemns this man for daring to proclaim the Nazarene as the* Messiah *here so close to the Holy Temple? I will!*

Abel pushed through the crowd, determined to berate the disciple, but the words froze on his tongue as Peter bar Jonah reached down, took the beggar by the hand, and lifted him to his feet.

The beggar clung to the disciple's hand for a moment. Then his eyes grew wide as he looked down at his legs and feet and gasped.

That gasp was echoed by those standing near the man. Instead of twisted and deformed, his feet and legs were whole and strong.

The beggar gingerly lifted one foot, testing it. "My feet," he whispered. He set that foot down and lifted the other. "They're whole." He lifted his tunic to look at the muscles of his legs, now straight and thick. "I'm healed," his voice grew, as he let go of Peter bar Jonah's hand and took several tentative steps. "I. Am. *Healed*!" He laughed. "I can *walk*!"

He continued walking in a circle, laughing at the crowd's expressions. He came to a puddle of water and *jumped* into it. "I can *jump*!" He twisted in a rhythmic movement. "I can *dance*!"

The crowd clapped and cheered; several joined in his dance while others—mostly children—jumped in the puddles of water.

He turned back to grab Peter bar Jonah's shoulders and hugged him. "Thank you!" He grabbed John ben Zebedee and then Michael, hugging the men and laughing as he wiped away tears. "Thank you all. You healed me."

The clamor of the crowd rejoicing with the beggar drew people from streets of the city.

It also drew people from the Temple. They shouted questions, wanting to know what had happened, and were astonished to hear of the beggar's healing. When they saw the lame man jumping and dancing and giving praise to Yahweh and to Jesus ben Joseph of Nazareth for his healing—they joined in, dancing, hopping, and splashing in the puddles of rainwater.

On one edge of the crowd, Abel saw Rabbi Nicodemus ben Melech and Rabbi Joseph bar Neriah; they were smiling at the crowd rejoicing with the beggar.

On the other edge of the crowd were more priests, including Rabbi Caiaphas, Rabbi Annas, Rabbi Gamaliel, and—Abel's mouth twisted in distaste—Saul Paulus. Behind them stood a line of Temple Guards, armed with spears. With the exception of Rabbi Gamaliel, as one, these priests folded their arms, their faces a study in righteous anger, as they listened to the crowd.

Abel stepped back, to avoid being seen by these men, but it was too late. *Caiaphas has the eyes of a hawk,* Abel thought, *to match his nose.* Abel noted the scowl on the High Priest's face as he stared at him and at the crowd's racket. *As if I were responsible for this pandemonium.*

The beggar apparently did not see the condemnation on the face of the High Priest. He continued to alternate between jumping and dancing and thanking the followers of Jesus ben Joseph for his healing. Abel was surprised when John ben Zebedee stopped the beggar.

"It was not by our strength or power that you are healed."

"Men of Israel..." Peter bar Jonah stepped into the center of the crowd.

Where he can be seen by all men, Abel sneered.

"...why does this surprise you?" he continued. "Why do you stare at us as if it were by our own power or godliness we made this man walk?

"The God of Abraham, Isaac, and Jacob, the God of our fathers, has glorified His servant Jesus." He turned and lifted a finger to point at the glowering Temple leaders. "*You* handed Him over to Pilate to be killed, even though the Governor had decided to let Him go." *You*," he jabbed, "disowned the *Holy and Righteous One* and asked Pilate to release a murderer to you. *You*," he jabbed again, "killed the *Author of Life*, but Yahweh raised *Him* from the dead. We," he extended his arms wide, "are all witnesses of this." Abel noticed Rabbi Caiaphas—eyebrows lowered as an angry bull—open his mouth, but the disciple pressed on.

"By faith in the name of Jesus, this man whom you see and know was made strong. It is Jesus' name and the faith that comes through *Him* that has given this man complete healing, as you can all see."

Abel saw the disciple smile—*as if he* cares *about these people*—before continuing to tell the crowd that they acted in ignorance and that the act of killing Jesus ben Joseph was a fulfillment of the prophecy that the Messiah would suffer. He admonished the people to repent of their sins and turn to Yahweh.

Peter continued talking; about how Jesus, as Messiah, was in heaven with Yahweh. He followed up by using scriptures—*twisting them*, Abel raged—to show how Yahweh will cut off anyone who does not listen to the words of Jesus and turn from their wicked ways.

Rabbi Caiaphas' face grew darker with each word the disciple spoke. At the final condemnation, he unfolded his arms and gestured at the Temple Guard.

The guards moved through the crowds, shoving people aside, butting heads, until they reached the two disciples. Abel grinned when Michael ben Nicodemus stepped in to block them, noting Rabbi Nicodemus and Rabbi Joseph were moving through the crowds to reach them. Abel grinned. *Your father's money and position cannot save your friends.*

The guards moved past Michael to grab the disciples. Michael—his face darkened—tried to remove the guards' hands from Peter and John's arms.

Keep fighting, Michael, Abel thought. *Perhaps you will see what the inside of the Temple prison cells are like.*

Rabbi Nicodemus and Rabbi Joseph had reached Michael. "Father, do something!" Abel heard Michael say.

He watched as the older two rabbis looked from the guards holding the Nazarene's disciples, to Rabbi Caiaphas and Rabbi Annas, then to Michael. Rabbi Nicodemus leaned in to speak to his son.

Michael glowered and gave a sharp nod. He glared, fists clinching as the Temple Guard—spears at the ready—prepared to lead the two disciples away.

Rabbi Nicodemus stepped to Peter bar Jonah and John ben Zebedee and spoke to them. Rabbi Joseph and Michael followed Rabbi Nicodemus to listen to the conversation.

Abel leaned in, as if he could hear the whispered conversation from this distance. *Perhaps they are discussing protecting the location of the Nazarene's body.*

After speaking to the disciples, Rabbi Nicodemus turned toward the line of Temple leaders. Known for his gentle manner, nothing reflected gentleness in the look the older man gave the High Priest.

Chapter 20

*M*ichael tried to control his rage as he watched Peter and John led away under guard as if they were dangerous criminals or members of the *Sicarii,* the radical sect of Zealots whose name means 'daggers.'

It was the *Sicarii* leader Jesus Barabbas—convicted of killing Roman soldiers—who had been released when Pontius Pilate had tried to placate the people gathered in the Antonia Fortress during the trial of the Lord Jesus. Rabbi Joseph had explained the governor was offering the crowd a choice between two Roman practices: the *indulgentia,* where a condemned prisoner—Barabbas—would be pardoned, or the *abolition,* where a prisoner—the Lord Jesus— would be acquitted before judgement was passed.

Despite the combined voices of the Lord Jesus' followers, it was obvious those who had arranged for the Lord Jesus' arrest had also paid the crowd to cry for the release of the *Sicarii* leader. Michael remembered Governor Pilate demanding an explanation from the crowd.

"If I release Barabbas—this murderer—to you, what shall I do with Jesus, the one you called the Messiah, the King of the Jews?"

"He cannot be the Messiah!" Mary's Uncle Joktan ben Philemon had screamed. *"When the Messiah comes, he will be strong. He will never allow himself to be captured."* He had jabbed a finger toward the Lord Jesus. *"He lied by claiming to be the Messiah! He lied to us! He lied to us! Release Barabbas!"*

"He's not the Messiah!" another man had yelled. Others joined in, decrying the Lord Jesus as a liar.

The governor had lifted his hands to silence the crowd. *"But what should I do with Jesus?"* he had asked.

Michael's gut still wrenched as he recalled Joktan screaming. *"Crucify him."*

That was the first moment when he realized that—in this situation—all his father's power, position, and wealth could do nothing. That was when he realized he had failed to keep his first promise to his beloved Mary; to save the Lord Jesus. Yes, in hindsight, the Lord Jesus was resurrected, but He suffered from torturous beatings and crucifixion.

Peter and John have done nothing. *They have not spoken against the Temple leaders. They have not disturbed the Temple by turning over the tables of the moneychangers. They were coming to the Temple to pray. All they did was speak healing to a man crippled from birth. Where is the crime?*

Michael recalled Peter and John's words just before the guards led them away. "Do not be anxious," Peter had said. "The Lord Jesus warned us to be on our guard against men. He said we would be arrested and brought before kings and governors."

"Peter speaks truth," John had said. "The Lord Jesus told us men would hand us over to leaders and councils. He said we would even be flogged in their synagogues."

Arrested. Just like now, Michael thought. *Flogged in the synagogues? Please, Lord Jesus, not that.*

"But," Peter had added, "The Lord Jesus also told us not to worry. He said the Holy Spirit would give us the words to say."

Michael looked at the faces of Peter and John. There was no fear; indeed, they radiated confidence.

He smiled, feeling hope kindle. Long before this day, the Lord Jesus had prepared His followers for events like the one happening now. *Lord Jesus, be with John and Peter and comfort them. Be with them as they are questioned by the Temple leaders.* He crossed to stand by his father and Rabbi Joseph. *Give Father and Rabbi Joseph, and myself the words to speak on their behalf. Through all of this, let Your Name be glorified.*

Chapter 21

"Itamar bar Reuben reported two of the Nazarene's disciples were arrested at the Temple. Did you attend the trial?"

Abel slanted a glance at his father's *scribe*. The other man, along with his son Aran, were setting up writing implements on a flat stone a few cubits away. *So now this man is bringing information to Father.* "Yes, sir. I was there."

"Wonderful!" Abel had not seen his father this—*happy*—since his cousin Lazarus' *supposed death* when he thought, as near kinsman, he would control his nephew's fortune as well as the futures of his nieces, Mary and Martha. He clapped his hands—or what was left of them—and reached down to get the basket of food. Sitting on the ground, he settled his garments beneath him, before removing a piece of bread from the basket and taking a bite. "The bread is better today. Tell your *racha* mother to continue sending me only this bread." He took a swig from the wineskin, apparently unconcerned by the blood-red droplets splashing his garments. "Now. Hand me the coins for Itamar and tell me everything that happened, beginning with the names of these men."

Abel forced himself to control a grimace as he drew the pouch of coins from his girdle and threw it to his father. "It was Peter bar Jonah and John ben Zebedee. They were walking to the Temple with Michael ben Nicodemus. They had reached the Beautiful Gate when the lame beggar cried out for alms."

Abel related what happened the other day, while his father peppered him with questions.

"Peter bar Jonah spoke to the beggar in the name of Jesus ben Joseph of Nazareth and proclaiming him as the Messiah and told the man to walk."

"How *dare* he name *that man* as *Messiah!* Is that when the Temple Guards arrested him?"

"No, sir. After he spoke to the beggar, Peter bar Jonah grabbed the man's hand and lifted him."

His father grabbed his sides, laughing. "Did the beggar fall down?"

"Noooo, sir. The beggar—uh—walked."

The levity vanished from his father's face. "What do you mean *he walked?*"

"Just that. The beggar walked."

"Did this Peter bar Jonah and John ben Zebedee *carry* him, so it *appeared* he walked?"

Abel glanced at the scribe. Under other circumstances, he would have confirmed what his father said. *I do not know what this Itamar is telling Father.* "No. The beggar walked on his own."

The scowl on his father's face deepened as Abel related the story of the beggar's healing; it eased only when he came to the part of the disciples' arrest. "Rabbi Caiaphas will not tolerate one of the Nazarene's followers stirring up the crowds, not after all the effort it took to have *that man* crucified. What happened next? Continue your story."

"As it was time for the *Tamid*, and too late to call the Sanhedrin for a trial, Rabbi Caiaphas had the men put in prison for the night."

"And when the High Priest convened the meeting the next morning, you stood in my place?"

"Yes." Abel had been there, but not in his father's stead. He was not concerned speaking this lie. Only the priests, rulers, elders, and teachers of the Law would be allowed to hear this trial; not his father's crippled scribe. "The High Priest had these two men brought before them and asked them by what power or what name they had done this."

"What did they say?"

"Peter bar Jonah addressed the rulers and said if they were being held and questioned for an act of kindness to a poor cripple and how he was healed, then they should know that the beggar's healing came through the name and power of the Nazarene."

"What!? He said that? What were his *exact* words? Itamar," he turned to the other man, "see that you write this down. Abel, repeat what this man said."

Abel thought for a second. "He said, 'It is by the name of Jesus of Nazareth, the Messiah, whom you crucified but whom Yahweh raised from the dead, that this man stands before you healed.'

"He went on to call the Nazarene the *stone that you builders rejected*, but which has become the capstone."

"What does that mean? Did you ask?"

"I did not question these men, Father, not in the presence of the High Priests and Temple leaders."

"Did he say anything else?"

Abel nodded. "He said, 'Salvation is found in no one else, for there is no other name under heaven given to men by which we must be saved.'"

"Saved? What does he mean by being *saved*?"

Abel shrugged. "I do not know, and no one asked him."

"What happened next? Did Rabbi Caiaphas command them to tell the location of the *Nazarene's* body?"

"No. The High Priest had the prisoners removed from the room. There was a *discussion* among the leaders and elders about what these men said. Many were surprised that these men presented their case carefully, even though they were ordinary men who had never been trained. The only thing that set them apart from other men was they had been with Jesus ben Joseph.

"To be associated with that criminal should have been sufficient for these men to be punished!"

"It appeared Rabbi Caiaphas and Rabbi Annas were concerned about doing anything when they had performed a miracle in front of so many."

"That is nothing! I am certain that the man was never lame and merely pretended to be, in order for people to give him money. Had I been present, I would have pointed this out. I am surprised no one else brought this up.

"No one did, and Rabbi Caiaphas appeared to believe a miracle had been performed. After conferring with Rabbi Annas, they had the two men brought back in and commanded them to stop speaking in the *Nazarene's* name."

"That command must have made an impact, after seeing what happened to the *Nazarene*. What was their response?"

Abel paused. *Father will not be happy with their answer.* While he was trying to frame his answer, his father erupted.

"What did these men say? Tell me, you *fool*!"

Fine! All concern for his father's feelings left. "They said, 'You be the judge. Is it right in Yahweh's sight that we obey you or Him? For we cannot help speaking about the things we have seen and heard."

Chapter 22

"Peter and John said *that* to the Temple leaders?" Mary asked Michael.

The night before he, along with Father Nicodemus and Rabbi Joseph, had brought home the news of Peter and John's arrest. They had sent word to the believers in Jerusalem and Bethany. Within the hour, many believers—including Lazarus and Abigail, Martha and Simon, and the remainder of the Twelve—had gathered to hear the news and to pray. After everyone left, Father Nicodemus invited Rabbi Joseph to his study. The two elders poured over the Law, making notes to use in defense of the disciples.

Michael, along with his father and Rabbi Joseph, had left for the Temple shortly after the second hour that morning. "Father is determined that the unlawful trial the Lord Jesus—may His name be blessed—faced will not be repeated today," Michael had told Mary.

Mary had made Michael promise to send back word as soon as he could. She and Ruth planned a long list of things to keep their minds occupied. They were surprised when the men returned before midday, with Peter and John.

Mary only had a moment to speak with Michael before sending Jemima to the kitchen for food while Ruth gathered clean clothes for the two disciples. Father Nicodemus escorted them to bed chambers to bathe and change, while Rabbi Joseph and Michael sent word to those who had gathered the night before.

Within the hour, the house was once again filled with believers rejoicing over the report of the trial and Peter and John's response to the questioning of the Temple leaders. They, in turn, were surprised to hear that word of the lame beggar's healing had spread throughout Jerusalem and Bethany, causing more to believe in the Lord Jesus.

"We are not certain of the exact number," Lazarus said, "but Simon and I think the number of believers is now about five thousand."

"This is wonderful news," Peter said. "And we thank you, Rabbi Nicodemus, Rabbi Joseph, and Michael for standing with us among the Temple leaders. However, we must also give thanks to the Lord."

Those gathered in the house bowed their heads.

"Sovereign Lord," Peter prayed. "You made the heaven and the earth and all that is in them. You spoke by the Holy Spirit through the mouth of Your servant and our father, King David, who said, *'Why do the nations rage and the peoples plot in vain? The kings of the earth take their stand and the rulers gather together against the Lord and His Anointed One.'* Indeed, Herod and Pontius Pilate met with the Gentiles and the people of Israel here in Jerusalem to plot against Your holy servant, the Lord Jesus, Whom You anointed. They did what Your power and will had decided should happen long ago."

When Peter grew silent, John spoke, "Now, Lord, consider the threat these people have made and give us strength and boldness to speak Your Word. Stretch out Your hand to heal and to perform miraculous signs and wonders through the name of Your Holy servant, the Lord Jesus. Amen."

Even as John's words were fading, Mary felt a tremor beneath her feet. Michael grabbed her hand, pulling her to his chest, as the house began shaking. She felt a familiar warmth radiating from inside, and she opened her mouth. "Thank you, Yahweh," she cried, "for Your great power, for protecting Your servants Peter and John."

"Thank you, Lord Jesus," Michael shouted over the sound of the quake, "for allowing them to speak of Your healing power to this man who has been lame for forty years, and to speak of Your saving power to all who were present yesterday and today."

"Indeed, Yahweh," Father Nicodemus added, "we pray You use this for Your glory and to further the message of Your Kingdom."

As the room continued shaking—without anything being broken or damaged—Mary heard the others in the room join in declaring the praise of Yahweh and of the Lord Jesus.

Chapter 23

"Wait." Mary was certain she had mis-heard. "Would you please repeat what you just said?"

It was supposed to have been a rare evening of family only. Martha and Simon, and Lazarus and Abigail were present, along with Father Nicodemus' oldest daughter Joanna and her husband Matthias and their young children, David and Deborah.

Elisheba had prepared a meal of roasted fish stuffed with garlic, onions, and olives. Side dishes included lentils, leeks, cucumbers, cheese, bread, figs and pomegranates. Mary had shared the recipe of her oat and honey cakes with the older servant. These were served after the meal, when everyone had moved to the family's private courtyard.

While Elisheba presided over the cooking and baking, Mary and Ruth had overseen the cleaning of the courtyard. Frescoes of palm trees and pomegranates decorated the walls, the colors echoing the gold, green, and red of the intricate mosaic tiles on the floor. A length of windows on the far wall had shutters that could be adjusted according to the season and weather; in the corner were stairs that led to the rooftop. Between the brightly burning braziers placed around the room were niches displaying antiques, delicate glassware edged with gold or silver, and amphorae filled with expensive fragrant oils. Tables were positioned around the room with thick cushions beneath, and should anyone wish to read, a shelf in one corner held scrolls.

There were also other things not normally seen in many homes: chairs. Made from polished ebony, they looked like a square stool with an upright piece of wood on one side for a person to lean back against. A year before he married Abigail, Lazarus had seen these on one of his journeys. When Father Nicodemus had learned of them, he commissioned Lazarus to purchase several for his home. He had explained to Mary that sitting upon the pillows beneath the tables was not easy for one of his age. "It is not the lowering oneself to the floor that is the issue," Father Nicodemus had said, "as it is rising."

The meal was delicious, with everyone enjoying several servings. As the family moved from the dining room to the courtyard, David and Deborah had been led away by a smiling Elisheba, ostensibly to be put to bed in Joanna's old bed chamber.

"However, I am certain," Joanna had told Mary, "Elisheba will ply them with your honey and oat cakes *before* putting them to bed."

The two children were not the only ones who had enjoyed the oat and honey cakes. There had been several trays piled high with oat cakes placed on the tables in the family courtyard. Now the trays held only crumbs.

As the oat and honey cakes had been consumed by the adults, the conversation had turned to what was happening to those who believed in the Lord Jesus.

Their numbers had grown over the months since the Festival of First Fruits.

Even though there were many believers, no one was in need, because other believers sold their property and took it to the Twelve to disperse, including Joseph bar Achaicus, who had sold a field and presented the whole amount to the Twelve. His generous gift, along with his encouraging spirit, caused the believers to call him "Barnabas," *Son of Encouragement.*

There had been some conflict about how the food was dispersed between the Jewish and Gentile believers. After praying, the Twelve had chosen Stephen ben Chariton, along with six other men, to oversee the food dispersal and other needs among the believers.

Although Mary tried to listen, her eyes grew heavy and her thoughts kept drifting toward her bed. Until something Lazarus said startled her awake.

"I wish to sell our family homes."

Certain she had been too sleepy to have heard correctly, Mary had asked him to repeat himself.

"I wish to sell our family homes." Her brother spoke as if he were talking of discarding an old garment and not the homes where she and her siblings had been born. The homes where they had grown up. Where their parents had died and where, just the year before, *he* had died.

"What?" Even after he repeated himself, she still couldn't believe it.

"Lazarus wants to sell our family's houses, the one in Bethany and the one in Capernaum," Martha echoed. Simply, without emotion.

A frown creased Mary's brow as she looked at her sister. "You knew of this?"

"I did."

"And why did you know before I did?"

"Because Martha and I are also selling our home," Simon said.

Mary's eyes widened. "What?" She looked at Father Nicodemus—who nodded—to Michael—who reached over to cover her hand with his. "You *all* knew about this?"

"I knew nothing about this," Ruth huffed as she crossed her arms.

Father Nicodemus frowned at his youngest child. "That is because this decision does not affect you, my daughter."

"Oh." Spots of scarlet burnt Ruth's cheeks. She dropped her arms and stared at the floor. Mary felt sorry for her sister-in-law; it was rare Father Nicodemus chided any of his children. She drew the attention away from Ruth. "Would one of you please explain what brought about this decision?"

"Mary, you knew we were planning to move to Cyprus," Lazarus said.

"And you knew we, along with Rabbi Joseph, were going to Gaul," Simon added.

"I knew you had *mentioned* leaving Bethany after the Lord Jesus' death and resurrection," Mary said. "But times were different then; we were all concerned about the repercussions of the Temple leaders toward the Lord's followers." She flung her arms wide. "But *nothing* has happened; indeed, there has been *favor* toward all who believe in Him."

Martha lifted an eyebrow. "You consider Peter and John's arrest and imprisonment to be *favor?*"

"Yes, well..." Mary stumbled, "but *they were released!* They were not flogged or..." she trailed off.

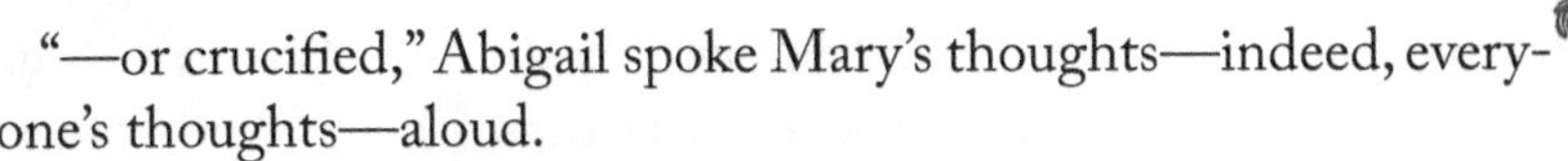

"—or crucified," Abigail spoke Mary's thoughts—indeed, everyone's thoughts—aloud.

"Yes," Mary felt the power of her argument deflate.

"You speak truth, my daughter," Father Nicodemus' voice was gentle. "There has been favor toward those who believe in the Lord Jesus, may His name be blessed. And thanks be to Yahweh that Peter and John were *not* flogged or…worse. However, as Michael will tell you, the disposition among the Temple leaders has never been *favorable* toward those who are followers of the Lord Jesus."

"The disposition of the Temple leaders is *not* why Abigail and I are still planning to go to Cyprus," Lazarus said. "We still believe that the Lord Jesus—may His name be blessed—is sending us there. We want to share the message of His love, of His sacrifice, and of His kingdom. We want to obey His last command and be His witnesses to the ends of the earth."

Simon placed his hand on Martha's. "That is what we wish to do as well."

Mary looked at Martha, "But, I thought," she looked at Lazarus, "we would all be near each other, and that our" she looked back at Martha, "*children* would grow up near each other."

"That would be wonderful," Martha smiled, lifting a hand to wipe away a tear. "But we must do as we believe the Holy Spirit is leading."

"We will not be separated *forever*, Mary, nor lose contact," Abigail blinked back tears. "We can write to each other. And Cyprus is not that far. You and Michael could come visit us."

"I would enjoy that," Michael said, squeezing Mary's hand. "I would also enjoy going to the lands of the Gauls. "Would you not, my Love?"

Mary let out a deep breath. "Yes, I would. Indeed, I have always dreamt of traveling to distant lands." She looked at her brother and sister. "But why sell our homes?"

"Mary, you heard the discussion of those believers selling land and other properties and bringing the money to the Twelve, in order to help those in need," Lazarus said.

She nodded.

"That is what we want to do," he said. "Rather than keep the houses, we want to sell them to help others. However, these houses do not belong to just Abigail and me. They are the homes of your childhood; they belong to you and Martha. Whatever price I get for them will be divided between the three of us."

"Lazarus," Martha frowned, "you do not need to do this," Her sister was obviously not aware of this decision.

Mary echoed her. "I do not need the money." She smiled at Michael. "My husband provides all I need."

"Nevertheless, that is what we are going to do." Lazarus smiled at Abigail. "We plan to give a portion of the sale to the Twelve in order to help those in need. Whatever is left, we will take with us to Cyprus, to help spread the word of the Lord Jesus there. In fact, I already have someone interested in buying our house in Bethany."

"And we have someone interested in our house," Simon said.

"So soon? Where will you live until you leave?"

"They are going to live here with us, Daughter," Father Nicodemus smiled. "It has been decided. We have plenty of room and this house will be all the more joyful for having them."

"That would be wonderful," Ruth said.

"Think of Elisheba's response to this news," Michael gave a wide, toothy grin. "I imagine she will be quoting her beloved grandmother from dawn until dusk for many days to come."

"Michael," Father Nicodemus' tone was gruff.

Everyone looked at the family patriarch. He lowered bushy brows at his son, who continued grinning. The elderly man's lips twitched before bursting into laughter. "I think she will as well."

Even as Mary joined in the laughter, she tried to digest her brother's news. *The homes of my childhood. Filled with so many memories. But what is keeping an empty house compared to helping others learn about the Lord Jesus? Like Aunt Naomi and my cousins. They need money; this would be the perfect opportunity to help them.* She looked at Lazarus. "That is a wise decision." She lifted her chin. "Michael, if it is alright with you, I too would like my portion of the sale," she gave him a knowing smile, "to help *those in need.*"

Her husband lifted her hand to his lips. "You are kind and loving, my wife. Yes, of course; you may do whatever you wish with your portion of the money."

Chapter 24

"What a beautiful day," Michael stretched his arms, closed his eyes, and lifted his head toward the sun.

"I agree the day is beautiful," his father smiled, "but I believe that for you my son, it is due to something beyond the sunlight." He turned to Rabbi Joseph. "Do you not agree, my friend?"

The other rabbi stroked his beard, his eyes twinkling as he studied Michael. "I do indeed. If I were younger and had finished my tasks at the Temple early, and was going home to be with my wife, I would think the day beautiful."

Michael grinned. "I am glad you understand." He glared at the congested street. "However, if the crowds would ease, we would arrive home even faster. Daniel," he leaned toward the driver, "could you perhaps take a different route?"

"The streets surrounding the Temple are always filled with people wishing to offer sacrifices and worship Yahweh," his father replied. "However, you have a good idea, my son. Daniel, please turn down this street. We can stop by Simon and Lazarus' warehouse."

"Yes, Rabbi Nicodemus." Daniel worked the reins.

"What?" Michael held on as their carriage made a sharp turn. "Father, why should we stop by the warehouse?"

"Lazarus and Simon might be finished with their work as well and I want to offer them a ride," his father replied. "I thought they might wish to get home to their wives as much as you wish to get home to Mary."

"Oh…well…but surely," Michael looked from his father—who had a toothy grin—to Rabbi Joseph—who copied his friend. After a moment, Michael threw his head back and roared in laughter, slapping his thighs. "I am certain they do wish it."

Within minutes, Daniel had pulled up to the warehouse and Michael jumped down to help his father and Rabbi Joseph descend. They walked to the door, smiling and greeting the people who were coming and going, before stepping inside the warehouse.

Built of cut stone, the front room on the lower floor was large, with walls of smooth clay and the floors tiled in alternating squares of blue, terracotta, and white. Designed for business, the room had no decorations, only niches for oil lamps in the walls. Beyond the main room were several smaller rooms for storage and a central courtyard.

They found Simon and Lazarus moving between the shelves along the walls that held merchandise and a long table in the center of the room with thick cushions beneath where sat several customers interested in the lengths of colorful silks that had been purchased from foreign lands.

Simon and Lazarus welcomed the offer of a ride to Nicodemus' house, "If you do not mind waiting while we finish with this business."

Michael opened his mouth, but his father spoke first. "Of course, we do not mind waiting." He slanted a glance at his son, "Do we, Michael?" Michael paused, caught his father's eye, and lifted his shoulders. "No, of course not."

"While we wait, we will go speak with the Twelve," Rabbi Joseph moved toward the stairs.

After the Feast of First Fruits, the upper room of the warehouse became the central location for the Twelve to meet. They used it for prayer, for teaching, for sharing their memories of the Lord Jesus, and to oversee the governing of *the Way*. That was the name that had been given to the burgeoning group of believers, taken from the Lord Jesus' proclamation, "*I Am the Way, and the Truth, and the Life. No one can come to the Father except through Me.*"

There were as many people in the Upper Room as there had been in front of the warehouse. Being taller than most men, it was easy for Michael to locate Peter. The fisherman, along with the other eleven disciples, were sitting beneath the windows. John Mark was seated nearby, writing implements set on a small table in front of him.

People were waiting in line for their turn to speak with the Twelve. Michael could tell, from the conversations overheard, that some were coming for advice, others to ask for healing prayers, while others brought family members or friends who wanted to know more about the Lord Jesus.

"Greetings Ananias ben Kenan," Peter was speaking to a short man with dark wavy hair. "The blessings of the Lord Jesus be upon you."

"And His blessings be upon you, Peter bar Jonah. My wife Sapphira and I have sold some property for three hundred denarii." The man handed a small chest to the disciple. "We wish to give it to you, for the *Way*." He folded his hands and smiled as those in the room commented on his generous gift.

Peter lifted the lid of the chest. The light from the window glinted on the coins. He closed the lid and looked up. "Three hundred denarii is a considerable amount." He glanced beyond Ananias. "Where is your wife?"

"Oh, uh," the man seemed confused at the disciple's question, "she had to buy some…herbs and, uh…fruit…for her mother."

"Herbs and fruit," Peter repeated, his eyes never leaving the other man's face.

"Yes."

Michael noticed Ananias shift from one foot to the other and reach up to wipe a trickle of sweat from his brow.

Those in the room were silent, their gaze shifting between Peter, Ananias, and the chest filled with coins.

"Ananias," Peter finally spoke, "how is it Satan has so filled your heart that you have lied to the Holy Spirit?"

"W-w-w-hat?" Ananias sputtered.

"You have kept for yourself some of the money you received for the land."

Ananias' eyes widened. "I—I did not—" he tried to interrupt the disciple, but Peter slashed his hand through the air.

"Did not the land belong to you before the sale? After you sold it, was not the money at your disposal?" He jabbed a finger at the other man. "What made you think to do such a thing? You have not lied to me," Peter placed a hand on his chest, "to us," he extended his arms to indicate the eleven disciples on either side. "You have not lied to men; but to Yahweh."

"I…" Ananias gaped at Peter. "We…" he looked at the other disciples. "You…" he glanced at those in the room who were staring at him. Suddenly, his eyes widened, he grabbed his throat, gasping for air, before collapsing onto the floor.

Several men rushed to help him.

"There is no need," Peter's voice resonated around the room. "He is dead."

Gasps rippled throughout the room. Several people stepped away from the body of Ananias. Several stepped from Peter.

The disciple did not appear to notice the blatant fear on the faces of many in the room. "Remove Ananias' body and take it to his family's tomb." He folded his arms across his chest. "We will wait for Sapphira."

No one had moved. No one had spoken.

For what appeared to have been hours—judging from the sunlight slanting through the window—Michael had stood with his father, Rabbi Joseph, Simon, and Lazarus. His two brothers-in-law had come running up the stairs when the men had carried out the body of Ananias for burial.

The eyes of everyone in the room shifted between the Twelve and the door.

Then, from below, came the sound of a door opening.

"Hello?" It was a woman. "Simon bar Hiram? Lazarus ben Jacob?" Footsteps echoed as someone crossed the tiled floor and ascended the stairs.

A woman entered the upper room. Petite, with ebony eyes and lips the shade of a ruby, Sapphira bat Teman wore a rose-colored tunic and a robe the shade of wine. Being newly married, Michael had learned something about women's clothing; he could tell the garments were new and her earrings expensive.

"Greetings, Peter bar Jonah. The Lord's blessings on you." She glanced around the room. "I am looking for Ananias. I understood he was bringing you a gift."

"Greetings, Sapphira bat Teman."

Michael noted Peter did not add the Lord's blessings in response. "Your husband was here. And he did bring a *gift*."

"Ah. That is good," Sapphira heaved a sigh and stepped further into the room. "We were so excited to bring the money to you, but I had to go to—"

"Let me ask you a question," Peter interrupted her. "Did you and Ananias sell the land for three hundred denarii?"

She nodded, her earrings jingling. "Oh yes. It was a large piece of land and has been in my family since my grandfather's grandfather's time. But that did not matter to us. We wanted to—"

"Sapphira," Peter cut through her words. "How could you and Ananias agree to test the Spirit of the Lord?"

"What?" She stared at him. "No, we did…"

The sound of the front door opening and feet crossing the tiled floor echoed through the room.

"Look!" Peter pointed at Sapphira, who had clutched her throat, gasping. "The men who buried your husband are here. They will carry you to be buried with him."

Chapter 25

"The actions of those foolish people of *The Way* are offensive!" Rabbi Caiaphas' lips thinned into a frown. "They treat this *unlearned fisherman* as if he were a prophet of Yahweh." His voice echoed around the marbled pillars in the colonnade.

Nearing the time for the morning *Tamid*, the Temple courts were filled with people, yet none of the worshippers approached the men speaking with the High Priest and his father-in-law.

"It is disgusting," Rabbi Annas said. "Abel ben Joktan reports of people bringing their sick, or those tormented by demons, into the streets and placing them so that this Peter bar Jonah will pass by them. What are they thinking? That perhaps his very *shadow* will heal them?"

Abel preened at the former High Priest's reference to him, but his smile slipped away when Saul Paulus spoke to him.

"Abel ben Joktan, did you question these people, to determine how they *made it appear* they had been healed by this Peter bar Jonah?"

Abel lifted his chin and folded his lips tight. *I do not report to you, Saul Paulus!*

"Answer him!" Rabbi Annas snapped.

Abel felt his cheeks heat. He lowered his chin but refused to look at Saul. "I…uh…did not, Rabbi Annas. I did not know you or Rabbi Caiaphas would wish me to question these people."

"Humph!" Saul Paulus folded his arms across his chest. "Had *I* been there, I would have *forced* these people to admit their duplicity."

"Look," Rabbi Caiaphas snarled. "They are using the Temple of Yahweh as their public gathering place."

Abel turned in the direction the High Priest was pointing. A crowd was entering into Solomon's Colonnade, following two men; Peter bar Jonah and John ben Zebedee.

"Look," Saul Paulus pointed to a tall man standing near the Nazarene's disciples. "That is the man I spoke of; Stephen ben Chariton."

"I do not see Nicodemus ben Melech nor his son Michael with *those* people," Rabbi Caiaphas said. "Neither is Joseph bar Neriah with them."

"I saw them enter the Temple earlier this morning," Saul Paulus said.

Rabbi Annas snorted. "They should attend to the Temple, rather than offer support to the followers of the Nazarene. Shhhh—" He hissed as his son-in-law opened his mouth to speak. "We need to listen for any words of blasphemy or treason."

Abel stepped aside to allow the High Priest and Rabbi Annas to move forward. He lifted his foot to fall in behind and tripped as Saul Paulus shouldered him out of the way. He glared at the Jew from Tarsus, but it was of no use; the other man did not even glance his way. Mumbling under his breath about men who think more highly of themselves than they should, Abel moved closer to the rabbis to listen to the two disciples of the Nazarene.

Peter bar Jonah and John ben Zebedee were talking to those in the crowd, discussing the weather, asking after their families and their needs.

Nothing that could be considered a cause for arrest.

Then someone in the crowd called out, "Peter! John! Would you tell us about *Jesus?*"

"We will," John smiled.

Going back and forth between themselves, the two fishermen began talking about the things Jesus ben Joseph said and did, beginning when he first appeared in the area to be baptized by John ben Zechariah.

Rabbi Annas and Rabbi Caiaphas scowled at the reference to the man known as the *Baptizer.* A little over three years earlier, this man had shown up in the area of the Jordan River, preaching a message of repentance and preparation for the coming kingdom of Yahweh. If that had been all he taught, nothing more would have happened. However, this John spoke against the Temple leaders, accusing them of abusing their power. Beyond that, he spoke against King Herod, for which he was arrested and later beheaded.

The Nazarene's disciples did not linger on the Baptizer. They spoke about Jesus' teachings, his *so-called* miracles, and of the events that occurred during the last Passover Feast.

"He was arrested by the," Peter turned to stare at Rabbis Caiaphas and Annas, "Temple leaders who—by Yahweh's purpose and fore-knowledge—handed Him over to the Romans, who put Him to death by crucifixion."

A soft groan rippled through the crowd. Anyone who lived in or visited Jerusalem had seen a Roman crucifixion.

John nodded at the crowd's response. "Jesus hung on the cross for six hours that day. He died at three in the afternoon." He lifted his hand, sweeping a pointed finger at the people in the crowd. "He died for your sins." He laid his opened palm against his own chest. "He died for my sins."

"But He did not stay in the grave," Peter's voice echoed around the colonnade.

Abel noticed the other three men with him perk up and lean forward. His lip curled in a jeer. *Do you really think these men will openly announce where they hid the body of Jesus?*

"No," Peter continued. "Yahweh raised Him from the dead, freeing Him from death's agony, because it was *impossible* for death to keep a hold on Him."

"King David wrote about the Lord Jesus in his psalms, when he said, '*You will not abandon Me to the grave, nor will You let Your Holy One see decay*'."

As one, the three men standing with Abel hissed.

"How *dare* these men claim a condemned prisoner is the Son of Yahweh!" Rabbi Annas snarled. Turning, he gestured to the Temple Guards and pointed to the two disciples.

The Guards, spears at the ready, moved in; within a few minutes, Peter bar Jonah and John ben Zebedee were arrested and led away.

"There," Rabbi Annas dusted his hands. "Let them spend tonight in the public jail. Caiaphas, send word to the Sanhedrin that we will convene tomorrow to try these men for their blasphemous comments. Oh and," he lifted a finger, "see that Nicodemus ben Melech and Joseph bar Neriah are the *last* to receive this message." The rabbi's slow smile reminded Abel of a cobra. "We would not want them to *worry* about their friends for too long."

Chapter 26

*D*awn was spreading its pale, grey light over the horizon when Abel left his home to walk to the Temple. He hunched his shoulders against the cold, clammy air, pulling the robe closer around his body. The cold did not help the empty feeling in his stomach. *If not for Father, we would still have money for food, and I would still be in my bed.*

Abel had visited the Valley of Hinnom the evening before, knowing Joktan would wish to hear of the disciples' arrest. His father had instructed Abel to leave for the Temple early this morning. Not to get an important seat—those were reserved for the seventy members of the Sanhedrin—but in order to give Rabbi Caiaphas a message.

Abel fingered the wax seal on the tightly wound scroll. He did not have to wonder about the message to the High Priest; he had heard his father instruct Itamar bar Reuben what to write.

> *As a member of the Sanhedrin,*
> *I find anyone who follows the Nazarene to be guilty of blasphemy.*
> *They should all be put to death."*

Once the scribe had finished, Joktan had demanded to hear it read before having the scribe seal it.

"Abel, give this to Rabbi Caiaphas before the trial. I wish him to know my position on the outcome."

"Father, you will not hear the testimony of the witnesses."

"*Racha!* I do not need to hear people speak lies! As my grandfather—may his memory be blessed—said, 'Where the head goes, the body follows.' These men are followers of the Nazarene. If he was guilty of blasphemy, his followers are also guilty of blasphemy. They deserve the same punishment he received: Death."

A cold rain was falling by the time Abel reached the Temple. He walked through the complex until he reached the Chamber of Hewn Stones.

The traditional meeting place of the Sanhedrin—especially when it functioned as a court—the Chamber of Hewn Stones was built into the north wall of the Temple, half inside the sanctuary and half outside, with doors providing access both to the Temple and to the outside. The chamber formed a semi-circle with a chair for the High Priest at the central point closest to the Temple. On either side of the chair were three levels of marble benches for the seventy members of the Sanhedrin. At the foot of the semi-circle were two tables with benches for clerks to sit and take notes. Beyond those benches were steps where the students of the teachers would sit and observe the proceedings.

At this hour, the Chamber was empty save for a few servants who were placing a small table with two cups and an amphora of water near the chair for the High Priest.

Abel waited until the servants left before crossing to place his father's message near the edge of the table. Glancing toward the doors, he reached down and *flicked* the scroll, so it rolled off the table, stopping when it reached his sandal. Lifting his foot, Abel *stomped* the scroll, feeling the same satisfaction he did when killing a scorpion. Bending over, he retrieved the scroll and stuffed it in his girdle.

His grin did not reach his eyes. *Yes, Father, I placed your message next to the High Priest's cup.*

The echo of sandals on tiled floors reached his ears. Abel hurried to the outside end of the chamber and turned, stepping beyond the outer door. Voices floating on the air as men entered the room, their conversation varying from discussions of their personal lives, their priestly duties, the Holy Scriptures, and the Traditions of the Elders.

After a long pause, Abel re-entered the room and casually walked to a spot where the students of Rabbi Gamaliel were gathered. *I might not be studying with him right now, but I am still one of the rabbi's students.* His teacher was talking with the students including—Abel frowned—Saul Paulus.

The Teacher saw him approaching and smiled. "Greetings, Abel ben Joktan. How are you this day? And how are your mother and sister, and…" his smile saddened. "…how is your father?"

"Greetings, Rabbi Gamaliel ben Simon." Abel tried to return the rabbi's smile. It felt awkward; smiling was not a common practice in his home. "It is kind of you to ask about my family. My mother and sister are doing well. My father—" he took a deep breath, "—is still hoping for a miracle."

"I know your family would be happy to have him restored to you. We are all hoping for a miracle for him as well, are we not, Saul Paulus?"

The Tarsuian looked at Abel, his one eyebrow drawn down over his nose. "Yes, of course we are, Rabbi Gamaliel." His countenance did not even appear to hide that lie.

Abel's lips tightened in a straight line. "Thank you."

"Abel, we were discussing today's examination of the two disciples of Jesus ben Joseph," Rabbi Gamaliel continued. "While I regret that illness kept me from being in Jerusalem for the last Passover, I am not sorry I missed the circumstances surrounding that man. An Execution—whether by crucifixion or stoning—is something I never wish to see. I did have an opportunity once to hear him speak and I confess I am interested in hearing what his followers have to say."

"That man's followers are everywhere," Saul frowned. "And not just those Jews who are from this area. There is a man, Stephen ben Chariton, who attends my synagogue, the one for freedmen. He is one of the Nazarene's disciples."

"Ah, yes. You have mentioned him before." Rabbi Gamaliel lifted his eyebrows. "Greeks are known for being skilled debaters. I would welcome the opportunity to speak with him."

Members of the Sanhedrin, arrayed in their priestly garb, continued to enter. Rabbi Nicodemus ben Melech and Rabbi Joseph bar Neriah arrived together with Michael. Approaching Rabbi Gamaliel, the three men greeted the teacher and Saul Paulus, but stared at Abel before giving a silent nod.

The Captain of the Temple Guard entered, followed by six of his men. Behind them Rabbis Caiaphas and Annas entered, followed by another half dozen of the Temple Guard. The Guard positioned themselves on either side of the chair of the High Priest, hands on the hilt of their swords or spears.

While the High Priest took his seat—and his father-in-law took the seat nearest him—the members of the Council found their places and the students crossed to sit on the steps.

After calling the room to silence and greeting the members of the Sanhedrin, Rabbi Caiaphas said, "Recently we arrested Peter bar Jonah and John ben Zebedee for preaching in the name of," he slanted a glance toward Rabbis Nicodemus and Joseph, "*the criminal,* Jesus ben Joseph. We commanded them to cease teaching in this man's name and to cease accusing the Temple leaders of putting to death one who claimed to be the *Son of Yahweh.*"

A murmur rumbled through the room. Except for Rabbi Gamaliel, all the members of the Sanhedrin had been present for the events of last Passover.

Rabbi Caiaphas nodded grimly. "The followers of this man have continued to spread their lies of Jesus ben Joseph being resurrected. They *claim* to have received power from this man to heal the sick and to cast out demons.

"However, they have not obeyed our commands to cease their actions in this man's name. Yesterday, Peter bar Jonah and John ben Zebedee were once again teaching in the Temple colonnade.

"We had them arrested and put in the public jail. We wanted to bring them before you, the leaders of the Jewish people, to allow you to ask your questions and determine whether they are guilty of disobedience and blasphemy." The High Priest sat back in his chair. His smile and tone left no doubt as to what he considered the judgement of the Sanhedrin would be. He turned to the Captain of the Temple Guard. "Send for the two prisoners."

The Guard saluted the High Priest and gestured for six guards to follow him.

Rabbi Caiaphas poured water into the cups and handed one to his father-in-law.

There was a low hum in the chamber as the priests and students talked among themselves while waiting for the return of the Temple Guard and the prisoners. Listening to Rabbi Gamaliel—who was discussing the legal aspects of the procedures with his students— Abel gently *leaned,* slanting a glance toward Rabbi Nicodemus, Rabbi Joseph, and Michael. Their position was too far away to overhear what they said, but Abel knew his father would demand to know why he did not put himself in a position to listen to their conversation. *As if they would discuss hiding the Nazarene's body here in the Chamber of Hewn Stones.*

The sound of sandals hurrying down the corridor drew everyone's attention. The Captain of the Temple Guard entered, but without his other men nor the prisoners.

Rabbi Caiaphas looked at his father-in-law and then back at the Guards. "Captain," he frowned, "where are the prisoners?"

The Captain looked uneasily at the High Priest. "Sir. I do not know."

"What!" Rabbi Annas surged out of his seat, his face reddening. "What do you mean, *you do not know where the prisoners are?*"

As the former High Priest, Rabbi Annas did not have the authority to question the Captain of the Temple Guard, but no one would dare to point that out. When Annas ben Seth spoke, all of Jerusalem listened.

The Captain's knuckles whitening around the hilt of his sword. "Sir, we went to the public jail. The prison guards were still standing watch as we had left them last night, but when they opened the door, the cell was empty."

Rabbi Caiaphas snorted like an angry bull. "What does the jailer have to say about this dereliction of duty?"

"Sir, he was as surprised as I. He has promised to question his men at length. For now, he sent his men, as I have sent my Temple Guard, to search for the prisoners."

The sound of running feet once again drew everyone's attention. A young Temple Guard rushed into the room. "Sir," he saluted, "we have found the prisoners."

"Where were they hiding?" Rabbi Caiaphas demanded.

The Guard shrank beneath the High Priest's frown. "They were not hiding, sir. We found them…in the Temple Courts."

"What? What were they doing?" Rabbi Annas asked.

"The Guard filled his lungs and, staring straight ahead, answered. "They were…teaching in the name of…*the Nazarene.*"

Caiaphas lunged from his chair. "How *dare* they!" His shout bounced off the walls. "*How dare they disobey our commands!* Bring them here!"

"The other Guards have arrested them and are bringing them here. I came ahead to inform you." Bowing his head, the young man crossed to the far end of the Chamber.

I do not blame him, Abel thought. *I too would move as far away from Rabbi Caiaphas as possible. He and Rabbi Annas are never easy to be around and never more so than when they are angry.*

From the quiet that descended upon the room, it was obvious to Abel that others agreed with him. Glancing beneath his lashes, he noted that some—like Rabbis Nicodemus and Joseph—exchanged looks with each other, but most of the men stared at the floor.

The sound of sandals and the clang of metal hitting tiled floor drew everyone's gaze to the doors. The other five Temple Guards entered the room, weapons at the ready, escorting Peter bar Jonah and John ben Zebedee. The hands and feet of the two disciples of the Nazarene were chained.

"Stop there," the Captain of the Temple Guard pointed to a spot before the High Priest. The Guards positioned the prisoners and moved to stand around the room, hands on hilts, as if enemies would slip into the Chamber of Hewn Stones.

Fingers clutching the arms of his chair, Rabbi Caiaphas glared at the prisoners, his gaze furious enough to peel away their skin.

The two disciples stood at their ease, as if they were hosts of a gathering instead of shackled prisoners standing before the highest authorities of the Jewish people.

"Peter bar Jonah, John ben Zebedee, you were put in jail yesterday, yet you escaped," the High Priest said. "How did you do that?"

Peter looked at John, who nodded. Peter looked at the High Priest. "We did not escape. We were released from the jail."

Rabbi Caiaphas' brow slanted into a deep furrow. "Who helped you? We command you to name this person!"

John lifted his shoulders in a shrug. "We do not know his name."

Rabbi Annas slapped the marble bench. "Then describe him!"

The two prisoners looked at each other and *grinned*. "He was tall," Peter said, "taller than me and broader than any man I have ever seen before. His hair was white, as were his robes, and they *glowed*, as did his body."

"The man was tall," Rabbi Caiaphas frowned. "He was taller and broader than most men," his voice increased in volume, "his hair and robes and body *glowed*?!" his voice echoed around the chamber. "What is this nonsense you are speaking? No man looks like this!"

Peter smiled. "I did not say he was a *man*."

"Not a man?" Rabbi Annas snorted. "Then what is he?"

"An angel."

Laughter erupted around the Chamber and, when the High Priest lifted his hand, quickly died.

"What is this nonsense?" he sneered. "An *angel* freed you from the jail?"

"Yes." John said. "During the night, an angel of Yahweh opened the doors of the jail and brought us out."

Peter took up the story, "He told us, 'Go stand in the Temple courts and tell the people the full message of the new life in the Messiah, Jesus ben Joseph.'"

"*Ah ha!*" The High Priest pointed a finger at the prisoners. "We gave you strict orders *not* to teach in this man's name. Yet you admit you disobeyed us and are filling Jerusalem with your teaching! You are determined to make us guilty of *this man's* blood."

Peter and John stood quietly under Rabbi Caiaphas' tirade. Then John spoke.

"Would you have us disobey Yahweh?"

Peter nodded. "We must obey Yahweh rather than men." Lifting his shackled hands, he pointed at Rabbis Caiaphas and Annas. "You killed the Lord Jesus by hanging Him on a tree. But the God of our fathers raised Him from the dead. Yahweh has exalted Him to His own right hand as Prince and Savior, that He might give repentance and forgiveness of sins to Israel." He turned his head to nod at John. "We are witnesses of these things, and so is the

Holy Spirit, Whom Yahweh has given to those who obey Him."

As the last word still echoed around the room, the High Priest leapt out of his chair, followed by his father-in-law. "Blasphemy!" He turned to the men seated on either side of the Chamber. "You have heard them speak blasphemy."

Rabbi Annas grasped the neck of his tunic and tugged, ripping it. "They deserve death, as did Jesus ben Joseph!"

The room exploded with priests crying:

"They are guilty!"

"Blasphemy!"

"Death!"

"No! They are not guilty!" Abel saw Rabbis Nicodemus, Joseph, and Michael trying to yell over the others. *Just as they tried to yell over the crowd when the Nazarene was on trial before Pontius Pilate.* He smiled and not pleasantly. He opened his mouth but froze when Rabbi Gamaliel stood.

All in the Chamber of Hewn Stones quieted. Honored by all the people, when Rabbi Gamaliel ben Simon spoke, everyone— including Rabbis Caiaphas and Annas—listened.

Crossing to stand before the High Priest, he bowed. "Rabbi Caiaphas, if you would have the prisoners escorted from the room, I would address the honored Sanhedrin."

Glancing at his father-in-law, who nodded, Rabbi Caiaphas turned to the Captain of the Temple Guard. "Remove the prisoners," he said and added, "to the small chamber down the corridor. Leave one of your men here, so I may send word when we are ready for them. And Captain," his gaze hardened, "make sure *they never leave your sight.*" He waited while the Temple Guard saluted and led the prisoners out of the room before turning back to the Teacher. "Rabbi Gamaliel. You may address the Council."

"Thank you, sir." Rabbi Gamaliel crossed to the center of the room. "Men of Israel," he extended his arms and turned in a slow circle, his gaze taking in everyone, "consider carefully what you intend to do to these men." His voice was soothing; all who studied under him agreed it was pleasant to listen to him.

"Permit this humble teacher," he smiled, laying his palm against his chest, "to present a brief history lesson. As you recall, some time ago, Theudas appeared. This man claimed to be someone important, indeed many people believed that he was. He drew about four hundred people to his cause. However, he was killed, all his followers dispersed, and nothing came of it.

"You will also recall when Rome demanded the census and tax be taken in Judea and how Judas the Galilean led a revolt in protest."

Many of the men in the room nodded. Few present had been alive to remember when Theudas appeared, but all the members of the Sanhedrin were alive to remember Judas the Galilean. Abel had heard of this man from his studies with Rabbi Gamaliel as well as from his own father.

About twenty-five years ago, the Romans had demanded a census be taken of the Jewish people and taxes levied. In protest, Judas the Galilean, together with a Pharisee named Zadok, led many men in revolt. Judas declared the Jewish state as a republic with Yahweh alone as king and ruler and His Law as supreme. The revolt spread, with major battles between the Romans and Jewish revolution-aries—who had named themselves *Zealots*. Eventually, the Romans overthrew the revolutionaries and Judas was killed. His followers scattered, but the spirit of the Zealots remained to this day.

"In the case before us today," Rabbi Gamaliel continued, "I advise you to leave these men alone! Let them go! If their purpose is from human origin, it will fail.

"However," he lifted his forefinger, "if it be from Yahweh, you will not be able to stop them." He turned in a slow circle again, "You will only find yourselves," stopping to look at the High Priest and his father-in-law, "fighting against Yahweh."

Chapter 27

"And the Sanhedrin agreed with Rabbi Gamaliel?" Mary asked. "Here are some towels." She removed several large linen towels from the shelves in the storage room and placed them in the basket at their feet.

"We will need some soothing ointments, too," Michael responded. "Yes, the Sanhedrin agreed with Rabbi Gamaliel, which is not unusual. I have never heard of anyone going against the honored rabbi's suggestion."

"Here is ointment made from olive oil and herbs. How did the High Priest and his father-in-law respond?

"You should have seen their faces," Michael laughed. "They looked as if they had a mouthful of spoiled grapes."

"They did not disagree with Rabbi Gamaliel? Here are some cloths for cleaning."

"What could they say?" He pitched his voice in a mocking imitation of the High Priest, "'I am sorry, Rabbi Gamaliel, but we do not trust Yahweh to handle this situation.' Where is the soap?"

"It is in this basket. Martha brought some of the special soap she makes when she and Simon came for supper the other night. I imagine the High Priest and his father-in-law were angry."

"They appeared to be," Michael nodded. "However, they had no choice but to let Peter and John go, after warning them not to teach anymore in the name of the Lord Jesus, may His name be blessed. It was a wonderful thing to witness."

"I am sure it was," Mary said, before furrowing her brow. "Michael?"

"Yes, my Beloved?" Michael lifted the basket filled with cloths, containers of ointments and oils, soap, and an amphora of water.

"If the High Priest and Sanhedrin agreed with Rabbi Gamaliel, why did they flog Peter and John?"

Michael frowned. "Father and Rabbi Joseph believe Caiaphas and Annas felt they had to do *something* in retaliation. So, instead of condemning Peter and John to death for blasphemy, they had them flogged for disobeying their command to not teach in the name of the Lord Jesus."

"*Those men,*" Mary fumed, folding her lips and arms. "It is hard to believe they are the leaders of the Holy Temple. First, they *crucified* the Lord Jesus and now they *flogged* His followers! I can only imagine the suffering Peter and John must have gone through. It must make it hard to walk. Is that why Father Nicodemus sent you ahead to gather ointments and bandages?"

"Actually, it is not what you would expect."

"What do you mean?"

"Peter and John do need the bandages and ointments," Michael smiled. "But they are delayed arriving because, after they left the Temple, the two wanted to stop at the homes of believers, to let everyone know they are rejoicing at their treatment."

Mary's eyes widened. "Rejoicing?"

"Rejoicing," Michael repeated, "that they had been found *worthy* to suffer for the sake of the Lord Jesus."

Chapter 28

"What do you mean they did not *kill* the Nazarene's followers?" His father raged, his face reddening. Several of the sores on his face oozed blood. "Did you not give my message to Rabbi Caiaphas?"

Abel swallowed hard to keep the bile down. "Yes, sir. I arrived early as you instructed and placed your message next to the High Priest's goblet on the table near his chair."

"And yet they released the men? Why?"

Abel lifted his shoulders in a slight shrug. "Rabbi Gamaliel presented a judgement they could not refute. If the High Priest had disagreed, it would be as if he did not believe Yahweh could deal with these men."

"*Racha!* Cowardly, stupid, *racha!*" Joktan slammed his fist into his other hand, causing the tip of an outstretched finger to fall to the ground. "The whole of the Sanhedrin is a batch of stupid, *racha* cowards! Is my punishment not proof enough that Yahweh wants us to wipe *that man's followers* from the face of the earth? It appears that *only I* will be strong enough to do something."

"What can you do?"

"I will let Caiaphas know I am displeased with the outcome. I will demand he change his decree and arrest not only these men, but *all* of the followers of Jesus ben Joseph."

Abel's eyes widened. *Father did not refer to him as* Rabbi *Caiaphas.* "Arrest *all* of them? Including—"

"Including your *racha* cousins," Joktan interrupted, "*and* Nicodemus ben Melech *and* Joseph bar Neriah. *Anyone* who disobeys Yahweh by following *that man* and spreading his lies." He stretched out his hand. "Did you bring more coins? My scribe needs more supplies."

Abel drew a small pouch from his girdle and tossed it at his father's feet. The coins inside barely clinked

Joktan picked it up, loosened the strings and peered inside. "This is not enough," he frowned. "Why did you not bring more?"

"Father," Abel extended his hands, "this is all we can afford. Even now Mother and Rebeca scrounge for food like beggars."

"I care not!"

"What?" Abel gaped. "We are to the point of *starving!*"

"I do not care!" Joktan grabbed tufts of hair on his whitened head and pulled, ripping them from his scalp. "I do not care if you all *starve!* The only thing that matters now is that these people are *destroyed*, and *I am healed*!"

Chapter 29

"Daniel, stop the horses," Mary said. "This is the home of my aunt and cousins."

The driver pulled up on the reins, stopping the carriage, and tied them, before jumping down to help Mary descend, and then running up the path to knock on the door.

Mary brushed the dust off her garments. She had chosen a plain blue tunic and robe with a cream head cloth; she did not want to shame her relatives by appearing to boast about her husband's wealth. Turning, she reached for the large basket from Jemima. "Thank you, Jemima. You wait here with Daniel. I do not need you to accompany me inside."

"Yes, mistress."

Mary reached the house just as the door opened far enough to reveal the face of a frail, older woman who peered fearfully at them. Mary forced a smile. "Greetings, Aunt Naomi."

The older women shifted her gaze from Mary's face, to the basket, to the driver, and to the servant in the carriage. She opened the door a little wider to gaze up and down the street before answering. "Greetings, Mary bat Jacob." She whispered before adding the traditional, "Peace be on you."

"And on you peace, Aunt. I have come to visit. I hope this is not an inconvenient time."

"Visit?" Her aunt's face clouded with what appeared to Mary to be a mixture of confusion and fear. "Noooo…it's not inconvenient." Yet she did not move.

Perhaps she is worried about not being able to offer me food. Mary lifted the basket. "I have brought a *gift* for you. May I come in?"

"Oh…uh…" Naomi's gaze darted up and down the street again.

"Uh…yes…" she stepped back and opened the door wider. "Please come in." Her gaze went to the servant standing next to Mary.

Mary turned to her driver. "Thank you, Daniel. Please move the carriage to that shady spot across the street. You and Jemima may eat your meal while you wait for me."

"Yes, mistress," the servant bowed his head.

Naomi stared wide-eyed as the driver turned to walk back up the path to the carriage.

Mary controlled her expression at her aunt's reaction. *I should have come alone.* It did not occur to her that her aunt would be unaccustomed to servants. She busied herself with adjusting the cloth over the basket until her aunt cleared her throat.

"Please come in, Mary."

"Thank you, Aunt." She touched her fingers to the *mezuzah* and stepped inside.

Mary could not recall the last time she had been inside her relative's home. She had grown up knowing her uncle was careful with his own money, even to the point of refusing to host guests. This was the only reason her parents—and later she, along with Lazarus and Martha—had hosted Passover each year and invited her uncle, aunt, and cousins.

From what she had learned of her aunt and cousins, Mary did not expect they could afford to offer even the simple traditional greeting for a guest of washing their feet, anointing their head with oil, and giving a drink of water. But what she saw as she followed her aunt into the house went beyond the result of frugality. The table in the front room had a large rock in the place of a missing leg and the pillows beneath it were threadbare and worn.

"Please be seated," her aunt said, as she hurried to light the two lamps at either end of the room. "Rebeca is in the cooking area. I will tell her to prepare some food and drink." She hurried across the room and down the hall.

Mary nodded, fighting the rising nausea from the smell of rancid oil. She removed a small bag from her girdle. Undoing the strings, she removed several peppermint leaves and popped them into her mouth. After Martha had told her drinking tea made from peppermint would help with the tender stomach of pregnancy, she had taken to carrying them with her to chew on them when needed.

Hopefully this nausea will ease as I get further into my pregnancy. Mary smiled at the thought of growing large with child—her and Michael's child. *Soon…soon I will tell him of our news. Now that things are settling down.* Her smile broadened as she imagined his reaction.

The sound of footsteps drew Mary back from her musings. Her aunt re-entered the room, followed by her cousin Rebeca. Her aunt carried a tray covered with a thin cloth and her cousin had a tray with a small amphora and three cups.

Both women were clearly related and even the most generous of people would not consider them attractive. Naomi and Rebeca were short, plain of face and figure, and dressed in grey tunics and dull brown robes and head coverings. Even though Mary was not skilled with a needle, it was easy for her to note the places where their garments had been repeatedly mended. *Uncle probably considered it waste to give them coins for new clothes.*

Before her uncle was cast out of Jerusalem because of his leprosy, he and Abel had often left the two women at home when attending public functions or private meals. Mary used to wonder if it was because Naomi and Rebeca were quiet to the point of embarrassment. She remembered even at family events, when they were noticed, they would look to her uncle for permission to answer a comment. As a child, Mary had remarked, "Aunt Naomi and Cousin Rebeca look like little grey mice hiding in corners." Even though her mother had chided her for her unkind remark, it was still the truth.

Her aunt spread her lips in a tremulous smile. "Rebeca was… *excited*… to learn you had come to visit us." She looked at her daughter and nodded.

"Uh…yes," Rebeca gaped at her cousin. "It was…kind…of you to come." She extended the tray. "We have brought food and drink."

Mother and daughter placed the trays on the table and settled themselves on the pillows. Mary had to control her expression when her aunt removed the cloth from the tray to reveal a platter with three small pieces of bread and a handful of what appeared to be dried olives. While Rebeca poured water into the cups, her aunt turned the platter so the largest piece of bread faced Mary.

The bread looked coarse. *It appears to lack sufficient flour*, Mary thought. Biting into it confirmed she was right. She nibbled at the food, washing it down with a sip of water, praying she would keep it down, while carrying on light conversation about the weather—it was a mild winter thus far—and Martha's and Abigail's impending births—their babies are due within a few weeks. Mary carried the weight of the conversation, with her aunt and cousin stammering the occasional noncommittal responses.

"Will you have more?" Her aunt gestured to the food.

"No, thank you, Aunt." Mary said. "I had breakfast before I came. But it was quite delicious." *Yahweh, please forgive this small lie. I could not embarrass my relatives by not eating more.* "I am sorry I have not come to visit before now. As an apology and sign of affection," she lifted the basket to place it in front of her aunt, "I have brought this." She removed the cloth.

The basket held bags of grain, blocks of cheese, figs, pomegranates, amphorae of olives, oil, and wine. Several fish were wrapped in cloths. It also had a platter of Mary's oat and honey cakes.

"I also have this special gift," Mary lifted a heavy bag that clinked. "Lazarus sold our home and gave Martha and me our portion of the sale. I want to give it to you."

Her aunt and cousin stared at the basket of food, and the bag of coins, their every blink slow and deliberate, reminding Mary of a frog.

Her aunt recovered her voice first. "Mary," she whispered, "I cannot...I do not...why are doing this? Your uncle..."

Holy Spirit, Mary prayed, *give me the words to say.* "Aunt, I realize my uncle said and did some *hurtful* things to Martha, Lazarus, and me. But I have *forgiven* him."

The older woman's brow furrowed. "Forgiven him?" She pronounced it with caution, like it is her first time speaking a language she had never heard before. "How can you forgive him?"

"I can forgive him," Mary smiled, "because the Lord Jesus—may His name be blessed—*forgave* me."

"Jesus?" Rebeca said. "Do you mean…"

"—the One who died on the cross," Mary finished her cousin's sentence. "Yes, I do. Only He is not dead now. He rose from the dead. I know. I saw Him." Feeling the familiar thrill she had come to associate with the Holy Spirit, Mary told her aunt and cousin about the Lord Jesus, how He was the Son of Yahweh Who had come to earth to die for the sins of the world. She told them about the miracles He performed—including raising Lazarus from the dead. How He had shown her that her value was not found in her appearance.

"My value is found in the fact that I am loved and created by Yahweh. This is true for you as well, Aunt, Cousin. Indeed, it is true for everyone. Yahweh loves us so much that He sent His Son Jesus to show us the Father's Kingdom and to die for us as the sacrifice for our sins."

"What are *you* doing here?"

Naomi's and Rebeca's face drained, their gaze darting beyond Mary before dropping to the floor as if they wished the ground would open up and swallow them whole.

Mary stood and turned in one fluid motion. She had not seen her cousin since the day the Lord Jesus was crucified, but even so, she barely recognized him.

Abel stood in the door, the grey light from behind him framing him like a specter. He had always been tall and muscular, with an assured and pompous air; but this man was gaunt, his garments hanging loosely. One hand grasped white-knuckled a basket filled with several small bags. The bones of his face framed eyes that kindled with anger and hatred.

Mary had never liked Abel, but she had never been afraid of him…until today.

"What. Are. You. Doing. Here?" He bit off each word.

"I…uh," Mary looked at her aunt, hoping the older woman would say something to diffuse the rage in her son, but she could see there would be no help from Naomi. "…I came to visit Aunt Naomi and Rebeca."

He lifted a boney hand to point at the basket on the table. "What is that?"

"Abel, Mary brought a gift. *Food.*" Rebeca had found her voice. "Enough food for ourselves and for *Father.*"

Mary noticed Abel grimace at the mention of her uncle. *Of course. They have been taking food to Uncle Joktan and probably more than they can spare. Please Rebeca,* she turned to look at her other cousin, trying to send a silent message, *do not mention the coins.*

But it was not to be.

Rebeca stepped forward and lifted the bag of coins. "And she has also brought a gift of *money.*" She shook the bag; it *clinked* heavily. "We will never have to worry about money *ever again.*"

"No." Abel's color was rising ominously.

"No?" Rebeca repeated, her brow furrowed in confusion. "But, Abel; she brought—" she dropped her gaze to the basket, "—*food.*"

Mary's heart ached for her cousin. *I will never again take food for granted.* She turned back to look at Abel.

His mouth worked, as he looked from the basket, to his sister and mother, and then back to Mary. "No. We will *not* take it. I will take care of my mother and sister."

"But, Abel," Mary said, "it is food. Your mother and sister are *hungry.*" She gestured to him. "You are *hungry.*"

"I do not care if we all *starve!*" He raged.

"What?"

He pointed at her. "Do you think we would take food from one of those responsible for my father being a leper?"

"What are you saying?" Mary shook her head. "I had *nothing* to do with Uncle Joktan's illness."

Abel stepped toward her. "My father's leprosy is a punishment from Yahweh," he took another step, "My father resides in the Valley of Hinnom because we did not deal with those who followed *that man!*"

"That is foolish!" Mary retorted. "Yahweh would not strike Uncle Joktan with leprosy because others chose to follow His Son!"

"Blasphemy!" Abel dropped the basket he held. The bags fell out, spilling a few handfuls of grain, some shriveled dates, and a small pomegranate. "How dare you speak *blasphemy* in my house!"

"It is *not* blasphemy." Mary said. "The Lord Jesus *is* the Son of Yahweh!"

"Get out!" He crossed the room in quick strides and grasped her arm.

Mary tried to pull away as Abel dragged her across the room and thrust her out of the door. "Get out of my house!" He went back into the house and returned, throwing the large basket at her. "We do not need your *gifts.*" The amphorae shattered as they hit the ground, spilling liquid and olives. The bag of flour exploded as it hit her—covering her from waist to feet—as the pomegranates hit her shoulder and chest. The coins from the bag scattered, *pinging* as they hit the ground.

Mary stepped away, turning, lifting one arm to shield her head and the other to shield her belly.

Out of the corner of her eye, she saw Daniel leap from the carriage and race across the street to place placed himself between her and Abel. Jemima was steps behind him, wrapping her arms around her mistress and shielding her from Abel's anger.

Her cousin raged, tramping on the basket, smashing the food, or stooping to pick something up to throw at her servants and her. "We do not need your charity!" He ground the coins into the dirt. "We do not need your help! We do not need *anything* from you!" He shook clinched fists at her. "Stop looking at me! Leave and *never* return to this house!"

He stomped back into his house, *slamming* the door behind him. The *mezuzah* shook under the impact of the door's rebound and fell off the frame. The box shattered when it hit the path, the tiny scrolls of Holy Scripture tumbling out onto the dirt.

Chapter 30

*T*he clouds were gray and heavy with rain. A wind blew from the north, moaning as it whipped around the buildings.

Abel's stomach tightened around his meagre breakfast. *Not that having a full belly would be a good thing in the Valley of Hinnom.* He wrapped his robe closer to his body, hunching his shoulders against the wind. His sandals slapped in cadence with the memories of his father's rage echoing in his brain, alternating with his own railing against his cousin Mary:

"I do not care if you all starve!"

"I do not care if we all starve!"

"If you all starve!"

"If we all starve!"

"All starve!"

"All starve!"

"All starve!"

Each step reverberated in his chest as he recalled all he had endured. His father's demands, yet not caring if his family died from starvation. Rabbi Caiaphas not caring whether he completed his Temple training. Saul Paulus sneering at his lack of success in finding those who had stolen the Nazarene's body. Now, his cousin Mary having the *audacity* to bring food and coins. *As if we were paupers begging at the Gate Beautiful,* especially *as all of this started the day the Nazarene showed up and began spreading his lies, and those* racha *fools—especially my cousins—began following him.*

He chewed his lip in deliberation, then his expression hardened. Lifting his head, he spun around, quickening his step as he headed toward the Temple. If he got there early enough, he might be able to talk with Rabbi Caiaphas before the morning sacrifices. He would get his father's priestly portion from the High Priest, buy some food at the Xystus Market, and take it home as a surprise for his mother and sister.

I will care for my family, even if Father will not.

Abel arrived at the Temple just as the sunrise was glinting off the walls. He passed a few priests in their somber attire as he walked through the corridors. He found the man he sought seated near the Brazen Sea, removing his sandals. Priests whose turn it was to serve would wash their hands and feet here before walking through the curtain, embroidered with a map of the world, into the Holy Place. The High Priest was, as Abel hoped, alone.

"Rabbi Caiaphas."

The High Priest looked up, wearing a sour expression. "Ah, Abel ben Joktan. Good morning. Peace be on you." His tone was a chiding reminder of Abel's rudeness.

Abel's face reddened. "Good morning, Rabbi, and on you peace. Sir, I need to speak with you."

The older priest glanced up at the sun, before favoring Abel with a thin smile, in which tolerance and contempt were nicely mixed. "I have little time before the morning sacrifice. What do you want?"

"I…uh…" Abel clasped his hands. This was going to be harder than he expected. He had never had to ask for money before, even money due to him.

"Abel ben Joktan, I have no time to waste upon '*Uh's.*' What do you *want?*"

Abel filled his lungs and expelled the air, replying in a single breath, "I need my father's priestly portion."

Caiaphas turned his attention to continuing to remove his sandals. "Your father does not have a priestly portion."

Abel frowned. "What do you mean?"

The High Priest lifted a shoulder. "Priestly portions are for priests who serve in the Temple. Since the day Yahweh struck your father with leprosy, he was no longer a priest. Therefore," he looked up, his lips drawn downward, "he does not have a priestly portion."

Abel felt a knot form in his stomach. Then a thought occurred to him. "What about my portion?"

Caiaphas lifted a contemptuous eyebrow. "*You* are *not* a priest."

"I was studying to become a priest."

"But you are no longer studying with Rabbi Gamaliel nor any of our teachers."

Abel gapped at the High Priest. "I no longer study with Rabbi Gamaliel because *you* commanded me to set aside my studies in order to search for the people who had taken the Nazarene's body. *I obeyed you!* Surely that is worth something."

"I did set you on that task," the other man nodded. "A task which you failed to complete. Do you expect to be *paid* for what you have not earned?"

The courtyard was filling, as other priests arrived for the morning sacrifice. Abel ignored them, his desperation and hunger outweighing his pride. "Sir, can you give me anything? After all," he pointed a finger at the High Priest, "you and Rabbi Annas gave Judas Iscariot thirty pieces of silver." *Thirty of these coins would provide for my family for four months.*

His barbed accusation missed its mark. "We did," Caiaphas smiled, and it was not pleasant. "But Judas brought us Jesus ben Joseph. *You* have brought us *nothing*."

Chapter 31

"What are your plans for the day, my Love?" Mary worked a comb through her waist-length curls.

"Stephen ben Chariton has invited me to go with him to the Synagogue of Freedmen."

Michael leaned over the bowl on the side table to splash water on his face.

"That sounds interesting."

"It does indeed. From the things he has said, the people at this synagogue are a curious mix of people. Some are like him; Jews from cities in Greece and Rome. Others are descended from Jews who had been made slaves under Pompey and later freed. Thus, the name: *Synagogue of Freedmen.*"

He grabbed a towel to dry his face. "With the Lord Jesus' command to be His witnesses to the ends of the earth, I want to learn as much as I can about peoples from other cultures and lands."

"You are wise, my Love," Mary set the comb aside and began braiding her hair. "Please send my greetings to Stephen bar Chariton. When you are finished at the synagogue, invite him to take the evening meal with us. Our table feels empty, what with Father Nicodemus spending time at Rabbi Joseph's home in Arimathea, and with Ruth visiting Joanna and Matthias and their children."

"It does indeed feel empty. I will extend an invitation to Stephen. I am certain he would appreciate a quiet evening here. He told me he misses being with his family."

"Family is important," Mary mused. "It was hard to lose Father and Mother—may their memories be blessed. Lazarus is the best of brothers, having to deal with two sisters who had different opinions about how things should be done."

"I can understand how he felt," Michael grinned. "I have sisters."

Mary slanted her eyes towards him. "But you have a beloved father who was responsible for your sisters. That was not how it was for us. We only had—" she paused, frowning.

"Your Uncle Joktan?"

Mary filled her lungs. "Yes," she nodded, "my uncle, who cared for only himself. I never realized how selfish he was until I went to visit my aunt and cousin. Michael, they are but one step from begging in the street. I thought for certain they would take the food and coin I brought, but Abel arrived." She frowned again. "Why would he refuse my gift?"

"Pride is a powerful master," Michael ran his fingers through his hair. "A man wishes to be the one providing for his family."

"Perhaps. Michael, what can I do? I still believe the Lord Jesus wants me to give this money to them."

"Let me speak with Father. He might have an idea."

"I am certain he will. Father Nicodemus is a wise man. Thank you, Beloved."

"Now that we have settled the matter of your kin, what are your plans for the day, Beloved? Spending it with your sister?"

"No. Martha and Abigail are busy making baby clothes with Elisheba. I am going to visit Leah bat Samuel," Mary glanced at her husband. "Did you hear she is pregnant?"

"I did not!" Michael laughed as he crossed to the chests that held their clothing. "I will have to wish Azariah bar Cleopas *mazel tov.*"

"They are excited. However, smells have made it difficult for Leah to cook. I asked Elisheba to prepare a basket of food for them."

"That is kind. I am sorry to hear she is not feeling well."

"I am as well, although it is common with pregnancy," Mary tied a cord around her braid and checked her reflection in the mirror, smiling to make sure she did not have anything in her teeth. "Most women experience a tender stomach early in their pregnancies. Although it has eased for Abigail, even now Martha still has it from time to time."

"I hope when you are *carrying our child,*" Michael slipped a tunic over his head and grinned at her, "you will not suffer this discomfort at all."

"Not being sick would be a blessing," she smiled. She crossed to the chests to select a soft blue tunic and a robe and veil in a deep rose. *I should tell him about our news. But not now, when we are both about to leave. Tonight; I will tell him tonight.*

Chapter 32

"*I* must confess, Stephen; I have never been to the Synagogue of Freedmen," Michael wrapped his robe tighter. The rain had stopped, but the wind was still brisk and chill. "I hope that does not offend you."

"That does not offend me," the other man lifted a shoulder. "Why should it? You were born in Jerusalem, to a powerful and noble house. You are the son of a wise and gracious priest who *considers* the comments and thoughts of others before responding. You have *nothing* in common with those who attend this synagogue." He grinned. "Forgive my jest. To speak truth; those who are members of this synagogue come from different backgrounds than you and often different backgrounds from each other. Some are like myself; Jews who were born in a Roman or Greek city."

"Like Saul Paulus," Michael said. "He has never spoken much of himself, but I do know he is from Tarsus."

Stephen nodded. "He is indeed. Saul attends this synagogue, when he is not at the Temple."

"Which is a rare day, indeed," Michael murmured under his breath. At least he thought it was under his breath, until he noticed Stephen's lifted eyebrows. "Forgive me. That comment was unkind. Saul Paulus' dedication to the Temple is…*commendable*. However…" Michael, spread his hands wide, at a loss for words.

"I am familiar with Saul Paulus' *dedication*," Stephen replied, "as, on those *rare days* when he is not at the Temple, he is at this synagogue. Your description of '*commendable*' is gracious indeed. I would say his dedication to the Temple is *extreme*, as is his interpretation of the Law given to Moses and the Traditions of the Elders."

"You are correct in your description of Saul Paulus."

The two men turned down the street leading out of the Upper City and into the Lower City, near the Pool of Siloam, where the Synagogue of Freedmen was located. The houses here were built after Roman or Greek influence.

"We know from the teachings of the Lord Jesus—may His name be blessed—that Yahweh no longer dwells within the Temple built by Herod. He dwells here," Stephen placed an opened palm on his chest, "within our hearts and spirits.

"While I do not *think* we are to do away with the Temple, we are learning more about what the Lord Jesus' death meant to the Law given to Moses and even to the Temple. John ben Zebedee shared that the Lord Jesus said if anyone loves Him, that person will keep what *He* taught, His Father Yahweh will love that person, and He and His Father will dwell with that person.

"As I mentioned to your father and to Rabbi Joseph, there are many Temple leaders who look upon those who attend the Synagogue of Freedmen as lower than proselytes. That sentiment causes many in this synagogue to feel slighted. As a result, some—such as Saul Paulus—are…*fierce*…in their adherence to the Law, to the Traditions of the Elders, and to the Temple." He drew his lips in a straight line. "Sometimes, this adherence goes too far."

Michael furrowed his brow. "Too far?"

Stephen's face was grim. "Once, during a meeting at the synagogue, there was a man who suggested the Temple needed to be cleansed. He was referring to a recent wind storm that had caused a vast amount of dust to settle on the Temple walls. There were many people present in the synagogue that day who wanted to have him flogged—or *worse*—until he was able to convince them that he merely wanted to help wash the dust from the Temple walls."

"What?" Michael gaped. "I had not heard about that. That *is* extreme."

"This is one reason I feel the Holy Spirit wishes me to share the Lord Jesus' story with these people," Stephen said. "If this type of response continues, who knows what will happen?"

Chapter 33

"Mary, thank you again for coming," Leah hugged her. "It was wonderful to see you and to get caught up on our lives."

Even dealing with the discomfort of nausea, Mary's friend was transformed. Beneath a leaf-green tunic and camel colored robe, Leah still had womanly curves, gently accented by early pregnancy, and she wore her long, curly hair in a neat braid. But the change went beyond appearance. Gone were the sharp giggles ending in a snort; gone was the young girl ripe for unchecked, frivolous fun; gone was the girl who was the despair of her parents. Now, Leah moved with grace and dignity and was a considerate hostess.

Mary did not have to look far for the source of Leah's transformation. Watching her friend smile when she spoke of her husband, Azariah bar Cleopas—how he was working hard with his father at their smithy, of their dreams and prayers for their unborn child—it was obvious.

Love. Love has transformed Leah, Mary smiled. *As it has me.*

"And thank you for this," Leah pointed to the large covered basket Daniel had placed on a side table. "Please extend my thanks to Elisheba. I know Azariah would wish me to add his thanks as well." She chuckled. "He has not commented on the simple fare we have been eating of late. I can only imagine his pleasure when he sees what we will have for the evening meal."

Mary grinned. "I will tell Elisheba. I am certain she will be most pleased. Until you are feeling better, I will continue to bring food."

Ready laughter sprang to Leah's eyes. "While part of me feels I should refuse your kind offer, I know my husband would consider it an answer to prayer."

The two young women dissolved into helpless laughter. When

they regained their composure, Mary bade her friend farewell and walked down the path from Leah's house to where Daniel and Jemima waited in the carriage.

Daniel jumped down to hand her up. "Mistress, did you have a pleasant visit with your friend?"

"I did, Daniel. It was good to see her again."

"It was kind of Mistress Leah to let us wait in her cooking area," Jemima helped Mary settle her garments and unfolded a light blanket to lay across Mary's lap. "Although the day is mild for Tivet, the wind has a crispness to it."

"It was also kind of her to leave some of Elisheba's cakes and a pitcher of milk for us," Daniel added.

"That was indeed kind of her," Mary said.

Daniel lifted the reins. "Home, mistress?"

"Not yet. Even though the air has a chill, the rain has stopped, and the day is beautiful. I would like to enjoy it. Please drive outside of the city."

"Yes, mistress," Daniel turned the horses and drove up the street.

Leah and Azariah's home was situated in the Upper City, where the homes of the wealthy were located, as was the palace of King Herod.

Herod—the one who had been called *Great* because of his many architectural projects, including the Temple—had overseen the construction of the palace. Built of white marble, it was strengthened by immense towers built into the city walls and named after his brother Phasael, his friend Hippicus, and his favorite wife, Mariamne, whom he had executed.

Mary turned away her eyes when Daniel drove past the palace, not wishing to see the location of one of the trials of the Lord Jesus.

I am thankful for the salvation Your death and resurrection bought, Mary prayed, *but I still cannot bear to remember what they did to You.* She felt a warmth echo through her. The awareness that the Lord Jesus was with her always was still new, but it brought comfort and peace.

Soon, they were outside of the city walls and driving along the road leading toward Bethlehem.

"Ahhh…" Mary lifted her head to feel the warmth of the sun, "what a beautiful day!"

The clouds looked like fat sheep grazing in the sapphire sky.

"It is indeed, mistress," Daniel replied.

Here and there, shepherds turned to watch their carriage pass, a few young boys waving and pointing.

"Do you think those are the shepherds that Mary bat Eli spoke of?" Jemima waved back. "The ones who came to see the Lord Jesus on the night He was born?"

"They might be, Jemima," Daniel smiled. "At least the older ones might."

"Could you imagine what it must have been like for the shepherds?" The younger girl said. "To see *a host of angels* in the sky, all proclaiming the birth of the *Messiah?*"

"That would have been amazing," Daniel said.

"I would have been terrified," Jemima said.

The two servants continued talking about the story Mary bat Eli had shared, wondering what it was like for the young couple; whether they would be able to determine which cave was the stable where the Lord Jesus was born; what the angels looked like.

Mary leaned back, absently listening to Daniel and Jemima while she stared at the countryside. *I cannot imagine what that must have been like for Mary bat Eli and her husband Joseph. Even with the promises and proclamations of angels, it must have been difficult. I am thankful the birth of our child will be easier.* She slid a hand over her belly. The wife of a noble house, she would never give birth in a place as humble as a stable. Her child will be born in her home, surrounded by the women of her family, with Michael in a nearby room, supported by his father. There will be a great celebration at their baby's birth, and after the delivery, Elisheba will oversee her and the babe's care, all the while quoting the things her grandmother had said.

A putrid smell pulled Mary out of her reverie. "What is that *smell?*" she pulled a corner of her head cloth over her nose and mouth.

Daniel sniffed and gagged. "That is from the fires of Hinnom," he nodded his head to where grey clouds hovered over the area southwest of the city walls.

Mary knew of the Valley of Hinnom, but like all residents from this area, her family had gone out of their way to avoid traveling near it. As a child, she had been taught about the valley's heinous past. It was there that King Solomon, led astray by his foreign wives, had built altars to Chemosh and Molech and offered sacrifices to them. Other kings followed Solomon's sin and had even offered their own children in the sacrificial fires of these pagan gods. King Josiah, who returned the people to following Yahweh, had destroyed the altars and rendered the valley unclean by covering it with human bones.

She knew the valley was now used to burn sewage and trash, but Mary could not rid her mind of the images of innocent babies being placed in the red-hot hands of a stone pagan god. *How could anyone kill an innocent child?*

"My father resides in the Valley of Hinnom because we did not deal with those who followed that man!"

Abel's accusation—springing unbidden to her mind—still rankled.

"That is foolish!" she lifted her chin, recalling her retort. *"Yahweh would not strike Uncle Joktan with leprosy because others chose to follow His Son!"* Mary frowned, remembering how her uncle *hated* the Lord Jesus and had rejoiced at His crucifixion.

"Yahweh blesses those who are insulted, persecuted, and even lied about because they follow Me."

That was what the Lord Jesus had taught that day on the slopes of Mount Eremos, outside of Capernaum. He had taught many other things, including how those who truly followed Yahweh are *happy* and *blessed,* even when people hated those who followed Him.

"Indeed," He had said, *"be happy when this happens to you, for your reward in Yahweh's kingdom will be great. For they did the same thing to the prophets of old."*

Another foul breeze wafted over her, carrying the image of her uncle, his body covered in open sores, digging for food and clothing among the burning fires of Hinnom.

"I do not know how I can be His witness to 'the end of the earth,' if I never leave Jerusalem," she had told her sister.

"Perhaps the Lord Jesus wants us to be witnesses wherever we are," Martha had replied. *"Starting with those closest to us. Family."*

Since that conversation with her sister, she had been praying for an opportunity to be the Lord Jesus' witness.

She had tried telling Aunt Naomi and her cousin Rebeca about the Lord Jesus; *They listened to me, until Abel came home.* She had been right in what she had told Martha, that he would not listen. Abel had driven her out of the house, trampling her gift of food and coin. *He rejected everything I said and did.* Mary furrowed her brow, remembering another comment of Martha's.

"I do not think the Lord Jesus would consider that a reason not *to try and tell him."*

Mary gave a sharp nod. She lowered the fabric from her nose and mouth. "Daniel, please turn the carriage around. Take me to the Valley of Hinnom."

Chapter 34

The rain had stopped by the time Abel reached Solomon's Porch. He barely noted the sun peeking out of the clouds, flashing off the plates of gold on the Temple walls, but wrapped his robe tighter against the chill wind whistling through the colonnade.

As he turned to walk through the East Gate, he heard his name called. Turning, he saw Rabbi Gamaliel approaching.

"Ah, good morning, Abel ben Joktan," the teacher said, "Peace be on you."

Abel bowed his head, "Good morning, Rabbi Gamaliel, and on you peace."

"I see you are leaving the Temple."

"I am. I had…*business* to discuss with the High Priest."

"Ahh…I see. Would you mind if I walked with you?"

"It would be my honor, sir."

The two men stepped through the Temple gate and turned down one of the streets.

"How are you doing?" the older man asked.

"I am…*well.*" Abel knew his lie was barely covered, but he would *not* complain of hunger and poverty before the only kind man he knew.

"That is good." The rabbi's smile was gentle. "How is your family?"

"They are also well."

"That is a blessing. Please give my greetings to your mother and sister, and also to your father, when next you see him."

"I will, sir. Thank you."

"You are missed among my students, Abel. I enjoyed your sharp mind and your dedication."

"Your words are kind, Rabbi." *Although I doubt anyone—save yourself—misses me.*

"Perhaps you will return to your studies, now that Rabbi Caiaphas no longer needs you."

"What?" Abel stopped in mid-stride. "Sir, what do you mean?"

"Forgive me," the rabbi lifted white bushy eyebrows. "From your expression, it appears I misunderstood."

"Rabbi Gamaliel, where did you get the idea that the High Priest no longer needs me?"

"I inferred it from something Saul Paulus said."

"Saul Paulus," Abel tried to control the fury constricting his throat. "What did he say about me?"

"He did not so much speak about you. He asked if he could increase his time with me, so as to finish his studies sooner. When I asked why he wished to do that, he mentioned he was undertaking a special task for the High Priest—that *another man* could not complete. I assumed—wrongly, it would seem—that Rabbi Caiaphas was releasing you from your task. I hoped you would be able to return to your studies."

"I know nothing of this."

"Ah, I have misunderstood. Pray forgive me."

"I will ask Saul Paulus myself." He turned back toward the Temple. "Is he studying with you today?"

"No. He mentioned he would be attending the Synagogue of Freedmen this morning before coming to the Temple."

"Then, if you will excuse me, Rabbi," Abel's eyes kindled, "I will go to the Synagogue of Freedmen and find Saul Paulus."

Chapter 35

*L*ocated within the area of Jerusalem where most people—including Jews—were from foreign cities, Michael was not surprised to learn from Stephen that the design of the Synagogue of Freedmen was patterned after the one in Capernaum. With two stories, there was a large main room on the first floor where the men would gather, and a loft for the women. Benches were placed along all four walls, where the men would sit to listen to the speaker, who would stand in the middle of the room.

"This synagogue has rooms for visiting Jews." Stephen pointed to an archway toward the back of the main room. "Down that hall are sleeping chambers, baths, and *mikvahs*. Saul Paulus stays in one of these chambers."

The main room was filling with men dressed in linen togas, girdles, and some with *palla*—the oblong shawls favored by Romans and Greeks—draped over their shoulders and arms. Michael, dressed in a cream tunic and headcloth with a brown robe and girdle, felt as if he were in a foreign country instead of the center of the Jewish world.

"Greetings, Stephen ben Chariton. Peace be on you." An older man approached them, with several other men trailing him. From the salting of grey in his beard and the familiarity with which he addressed Stephen, Michael estimated the man to be older than himself; probably of Stephen's age. From his expression—reeking of barely contained condescension and contempt—Michael judged the other man did not like Stephen.

"Greetings, Adalia Gaius. And on you peace." Stephen's smile and greeting took in those with Adalia. He extended a hand toward Michael. "This is my friend, Michael ben Nicodemus. Michael,

Adalia is a Jewish brother whose father had been cruelly enslaved by a Roman; but thanks be to Yahweh, at his master's death, he was freed."

"Greetings, Michael ben Nicodemus," the other man nodded. "Peace be on you. Welcome to our humble synagogue. All have heard of *your* noble father." He glanced beyond Michael's shoulder, "Will he be joining us today?"

"Greetings, Adalia Gaius. And on you peace. No, my father is not with us today. He is visiting the home of Rabbi Joseph bar Neriah in Arimathea."

"Perhaps, once he has returned to Jerusalem," Stephen said, "he will visit our humble synagogue."

"His presence would honor us," Adalia smiled at Michael. "He and Rabbi Joseph bar Neriah are renowned teachers of Israel. Many," he slanted a glance toward Stephen, "would be wise to *follow their dedication* to the Temple and the Holy Scriptures."

Michael fought to control his expression. The man's accusation toward Stephen was as thin as one of Mary's veils.

"I agree with you about Rabbi Nicodemus and Rabbi Joseph, my brother," a smile hovered around Stephen's mouth. "All who *truly know* them are careful to listen to their teachings."

Michael bit his lips to keep from laughing aloud. Stephen was known for his skills in rhetoric and debate, including never allowing another to cause him to speak without thinking.

"Indeed." Adalia's brows slanted over his hooked nose. "Stephen, there are some here who would like you to read the Holy Scriptures and share your thoughts." He turned slightly to indicate the men standing next to him.

Stephen bowed his head. "It would be my honor to do so."

After escorting Michael to a bench, the Hellenistic believer crossed to where the attendant was placing the scroll on a stand.

Although the architecture of the Synagogue of Freedmen might be different to Michael, its purpose was the same as other synagogues. Whereas prayers and sacrifices were offered up at the Temple, synagogues were used for all Jews to read the Holy Scripture and to learn about Yahweh's commands.

Stephen stood behind the scroll and closed his eyes.

Lord Jesus, Michael prayed, *direct Stephen to the Holy Scripture You wish read.*

Opening his eyes, Stephen unrolled the scroll. Those in the room waiting while he scanned the passages, until finally he stopped.

"A reading from the prophet Ezekiel," Stephen said.

"*'I will make a covenant of peace with them; it will be an everlasting covenant.*

I will establish them and increase their numbers, and I will put My sanctuary among them forever. My dwelling place will be with them.

I will be their God; and they will be My people.

Then the nations will know that I the LORD make Israel holy, when My sanctuary is among them forever.'"

He rolled up the scroll, gave it back to the attendant, and crossed the floor to sit next to Michael. He turned to smile at Michael. "Pray for me," he whispered.

Michael nodded. *Lord Jesus,* he prayed, *guide Stephen as he tells these, our brothers, about You.* Looking at the room, he frowned; Saul Paulus was standing in the archway, staring at Stephen.

In the time spent studying with Rabbi Gamaliel, Michael had grown accustomed to Saul's intensity. *Dedicated* he had described Saul to Stephen. *Fierce,* Stephen had responded. But now, looking at the Jew from Tarsus, Michael felt both descriptions fell short. The image of a leopard stalking its prey leapt unbidden to his mind. He lifted a hand toward his friend, but Stephen had begun speaking.

"This prophecy was fulfilled in the person of the Lord Jesus," he lifted his gaze toward the ceiling, "may His holy name be blessed."

Michael held his breath as Stephen's words echoed around the room. All eyes were fixed on his friend.

"Are you claiming," Saul Paulus broke the silence, his eyes kindling, "that *this man*; the Nazarene; that Jesus ben Joseph, is the Messiah? The Son of Yahweh?"

Stephen lowered his gaze to Saul's face. Michael noted his friend's gaze was as direct as his words and as unbending.

"I am."

Chapter 36

"Mistress, I must protest," Daniel said. "You should not be in this place of death and decay."

Mary had waited with Jemima in the carriage while Daniel had gone to locate her uncle in the Valley of Hinnom. Now, at her insistence, he held her elbow, guiding her past feral animals, vermin, through the piles of burning refuse and past the poor wretches digging in them. The putrid stench she noticed earlier was now overwhelming. The few sprigs of mint leaves she had slipped between her nose and veil did nothing to block it. She took shallow breaths, fighting the bile rising in her throat, and concentrated on where she placed her sandaled feet. The descent into the ravine had been steep and the stones where they walked sharp.

"What would my master, Michael ben Nicodemus, say about me bringing his wife to this vile place?"

"Daniel, I am certain *my husband* would tell you to *obey* his wife." Mary snapped. Seeing the pained expression on her servant's face, she softened. "Forgive me. I appreciate your concern for my well-being, as would Michael. However, this is something I feel I *must* do, and I know he would agree with me. Now, where is the location of my uncle's...*dwelling*?"

Daniel frowned before pointing. "This way, mistress."

Mary shifted her hand to grasp Daniel's muscular arm as he led her around heaps of burning trash. He stopped to pick up a thick stick and a handful of sharp rocks. The stones he threw at carrion eaters; the stick he shook to scare off beggars who dared approach them. Mary lowered her gaze from those sad creatures; she had nothing to offer them, except her prayers.

After several minutes, Daniel stopped before a line of stones placed on the ground. "We are here, mistress."

Looking up, she saw a bank of caves. Here and there, people scuttled in and out of them, carrying armfuls of debris, while others huddled before small fires. From their ragged clothing, open sores, and skin as white as maggots, it was easy to identify those people as lepers. Try as she might, however, Mary could not identify her relative.

"Daniel," she whispered, "which one is my uncle?"

"None of these." Cupping a hand around his mouth, he called, "Joktan ben Philemon!"

Mary removed her hand from her servant's arm. "Thank you, Daniel. Please wait for me in the carriage with Jemima. I will call from the edge of the ravine when I am finished speaking with my uncle."

"*Mistress!*" his eyes widened. "I cannot! I *will not* leave you *alone* in the Valley of Hinnom!"

"Daniel, my uncle has been struck with leprosy. I would not wish him to feel shame by having a stranger see him thus." She smiled, "Besides, I am not alone. The Lord Jesus—may His name be blessed—is with me. Remember what He said on the day He ascended into the clouds: *I will be with you always, to the very end of time.*"

Daniel opened his mouth, but when Mary lifted her chin—and a single eyebrow—he closed it. He took a deep breath. "Yes, mistress."

Mary watched until he was out of sight before turning back. She lowered her veil from her mouth and nose; beyond not wanting to be seen by strangers, she did not wish to shame her uncle with the suggestion that she was revolted by her surroundings. She smoothed her dress, folded her hands before her, and waited.

After a moment, a man, stepped from one of the caves. He gazed at her curiously, until angry recognition crossed his face. A gathering frown on his face, he walked to the line of stones.

Mary bit her tongue to keep from screaming at the horror that stood before her. What was left of her uncle's hair and beard was whiter than his skin which was covered in oozing, ulcerated sores. Several fingers were missing, and—from his uneven gait—it appeared parts of his feet were gone as well.

Crossing his arms, Joktan ben Philemon glared at her. "Mary bat Jacob. Why are you here?" His speech was garbled, due to part of his lips and half his tongue missing.

Mary lowered her hands to grasp the sides of her robe. She swallowed hard. "I am here to see you, Uncle."

"Here to see me?" Joktan frowned. "Why?"

She exhaled a deep breath. "I want to tell you about the Lord Jesus."

Chapter 37

*P*ale light leaked between the torn flesh of the clouds as Abel left the Temple area and turned down a street leading toward the Lower City. He lengthened his stride, scanning the people on the streets, determined not to miss Saul Paulus. His countenance darkened as memories circled like vultures, picking away at him.

"Why have you not discovered these people?" Saul Paulus had demanded of him and, moments later had asked the High Priest to be given Abel's task. *"Let me find these people who defy the law, Rabbi Caiaphas. I will not take seven weeks to find them."*

On another day, Saul had challenged him, *"Abel ben Joktan, did you question these people, to determine how they made it appear they had been healed by this Peter bar Jonah?"* When commanded by the High Priest to reply, Abel had confessed he had not. *"Had I been there,"* Saul had scorned, *"I would have forced these people to admit their duplicity."*

"You are correct, Rabbi Gamaliel." Saul had said on yet another occasion. *"My studies are important."*

"…he said he was undertaking a special task for the High Priest," Rabbi Gamaliel had said, *…that another man could not complete."*

Abel fumed. Saul Paulus, who had no family to care for, who had no responsibilities beyond his studies, had the temerity to sneer at his failure in completing the task assigned to him by the High Priest. A failure that not only humiliated him, but brought shame and poverty to his family.

He seethed as the memories turned from Saul Paulus' insults, to the High Priest's dismissal of his efforts—*"Judas brought us Jesus ben Joseph. You have brought us nothing"*—and his own father's insults, *"It appears that only I will be strong enough to do something."*

"It is not my fault," Abel growled. "I have striven all my life to follow the Law Yahweh gave to Moses. I was dedicated in my studies, so I could serve as a priest in the Temple. I have done all I could to please my father, to please Rabbi Caiaphas, to please Yahweh.

"Yet, none of it matters." He kicked a rock, sending it *pinging* across the street. "The High Priest dismissed me from my pursuit of the priesthood. My father considers me *racha* and cares not whether my mother, my sister, nor I starve. Even my cousin Mary refused to obey her father's wishes and marry me. *Why?* What have I done?"

Abel stopped in mid-stride, awareness shooting through him like a wandering star in a dark night sky.

I have done nothing. The fault for everything—all he had suffered, all his mother and sister had suffered, even all his father had suffered—could be laid completely at the feet of Jesus ben Joseph and his followers.

His mouth tightened as he realized his father was right.

Jesus ben Joseph is dead. The only thing that matters now is that His followers are destroyed.

The sound of angry voices pulled Abel out of his reverie. He looked up to see a mob coming up the street, cries of, "Blasphemy!" "Death to the Blasphemer!" rising from them. In their midst, he saw Saul Paulus who—along with another—were dragging the man, Stephen ben Chariton. Behind them, yelling, trying to pull their hands off the Hellenistic Jew, was Michael ben Nicodemus.

Chapter 38

*T*he crowd dragging Stephen roiled like an angry sea. It grew as it moved through the streets towards the Temple, gathering people drawn to the cries of "Blasphemy! Stone him! Kill the blasphemer!"

Michael, desperate to reach his friend, tried forcing his way through the mob, crying Stephen's name, demanding Saul release his friend; but those on the edge of the crowd shoved him, blocking his way.

Never had he felt so helpless.

No. There was another time. That unspeakable night when the Lord Jesus had been arrested. In a painful heartbeat, Michael recalled the nightmares of those endless hours. The Teacher, weary from lack of sleep, bruised from beatings, bloodied from the crown of *nabk* vine shoved onto His brow, cringing as He was flogged with a Roman *flagrum taxillatum*. The whip's multiple ropes, with sharp tips of bone or metal tied along each strand and hooked on the end, had ripped the flesh from the Lord Jesus' body.

More terror-filled memories. The screams of "Crucify Him!" had echoed from those in the courtyard of the Antonia Fortress. Mary bat Eli wailing, "You cannot! You *cannot*!" as she had heard Pontius Pilate's judgement of death. Rending the neck of her tunic, she had fallen to her knees screaming, "My son! My *Son!*"

Standing next to her was Mary. His Mary.

Michael remembered running to the back of the fortress's courtyard, with his father and Rabbi Joseph steps behind him.

Mary had dropped to her knees next to the Lord Jesus' mother, to cradle the other woman's head against her shoulder. "Shhhh," Mary had murmured. "Do not cry. Something can be done." She had looked up at Michael, lifting an eyebrow in a pleading question.

Even months later—even after all the wonders that had resulted from that day—Michael's stomach still clinched, knowing the Governor's pronouncement had doused any flames of hope for the Lord Jesus' release. Michael had shaken his head in response to her question.

Tears had filled his Mary's eyes, dripping from her long lashes. Lowering her head to Mary bat Eli's shoulder, she had sobbed.

The sound of the two women's grief had constricted his throat, leaving his chest aching. He had slid his hands over his head covering and looking upward, his mouth opened in a silent scream. *Yahweh! Help us!* he had pled. *Help Jesus! Help me! This was the first time Mary asked me to do something, and I have* failed *her!*

The atrocities in the following hours, culminating in the Lord Jesus' death, continued to flash through Michael's mind. Even though, three days later, the Lord Jesus would come forth from His tomb as the resurrected Messiah, the pain and heartache of those terror-filled hours reverberated through Michael's memory and heart.

It did not take contemplation to realize who was responsible for all this pain. For what happened to the Lord Jesus and what was happening to his friend, Stephen.

"Caiaphas. Caiaphas and Annas," Michael growled, refusing to add the honorific, "Rabbi." *This is all their doing. They hated the Lord Jesus and they hate all who follow Him. Something* must *be done to help Stephen.* He paused. *Father and Rabbi Joseph are not in Jerusalem.* He set his jaw. *It matters not. I am Michael ben Nicodemus. If I must do it alone, so be it. I cannot, I will not, allow another friend to suffer from the lies and manipulations of those two.*

With renewed strength, he attempted to push his way through the crowd to reach Stephen. "No! You cannot! Stephen is innocent! Saul Paulus! Let him go!" Michael grabbed at two men at the back of the crowd. "Get out of my way!"

As one, the men shook off Michael's hands and turned, standing shoulder to shoulder to face him. Both men were muscular; one was as tall as Goliath, the other had a crooked nose. *Probably broken in a fight.* Michael did not recall seeing either of these men at the

Synagogue of Freedmen. *They are like leeches, drinking the misery of another's distress.*

"Move!" Michael pushed against them. "Get out of my way!"

The men stood implacable. Goliath folded massive arms across his chest.

Michael moved to sidestep them.

Broken Nose stepped to block him.

Michael shifted to go the other way.

The men grabbed him.

The crowd leading Stephen moved further down the street.

Michael tried to shake off the men's grasp. "How dare you! Take your hands off me! At once!"

"Why should we?" Broken Nose sneered. The giant flexed his muscles, his gaze taunting Michael to try his luck.

"I am Michael ben Nicodemus, the son of Rabbi Nicodemus ben Melech!"

"And I am the High Priest Caiaphas ben Joseph. Leave now…" Goliath shook a balled fist under Michael's nose, "or do I need to *encourage* you?"

Michael paused. He stepped back, lifting his hands and shaking his head, and turned as if to walk away; then, in one fluid motion, shifted to dart around the two men. Success coursed through his veins, *I am coming, Stephen!* until a hand like iron gripped him and threw him aside as a woman tosses a soiled rag.

He stumbled and twisted as he fell, his vision exploding as his head rebounded against the stone façade of a house. The last thing Michael heard before the world went black was the crowd screaming for Stephen's death.

Chapter 39

"*You dare*," Joktan's face contorted, "speak to me of *that man?*" Fear shot through Mary. She took a half-step back; years of honoring Joktan as the patriarch of her family was a hard habit to break. In a heartbeat, she remembered, *I am wife of Michael ben Nicodemus. I no longer must answer to my uncle. Help me, Lord Jesus.* She lifted her chin. "Yes. I have come to tell you about Jesus ben Joseph. To tell you about His love and sacrifice for you."

She jumped as her uncle spat. The spittle barely missed her.

"The last time I saw you—the last time I acknowledged you as my kin—you chose to dishonor the wishes of your father. You refused to obey me." His color was rising ominously. "You chose instead to follow *that man.* Because of you, because of your *racha* brother and sister—because of all who followed the Nazarene—I was punished by Yahweh! It is your fault I am a *leper.*"

"That is absurd!" She retorted. "Lazarus, Martha, and I are not responsible for what happened to you. None of those who love the Lord Jesus are responsible." She took a deep breath and softened her voice. "Uncle, you can still receive forgiveness, and perhaps even healing. The Lord Jesus healed Simon of his leprosy. You can be healed too." Her voice picked up speed in her excitement. "All you have to do is ask the Lord Jesus to forgive you."

"Ask *Jesus ben Joseph* to forgive *me?*" Joktan's brow furrowed.

Mary took that as a good sign. "Yes, Uncle. The Lord Jesus is the Son of Yahweh. He is the promised Messiah, the one spoken of by the prophets of old. When He died on the cross, it was for the sins of the world. But He did not die. After three days, He rose from the dead. I saw Him. Martha and Lazarus saw Him. We spoke with Him many times. We were there the day He ascended into the clouds to be with His Father Yahweh. The last command He gave was to share His story with everyone. That is why I have come." She extended her hands towards her uncle. "To tell you about Him."

She waited, her heart joyously beating at being the Lord Jesus' witness, here in Jerusalem, and sharing the message of His salvation with her uncle.

"Blasphemy." His voice was still and cold as the grave.

Mary tilted her head. *I mis-heard. He cannot speak well, due to the leprosy.* "What?"

"Blasphemy! You speak blasphemy by naming this *man*, this *criminal*, as the Son of Yahweh!" He pointed a maggot-white hand at her. "Renounce him. Tell me who took his body and where they hid it. As your uncle, your eldest kin, I command you. Renounce him and ask Yahweh to forgive you for this blasphemy."

"No." She shook her head. This was not going as she had planned, but there was no question about obeying her uncle. *It is hopeless. Uncle will never accept the Lord Jesus.* "I will *not* renounce the Lord Jesus. I will *never* renounce Him. He is *alive*. He is the Messiah. He is my friend. He loves me. I would rather die than renounce Him."

Mary turned to leave. She had taken only a few steps when her uncle spoke again.

"Then die."

She heard the crunch of a footstep behind her. She turned to see her uncle had crossed the line of stones and was following her, rage suffusing his face.

Chapter 40

Abel flattened his back against the Temple walls, eyes sweeping up and down the corridor, ears straining listening for sounds of approaching footsteps. Holding his breath, he eased away from the wall and peered around the corner. No one. Filling his lungs with a quiet sigh, he slipped around the corner into the hallway leading to the Chamber of Hewn Stones.

I studied to be a priest, trained by Rabbi Gamaliel; yet here I am, skulking around the Temple of Yahweh as if I were a thief. Will my shame know no end?

Yet he would not stop. He had to know what was happening to Stephen ben Chariton.

Abel had watched the crowd grow as they dragged the Hellenistic Jew, screaming for his death. He had seen Michael ben Nicodemus confront those two louts and suppressed a smile when the larger one knocked him against the stone wall. As the crowd moved on, Abel had crossed the street to kneel by Michael.

He was lying at a twisted angle, his breath shallow and rasping, blood pooling behind his head. His skin was turning an odd gray color, like wood ash left over after a hot fire.

Abel was not trained in medicine, but it was obvious Michael needed help. He stood, looking around. He saw two boys, beggars from the looks of them, staring wide-eyed from him to Michael. Abel opened his mouth to send one of them for help. Then he paused, his hand sliding to finger the money pouch hidden in the folds of his girdle. The boys would likely expect a coin in exchange and Abel had only a few copper pennies in his pouch. Pennies he needed to purchase food for his mother and sister.

Like the widow of Zarephath. After we eat our meal, we will die.

Abel stared at the man lying unconscious at his feet. Michael ben Nicodemus, the son of a rich and noble family, had everything he did not. Michael had plenty of food, a palatial home, and a father who loved him. He also had a beautiful wife with a rich dowry.

That wife should have been mine! Abel's lips spread in a dark smile. *Yet, here he lies bleeding to death. He is a follower of the Nazarene. Father would say he is being punished by Yahweh. Who am I to stand in the way of the Almighty's judgements?*

Turning, he started walking up the street, lengthening his stride to catch up with the crowd. He glanced back as he turned the corner and saw the boys creeping towards Michael's inert body.

The crowd had dragged Stephen into the Temple by the time Abel arrived. He passed through Solomon's Porch, through the East Gate, and the Court of Women, up fifteen steps to the Gate of Nicanor and into the Court of Israel, where only Jewish men were allowed. Temple Guards stood, spears at their side, blocking the Court of Priests. Abel knew these men and nodded at them as he prepared to cross the marbled floor.

"Hold," One guard slanted his spear in front of Abel, blocking his way. "You cannot go in there, Abel ben Joktan."

Abel gaped at him. "What do you mean?"

"Only priests are allowed beyond this point. Rabbi Caiaphas informed us this morning that you are no longer studying to be a priest. So," he shrugged his shoulders, "you cannot go in there."

Abel felt his cheeks burning. *Rabbi Caiaphas cares not if I am shamed. All he cares about is dealing with those who follow the Nazarene.* He frowned. *I will prove to him—and to Father and even to Saul Paulus—that I can complete the task, beginning with Stephen ben Chariton.*

All of that flashed through his mind in the time it took to feel the blood suffuse his face. Controlling his anger—Abel realized he was no match for the Temple Guards and their weapons—he stepped back, spreading his hands wide, and turned to walk away.

He walked away from the Guards and found a spot in the shade to study the crowds in the Temple court. After a moment, he noticed a young man carrying a cage with two small doves, the substitute for those who could not afford the prescribed sacrifice.

Fingering his money pouch, Abel's eyes slanted from the man to the Guards. *Food for Mother and Rebeca? Or proving I am worthy to be a priest of Yahweh?* After a moment, his face hardened. He pulled the pouch from his girdle and crossed the courtyard.

Several minutes later, Abel watched as the young man ran up to the Temple Guards, yelling, "Hurry! A band of Gentiles are approaching the Temple."

The Guards did not even question the man. Lifting their spears, they ran through the courts.

Abel crossed to the edge of the Court of Israel and handed the young man a second coin. "Go." Watching until the young man left the Temple, he turned to hurry through the Court of Priests and turned down the arched doorway on one side. He increased his steps, pausing now and then to listen, checking down hallways, until he arrived at the entrance to the Chamber of Hewn Stones.

Abel looked down, pulling the edge of his head cloth to cover his face, and slipped into the back of the people crowded in the room. He glanced side-to-side, watching for any sign that someone had noticed him. He saw Saul Paulus across the chamber, standing next to Rabbi Gamaliel. From his demeanor, arms folded, dark eyes kindling as he listens to the man on trial, it was obvious to Abel that Saul had not seen him. *If he had seen me,* Abel's frown deepened, *I do not doubt he would have drawn attention to me.*

All eyes were on the man standing in the middle of the room—Stephen ben Chariton.

Abel realized he had missed hearing the charges brought against the follower of the Nazarene. At this point in the trial, the High Priest would have given the accused an opportunity to deny or confess to the charges brought against him. From his words and bearing, however, the Hellenistic Jew behaved as if he were the prosecutor and not the one on trial.

Stephen ben Chariton spoke at length of the history of the Jewish people, beginning with their faithful patriarch, Abraham, and how God had led him from a pagan land into the land of Israel, where He made a covenant with him. He spoke of the journey of his people, through Joseph's sojourn in Egypt to their deliverance by Moses 400 years later. He spoke of how Moses had met God in the wilderness of Midian in a burning bush, and how God had empowered Moses to lead His people from idolatry and slavery to freedom in the Promised Land. He reminded them of how, despite the mighty works and provisions of Yahweh, their ancestors had time and again rebelled and even turned to idolatry. By his words, it was obvious he was accusing those present of being complicit with the acts of their ancestors.

He spoke of Israel's failure to recognize Jesus ben Joseph as their Messiah, how they rejected and *murdered* him, just as their ancestors had murdered Zechariah and other faithful prophets and godly men.

"You stiff-necked people, with uncircumcised hearts and ears!" Stephen spread his arms wide, turning in a circle to look at all present. "You are just like your fathers. You always resist Yahweh's Holy Spirit! Was there ever a prophet that your fathers did not persecute? They even killed those who foretold the coming of the Righteous One. And now you," he stopped and pointed at the High Priest, "have betrayed and murdered Him. You have received the Law that was put into effect through angels, but you have not obeyed it."

No one moved as Stephen ben Chariton's words faded. Everyone's gaze shifted from the accused to Rabbi Caiaphas ben Joseph. The knuckles on the High Priest's hands were white as he grasped the arms of his chair, his face working as he gnashed his teeth. Standing, Rabbi Caiaphas lifted a hand to point at the accused. He opened his mouth, but before he could speak, the Hellenistic Jew looked up.

"Look," he pointed. "I see Heaven open," Stephen's voice echoed around the Chamber, "and I see the Son of Man standing at the right hand of God."

Abel looked upwards—as did all those standing in the chamber— and then lowered his eyes to the face of Stephen. The Hellenistic Jew looked straight at him. Abel could not look away, as the man's face faded from his view to be replaced with a face covered in blood beneath a crown made of thorns. Eyes filled with pain and with something else. Eyes staring into his soul.

No! Abel clasped his hand over his mouth, to keep from screaming. *Not here! Not now! Stop looking at me! Stop looking at me!* Turning, he ran from the chamber.

$\mathcal{M}$ary had seen her uncle angered before, even angry with her; but she had never seen this rage. Face contorted, the pulse beating at his temple, hands clinched, gaze black, Joktan appeared consumed as he pursued her.

"Uncle! What are you doing?" She picked up her steps.

His steps did not slow. *"Take the blasphemer outside the camp,"* spittle flew from his mouth. *"All those who heard him are to lay their hands on his head, and the entire assembly is to stone him."*

She recognized the scripture he quoted. *Surely, he cannot mean to…* Mary felt a rising tide of panic. "No, Uncle! Stop!" She picked up her pace. "You have no right!"

He continued stalking her, *"Take the blasphemer outside the camp,"* even with his limp, he was gaining ground. *"…and stone her."*

Mary lifted the hem of her garments—modesty did not matter— and blindly ran. She zig-zagged around the fires, stumbled in holes, throwing out her hands to regain her balance, the jagged stones cut her feet; but she kept running, desperate to be anywhere but in this valley of death.

"Daniel! Jemima! Help me! Daniel!" She screamed, but the wind was in her face and her words were thrown back at her. "Oh, Lord Jesus, help me!"

Mary reached the slope of the ravine and began climbing, grasping rocks, exposed roots, digging into the dirt, anything to get a handhold. She tripped, losing her footing as she stepped on the hem of her robe. She slid down the edge of the slope, until she hit a boulder. She opened her mouth to scream, but she could not breathe. Grasping the linen, Mary jerked, rending the garment.

A pain shot through her shoulder, and then her temple. A rock whizzed past her and *pinged* off the boulder in the slope. Another rock hit her hand; blood oozed from the wound. She looked back.

Her uncle stood near a fire at the foot of the slope, picking up rocks, and throwing them at her. "*Take the blasphemer outside the camp,*" her uncle screamed like a hawk attacking its prey, "*and stone her!*"

Chapter 42

*W*armth. Michael felt embraced. Peace. Floating. It must have been night, because there were countless bright stars all around him.

Suddenly, ice shot through his veins. He felt *yanked* down.

"Michael. *Michael!*"

He did not want to move. Everything *hurt*. He felt the pressure of a hand on his forehead. He heard voices mumbling. *Something* washed over him.

"Michael, wake!"

With effort—his eyelids felt heavy—Michael peeked through his lashes. A face. Two faces, their beards inches above his face. Frowning. Opening his eyes, he stared at the men. Recognition. "Peter?" His voice sounded faint. "John?" He licked his lips; his mouth felt as if he had swallowed a desert.

The disciples heaved a sigh of relief. John smiled as Peter dashed a hand across his eyes.

John nodded. "It is us."

Peter slid a hand beneath Michael's shoulders and helped him sit, leaning him against the wall. John handed him a wineskin.

Michael took a sip. He looked around, still dazed. Beyond Peter and John stood two boys, dressed in rags. He started to ask the identity of the lads, when he glanced down and saw the pool of blood beneath him. "What...? Is that..." He took a breath and grimaced; his lungs ached, "...*blood?*"

"It is." John looked at Peter, who nodded. "Your blood. You were hurt."

"How did you know?"

"Benaiah bar Hirah and his brother Jadon," Peter pointed towards the boys. "The brothers and their mother are believers in the Lord

Jesus, and they have seen you at the teachings. They witnessed what had happened and saw you needed help. Benaiah left Jadon to stand watch over you while he ran to find us."

Michael smiled at the brothers. "Thank you."

The boys blushed, shifting from one foot to the other.

"You are welcome," Benaiah nodded his head.

"Taking care of our brethren is what the Lord Jesus would have wanted," Jadon added.

"While the boys told us about you being knocked down by the brute," John said, "what they did not know was why. Michael, what happened? Why were you fighting?"

Fear spiked through Michael. "Peter! John! Help me up! We must hurry!"

"Michael, you must be careful," John said. "You were hurt. In fact, it appeared that—"

"—that does not matter," Michael interrupted him. "Stephen was accused of *blasphemy*. The crowd was dragging him to the Temple to be tried before the Sanhedrin. I must go and speak for him!" He struggled to stand and turned towards the street leading to the Temple, until Peter put a hand out to stop him.

"Michael, wait. It took a long time for Benaiah to find John and me and bring us back here. By now, the trial would be over. If Stephen was found guilty of blasphemy, there would be only one punishment."

"*Stoning*!" Michael felt panic rising. "I know!" He grabbed John's forearm. "We have to *help him!* We have to go!"

"We will go," Peter said, "but not to the Temple."

"Michael, if Stephen was found guilty," John said, "they will take him in the Kidron Valley."

"Then let's go there."

"You go to the Kidron Valley," Peter said. "You are the son of Rabbi Nicodemus; that should carry weight. John and I will try to gather as many of the Twelve as we can."

"Take them to my house," Michael said. "Mary should be home by now. She will prepare whatever is necessary."

$\mathcal{A}$bel stomped up and down the street leading from the Temple, anger consuming him. Anger shot from his belly, up through his chest, down his arms, making his hands twitch to *hit* something.

Anger at life, that he should go from being a promising young priest to a man skulking around the Temple courts. Anger at Caiaphas, who looked upon him as a worthless tool to be tossed aside. Anger at Saul Paulus, who succeeded at what he himself had sought to achieve. Anger at his father, who did not care about his own family. Anger at the followers of the Nazarene—especially Mary—who rejected him as a husband and chose to marry a richer man. Anger at himself, for not being able to do anything about his situation.

Anger at Yahweh. Abel had been raised to believe if he obeyed the Law given to Moses, he would please Yahweh, Who would see that he prospered and nothing bad would happen to him.

Humiliation wrestled with the anger; humiliation that the memory—the nightmare—of Jesus ben Joseph's face would send him running from the Temple like a *frightened woman*.

The sound of sandaled feet and raised voices stopped Abel's pacing.

A crowd emerged from the Temple. Stephen ben Chariton was at the front, stumbling—hands and feet bound—between two Temple Guards. The Guards on either side of Stephen grasped his arms with one hand and held short swords with the other.

Scanning the enraged faces in the crowd that followed, Abel noted the High Priest was not among those screaming, "Stone him! Stone the blasphemer!" *The death of a foreign-born Jew is not worthy of Caiaphas' attention.* Several members of the Sanhedrin were behind the Guards and their prisoner; they sneered at Abel as they passed.

At the back of the crowd was Rabbi Gamaliel. Unlike the others crying for Stephen ben Chariton's blood, the Teacher of the Law followed silently. He looked at Abel and gave a single nod, his mouth stretched in a sad smile. *"An execution,"* the Teacher had said to him, *"whether by crucifixion or stoning, is something no one wishes to see."*

Saul Paulus' steps shadowed the Teacher's, but his screams echoed the crowd. As the roiling throng turned the corner, Saul caught Abel's gaze. Raising his single brow and his chin, Saul spread his mouth in a toothy, superior smile.

Abel's cheeks burned. *Arrogant! Spiteful!* He took a step, fist clinched. *Racha! You think you are better than me! I am the son of Joktan ben Philemon.* He lifted his chin. *Our family has been serving as priests of Yahweh for generations. Your family is unknown. I will prove to you.*

Crossing the street, Abel hurried down an alley.

I will prove to you. I will prove to all. At the end of the alley, he turned down a second street. *Father thinks he is the only one strong enough to do something about the Nazarene's followers.* He picked up speed, *I will do something,* lengthening his strides, *I will show all of them,* dodging people on foot—or pausing only seconds for those driving carriages or riding horses—before launching down the street again.

He ran through the Lower City, passed the Pool of Siloam, and out of the Water Gate. Only then did he stop, hands on knees, his heart pounding, gasping in air, at the edge of the Kidron Valley.

A steep slope led down into the valley. At one time, the Gihon Springs had filled it, but the builders of Jerusalem had diverted the water into pools and channels to be used by the city. Now, only the Kidron Brook flowed there.

King David had passed through this valley after his son Absalom had taken over the city. Two kings, Asa and Josiah, had burned idols and pagan altars near the Kidron Brook. During King Hezekiah's rule, when the Temple was purified, the priests used the Kidron

Valley to discard the unclean things that had been used in the Temple.

It was to this valley those guilty of sins that Yahweh's Law condemned to death were brought. To be stoned.

When Abel could draw breath without pain, he began walking around, collecting large stones and piling them on the edge of the slope. *I will do it. I will rid the earth of this man's followers, and then Yahweh will bless me, and the nightmares will go away.* He had gathered several dozen stones when the howling crowd arrived.

The two Temple Guards dragged Stephen ben Chariton. They paused long enough to check the ropes binding the prisoner's hands and feet before throwing him over the edge.

A cheer rose from the crowd as they watched the Hellenistic Jew fly out about six cubits and then fall, hitting the slope with a *thud*, and begin rolling downward. They clapped every time Stephen ben Chariton cried out as he hit protruding rocks and tree roots, until he landed in a heap in the valley.

The crowd moved to the edge of the slope, watching the inert body of Stephen. Several asked, "Is he dead?"

"No, look!" Saul Paulus pointed, "He is moving! Gather rocks!"

That was what Abel had hoped for. Crossing to the Tarsuian Jew, he removed his cloak—he did not want his right arm impaired— and tossed it at the feet of Saul Paulus.

"Here," Abel sneered, "watch my clothes." Not waiting for a reply, he walked to the pile of rocks he had gathered, chose the largest one, and looked over the edge.

The condemned man had managed to lift himself up, resting on his forearms, blood dripping from his face.

Abel stepped back several paces, lifted the rock, and then rushed towards the edge, throwing the rock. It shot down, hitting Stephen ben Chariton's face. The *crunching* of bones breaking echoed around the valley. "Death to the blasphemer!" Abel screamed.

Chapter 44

"*D*eath to the blasphemer!" Joktan screeched. He stooped to pick up another rock and threw it.

Mary screamed as it hit the back of her legs. She collapsed against the slope of the ravine. Glancing upwards, she did not see either of her servants. *Where are they?*

Another rock *pinged* near her.

Gulping a breath, she shoved her fingers into the dirt, seeking a handhold, biting her lips as her nails broke and skin tore off. *Lord Jesus, help me*—she did not have the breath to cry out—and dragged herself up a handbreath.

"Kill her!" Joktan screamed. "Stone the blasphemer!"

Reaching up, Mary grabbed a protruding tree root. *Almost there. One more*—screaming as pain erupted in her back.

"Kill her!" Joktan's laughter echoed beneath her. "Kill the blasphemer!"

Terror shot through Mary's veins at the sound of wood splintering. She looked at her hands, her eyes drenched with horror as the tree root split, giving away. She scrabbled, trying to grab another root, a rock, *anything*. Her vision exploded as pain shot through her head as another rock hit her.

She fell, rolling down the slope, unable to stop her fall, moaning as she hit rocks, protruding roots and sticks, hearing the crazed laughter of her uncle.

Lord Jesus, help me. I am going to die in the fires of Hinnom.

The world went black.

$\mathcal{A}$s Michael dashed through the Water Gate, he heard the blood-thirsty shrieks of the crowd. Dread of what was happening to Stephen and memories of the Lord Jesus' sufferings twisted his gut. Ignoring his own screaming lungs, Michael lengthened his stride. *I am the son of Nicodemus ben Melech; I can do something. I can stop them.* Sharp gusts whipped his hair into little needles that jabbed at his face. *Lord Jesus, help Stephen.*

Screeching and cheering like spectators watching a race, the people in the crowd paused only long enough to find a rock and push their way to the edge of the ravine. Taking aim, they threw them at the man in the valley, and ran to find more rocks.

"No!" Michael shoved a man holding a boulder, knocking him down. Pivoting, he rammed another man, "Stop!" He elbowed his way through the crowd—punching, shoving, and tripping—to the edge of the valley, where honored members of the Sanhedrin mingled with rabble, all squawking like vultures. Across the crowd, he saw the two men who had attacked him earlier—Goliath and Broken Nose. The two brutes were clapping the shoulder of Adalia Gaius—the older Jew from the Synagogue of Freedmen—praising his aim. Several paces away was Saul Paulus, with a pile of robes at his feet. Standing next to the Tarsuian was Abel ben Joktan, chest heaving.

Looking into the valley, Michael's mouth fell open in horror.

At the base of the ravine was Stephen, covered in blood, clothing and skin shredded, bones broken. He moaned as he pulled himself upright. Lifting his gaze to scan the faces of his attackers. He paused when he saw Michael, stretching his bruised lips in a slight smile.

Michael's throat tightened against tears as he looked at Stephen's face. Gazing at his friend, Michael recalled standing on the hilltop of Golgotha, staring into the eyes of the Lord Jesus. As it had been on that day—in Stephen's eyes—Michael saw the same sadness as he had seen in the Lord Jesus' face, he saw the same pain. He also saw something more; the same *acceptance*, the same *strength*, the same *determination*, the same *trust*, as he had seen in the Lord Jesus' face. Michael filled his lungs and nodded, returning the gaze of his friend and brother in the Lord Jesus.

Stephen nodded before lifting his eyes to the grey sky. "Lord Jesus," his voice echoed around the walls of the Kidron Valley, "receive my spirit." Lowering his gaze, he looked straight at Abel ben Joktan. "Lord, do not hold this sin against them."

Closing his eyes, Stephen crumpled to the ground.

The crowd on the edge of the valley silenced, studying the inert body.

"Is he dead?" someone asked.

"I think so."

"I do not see him breathing."

"Someone needs to check to make sure he is dead."

"I am not going to touch a dead body. That would make me unclean."

Michael lifted a foot to take a step when a hand touched his back. Spinning, fists raised, he startled to see Lazarus and Simon. Beyond them was Daniel, his father's driver.

"Lazarus! Simon!" He grasped his brother-in-laws' forearms. "I tried to help Stephen. I did, but…" he could not form the words.

"I know, Michael," Simon's were rimmed red and his mouth turned down. "I am sorry. But you must come now."

"Come?" Michael shook his head. "*I* cannot leave, *we* cannot leave," he flung a hand towards the valley. "*They* will not give him," he choked, "an honorable burial."

"We will do what we can for him; but, Michael" Lazarus dashed a hand across his eyes. "You must come now."

"Lazarus! Simon! I cannot *go*!" Michael said. "It is *Stephen*!"

"Michael, you must *come*!" Lazarus tightened his grasp on Michael's forearms, his voice breaking, "It is *Mary*."

Chapter 46

Abel bent over, his left hand on his knee; his chest heaving as he gulped in air. Although others from the crowd had participated in stoning Stephen ben Chariton, he himself had thrown more stones than all. His right hand ached around the jagged rock he held.

He had noticed Michael ben Nicodemus arrive and had watched with grim satisfaction the other man's futile attempts to stop the storm of rocks pummeling the man in the ravine. *Your father's wealth and name have no power here. The blasphemer will die as all blasphemers must die.*

Abel's lips spread in a toothy grin as he glanced at Saul Paulus, a mound of robes at his feet. *For once, others followed* my *example.*

He turned his gaze from where Rabbi Gamaliel stood, his smile fading. *"Stoning is something no one wishes to see."* The elderly teacher was the kindest man he knew, and was one of the reasons Abel studied as hard as he did. He did not want to see sadness—or worse, disappointment—in the rabbi's eyes.

"Lord Jesus."

Abel startled; he turned to look at the criminal in the ravine. Bloodied, his body twisted and broken, Stephen's face was lifted towards the sky. "Receive my spirit," Grimacing as he took a breath, he lowered his eyes and looked straight at Abel. "Lord, do not hold this sin against them." The condemned man slumped to the ground.

Stephen ben Chariton's bloodied face faded before Abel's eyes to be replaced by another bloodied face; one wearing a crown of thorns. Abel was unable to break his gaze away from the onyx eyes filled with pain looking into his own eyes; into his soul.

"No." Abel screamed. He ran to the edge of the ravine and slid down, stumbling, cutting his body on protruding roots and jagged rocks. "No, no, no, no! Leave me alone!" Reaching the bottom of the slope, he lifted his arm as he ran to the inert body. Throwing the stone, it smashed Stephen's face. The onyx eyes of the Nazarene gazed at him. "Stop looking at me!" He picked up another rock and threw it, smashing it into Stephen's chin. The face of Jesus ben Joseph remained. "Leave me alone!" Abel picked up another rock; and another rock; throwing them at the face gazing at him. "Stop. Looking. At. Me! Leave! Me! Alone!"

Chapter 47

*N*oises.

Faint, muted.

Mary tried to open her eyes, but her lids were heavy.

Her body was cool. *No*, she moves a finger, *I am lying in coolness.*

The noises take shape. Voices. Words.

"Mary. *Mary*, Beloved. Please wake up."

Michael? She frowned—or at least tried to frown. Her face felt heavy as her eyelids. Her brow moved against a cool, wet cloth.

Other voices.

"Mary." That was Martha's voice; she echoed Michael's concern. "Please, you must wake up."

"Peter, John," that was her brother. "Can anything else be done?"

The disciples are here, my family is here—thought solidified—*in the Valley of Hinnom? Hinnom! My uncle! Stoning! Me!* Parting her lips was as difficult as rolling a stone from a tomb.

"Help me!" She forced her eyes opened. "Help me!" She meant it as a cry; in her ears, her voice sounded thin and quivery.

"Mary!"

In an instance, she was wrapped in Michael's embrace. It felt strong and solid. It felt safe. Over the shoulder of her husband, she saw that the room—*their room*—was filled. Martha was kneeling by the bed, a damp cloth in her hand. Lazarus and Abigail were standing nearby. The two disciples, Peter bar Jonah and John ben Zebedee stood at the foot of the bed. Elisheba was next to the wash table, pouring water from the pitcher into the bowl, with Jemima at her side. Near the door was Daniel, her driver.

"Daniel? Jemima?" she whispered. "How? My uncle...*Michael*," fear etched her voice, "my uncle *stoned me!*"

"I know." Michael's embrace tightened around her. "I am sorry, Beloved. But you are safe. You are home."

It hurt to shake her head. "But how?"

"Daniel and Jemima," Martha said. "They saved you."

"Saved me?" Mary looked towards her servants. "I sent you back to the carriage."

Color bloomed in Daniel's face. "I…that is…we…" he glanced at Jemima.

The young girl spoke up. "We disobeyed you, mistress. When Daniel came back to the carriage, he told me what you had instructed him to do." She lifted her chin. "You are a kind lady, and never give thought to yourself. *We,*" she nodded towards the driver, "determined *not* to leave you alone in that valley of death. We were climbing down by a different path when we saw your…" she paused and looked towards Michael.

"When they saw your uncle stoning you." Michael's countenance was like flint; a vein throbbed in his forehead. "They rushed to protect you." He nodded towards the two servants. "Jemima threw herself over you, shielding you with her own body. Daniel picked up a large stick and drove your uncle away. They carried you back to the carriage and brought you home."

"They were hurt themselves," Martha said, "but refused to allow Elisheba to tend their wounds until the disciples were sent for," she nodded towards Peter and John, "and Lazarus was sent to find Michael and bring him home."

Mary looked at her two servants. *They risked their lives for me.* "Thank you."

Daniel's face reddened. He shifted from foot to foot.

"We love you, mistress," Jemima smiled, wiping away a tear. "It is what the Lord Jesus would want us to do."

"I share my wife's thanks," Michael smiled at the servants. He turned to Mary, "They have never strayed far from your door."

Mary spread her lips in a weak smile. *'They have never strayed far from your door.'* Her brow furrowed. *Wait!* She glanced towards the window; from the slanting of the sun, it was early morning. *That cannot be right.* "How long have I been unconscious?"

Michael looked at Martha and Lazarus. Her sister nodded. "Three days," Lazarus said.

"Three days?"

"Three days," Martha repeated. "Your wounds were severe. Had it not been for the prayers of Peter and John…" she blinked away the sheen of tears gathering in her eyes. Drawing a ragged breath, she continued, "But, they came and prayed for you."

"The Lord Jesus heard our prayers," John ben Zebedee smiled, "and healed you."

"May His name be glorified," Peter bar Jonah said.

All in the room echoed the disciple's words of praise.

"May the Lord Jesus be praised, indeed," Elisheba crossed the room, the fabric of her sand-colored tunic whispering over broad hips. "But, as my grandmother—may her memory be blessed— always said, 'A pillow is as important as a prayer.' Mistress Mary needs to rest.

"Jemima, you stay here while I prepare a meal for her. Mistress Martha, Mistress Abigail, you both need to eat and rest yourselves." She stopped in front of Michael, her fists on ample hips. "You too, Master Michael." She lifted a hand when he opened his mouth. "I know Mistress Mary is your wife, but the care she needs right now, you cannot give."

Michael straightened, but he was no match for the elderly servant gaze. "As you say, Elisheba." He lifted Mary's hand to his lips. "Beloved, I will spread the news of your recovery. Many believers have been praying for you."

As Elisheba shooed the people from the room, Jemima poured a cup of water. She held it to Mary's lips and then helped her lie back against her pillows. "After you are rested, mistress, I will help you bathe."

"Thank you," Mary said. "A bath would be nice." She slid her hand down the bed linens. "I feel…" Her tongue froze as her fingers touched the folds of cloth placed between her thighs. She lifted her eyes to her servant.

Jemima nodded. "Your monthly flow started when Daniel and I were bringing you home. Mistress Martha and I have been changing your cloths."

Mary's eyes widened in horror as her mouth stretched around a silent scream. *My baby!*

PART TWO

Chapter 48

*A*bel shoved a stick into the campfire, sending sparks flying like lost souls reaching for the wraith-silver moon hanging amidst the stars in the lonely sky.

From childhood, he had been drawn to the stars and had spent many nights on the rooftop of his home learning to identify the *mazzaloth*, the pictures formed by their arrangement. Abel searched the sky, noting the Ram; the Great Bear followed by its cubs; the Twin Brothers; the Hunter and his two dogs chasing the Bull.

The Hunter. That is what I am now. Only it is not bulls I am hunting. He poked the fire again. *It is blasphemers; followers of the Nazarene.*

He looked at the man sitting across the fire from him. Saul Paulus was opening a basket of food, drawing out containers of olives, figs, cheese, and bread.

Saul called to the Temple Guards, who had been tending their horses.

As the men reached them, Abel put the stick down and joined the others in speaking the prayer of blessing. Then Saul selected a piece of bread and a single fig before handing the food to Abel.

It took the strength of Samson for Abel to not snatch the rest of the food for himself. Even after months of having the money the High Priest provided for their journey, his stomach still ached as he remembered the meager meals his mother and sister had prepared. Filling his lungs, he followed Saul's lead and selected only a small portion before handing the rest of the food to the Temple Guards, who took the basket to sit by their blankets. It was obvious they preferred their own company to that of his and Saul's.

Not that I blame them. Biting into a piece of cheese, Abel studied the other man.

The Jew from Tarsus was shorter than he and of moderate size. He was only several years older than Abel, yet the raven-black hair on his head was sparse. He had a single brow that spanned his face and a long, hooked nose. But appearance was not what people noticed about Saul Paulus. What made him stand out was his focus and passion to uphold the Holy Scriptures and the Law given to Moses. Abel had always considered himself to be dedicated to the Law and the Scriptures. But, in Saul Paulus, he met someone who exceeded him. *Father would have preferred him as a son over me.*

Opening a wine skin, Abel took a drink before passing it to Saul, who grunted a thanks.

"Saul Paulus," he picked up a fig, "why did you ask me?"

Saul studied him, frowning. "What do you mean, Abel ben Joktan?"

"Why did you ask me to come with you? You do not like me."

Saul *harrumphed* and drank from the wine skin before answering. "*Like* had nothing to do with it. The High Priest commissioned me to," he glanced at Abel, a hint of a sneer on his face, "find and arrest those blasphemers who proclaimed Jesus ben Joseph was the Son of Yahweh. I needed someone whose passion met mine. You showed passion in stoning Stephen ben Chariton." He squinted. "Let me ask you? Why did you agree to come with me?"

Money. Abel thought, biting into the fig. *I would not have come if it was not for money. No,* he corrected himself, *there was another reason.*

He remembered that day, months ago, in the Kidron Valley. Stoning Stephen ben Chariton. Abel had felt a satisfied elation each time Stephen cried out from the rain of stones lacerating his body and breaking his bones. With each stone he threw, Abel knew he was one step closer to ridding the earth of these blasphemers. With each stone, he was one step closer to earning Yahweh's forgiveness, and—almost as important—he was one step closer to earning His father's approval.

When Stephen ben Chariton cried out, calling the Nazarene, "Lord," and asking, "do not hold this sin against them," before slumping to the ground, Abel thought he had achieved his goal. But it was not to be. The bloodied face of Stephen had been replaced by the bloodied face of Jesus ben Joseph. Looking at him. Abel still felt the fear and hate that had consumed him like the flames of a fire. He remembered sliding down the ravine to continue pelting the dead man, screaming, "Leave me alone! Stop looking at me!"

When exhaustion deadened his rage and his arm, Abel looked up. Saul Paulus alone stood on the edge of the ravine, watching him. He stayed as Abel climbed out of the Kidron Valley. Saul bent over and picked up Abel's robe where it lay at his feet and handed it back to him.

"Rabbi Caiaphas and Rabbi Annas have commissioned me to find the followers of Jesus ben Joseph and bring them back for trial. Do you wish to come with me?"

"No." Abel snatched his robe from Saul's outstretched hand. "You have *taken*," his tone meant '*stolen*', "that task from me. Why should I go with you?" He looked down as he shook the dust from his robe.

"Money."

Abel's gaze shot up. "What?"

There was the hint of a smile around Saul's mouth. "In addition to providing money for our journey, the High Priest is paying a ten drachma bounty for each follower of *The Way* arrested and sent back for trial." He paused, studying Abel. "I will pay you half of that."

Five drachmas! Abel's eyes widened at the amount and then narrowed as he considered Saul's offer. He did not like that it would mean being in the company of the Jew from Tarsus and taking orders from him. However, it would mean ridding the earth of the blasphemers. Both considerations were secondary to the thought of all he could do with a continual flow of drachmas. His mother and sister would no longer be scrounging for food; they would no longer wear old, twice-mended clothing.

Looking at the Jew from Tarsus, Abel said, "I need to make arrangements for the care of my mother and sister—and my father—while I am away. But," he nodded, "I will come with you."

"Make your arrangements quickly," Saul said. "We leave the day after the Sabbath."

Abel had gone straight from the Kidron Valley to see his father. He told him about the stoning of Stephen.

"Good!" Joktan spat. "One less blasphemer; one step closer to Yahweh forgiving me and healing me."

When he told his father about traveling with Saul Paulus, Abel made it *sound* as if *he* had been commissioned by Rabbi Caiaphas and not the Jew from Tarsus. *I do not want him to know that neither he nor I are no longer considered priests of the Temple.* He also left out the mention of the bounty. Abel knew his father would demand the money be sent directly to him, without any thought his wife or daughter.

"It is good the High Priest has commissioned you for this task," his father said. "Who but my son would have the passion to over-see such a task? Arrange with your mother and sister to see to my daily needs. And tell those *racha* women to make sure my food is fresh and my clothing clean!"

All of that flashed through Abel's mind in the time it took to eat the fig. "Passion," he responded to Saul's question. "As you say, I am passionate about dealing with these blasphemers. They are responsible for my father being a leper. These people's actions have affected my family and my own studies in the Temple."

"And caused you the loss of a rich wife?"

Abel frowned. "What do you mean? I said nothing about a wife."

Saul's mouth spread in a smile, and it was not pleasant. "I am not blind. Nor am I deaf. When he was still serving in the Temple, I heard your father tell others that you were to marry your cousin, Mary bat Jacob. It had been less than a year since she married the son of Rabbi Nicodemus ben Melech. Now, she is the wife of a wealthy man." He waved a hand when Abel opened his mouth. "Do not attempt to explain the situation to me. A wife is only good for bringing wealth, position, and children," he frowned, "I do not consider that you have lost much."

Abel studied the other man's face before answering. "You speak as if a woman refused *your* offer of marriage."

Saul's frown deepened. "That is a story I do not wish to share." He tossed a half-eaten fig into the campfire. The flames consumed it like hungry dogs. "Tomorrow, we will arrive in Capernaum. I have traveled through there when coming from Tarsus, but never stayed there for long.

"We might be in Capernaum for several days. We will buy more provisions from the marketplace and find a place to stay before approaching the leaders of the synagogue. From my correspondence with the synagogue leaders, this town was favored by the blasphemer, Jesus ben Joseph. He spent much time here and is… *alleged*…to have performed many…*miracles*," his mouth pursed as if he had eaten an unripe persimmon. He took another swig from the wine skin.

"That is what I have heard," Abel said.

"I understand from Rabbi Caiaphas that your uncle built a house in Capernaum." Paul glanced at him from beneath his single brow. "Would we be able to stay there?"

"No." Abel ripped the bread in two, shoving one part into his mouth. "If you know of my cousin Mary turning me down, surely you heard my father complain about my Uncle Jacob." *I will not bless his memory.* When Saul shook his head, he continued. "He left his training in the Temple to become a merchant. He traveled much and built a house patterned after the ones in the pagan lands he visited. My father refused to stay in the *house inspired by Gentiles*."

"From all aspects, your father was faithful to the Law given to Moses—

Abel leapt up, crushing an olive in his fist. "My father is *still* faithful to the Law given to Moses!"

"—and yet," Saul continued as if Abel was not looming over him, "Yahweh struck him with leprosy." He squinted at him. "I wonder what law He broke?"

Saul's arrow missed its mark. "He did not break any law. He was present for *that man's* trials and even witnessed his crucifixion. I remember." Abel remembered that day as clearly as if it had just happened. From Jesus ben Joseph's arrest in the Garden, when he *healed* Malchus' ear, to the endless night of trials, the flogging, the Game of the King played by the Roman soldiers. Dragging a heavy cross through the streets of Jerusalem to Golgotha. Thick nails piercing hands and feet before lifting the cross and dropping it into a hole. The hours watching while *that man* hung on the cross, speaking to his followers, asking for a drink. Looking at him.

That face still haunted his dreams and now his waking hours. "I remember," Abel rasped, "because I was there. For all of it."

"You were there for all of it," Saul's words were as smooth as a snake's skin, "but was your father?"

Abel startled, drawn from his memories. He looked at Saul, who held his gaze, waiting. "My father…had *responsibilities*…to see to; he had to report back to the High Priest. He left me to watch the crucifixion to make certain the Nazarene's men did not attempt to rescue him."

Saul's single brow arched. "Your father thought a small group of Jews," there was a hint of mockery in his voice, "would be able to overcome Roman soldiers armed with swords and spears, and free the Nazarene from the cross? And—if they did attempt a rescue— he thought you alone would be able to do something about it?" His mouth spread in a derisive smile. "Your father thinks highly of you.

"Enough," Saul said before Abel could respond. "It matters not why you came with me. What matters is that we arrest these people and send them back to the High Priest to be tried. I am determined not to return to Jerusalem until all those who follow Jesus ben Joseph are arrested and punished." He paused. "What is strange is that it has not been as hard discovering these people as I had thought."

Abel nodded. On this point, he agreed with Saul. Over the months since they had left Jerusalem on this journey, they had arrested scores of people who were followers of Jesus ben Joseph. He and Saul had planned different ways to uncover them. In each town, they would meet with the leader of the synagogue and get a list of names of people suspected to be followers of *The Way*. They would go to these people's houses and accuse them of believing the Nazarene was the Messiah. They had a plan to force a confession, but there had been no need. Not one of the people denied it.

"They readily confessed it," Abel said. "You would think they would lie, but they did not; not even the children."

These people made their task easier. After arresting the people for blasphemy, Saul Paulus would put them in the custody of one of the Temple Guards, who would take them back to Jerusalem for trial. When the Guard returned, he would bring a bag filled with the bounty of drachmas. As he had promised, Saul gave Abel half of the bounty.

Abel kept a small portion for his own needs and arranged for the rest to be sent to his mother and sister.

"I am tired," Saul stood and dusted the crumbs from his garments. "Good night." He took several steps before turning back. "There is another thing that has made our task easier. You."

Abel startled. "Me?"

"You seem to have the ability to identify these followers of Jesus ben Joseph, often before we even speak to them."

Abel's gaze turned inward. *That is because I see* his *face on their faces. Like the day when the sound of the wind and the fire came from the upper room of Lazarus' warehouse. Or from Mary's servant girl. Or,* he swallowed, *the dead face of Stephen ben Chariton.* He squeezed his eyes shut, as if he could crush these visions from his memories. *If I rid the earth of these people, the nightmares will stop.*

"I will not demand an explanation of how you do this," Saul's voice broke into his thoughts. "What matters is your ability makes our task easier."

Chapter 49

*M*ary runs through the Valley of Hinnom, dodging the burning mounds. But the piles are not debris and refuse; they are people—the poor and the lepers. They writhe, reaching out to her for help as the dancing flames consume their bodies. She shakes her head and side-steps their grasps as she continues running. Her sandal slips and she falls, groaning as the sharp rocks slice through her garments and flesh.

She lays panting, the beating of the blood in her ears drowning every sound, save one. A sound from the pit of Hades, a scream from a demon, echoes around her. She turns.

Uncle Joktan. Taller than the misshapen trees that line the valley, he is a grotesque monster. His face is half gone, the gaping mouth revealing knife-sharp teeth. He laughs as he tears the flesh from his own body and shoves it into his mouth. He has an extra arm and two more legs; he has the speed of a lion as he chases her, screaming, laughing, as he scoops up rock after rock to throw at her.

Gasping and groaning, Mary pulls herself up and continues running. It is not fear that drives her. Beyond the screams of the monster chasing her, she now hears a cry.

The cry of a babe.

"Lord Jesus," she screams out a prayer, "please help me. Help me find her." She runs through the Valley of Hinnom, hunting for the baby.

She screams as arms grasp her. "Mary! Mary! Wake up!"

She wakens to see Michael bending over her, his face silhouetted by the moonlight streaming through the window of their bed chamber. She stares at him for a moment, before grabbing his forearms. "Michael!"

Michael pulls her against his chest as she sobs. She feels the warmth of his skin, hears the beating of his heart. "Shhh…" he whispers, "Beloved, do not be afraid. I am here. You are safe."

"No!" she shakes her head against his chest. "It is not me. It is *her!* Michael, you must find her! You have to find her! She is crying!"

Chapter 50

Michael's family had gathered earlier that evening to celebrate the birth of its two newest family members. Three weeks earlier, Abigail and Lazarus had welcomed a son, whom they named Jacob, after his and his sisters' father. Two days later, Martha gave birth to a son, whom they named Hiram, to honor the memory of Simon's father.

"How wonderful to have so many of my family—and those we consider family—" Nicodemus nodded to Joseph bar Neriah, "around our table."

The rabbi from Arimathea smiled. "It is a privilege to be part of this celebration, my friend."

"My beloved Hannah—may her memory be blessed—would have rejoiced to see our family growing."

Michael grinned as he watched Joanna and her husband Matthias attempt to keep the tray of grapes out of the reach of their children, David and Deborah. *One day, that will be Mary and me.*

They were finishing the meal when the servant Baruch entered the room.

"Rabbi Nicodemus, Peter bar Jonah and John ben Zebedee are in the hall. They have asked to meet with you."

"I will ask them to join us in the family courtyard," Michael's father said. He returned to the dining room a few minutes later. He was smiling, but Michael could see it was forced. "Michael, Lazarus, Simon, Joseph, Matthias, would you please come with me? We must confer with the Apostles over matters relating to the body of believers.

"Daughter," he smiled at Mary. "Earlier, I was certain I smelled some of Elisheba's oat cakes. Would you and Ruth please ask her to send those along with other food and drink to my sitting room?

You can arrange for some to be sent to the family courtyard for you, your sisters, and the children."

Michael turned to help Mary stand. She felt frail under his hand. He frowned. She had never been one to eat large portions, but since the incident in the Valley of Hinnom, her appetite had disappeared. It had become common for him to spend most of each meal quietly encouraging her to eat. Tonight, she had only eaten a single piece of cheese and a small olive.

"Beloved, I must go with Father. Will you eat something?"

"I am not hungry."

"Please, Beloved." He glanced to see his father and the other men waiting for him. He lifted a single finger and turned back to his wife. "Please…try to eat something," he smiled, *"for me?"*

Mary's lips spread in a tremulous smile. "I will eat something… for you." As she turned away, she sighed, "There is no one else."

Michael opened his mouth to question her and paused. She and Ruth had begun discussing food as they walked towards the hallway leading to the kitchen. *I will ask her later.* He crossed the room to where his father and the other men waited.

His father turned to the Apostles. "Peter bar Jonah, John ben Zebedee," he nodded to Rabbi Joseph, "my friend, if you will follow me. My sitting room is comfortable and will allow us privacy to discuss this further."

Michael's father led the way through the corridors, up the stairs, and down the hall to the small sitting room adjacent to Nicodemus' bed chamber.

Flames danced in the lamps that stood in the four corners. Through the long window on the far wall, the moon hung like a large pearl in the sky. In the center of the room was a low table with thick pillows placed around it.

"I see Elisheba bat Penuel has anticipated our needs," Nicodemus smiled, extending a hand towards a side table with trays of cheeses, figs, clusters of grapes, and bread, along with *amphorae* and cups. "Please, eat. We will talk of this situation in a few moments. As my mother—may her memory be blessed—used to say, 'Bad news will keep; bread will not.'"

Michael smiled. Even in the midst of crisis, his father was the perfect host, waiting until the others had selected their food and drink before getting anything for himself. While they ate, the elderly rabbi kept the conversation light, talking about his new grandchildren, asking the Apostles about their families, or encouraging them to take more food.

Once all the men had assured him they could not eat another bite, only then did he ask the Apostles to share the news that had brought them to his house at this late hour.

"The *persecution* against those who are followers of *The Way* continues to grow," Peter said. "John," he gestured towards the other Apostle, "received a letter from his father in Capernaum."

John nodded. "Father wrote of two men—accompanied by Temple Guards—going house to house, questioning people and arresting anyone who professed to be a follower of the Lord Jesus. He learned one of these men is Saul Paulus. The other is a man named Abel ben Joktan."

"Abel?" Lazarus' eyebrows climbed towards his scalp.

"Is this Abel your…?" John asked.

"He is my cousin," Lazarus answered. "I have not seen him since," he filled his lungs, "the Lord Jesus' death. I know from my father-in-law," he looked at the older man, "that my cousin is no longer studying in the Temple. As my uncle was driven from the city as a leper, I assumed Abel would be working to provide for his mother and sister.

"It appears he is doing that," John said. "My father heard rumors these two men are being paid for each believer they arrest and send back to Jerusalem."

"If they are accompanied by Temple Guard," Rabbi Joseph said, "it is not difficult to determine who is paying these two men to hunt down believers."

"Caiaphas," Nicodemus said.

Joseph nodded, adding, "And I do not think he acts alone."

"I agree, my friend," Nicodemus said. "As all of Jerusalem knows, where Caiaphas places his foot, Annas has already trod."

"I am ashamed my kinsman is party to this action towards

believers in the Lord Jesus," Lazarus said. "Father Nicodemus, what will Caiaphas and Annas do to them?"

The room fell silent, the men looking at each other.

There is no need to answer Lazarus, Michael thought. *Those who crucified the Lord Jesus would do no less to his followers.*

"I do not think," Rabbi Joseph looked at his host, "there is any reason for you nor I to be concerned on our behalf."

"I agree with you, my friend." Nicodemus said. "Our wealth and position in the Council holds weight. They would hesitate to arrest us or our families. However…" he looked at Peter and John.

"Rabbi Nicodemus, thank you for your concern," Peter said. "John and I—along with the rest of the Twelve—have prayed about it. We believe the Lord Jesus wants us to leave Jerusalem."

"After all," John said, "on the day He ascended, the Lord Jesus told us to be His witnesses in Jerusalem, in Judea, and Samaria, and to the ends of the earth." He spread his hands out, "We have obeyed the first part of His command. Now, it is time to obey the second part. I will not be surprised if other believers join us."

"Where will you go?" Rabbi Joseph asked.

"Capernaum first," Peter said. "Our families are there. We will not leave them to face arrest. After that…" he shrugged, "wherever the Holy Spirit leads."

"That is wise," Nicodemus said.

"Martha and I still wish to go to the lands of the Gauls," Simon looked at Rabbi Joseph. "Sir, you mentioned wishing to accompany us. We would be pleased to have you journey with us."

"I would be honored to join you." The rabbi from Arimathea nodded. "When do you plan to leave?"

"Could you be ready in three weeks?"

"I could."

"I think it is time Abigail and I go to Cyprus as planned," Lazarus said. "Our houses have been sold; our son has been born." He looked at the Apostles. "I would appreciate your wisdom."

"I have never been known as a man of wisdom," Peter glanced at John—who was grinning. "I do, however, know the wisdom of praying over a matter."

The men in the room bowed their heads as the Apostle prayed, asking the Holy Spirit for comfort for those believers who had been arrested, for protection for them and for all who followed the Lord Jesus, and for wisdom for Lazarus and Abigail. After the final, "Amen," Peter looked at Lazarus. "I believe your decision is what the Lord Jesus wishes."

"Then we will leave when Simon, Martha, and Rabbi Joseph leave. We can travel together until our paths separate."

"You will be missed, my son," Nicodemus said, "but you are wise."

"I agree with Father," Michael said. "You will be missed; especially by Mary. Although you have traveled much, this will be the first time she has been separated from her sister. She has leaned on Martha and Abigail since—" he swallowed, "the incident in the Valley of Hinnom."

"Michael, how is your wife?" John ben Zebedee asked. "I have not seen her at many of the gatherings."

"She appears *well*," Michael drew the word out, "and yet, she does not." He held out a hand to John and Peter. "I am not saying she was not healed by your prayers. Her wounds healed before our eyes, without any scars. It is just…there appears to be a sickness of her spirit."

"That is not good," John said. "Let us seek the Lord on her behalf." He bowed his head.

Michael closed his eyes, extending his hands waist-high, palms upward.

"Lord Jesus," John prayed, "we come to You on behalf of our sister, Mary bat Jacob. We thank You for protecting her during the attack in the Valley of Hinnom. We thank You for Your miraculous touch that healed her of the wounds. Now, Lord Jesus, we come to You asking for wisdom for this sickness of spirit that her husband has observed." The Apostle paused.

Michael felt a shift in the room. There was no wind, no dancing flames, but he recognized the presence of the Holy Spirit. He heard the beating of his blood in his ears as he waited.

"The Holy Spirit tells me Mary is not experiencing sickness," John said. "It is grief."

"Grief?" Michael shook his head. "For whom? Stephen ben Chariton?"

John shook his head. "I do not know. All I heard from the Holy Spirit was the word, *grief.* I am sorry. We will continue to pray for your wife. For now, it is late." He glanced towards Peter. "If we are to leave Jerusalem, we must make plans."

Michael left Rabbi Joseph to discuss plans with Lazarus and Simon. He lit two small lamps so he and his father could escort the Apostles to the front door.

Walking back towards their bed chambers, his father said, "It appears our life is going to be changing." He stifled a yawn. "I am certain the ladies have settled the children down for sleep. That is what I am going to do." He patted Michael's arm. "I will see you in the morning, my son. May the Lord Jesus bless your sleep."

"Good night, Father. May the Lord Jesus bless your sleep." Michael turned to walk down the hall towards his and Mary's bed chamber. He was near their room when the door opened, and Martha stepped into the corridor.

"Martha? What are—" He paused when she lifted a finger to her lips, glancing back at the closed door.

She gestured to Michael and walked past several doors before stopping. "I assume from the length of your meeting that Peter bar Jonah and John ben Zebedee brought news of import."

"They did." Michael told her of the arrests.

"So Abel is arresting believers," she frowned. "That does not surprise me. He and my uncle hated the Lord Jesus; why should they not also hate those who follow Him?" She nodded. "I am glad Simon and Rabbi Joseph are making plans to leave." She glanced at down the hall. "I will miss my sister and brother."

"She will miss you as well," Michael said. "Martha, what were you doing in our bed chamber?"

"I heard Mary," Martha folded her lips. "She was crying out in her sleep."

"She has been having nightmares of late," Michael said. "Almost every night since…" he paused, "that day your uncle attacked her. When I wake her, she cries out that "she" is crying, and I must find her!' I do not know what to do except to comfort her and promise I will find whoever this woman in her dreams.

"Martha, I am concerned about Mary. She does not eat; she rarely smiles and never laughs; she refuses—" he bit back the words, *my embrace.* He felt himself blush to the roots of his head. "I thought she was sick and asked Peter and John to pray for her. They said the Holy Spirit told them it was not sickness, but *grief.*" He shook his head. "Stephen ben Chariton's death was horrible, but I did not realize she felt that close to him."

"She was not."

"Then who? For whom is she grieving?" Michael shook his head. "Perhaps John heard wrong. Perhaps she is sick."

Martha filled her lungs and let the air out. "What Mary is experiencing is from the day when…my uncle…attacked her."

"But, Martha, the Apostles prayed for Mary after the attack. I watched her wounds heal right before my eyes."

"Michael," she swallowed, "it is not sickness nor something lingering from her wounds. John ben Zebedee heard the Holy Spirit clearly; this is grief." Martha laid a hand on his forearm. "When Mary went to see our uncle, she was with child. That day, in the Valley of Hinnom…she lost the baby."

He stared at her. It felt like all the air in his lungs had been sucked out. He shook his head.

Martha nodded. In the light from the flame, he saw a sheen of tears in her eyes.

"With child?" Michael pronounced the words with caution, as if it was his first time speaking a new language.

Chapter 51

"Look at that house," Saul Paulus frowned. "It must be the home of a wealthy Roman."

Abel bit back a sigh. The further they traveled from Jerusalem, the more the Jew from Tarsus found to point out examples of Jews being influenced by Gentiles or not following the Law given to Moses. *Or at least not following the Law as* you *follow it, Saul Paulus.* He looked where the other man was pointing; a house on the shore of the Lake of Galilee.

The building was two-storied and formed a large rectangle. On the front was a verandah with low marble walls and sculpted pillars to support the roof. Abel did not need to draw closer to know that the floor of the veranda had blue tiles, or that inside the two floors opened onto an atrium with containers of fragrant flowers and herbs and an ornamental pool at one end.

This was the house his Uncle Jacob had built as a gift for his wife, Esther bat Abrahim, who had been born in Capernaum. Each summer Aunt Esther and Uncle Jacob would bring Lazarus, Martha, and Mary to spend the warm months in this house. It had additional bed chambers, *mikvahs*, a large cooking area and dining room to allow the family to host many guests.

He had seen the house on the occasions he had traveled to Capernaum with his father, but he had never stayed there as a guest. His father often pointed to this house as evidence of Jacob having been influenced by the pagans he had met on his many travels. While Abel's father had, on several occasions, gone to the house to meet with his brother—and later his nephew or nieces—he refused to stay there.

"There are Romans in Capernaum, just as there are in Jerusalem,"

Abel said. *I will not tell him that is my cousins' house. I will not give him opportunity to denounce me or my family.* "Both cities have a Roman garrison."

"True," Saul sneered, "but in Jerusalem, you would never see a mix between those who follow Yahweh and the ways of the pagan Gentiles."

You are such a mix, Abel thought. *You are a Jew* and *a Roman citizen.*

He closed his ears to the sound of Saul Paulus' continued tirade and glanced out over the lake. The waters were soothing and mesmerizing, reflecting the cerulean sky, and cool where they washed over his feet. When his Aunt Esther was living, she would often talk of the lake and how people would claim, *"Although Yahweh created the seven seas, He has chosen Lake Galilee as His special delight."* Looking inland, he saw they were approaching the marketplace of Capernaum.

Not as large as Jerusalem, Capernaum had about a thousand people living in or near it. Located on the northwestern shore of Lake Galilee, the village was known as a stopping point for caravans going from Damascus to the ports on the Great Sea and on to Egypt. A busy trading center, it was famous for its variety of fish or the abundance of wheat that grew on the nearby plains.

Pausing in the marketplace to ask directions, Saul led their small group through the streets of Capernaum to the synagogue. What he saw caused the Jew from Tarsus to gape in disbelief.

Rising sixty-five feet long and two stories high, the synagogue was made not from the local black basalt, but of white limestone and designed with figures and carved pillars bearing ornate capitals.

"*This is what I meant!*" he spat. "I was dubious when Rabbi Caiaphas told me a high-ranking Roman official—whom he described as a man of faith and kind towards our people—had used his own monies to build a synagogue in Capernaum. But *this!* This is more pagan temple than a synagogue to worship Yahweh! No wonder these people are easily tempted to follow other gods."

"Come," he patted his garments to remove the dust from them. "Let us speak to the leader of the synagogue at once. It is obvious this place has strayed from the ways of Yahweh. I would not be surprised if there are many in Capernaum who are followers of *The Way.*"

After instructing the Temple Guard to remain outside with their horses, Saul walked to the synagogue, pausing at the threshold to touch his fingers to the *mezuzah*—the box on the doorposts that contained sacred Scriptures—before entering.

Abel followed Saul into the main room, where they found a group of men praying. Saul stopped near the door, signaling for Abel to do likewise.

Abel shifted his body so that he could bow his head yet still watch the men in the room. He studied each man, waiting to see if that face—*that bloodied face*—would float over the faces of those present. Nothing happened.

After the final "Amen," was spoken, Saul waited until all had left save one; a tall man with more gray than black in his beard.

This man watched them as they approached. "Peace be on you," he said. "Welcome. I am Adriel bar Kalev; I am leader of this synagogue."

"And on you peace," Saul returned the man's greeting. "I am Saul Paulus and this," he extended a hand, "is my traveling companion, Abel ben Joktan."

"Welcome, Abel ben Joktan," the synagogue leader bowed his head. "Peace be on you."

"And on you peace, Adriel bar Kalev." As Abel bowed his head, he noticed Saul grimacing. *He wants to observe propriety, but does not wish it extended to me.*

"I—*we*," Saul added, "have been commissioned by *Rabbi Caiaphas ben Joseph* to complete a task. He instructed me to show this letter to the synagogue leaders in every town we visit." He reached into his girdle and drew out a small scroll—the parchment was creased and soiled—and handed it to the older man.

Adriel bar Kalev frowned as he unrolled the scroll.

A letter from the High Priest never portends glad tidings, Abel thought. He watched the synagogue leader's eyebrows creep towards his scalp as he read the letter. It was not surprising; receiving a letter from the High Priest was not an everyday occurrence. This letter held special significance; Saul had shown Abel what Caiaphas had written:

To the leaders of the Jewish synagogues,
From Caiaphas ben Joseph, High Priest of Yahweh.
Greetings:
Under my authority, Saul Paulus is seeking those who are members of the false sect known as The Way, in order to arrest these blasphemers and send them to Jerusalem for trial.

You are to give him whatever aid he requires. To refuse him is to refuse me. Saul Paulus will bring to my attention anyone who refuses this help. I will see they are punished.

After the synagogue leader finished reading, he rolled up the scroll, and handed it back to Saul before speaking. "That is an… *interesting*…commission, Saul Paulus; to have the full support of the High Priest speaks of the weight of this task. How may I help you?"

"You may provide lodging and food for us and the Temple Guards who are with us, as well as for our horses," Saul tucked the scroll back into his girdle. "But first; tell me if you know of any of these blasphemers. Direct us to their homes and we," he turned slightly towards Abel, "will do the rest."

Chapter 52

"Elisheba, this will be the…last…meal with my brother and sister and their families before they leave. I want it to be special, but," Mary put her hand to her forehead, "I cannot think what foods to prepare."

"Do not worry, mistress; you have been…*unwell*." The older servant gave a motherly smile. "Mistress Martha and I have had several occasions to talk about household matters, including cleaning practices and recipes. She graciously shared some of your family's recipes with me.

"I will roast some grain to whet everyone's appetites. For the meal, I will prepare your honored sister's recipe of fish, stuffed with garlic, onions, and olives. For side dishes, there will be leeks, cucumbers, lentils, cheese, and bread. To finish the meal, figs, pomegranates, grapes, and—if you like—your honey oat cakes."

"That sounds wonderful. I will come later to help with the meal. Martha and Abigail are busy with their babies and with packing for the trip. Ruth is visiting with Leah bat Samuel, who just," Mary swallowed, "gave birth to a son." *Was not it just yesterday that Leah announced her pregnancy? It was the day that—No! Do not think of that day!*

"Now, Mistress Mary," Elisheba put hands on her hips. "As my grandmother—may her memory be blessed—used to say, 'Leave gutting the fish to those who wield the knife.' Let me tend to the meal; I am certain you would wish to rest before the evening meal."

"How kind," Mary forced her lips into a smile. "Thank you. I appreciate your consideration. I know my family will appreciate the meal."

"Thank you, mistress."

Mary left the kitchen, with Jemima shadowing her steps; since that day in the Valley of Hinnom, the young girl was never far from her side. Martha had confessed to her that she had told Michael about losing the baby. Mary had never spoken to her husband of their baby; it was useless. Words were like pennies, fallen into corners and down the cracks, not worth the effort of collecting.

It was about that time Jemima began following her around the house. *I am certain Michael instructed her to watch over me, as if I was a child. No,* she furrowed her brow, slanting her eyes towards the servant, *that is unkind. Jemima and Daniel risked their lives for me. They are concerned for me. My husband loves me. I wish I could regain my strength and resume caring for my husband and our home.*

Since her marriage, she had been determined to learn how to run this large household. It had been a challenge, but one she had pursued. But now, even the thought of what that entailed made Mary long for her bed, long for sleep.

Except sleep brought nightmares. Of the baby crying. She slid her hand over her abdomen. *My baby,* her throat tightened as tears gathered in her eyes. *Our baby. Why, Lord Jesus? What did I do wrong? What sin did I commit that my baby died? I only wanted to tell my uncle about You. You raised Lazarus from the dead. Why did I live and my baby die?*

Silence.

Mary shook her head, knowing if she did not change the path of her thoughts, she would begin screaming. Looking around the corridor, she noted vases of flowers placed on marble tables. She loved flowers and one of her chief delights had been seeing the rooms of this house filled with fragrant flowers. During her *weakness*—she did not know what else to call this lethargy of body and spirit—someone had seen that the vases were filled.

I must *resume my responsibilities to my husband and the household.* Today. Now.

"Jemima," she turned to the young girl, "I will be in Mother Hannah's garden, tending to the flowers. No," she lifted a hand when the servant opened her mouth, "I wish to be alone. Please go to my bedchamber and select something for me to wear for the evening meal. *No, wait,*" she thought for a moment, "I will wear the cream-colored robe and rose tunic." Even selecting her clothing took effort, but it felt good. "Come for me when it is time to prepare for supper."

The servant bowed her head. "Yes, mistress."

Mary walked through the house, passed several courtyards, public reception rooms, and ceremonial *mikvahs*, up the stairs, down the corridor to the small courtyard with Mother Hannah's flower garden.

She crossed to the small chest and removed the large apron, wrapping it around her waist. There were several amphorae near the chest; lifting the lid of one, she saw it held water. She put the pruning knife in a basket and lifted an amphora. It was early in the growing season, too early for regular pruning, but it had been a while since she had been in here—*weeks? Or was it months?*—and she might need to clear away old growth.

She moved among the containers, watering the plants, cleaning up dried leaves, rotating the containers in order that all sides of the plant received sunlight. She worked her way through the garden, to the long window, where her roses were sprouting red leaves. They would be forming buds soon.

When she came to the end of the window, she gasped, "My jacinth!" The soil covering the plant bulbs was cracked and dry. Whoever had been caring for her garden must not have been aware there were bulbs in that container.

Mary dug her fingers in the soil until she found a bulb. Moving the dirt away, she saw it was shriveled like an old onion.

"No!" Patting the dirt back over the bulbs, she lifted the amphora to empty the water into the container. "Please, do not die!" She ran back to get another amphora and carried it back to pour over the soil; water drained out of the bottom of the container, bleeding muddy water over her feet. "Please! I cannot lose this too!"

$\mathcal{A}$bel shoved a cloth into the container of water and swiped at the blood on his hands and on his garments. Some of the blood was his own; the rest was from the prisoners whose faces he had stuck.

He confessed to himself, it was not the faces of the prisoners he had been hitting. He had struck the bloody face of the man wearing a crown of thorns.

He looked to where a prisoner lay on the ground; hands and feet bound; his white hair and beard matted with the blood oozing from his nose.

Saul Paulus gestured to the Temple Guard, who grabbed the rope wrapped around the man's hands and hauled him upright.

The prisoner moaned.

The Jew from Tarsus circled the old man. "Where is the body of Jesus ben Joseph? Where have you hidden it?"

The prisoner grimaced as he drew breath. "I do not have the Lord Jesus' body," he spit out blood, "because He is not dead. Yahweh raised His Son from the dead." He looked upward, smiling. "He is alive!"

Saul nodded to the Temple Guard, who slapped the man, causing him to fall. Grasping a rope wrapped around the man's neck, the guard jerked him back up.

The man twisted his body, scrabbling to reach the rope that was cutting off his breath.

"Blasphemy!" Saul screamed. "To speak of *that man* as *the Son of Yahweh* is *blasphemy*! Unless you repent, unless you tell us *at once* where the Nazarene's body is hidden, you will be taken to Jerusalem, tried before the Sanhedrin, and *stoned!*"

The elderly man stared at Saul. He shook his head, grimacing as he tried to fill his lungs. "I will *never* deny the Lord Jesus," he whispered.

Saul nodded to the Temple Guard.

The guard struck the man with the hilt of his sword and dropped him. The prisoner's head rebounded when it hit the ground.

The elderly man lay there, eyes shut, breath shallow and rasping.

Saul Paulus turned to look at the group of people tied by ropes to the horses of the Temple Guards. Men, women—some old like the unconscious man on the ground—even children. All were bound with ropes. All were bruised and bleeding. None had denied that they were followers of Jesus ben Joseph.

Not that Abel needed to hear them confess it. On each prisoner—even the youngest ones—he had seen the face of *that man.*

"Captain," Saul Paulus said, "take these prisoners to Jerusalem. Tell Rabbi Caiaphas they are all blasphemers. Leave several of your guards with Abel ben Joktan and me. Tomorrow, we leave Capernaum for Damascus."

Chapter 54

*M*ichael sat up in their bed, his back against pillows, holding his sleeping wife in his arms. He had awakened to her twisting and moaning in the grips of another nightmare.

He had laid a hand on her arm, whispering her name. She had startled awake, eyes wide and darting around the room.

"Mary, you are alright. It was a dream."

"Michael!" She gave the involuntary intake of breath of someone who has been sobbing her heart out, before grasping his forearms. "She is crying, Michael! You must find her! You must find her!"

He had sat up and pulled her to his chest, gently rocking her, murmuring her name, telling her that yes, he would find this babe who was crying. There had been no need to light a lamp; since her attack, she always wanted a lamp lit against the night.

After a while, her cries settled, and she fell asleep.

Michael watched Mary sleep, tears drying on her lashes. *I thought she was getting better. During the evening meal, she had seemed to be her old self.*

That afternoon, he had passed Elisheba in the corridor and the servant informed him that Mistress Mary had spoken to her about the farewell feast. He had gone to their bed chamber to dress and found Mary getting ready. She had chosen a beautiful garment to wear, even if it did hang on her thin frame, and Jemima was braiding her hair. As he leaned over her to greet her, he smelled rose oil wafting from her. During the feast itself, she had seemed happier, smiling, and even laughing at Daniel and Deborah begging their mother for another oat and honey cake.

After the meal, everyone had walked to the stables where camels and horses, laden with bags and pouches, were waiting. The moon hung like a creamy sliver in the sky. Lazarus and Simon knew from their many travels that it was best to begin a journey across the desert at night.

After hugs and kisses, Joanna and Matthias had carried their children back into the house to put them to bed.

Michael watched Mary closely as she made her farewells. This would be the first time in her life she would be separated from her sister and he expected her to weep; yet, she had not. In the torches' flames, he had seen tears shimmering in her eyes and her lips forced into a smile. But she had joined in the farewells with hugs and kisses, and prayers for safety and promises of letters, and stood by his side, waving goodbye until the travelers could no longer be seen.

He adjusted his position against the pillows, his arms aching from holding Mary, but he did not let go of her. Since that day in the Valley of Hinnom, the only time she reached for his embrace was after the nightmares. Then, she clung to him.

She sighed and nuzzled her cheek against his arm, her hand moving across his chest. In the torchlight, he could see her nails were short, broken—he knew—from time spent in his mother's garden. He was pleased she was doing something again, *anything* other than sleeping, not eating, and crying. Yet, while she tended all the plants in the garden, she was concerned over the jacinth as if it were a child.

A child. His throat worked. *How did I not know she was with child? I never even had the chance to rejoice at the knowledge of our child; all I have had is sorrow. Lord Jesus, Mary and I need something to rejoice over.*

Michael realized they were not the only ones to suffer, nor was their grief beyond that of others. *Stephen.* He still could not remember that day without sorrow—and rage—shooting through him. He had failed in his attempts to help the gentle Hellenistic believer who only wanted to share the story of the Lord Jesus with other people. After he had told Mary about Stephen's death, she had sighed, "So many lost that day."

Now, many believers were fleeing the area, even of his own family. Michael had grown up with the knowledge that his family's wealth and his father's position in the Sanhedrin would protect his family. He extended a finger to stroke Mary's cheek. But that protection did not extend to his wife's family. *I can only imagine how Father must feel that his position could not protect Abigail's husband and their child.*

Our child. Michael's eyes filled. *Wealth and position did not protect my wife nor my child. Lord Jesus, why would Yahweh allow such a thing to happen to my Mary? To our child? King David lost a child as a punishment for his sin of murder and adultery with Bathsheba. What have I done? What has Mary done? She just wanted to share Your love with her uncle.* Rage filled his heart. *Joktan should be made to pay for what he did. He deserves to die. The Law states, 'A tooth for a tooth. An eye for an eye.'*

The sound of a soft knocking on the door of their bed chamber drew him out of his reverie. He frowned. *Good news waits until morning,* his mother used to say, *while bad news comes at all hours.*

Shifting his body, he laid Mary down, pausing to kiss her cheek and smooth her hair away from her face. He bit back a cry from the painful tingling rushing through his arms. Crossing the floor, he lifted a lamp, and opened the door. Their servant Baruch was standing in the corridor.

"Baruch," he whispered, stepping into the corridor and softly closing the door. "What is it?"

The servant bowed his head. "Forgive me, sir. Mistress Mary's kinswoman, Rebeca bat Joktan, is here."

"Rebeca?" *I will not speak her father's name.* "What does she want?"

"She said her mother is ill. She begs to see Mistress Mary."

See Mary? Michael frowned. *No. I do not care that your mother is ill You cannot see my wife. Your father tried to kill her; he killed our child.*

Then a memory rushed in: Mary distraught about the poverty of her aunt and cousins. Mary wanting to do something to help them. Mary weeping as she told him of Abel refusing her gift and driving her away. Another memory washed over him: that of the Lord Jesus teaching, *"Love your enemies, do good to those who hate you, bless those who curse you, pray for those who mistreat you."*

If I refuse Rebeca, Michael thought, *if I wish her and her mother harm, how would I be different than Abel or Joktan?*

All of that flashed through his mind in the time it took him to draw breath. He nodded to the servant.

"Thank you, Baruch. Please escort my wife's kinswoman to the kitchen. Wake Elisheba and ask her to offer Rebeca food and drink, and to gather her medicinal herbs. I will wake my sister Ruth and my father."

Chapter 55

"There is our destination," Saul Paulus stopped his horse to point at a city in the distance. "Damascus."

Abel looked where Saul pointed. He knew about Damascus, but was unprepared for its beauty. Situated in an oasis, the city's white buildings amongst the dark green gardens looked like a gem in a verdant setting. Beyond it, he saw the sparkling blue waters of a river.

Saul turned to look at him. "Have you ever been to Damascus?"

Abel shook his head. "The farthest I have been from Jerusalem is Capernaum."

"Ah, well, the city has been here for millennia," Saul's voice took on the tone of a lecturer. After spending several days in close proximity, Abel realized the Tarsuian Jew was not only a dedicated student, but also a natural teacher. Beyond being conversant in the Law and the Traditions of the Elders, due to his being born abroad, Saul knew much of history, geography, and other cultures.

"Damascus is bordered by the desert on two sides, but due to the oasis and the seven routes that lead to it, many consider it one of the most important trade cities in the land. The river," Saul pointed, "is the Barada, which means 'cold.' In the Hellenistic language, it is called *Chrysorrhoas*, which means, 'streaming with gold.' Do you recall the story of Naaman the Leper who came to Elisha to be healed?

Abel gave a curt nod. He might not be familiar with geography, but he knew the history of his people.

"Naaman was the commander of the army of the king of Aram," Saul continued as if Abel had not responded. "He was a great soldier, and highly regarded by the king, but he had leprosy. Through his wife's servant girl—a Jewish girl who had been taken captive—Naaman had heard of the mighty prophet Elisha. The servant girl told her mistress if Naaman went to see Elisha, the prophet would pray for him and he would be healed of the leprosy.

"The soldier received permission from the king and traveled to see Elisha. When he arrived, the prophet would not even come out to see him, but sent a messenger telling Naaman to wash seven times in the Jordan River.

"Naaman was insulted that the man of Yahweh had not even come out and waved his hand over his leprosy. He commented, 'Are not Abana and Pharpar, the rivers of Damascus, better than any of the waters in Israel?'" Saul pointed towards the river beyond Damascus, "*Abana* is another name for *Barada*.

Saul glanced skyward, his hand shielding his eyes from the sun. "It is nearing midday. Come," he said, gathering his horses' reins, he *clicked* his tongue. "There is an inn on the Straight Street near the synagogue. I have sent word to the innkeeper, Judas—Aiiii!" Saul Paulus screamed as a blazing light flashed all around him.

The world tilted as Abel's horse reared in terror. He fell, groaning as his head hit the ground. He lifted one hand to his head and the other to shield his eyes against the blinding light. He looked around. The two Temple Guards were as he, lying on the ground, hands covering their faces. Their horses had not run off, but were standing nearby, their flanks trembling, heads lowered, eyes wide with fear. Abel looked towards Saul.

The Tarsuian Jew was splayed on the ground in a ring of dazzling light so brilliant it made the desert appear to be in evening shadows. Unlike the rest of them, Saul was not shielding his eyes against the light, but gazing—stunned—into it.

But it was not the surreal light that dried Abel's tongue and made his heart pound. It was the sound *crashing* like thunder around them.

"*Aiii!*"

Abel glanced at the Temple Guards.

They shook their heads, hands clasped to their ears. "What is that sound?"

He looked back at his traveling companion.

Saul gaped as the sound continued. He licked his lips. "Who

are you, *Lord?*" he rasped. His eyes widened as the sound *rumbled,* growing louder until it *boomed* over their ears.

The flashing light disappeared.

Abel blinked against the dancing images burning in his vision.

The Temple Guards scrabbled to stand upright and ran to their horses. Within moments, they were galloping away into the desert.

Abel watched until they were specks in the distance. Turning back, he saw Saul Paulus still lying on the ground, his hands covering his face. Standing, he stumbled to the other man. "Saul," he whispered. Swallowing, he tried again. "Saul Paulus?"

Saul lay motionless for a moment and then lowered his hands and opened his eyes.

Abel gasped. The other man's eyes were covered with something that looked like—*scales from a fish.*

"Abel," Saul waved his hands in front of his body. "Abel ben Joktan, help me. Please. I cannot see."

Chapter 56

Michael helped his father into the carriage and turned to his sister. "Ruth, if Mary should wake while I am gone, will you please tell her…" he paused, not knowing what he wanted her to say.

"Michael," she laid a hand on his forearm, "do not worry. I will have Jemima tell me the moment Mary awakens. I will think of *something* to say to her. Now go," she stepped back.

"Thank you." Michael climbed into the carriage and nodded to the driver. "Daniel, please take us to the home of my wife's cousin."

As the carriage lurched into motion, Michael turned to see Elisheba fussing over the other passengers.

"Mistress Rebeca, tuck this blanket around you. Rabbi Nicodemus, here is a blanket for you as well."

Michael grinned when the elderly servant turned to him with a blanket. *No matter how old I am, Elisheba will always treat me as a child.*

"Bilhah," Elisheba turned to the servant girl seated next to her, "give Mistress Rebeca some of the bread. It is fresh and warm."

"Oh, no," Rebeca whispered. "Thank you, but I cannot. My mother…"

His father intervened. "I am certain your honored mother would wish you to eat." In the moonlight, Michael saw his father's gentle smile. "How can you care for your her if you are weak? Besides, if I know Elisheba bat Penuel, she has made sufficient food for everyone in your household as well as ours."

Rebeca looked from him to Elisheba, who nodded. "Well, if there is enough for Mother, then…thank you," she said. Selecting the smallest piece of bread, she paused before *shoving* it into her mouth, consuming it in a few bites. A few moments later, at Elisheba's insistence, she was selecting another piece.

Michael turned his head, thankful the darkness of night hid his shock. He had grown up seeing the poor begging on the streets of Jerusalem—and had even given them coin—but he had never personally known someone who was starving.

His father and Elisheba did not appear to share his shock. His father carried on a conversation with her while Elisheba offered more food. By the time the carriage was pulling up to Rebeca's house, she had eaten several pieces of bread, along with cheese and dates.

Michael jumped down to help his father and Rebeca step out of the carriage, while Daniel helped the two other two women.

Elisheba smoothed her garments and took control of the situation. "Thank you, Daniel," she said. "Please give that basket of food to Bilhah and hand the basket of medicines and herbs to me. Rabbi Nicodemus, if you and Master Michael will carry the blankets and the amphorae of water and wine. Now, we are ready. Mistress Rebeca, if you would please lead us to your mother."

Michael grinned as his father, a wealthy and honored Temple leader, followed the servant's instructions. He himself knew better than to question Elisheba's instructions. Touching the *mezuzah* on the doorposts, he followed the others into the house.

Rebeca had lit a small lantern; the flame danced fitfully, the smoke wafting a rancid smell. After she had extended the briefest of host greetings, Elisheba spoke.

"And on you peace, Rebeca bat Joktan. I know Rabbi Nicodemus and Master Michael will be happy to wait here while Bilhah and I follow you to your mother's bed chamber."

Michael suppressed a grin as Rebeca's eyes widened at the elderly servant taking charge, her eyes shifting between Elisheba and his father. His father—ever the gentle man—intervened.

"Elisheba is right, Rebeca bat Joktan. It is best if she sees your honored mother now. Michael and I will wait here and pray." He crossed to sit on a pillow, nodding for Michael to follow his example.

Rebeca nodded and lit another lamp in the corner before turning to the servant. "If you will follow me."

As the three women walked down the corridor, Michael looked

around. He had never been inside the home of Mary's relatives, but she had told him even though her uncle—*I will not speak his name*—had some wealth, he had always been careful with his own money. Yet even that knowledge, and what Mary had told him after her last visit to this house, did not prepare him. The room did not look as if it were the home of a member—*former member*—of the Sanhedrin. It had few furnishings—and even those needed repair—and threadbare pillows. Movement caught his eye; turning his head, he saw a rat scurrying out of a room. He jumped up. "Father—"

"Sit down, Michael."

"But Father, I saw—"

"I saw it as well, Michael." His father looked at him from under bushy eyebrows. "Surely you are not going to allow a rat to keep you from praying for your wife's kinswoman?"

Michael exhaled. "No. I am not." He sat on the pillow. "Now I understand Mary's distress over her kin. Surely, we can do *something* to help them," he glanced towards the corridor and lowered his voice, "in a way that will not offend them."

"I am certain we can think of something. We will speak of it tomorrow. But now, we must pray for Naomi." Extending his hands, palms up, he began praying.

Michael copied his father and began praying for his wife's aunt. After a few minutes, the sound of footsteps drew their attention. They looked up to see Elisheba in the doorway.

"Elisheba," his father asked, "how is Naomi bat Simeon?"

The woman shook her head. "I cannot identify what is wrong with her, but I can tell she is beyond my aid. Sir, if any of the Apostles are near Jerusalem, you had best send for them to pray for her."

Michael glanced at his father, who shook his head. "Elisheba," he said, "all of the Apostles left Jerusalem months ago, after Stephen ben Chariton was…*stoned*."

"Rabbi Nicodemus, Master Michael; would you come pray for her? You are priests in the Temple of Yahweh. You are followers of the Lord Jesus. Surely, Yahweh and the Lord Jesus will listen to your prayers."

Michael's eyes widened. He had seen the Lord Jesus heal. He

had been in the room when the Apostles had prayed for Mary, and for Daniel and Jemima, and had seen their wounds heal. But he had never been witness to anyone else praying for healing. *How can I pray? Our child died; surely, I committed some sin.* He looked at his father. "Father?"

His father stared towards the corridor and filled his lungs. "Yes," he stood and nodded to the servant. "Yes, of course. Come, Michael."

They followed Elisheba down the corridor and into a room. They crossed the floor to where Rebeca and Bilhah knelt by the bed, a lumpy pallet placed on a cracked frame. On it—covered by a thin blanket—lay Naomi, her breathing shallow. Rebeca held her mother's hand while Bilhah dipped a cloth into a bowl of water and wiped her brow. Rebeca looked at them when they entered the room. In the flickering light, Michael could see the sheen of tears in her eyes. She turned to lean over her mother.

"Mother," her voice cracked, "Rabbi Nicodemus and Michael bat Nicodemus are here to see you." She looked at them. *"Please."*

Michael had been a child when his own mother died, but he never forgot the smell, he never forgot the rasping, ragged, gurgling breath. Nor had he forgotten the fear, the desperation for something—*anything*—to be done to save his beloved mother. Looking into Rebeca's eyes, he saw that same desperation.

His father knelt by the bed. "Greetings, Naomi bat Simeon," he spoke as if they were meeting in the marketplace. "Your daughter has told us you are not feeling well. Michael and I have come to pray for you." He extended his hands over Naomi.

"Yahweh, Lord of all creation, Father of our Savior. We come to you for Naomi bat Simeon. You created her; You love her, and You love her family. Your Son died for her; for her healing, body and soul. As Your prophet, Isaiah, wrote, *'But He was wounded because of our transgressions, crushed because of our iniquities; the chastisement of our welfare was upon Him, and with His wounds we were healed.'*

"Heal her, Lord, according to Your mercy, and restore her to her loved ones. In the name of the Messiah, Who is Your Son; our blessed Lord Jesus. Amen."

Michael heard the sound of a wind coming through the corridor and into the room. At first, it was a sigh, brushing his face with a soft touch. Then it picked up strength. He held his breath as it whistled around the room, flattening their garments against their bodies, extinguishing the lamp, and rattling the shutters as it blew out the window.

Michael let out his breath. The wind had blown away the rancid smell of the lamp. The room was silent; Michael did not hear the rattling gurgle from the woman lying on the bed. *Oh no!* His heart sank. *She is gone. Poor Rebeca; that sad, frightened girl. Surely, we will—*

"Rebeca?" The voice was thin.

"Mother?" Rebeca leaned over the bed.

"Daughter…I am so thirsty. May I have some water?"

"Certainly!" Rebeca laughed.

Michael's hand shook as he relit the lamp. *She is healed. Father prayed for her and she is healed. Thank you for her healing, Lord; but, why not our child?*

Rebeca filled a cup and held it to her mother's lips, while Bilhah helped her sit upright. After Naomi drank two cups of water, she looked around, her eyes widening at the other people in her bed chamber. "Rabbi Nicodemus, Michael ben Nicodemus; welcome to our home," her voice was soft. "Peace be on you."

"And on you peace, Naomi bat Simeon," his father responded.

"Why…why are you here?"

"Mother," Rebeca said, "you were…*not well*…I went to see if my cousins Mary or Martha could help you. Martha is no longer in Jerusalem and Mary…," she glanced at Michael.

"My wife is not well herself," Michael said. "Father and I have come in her stead, and brought our servants, Bilhah and Elisheba bat Penuel." He smiled at the elderly servant, "Elisheba raised me after my mother's death—may her memory be blessed."

"Not well?" Naomi lifted a hand to her brow. "I remember going to the Valley of Hinnom." She paused, glancing at them.

Michael's father spoke. "We are aware of your husband's sad condition, and have been praying for him."

Naomi arched a brow.

She is not ignorant, Michael thought, *of what her husband has done to my wife's family.*

"Thank you. Since my son—*is away*—" she paused.

We know where your son is. Michael looked away. *We've heard the reports of what he and Saul Paulus are doing.*

"Rebeca and I have been taking food and drink to my husband."

Michael's eyes widened as he listened to Naomi. *How could any man require his wife and daughter to go to the Valley of Hinnom? To be exposed to contagion and to people who would not hesitate to harm them!*

"I remember coming back and not feeling well," Naomi said. "I remember lying down. That was—" she looked to Rebeca, "yesterday?"

Rebeca took her mother's hand, "Mother, that was last week."

"Last week?" Naomi eyes widened. "Your father's food—"

"I took food and drink to Father," Rebeca put a hand on her mother's arm. "I tried to care for you myself. When you were not getting better, I went to my cousin's house."

"I remember being hot." Naomi stared at the lamp. "I ached. My lungs were heavy…it felt like I was…*drowning.* It was dark, darker than any night. Then the…*wind*…it blew into me, into my lungs. I felt a—*hand*—lifting me, bearing me towards—a *light.* And the *voice.*" Her gaze focused and she looked at them. "Rabbi Nicodemus, it mentioned you."

"Me?"

She nodded. "The *voice;* it said you would tell me—tell us," she took her daughter's hand, "about *Jesus.*"

Chapter 57

$\mathcal{A}$bel stood at the window, staring down on Damascus. In the shape of an oval, the city was cut down the center by the Straight Street. The innkeeper had boasted the street was over three thousand cubits long and fifty-six cubits wide. Abel could barely conceive of a city street whose length was half the distance of Jerusalem to Bethany. And its width—*the Holy Temple measures sixty cubits by twenty cubits.* The street was lined on both sides with covered porticoes containing shops with people popping in and out, like bees to flowers.

He would like to visit some of those shops, to see what the merchants were selling. Maybe find something to send back to Mother and Rebeca. Perhaps fabric for new garments. After all, he had money now.

A moan from behind him broke his reverie. He let out a deep breath. *I cannot do that as long as* he *needs me.* Abel turned.

Saul Paulus was waking.

Since the moment, three days prior, when that light flashed brilliant-white around him—after the two Temple Guards deserted them—Abel had cared for the Jew from Tarsus. He had helped Saul onto his horse—*thank Yahweh their horses had not run off*—and led him into Damascus. When they passed through the city gates, people began pointing at Saul, calling to Abel and demanding to know whether the scales were signs of leprosy. Abel had stopped to rummage through their bags to find another headcloth; this he wrapped around Saul's eyes.

Abel wished he could have wrapped another cloth around the other man's mouth. After asking—*begging*—for his help, Saul had not stopped talking. But Saul was not talking to him. He was *praying*. Saul cried out to Yahweh, beseeching Him to show mercy, to forgive him, to heal him. Sometimes, Saul babbled in what sounded to Abel like another language; *Greek, perhaps?* Saul's babbling—as much as his eyes—drew people's stares.

He had been concerned about finding the inn where Saul had said he had made arrangements for a room. A street as long as the Straight Street would have several inns; thankfully, there was only one inn near the synagogue. A young boy sat by the door, scratching a dog's ears.

"You there, boy," Abel said. "I am looking for an inn owned by a man named of Judas. Is this his inn?"

The boy gaped at Saul.

Abel sighed and reached into the folds of his girdle to draw out a leather pouch. He removed two coins and extended them to the boy, repeating his question.

The boy took the coins, bit one of them, nodded to Abel, and ran through the door. He returned several minutes later with a man, whom the boy called, "Father." Older than himself, the man's dark beard and hair were clean, as was the crisp white cloth tied around his waist.

"Welcome to my inn," the innkeeper bowed. "Peace be on you. I am Judas bar Tammus." He glanced beyond Abel. "*Saul Paulus!*" he gasped. "Sir! What has happened? No wait; let us get him inside. Zerach," he turned to the boy, "take the horses around to the stable and have your mother bring food and drink to the guest chamber we prepared for Rabbi Paulus. Oh, and have her bring her healing ointments."

"Yes, Father."

Within a short time, Abel and Judas were attempting to get Saul settled; but to no avail.

He let them wash and anoint his eyes, but he would not lie down on the bed. He refused food and drink. All he wanted was to kneel on the floor—or lie prostrate—and pray.

For the last three days, Saul had continued to refuse the food and drink the innkeeper sent up for them. The food was delicious and plentiful; after eating his fill, Abel would store what was left in his bags. *Would the memory of hunger ever leave?*

Abel stayed in the room, in order to be near should Saul need him. Each day, he helped him bathe and get into clean clothing. He washed and anointed Saul's eyes, but that was the most the other man would allow him to do.

"Saul Paulus is blessed to have a friend such as yourself," Judas had said to him that morning. "As it is written in the Holy Scriptures, *'There is a friend who stays closer than a brother.'* Let me know if you need anything else." He bowed his head and left.

Abel crossed the floor to where Saul was turning over—it had been during the third watch of the night when the Tarsuian Jew had succumbed to sleep, sprawled on the floor, his arms over his head, his snoring ragged.

"Abel ben Joktan, are you here?"

"Yes, Saul Paulus, I am here. Would you like to eat? Judas bar Tammuz brought hot bread, cheese, and goat's milk. His wife is an excellent cook."

"No," the other man shook his head, "thank you. If you would please help me wash and change clothing."

"Of course," Abel crossed the floor to where he had stashed their belongings. Opening Saul's bag, he removed a fresh robe and tunic. "We are both running out of clean garments. I will ask Judas's wife if she will launder our garments."

Saul nodded. "I have coin in my bag; give her some for my garments and for yours. You have been *kind* to stay with me."

Abel stretched his mouth into a thin line. *It is not* kindness *that has caused me to stay with you. I need the money we get for arresting the blasphemers.* Yet, he knew it was more than money. Yahweh was angry that they had not finished the High Priest's commission sooner. Not only was he tormented by the visions of the Nazarene's face, now Saul has been struck blind. *We need to rid the land of these followers of Jesus ben Joseph. Then Yahweh will forgive us.*

He opened Saul's leather pouch; their supply of coins was greatly reduced. He guessed there was enough for a week more at best. The scroll from the High Priest was in the bottom of Saul's bag. The letter identified Saul as having the High Priest's authority. *What if I went to the synagogue leader and told him Saul was busy, and I was acting on his behalf? I do not need Saul to continue our task; I can identify the followers of Jesus ben Joseph. When I have completed our commission, I will return to Jerusalem and complete my training as a priest. Then I will be able to care for my mother and sister.*

"There are a few things we need," he lifted the scroll and put it into the folds of his girdle. Turning, he carried Saul's garments to him. "After I speak with Judas' wife, I will go to the marketplace."

Able was anointing Saul's eyes when he heard a knock. Crossing the room, he opened the door. The innkeeper stood in the doorway. Behind him, another man stood in shadows of the corridor.

"Abel ben Joktan, a man came to the inn. He is looking for Saul Paulus."

"Looking for Saul Paulus?" Abel frowned. *Other than yourself and your family, no one knows we are in Damascus.* "Who is he?"

The man stepped forward. He was short and slender, wearing a simple brown tunic and white robe. "I am Ananias ben—"

Abel's strangled gasp cut off the man's words.

Floating in front of the man's face was *the face*; the one covered with blood dripping from a crown of thorns.

"No!"

"Sir!" the innkeeper glanced between him and the other man. "Sir, what is wrong?"

"Go away! Leave us alone!" Abel shook his fist at the bloody face. "Leave me alone!"

"No! Stop!" Saul rose to his feet. "Abel ben Joktan, let him come in."

"Saul Paulus," Abel crossed to his companion in quick steps. "You do not understand. This man is *one of them*," he hissed. "He is a follower of *Jesus ben Joseph*."

Saul nodded. "I know. I have been waiting for him."

Abel's brows climbed to his scalp. "You have been *waiting for him?*"

Saul turned to walk across the floor, hands outstretched, until he reached the door. "Sir, be welcomed."

Abel stepped backwards—his eyes never leaving the newcomer's face—until his back was against the wall. *What is happening? What did Saul mean he was expecting this man? Why is he welcoming him as if he were a friend? Wait! What if this Ananias is a leader of the blasphemers here in Damascus? What if Saul heard of him and contacted him—pretending to be another follower of the Nazarene—and arranged to have him meet us here, so he could arrest him? Yes,* Abel relaxed. *That must be what is going on.* He leaned against the wall, as if he had no care, but kept a close watch on the newcomer; this Ananias.

Saul turned to the innkeeper, who was clearly bemused. "Judas bar Tammuz, thank you for escorting my guest to me."

"You are welcome, sir." He looked from Saul, to Ananias, to Abel.

Abel forced his mouth into a smile and shrugged his shoulders, as if to say, *"I have made a mistake."*

The innkeeper nodded in response. "Well, if you need anything else, please let me know." Bowing his head, he quietly closed the door.

Able forced himself to maintain his outward calm; inside, he suppressed the scream crouching in the base of his throat, like a lion waiting to pounce.

Saul Paulus ran a hand along the door, as if to check that it was completely closed, and then turned. Abel could see the muscles in the man's throat work. "Ananias—" he paused. "Ananias bar—" he cleared his throat. "Ananias—I" He fell to his knees. *"Please!* Tell me what I must do!" His face crumbled; Saul Paulus began crying.

Abel gaped, his feet rooted to the floor, unable to do more than watch as—in a heartbeat—Ananias dropped to his knees to embrace Saul. He held the Tarsuian Jew until his cries subsided. Only then, did the stranger release Saul. "Tell me what happened."

Saul Paulus lifted a corner of his headcloth and wiped his brow. "We—Abel ben Joktan and I—were on the way to Damascus."

Ananias glanced at Abel as Saul continued.

"We had been given a commission from the High Priest Caiaphas to…" he paused.

"—to arrest those who are followers of the Lord Jesus," Ananias finished. "I know. We have heard reports of you. Please continue."

Saul nodded. "We were outside of the city…Abel, how long ago was that day?"

Ananias—the bloody face still floating—looked at him.

Abel licked his lips. "Three days ago." His voice sounded weak in his own ears.

"Three days?" Saul repeated. "It feels longer. Three days ago, we were approaching Damascus when…suddenly, a *blinding* light flashed all around me. My horse reared in terror, throwing me to the ground. Then, I heard the *Voice.*"

Abel's eyebrows shot upward. He remembered that day. He had heard a rumbling, the sound of thunder. *Saul had heard a voice?*

Saul continued. "The Voice said, 'Saul, Saul, why do you persecute Me?'

"I said, 'Who are you, Lord?'

"The Voice said, 'I am Jesus, Whom you are persecuting. Now, get up and go into the city, and you will be told what you must do.'

"Those who were with us ran off, but Abel stayed with me. He helped me on my horse and led me into Damascus and to this inn, where I had made arrangements to stay. Abel has taken care of me for these three days. I have eaten nothing, I drank nothing, I have only prayed, waiting for the one who would come to me. And now, Ananias, you are here. Sir, please tell me; what must I do?"

The other man gripped Saul's shoulders, staring at him. Then he looked up. "Yahweh, praise be to Your holy name!" He lowered his gaze to Saul's face. "Saul, I am a follower of the Lord Jesus ben Joseph, the Messiah, the Son of Yahweh. This morning, while I was sleeping, the Lord called to me in a vision.

"'Ananias!'"

"I answered Him, 'Yes, Lord.'

"He told me to go to the house of Judas, at the inn on Straight Street. He said, 'Ask for a man from Tarsus named Saul, for he is praying. In a vision, he has seen a man named Ananias come and place his hands on him to restore his sight.'"

"I said, 'Lord, I have heard many reports of this man and the harm he has done to Your saints in Jerusalem.' We had heard that you and," he glanced at Abel, "those with you, were coming here. We heard you had authority from the High Priest to arrest all who called on the name of the Lord Jesus.

"But the Lord said to me, 'Go! This man is my chosen instrument to carry My name before the Gentiles and their kings, and before the people of Israel.'" Ananias swallowed and then continued; his voice lower. "He said, 'I will show him how much he must…*suffer*… for My name.'"

"When I awoke from the vision, I did not wait. I came here and asked Judas bar Tammuz if he had a man staying here named Saul Paulus. And he brought me to you."

He reached up to remove the cloth tied around Saul's eyes and dropped it. He did not flinch at the scales covering Saul's eyes, but laid his hands over them and filled his lungs. "Brother Saul, the Lord—Jesus, Who appeared to you on the road as you were coming here—has sent me so that you may see again and be filled with the Holy Spirit."

Abel felt a breeze blow in through the window and rush past his cheek. The wind grew stronger, whistling around the room. He watched Saul turned his face towards the ceiling; the wind whipped his hair around his face, before rushing out of the window.

Saul lifted his hands to smooth his hair and then lowered his face. He turned towards them.

The scales were gone.

Abel would have gulped, except his throat had grown too parched to produce spittle.

Saul blinked. He turned his head and blinked again. He lifted his hands in front of his face. "I can see," he whispered. "I can *see!*" He shouted. Turning, he embraced Ananias, "Praise be to the Lord Jesus!" He jumped up and started laughing and clapping his hands. "Praise be to the Lord Jesus!"

Ananias stood, laughing. "Praise be to the Lord Jesus!"

"Abel," Saul turned to look at him. "Able ben Joktan. I can see!"

"No," Abel shook his head.

"Yes, Abel," Saul nodded. "I can see. I can see you." He saw the tray on the table near the bed. "I can see bread, cheese, and—" he crossed to lift the cup to his lips to drink, "—mmmm, goat's milk."

"No!" Abel gaped at the countenance floating over Saul's face. A face covered in blood and wearing a crown of thorns. "No! Saul, you cannot be *one of them!* You cannot believe…that Jesus…" he licked his lips.

"I cannot believe that Jesus ben Joseph is the *Messiah*, the Son of Yahweh?" Saul smiled. "But I do. I do believe! He healed me! He has forgiven me. He *loves* me. He *died* for me. Abel," Saul extended a hand, "He died for you. He loves *you*."

Abel avoided Saul's hand as if it was a cobra. "No." He shook his head. "He is not the *Messiah!*" Abel lurched across the room. "You cannot…I cannot…No! Leave me alone!" He grabbed his bags, and rushed out the door.

"Wait, Abel! Please! Do not go!" Saul cried. "He loves you!"

"No! No! Leave me alone! Leave me *alone!*" Abel stumbled down the stairs, running from the echoes of Saul Paulus' cries.

"He loves you, Abel! The Lord Jesus *loves* you!"

Chapter 58

"Welcome, Gamaliel ben Simon," Michael's father bowed his head. "Peace be on you."

"And on you peace, Nicodemus ben Melech," the renowned teacher returned the bow, and turned to smile at Michael, "and on you Michael ben Nicodemus. While I am pleased you finished your studies and have taken up responsibilities as a priest of Yahweh, I do miss having you as a student. Your comments were always well-thought-out and carefully presented. A habit that is rare among younger men."

Michael bowed his head. "I am honored by your kind words, Rabbi."

"If you would please come with us," Michael's father said, "we have food and drink prepared."

"That sounds delightful," Rabbi Gamaliel said.

Michael followed his father and his former teacher through courtyards, public rooms, and up the stairs of their home. A gracious host, his father carried on a light conversation with their guest; discussing the recent weather, their common acquaintances, and the antics of his grandchildren.

The last topic made Michael frown. He loved his nieces and nephews, but... *if not for* that *man—I will not speak his name—Father would be discussing Mary's and my children. Now, only Yahweh knows if we will have any at all.*

The wind blowing through the family courtyard was light. Beyond the window, whispy clouds floated in the azure sky.

On the low table in the center of the room were bowls of cheese, dates, and oat cakes, along with an amphora and three cups. After seating their guest on a thick pillow, Michael's father spoke a blessing and continued the conversation while they ate.

After Rabbi Gamaliel would eat no more—and extended his compliments to Elisheba's cooking—he wiped his mouth, set the napkin aside, folded his hands on the table, and turned to Michael and his father.

"Nicodemus, as honored as I am to have been invited to your and Michael's home, I *sense* there is something you wish to discuss with me."

"Ahh…I have heard people speak of you as 'Gamaliel the Wise,'" Michael's father smiled, "and I agree with them. You have *sensed* correctly. There is a situation about which my son and I wish to ask your opinion. Michael, as it is your wife's family, perhaps you should explain it to the rabbi."

Michael nodded. "Rabbi Gamaliel, my wife, Mary bat Jacob, is niece to Naomi bat Simeon."

"I know of Naomi bat Simeon," the teacher said. "She is wife to Joktan ben Philemon, and has two children; a daughter and a son, Abel, who studied along with you to become a priest. Is this whom you mean?"

"She is," Michael folded his lips. *Focus on Naomi and Rebeca,* not on *that* man.

"I was sorry to hear about what happened to Joktan ben Philemon," Gamaliel shook his head. "Leprosy is a sad condition. I have told Abel I continue to pray for his father's healing."

"That is…*kind*…of you," Michael's father slanted a glance at him. "Is it not, Michael?"

"It is kind; thank you, sir." *Do not be abrupt with the rabbi. He does not know what happened.* "My wife learned that, since the day her uncle was struck with leprosy, her aunt and cousins have been struggling." He remembered Mary weeping over her aunt and cousins reduced to poverty. "She is concerned for her kin and wants to help them. Father and I have not seen…Abel…at the Temple." He took a breath. "My wife's brother, Lazarus ben Jacob—"

Gamaliel interrupted. "Lazarus! I heard he is the one who was…" he lifted an eyebrow.

"…raised from the dead?" Michael smiled. "He was indeed. By the Lord Jesus. Several months ago, Lazarus decided to leave

Bethany. He sold the home that he, my wife, and their sister Martha had grown up in, and divided the money between the three of them.

"As my wife, Mary has no need for this money. She would like to give her portion to her aunt and cousins, as a blessing gift. As I mentioned, Father and I have not seen…Abel…at the Temple for a while." He suppressed a frown, remembering Abel rejecting Mary's gift. *If it were not for her aunt and Rebeca, I would not care.* "She does not wish to offend her kin." He looked from his father to his former teacher. "We do not know what to do."

"Your wife's desire to help her kin and not injure their pride is a kindness indeed," Gamaliel's smile was gentle. "As long as Joktan ben Philemon is a leper, he cannot serve as a priest in the Temple of Yahweh. That means he no longer receives his priestly portion. You have not seen Abel ben Joktan at the Temple because he has been on a…" he glanced between Michael and his father, "*special commission*…by Rabbi Caiaphas. I do not know about the arrangements between the High Priest and Abel, nor do I know if Abel has the ability to send any money back to his mother and sister.

"Hmm…" Gamaliel stroked his beard, his gaze turning inward, "how can we offer this money to Naomi bat Simeon and her daughter, and how can we explain it?"

Michael glanced at his father—who lifted a finger to his lips— and back to his former teacher.

After several minutes, Gamaliel looked at them. "What if I sent a note to Naomi bat Simeon and mentioned I learned of some money that was due Abel. As I do not know where he is, I am sending the money to them. I would word the note to *suggest* that, as a good son, I am certain he would want his mother and sister to have it and am certain her husband would wish that as well."

He looked at Michael. "You know your wife's aunt. Do you think she would believe that?"

Michael thought for a moment. "Yes," he nodded. "I think they would believe that. I will get you the money before you leave. Thank you, sir. I know Mary will be relieved her aunt and cousin will be cared for."

"I am happy to help in such a generous task," Gamaliel smiled. "Now, there is something you can do for me."

Michael raised his eyebrows. "I would be happy to learn what I can do for you, Rabbi."

"You can tell me about *Jesus ben Joseph*," the teacher looked between Michael and his father, "and why you call him, 'Lord.'"

$\mathcal{M}$ary secured a strip of linen around the end of her braid and tossed her hair over her shoulder. She tied her sandals on her feet and stood to carry her sleeping garments to the basket where their soiled clothes were kept. The basket was nearly full.

I will have Jemima launder our garments. There had been a time when—even with household servants—she loved caring for her and her husband's garments. Now, the mere thought of laundry *fatigued* her.

What will you do with your day, Mary bat Jacob? Michael left for the Temple hours ago. What will you do? Will you go and see your friend Leah and her new son? No, I cannot do that. She would see the pain in my eyes, and I cannot hurt my friend. Will you wander around the house, pretending to oversee Elisheba and the other servants? Will you go to Mother Hannah's garden and plead with a jacinth bulb to bloom?

What would Martha think of me if she were to see me now? She has a new babe, and I am certain she does not lie about for hours. What would she say to me? Her mouth set in a straight line. *She would chide me and tell me to get up and do something. Just like she did when I was unmarried.*

Just like the time we were celebrating Lazarus' resurrection and Simon's healing, when I was sitting at the feet of the Lord Jesus.

Mary remembered that day. Martha had been in her element, with many people in their house and everyone eating their food. Mary had wandered around the rooms, offering a tray of food and encouraging their guests to eat. She had walked into the room filled with people, all focused on where the Lord Jesus was sitting on a bench, talking to Rabbi Joseph and Father Nicodemus.

She had always been drawn to the sound of the Lord's voice, rich and well-modulated. Without even realizing what she was doing, Mary had dropped to the floor to sit at the Lord's feet to listen to Him. He had been talking about being the good shepherd and laying down His life. *Now* she understood what He was speaking of—His coming sacrifice—but *on that day* she had leaned in to listen, trying to discern what His words meant.

"Mary bat Jacob!" Martha's voice had echoed around the room. "What do you think you are doing?"

All eyes had looked to where her sister stood in the doorway to the room.

Martha had blushed furiously—it took a great deal to discompose her sister—and looked at the Lord Jesus. "Teacher," she had said, "does it not matter to you that Mary is sitting there, doing nothing, while I have been doing all the work? Tell her to get up and help me."

"Get up!" Mary folded her arms. *That is what Martha would say if she saw me. "Get up! Do something!"*

"Well and good!" Mary straightened. "I will do something." Bending, she picked up the basket and turned. The basket hit her dressing table, knocking her mirror askew, and scattering her combs, bottles of perfume, and her jewelry box. Her alabastron tipped over and spun lopsidedly toward the edge. Mary dropped the basket and lunged to grab it before it fell off the table.

Clasping the delicate bottle to her chest, she slumped to the floor, her heart pounding, tears stinging her eyes. *What if it had fallen off the dressing table? What if it had hit the floor? It would have shattered. I would have lost it forever.*

"I cannot lose anything else," she sobbed. "I cannot lose anything else."

Chapter 60

*T*ime lost all value to Abel. Days flowed into nights; nights flowed into days. Nightmares chased him; panic drove him. He stopped only to rest and feed his horse. He slept when he collapsed and ate when he remembered he had food; when the food was gone, he did not think about it again.

Leaving Damascus, he galloped to Capernaum, crossed the Jezreel Valley and the mountains of Samaria, focused only on reaching Jerusalem. He avoided people, skirting around the towns; but that was not because he wished to sidestep distraction. As much as he was racing towards the Holy City in order to report Saul Paulus' desertion, he was fleeing from faces. *No,* he confessed, *The face.*

The sun was hanging low in the western sky when Abel reached the edge of the Kidron Valley. He pulled back on the reins, slowing the horse to a canter. Only a fool would race towards the corner of Jerusalem where the Temple and the Antonia Fortress—with its 600 Roman soldiers—were located.

He pondered his next move. By this time of day, Caiaphas would have left the Temple. Abel had two choices; either wait until morning or go to the home of the High Priest now. *Caiaphas will probably berate me for disturbing him at his home. But,* Abel frowned, *he will probably berate me if I waited until morning to report about Saul Paulus.* He shrugged. *Either way, he will berate me.* He turned the horse towards the west.

Following the northern edge of the city walls, he passed the Fish Gate and turned south. He would enter Jerusalem through the Essene Gate in the southwest corner. Caiaphas' house was located nearby, in the Essene Quarter.

He had reached the edge of the main road when he heard a sound, like a deep murmur, beneath the horse's hooves. Abel straightened, his eyes widening, his hands tightening on the reins; he knew what that sound meant. He jumped off the horse and tried to calm the animal.

The sound began swelling and growing, shooting upwards. Around him, rocks and pebbles were bouncing, and the trees were swaying violently. He felt a rush as the murmur changed to a roar and the earth exploded.

Abel was knocked to his knees as the earthquake made the ground heave as a stormy sea. He threw his arms over his head and curled up in a ball to protect himself from the rocks—some were breaking from the force of the quake—and from the horse, who danced in fear before being thrown down next to him.

The shaking stopped. Abel stayed where he was; he had experienced earthquakes before and knew a second tremor might be more deadly than the first. After several minutes, he cautiously pushed himself up, and planted his feet wide to regain his balance. The horse scrambled up, flanks trembling, its nostrils flaring.

His ears ached from built-up pressure and felt as if they were packed with wool. Closing his mouth, he pinched his nose, and blew, causing a high-pitched squealing and then a *pop*. He sighed as the pain eased and sound returned.

"Abel."

"What?" He turned around, wondering who was calling his name. There was no one. *It must be noise left from the earthquake.* He reached to grasp his horse's reins.

"Abel."

He spun around. There was no one. The haze was settling and there was no place anyone could hide on this barren, rocky hill. *Wait.*

First, he was haunted in his dreams. Then he began seeing *his* face. Now he heard a voice. *The* voice. He had heard it at his cousin's house. In the Temple's court. In the streets of Jerusalem. From a cross.

His heart pounded as he looked around. He *knew* this place. He had been there before. He was on the slopes of…Golgotha.

"Abel ben Joktan."

Groaning, Abel dropped to his knees. He felt the weight of someone's gaze. He knew whose voice he heard, but he was too weary to resist, too weary to run away from it; even if it meant he would die.

Turning, he looked directly into the eyes of Jesus ben Joseph. His hair matted with blood beneath a crown of thorns, face ravaged with pain, dark eyes staring into his eyes; into *his soul.*

As on *that* day, Abel was unable to break his gaze. He stared into the Nazarene's eyes. He saw pain. He saw sadness. But there was something more. Something he could not identify. Something that left an ache in his heart. He looked deeper into the Nazarene's eyes and saw…*kindness? Acceptance? Yes, but there was something more.* Abel's eyes widened. *Could it be?* He remembered the last words he heard from Saul Paulus

"He loves you, Abel ben Joktan!"

Love! Abel felt a thrill of something *shoot* through his veins. *Love?* He had never experienced *love* from his father. His mother—and maybe even Rebeca—*loved* him, but their fear of Joktan over-weighed everything else.

Love! This is what he saw in the man's eyes. *Love.*

He licked his lips. "For me?"

Jesus smiled. "For you."

A hard knot exploded in Abel's chest. *He loves me.* It was as if he were lit from within, bright and glorious like the sun on a new day. He smiled. "I…*love*…you…Lord Jesus."

The face faded. Abel knelt on the slopes of Golgotha, the Lord Jesus' smiling eyes burning in his vision, in his memory, in his soul, until a wet nose nudged his arm.

Looking up, he saw the horse staring at him. The animal leaned down and nudged him again.

Able laughed. A pure, clean laugh. He laughed again and reached up to stroke the soft nose. "Horse, the Lord Jesus loves me," he said. "He *loves* me. The Messiah *loves* me. He…*died* for me. He died for *everyone.* For my mother, my sister…" his smile faltered, "…even my father." *Father does not know.* His thoughts began racing. *He does not know that Jesus ben Joseph* is *the* Messiah, *the Son of Yahweh. Father does not know that the Lord Jesus* loves *him. He needs to know.*

"Come horse," he grabbed the reins dangling in front of his face and stood. "I must go tell Father."

Jumping on the horse's back, Abel rode, following the city walls, turning right at the Gennath Gate, turning left when he came to the three towers of Herod's palace. He continued following the city walls until he rode past the Essene Gate and out to the edge of the Valley of Hinnom. Tying his horse to a tree—and whispering a prayer that it would still be there when he returned—he lifted his bag over his shoulder and descended the steep ravine.

He found his father seated outside his cave, warming his hands—wrapped in strips of cloths—before a small fire. Beyond his father, sat Itamar bar Reuben—the man who worked as his father's scribe—and his son, Aran.

Abel stepped up to the line of rocks. He licked his lips. *Yahweh, Lord Jesus; help me.* He filled his lungs. "Father?"

The other man lifted his face.

Abel gasped.

His father's hair and beard were gone, as was his right eye and bottom lip. The skin of his face was maggot white and oozing in ulcerated sores. When he stood, his body was hunched and crooked. His steps were uneven and, where he trod, he left smears of blood and pus. Crossing his arms—Abel noted his father's hands were half gone—he spoke.

"Abel. What are you doing here?" His words were slurred.

"Father," Abel started to lick his lips again, experiencing the remembered anxiety, but then stopped. *I am not afraid of Father anymore.* He recalled the Lord Jesus' gaze and felt something stir in his heart. *The Lord Jesus* loves *me. And He loves Father.* "Father, I have come home."

"Home," he harrumphed. "Did you bring me food or drink?"

"No Father, I do not have any food or drink."

"*Racha.* Do you have money? I will send Itamar or Aran to buy some."

Abel reached in his girdle and drew out his coin purse, thankful he had left the bulk of his coins in the bag on his shoulder. He tossed it across the line of rocks. "Here. I will arrange for food and drink to be brought to you. I do not wish Mother or Rebeca to come to this place again."

"I do not care whether I see those *racha* women ever again." His father picked up the purse and opened it to count the coins. "You are back. That means you and Saul Paulus finished your task."

"Not exactly."

"What do you mean?" His father looked up, frowning. "Did you arrest the followers of *that man?*"

"Yes…some of them."

"Good. Did you compel them to tell you where they had hidden the Nazarene's body?"

Abel shook his head. "No."

"No? You were commissioned by the High Priest Caiaphas to arrest the followers of *that man* and to force them to tell you where they had hidden the body. You say you have not completed that task." He pointed a hand—missing two fingers—at Abel. "Until you do, Yahweh will not forgive me and heal me."

"But He *will* heal you," Abel said.

"What?" His father lifted his eyebrows, or at least he lifted the skin where his eyebrows had been. "What are you talking about?"

"Father," Abel felt the rush, the thrill he had experienced only a short time before. "Yahweh wants to forgive you. *I know.* He forgave me. He loves you, as does His Son."

"Loves? What nonsense is this? What do you mean," his father's one eye narrowed, "His…*Son?*"

"Yes," Abel nodded, "Yahweh's Son; the Lord Jesus."

His father gaped. "What?"

"Father, He *is* the Messiah, just like Saul Paulus said. He loves me. He died for me. He loves you, too. He died for you. But He did not stay dead. The Roman soldiers spoke the truth when they said He was alive. He is alive! He just spoke to me! That is why we were never able to find His body. You speak of healing. He healed Saul Paulus; I witnessed it. He can heal you, too." He held his hands out towards his father. "If you only believe."

"Blasphemy." His father growled. "Blasphemy! You speak *blasphemy* by naming this *man* as the Son of Yahweh! Is my whole family *racha*?" He shook a fist at Abel. "Renounce him! As your father, I command you! Renounce him and plead with Yahweh to forgive you for this blasphemy." He spewed curses at Jesus of Nazareth. "Renounce him! Now!"

"No."

His father's eyes—even the blind eye—widened. "What," his voice was soft as a serpent's hiss, "did you say?"

"I said, 'No.'" Abel lifted his chin. "I will not renounce Him. I have never felt the way I do. I never felt the *forgiveness*, the *acceptance*, the *love*. Father, there is nothing that will make me renounce Him."

"You are dead."

Abel shook his head, startled. "What?"

"You are dead!" His father spat. "You are dead to me!"

"But, Father!"

"Go! Leave me!" His father crossed the line of rocks.

Abel took a step back. "Father, please, no. The Lord Jesus—"

"Silence! You will never speak that name to me again. Leave here and never return. Blasphemer!"

His father bent over, picked up a rock, and threw it at him. It hit the edge of his shoulder. There was no force in it, but the pain of his father attempting to stone him cut deeper than any rock.

"Father, stop! Do not do this!"

His father spit and picked up another rock; it missed. "I have no son!" He threw another rock. "You are dead! My son is dead!"

"Stop!" Abel stepped back, lifting his hands. "I will leave, Father." He turned and walked away, lifting a hand to wipe the tears from his eyes.

"Do not call me, Father! I have no son!" The man behind him screamed, the wind carrying each word across the fires of Hinnom. "I. Have. No. Son!"

Abel climbed out of the valley with leaden steps. He breathed a prayer of thanksgiving to find his horse still tied where he had left it. Mounting it, he turned the animal around and rode back towards Jerusalem.

It was full dark by the time he stopped in front of his home. He led the horse to the side of the house, where several trees provided shelter. Opening his bag, he drew out one of his robes and laid it across the animal's back.

"I will bring water and food in a bit," he said, "after I see about my mother and sister."

Walking back around to the front, he touched the *mezuzah* before knocking on the door. "Mother?" he called, "Rebeca? It is me. Abel. I am home."

After several moments, he heard footsteps from within. "Abel? Is that you?"

"Yes, Mother. Do not be afraid. It is me."

The door opened far enough to reveal the face of his mother. "Abel?" She looked beyond him. "You are alone?"

He nodded. "Yes, Mother. I am alone. Please, may I come in? I have traveled far, and I am weary."

"Oh," she gasped. "Forgive me. I am just surprised to see you." She opened the door wider. "Come in, Son. You are just in time. Rebeca and I have been cleaning up after the earthquake and are about to eat our supper."

He followed his mother into the main room. In the flickering light of a single lamp, he saw his sister kneeling on the floor, a basket of soiled cloths nearby.

"Rebeca," his mother said, "look who has returned. Abel."

She sat back on her heels and lifted a hand to wipe her brow. "Welcome home, Brother."

"Mother, it is dark in the room," Abel said. "Would you please light another lamp? I have money and will buy more oil for the lamps tomorrow, and anything else that was damaged by the earthquake."

"As you wish, Son. Rebeca, please light the other lamp."

"Yes, Mother." She picked up the lamp and carried it to another lamp. She carried the lamps back and placed them on the table, before moving to stand by her mother, silently studying him.

Both women were dressed in soft cream tunics and dark robes. Although soiled from cleaning up, Abel did not see any sign of mending on their garments. *At least they used some of the money I have sent home to purchase fabric for new garments.* Then he looked at their faces.

It had been some time since he had seen his mother and Rebeca, yet there was something *different* about them. They would never be considered anything more than plain, but they no longer gave the appearance of scared, timid mice. *There is,* he narrowed his eyes studying them, *peace.* His eyes widened. *There is peace in their countenances.* He spread his lips in a gentle smile.

"Abel," his mother smiled as she reached up to touch his cheek, "you have met the Lord Jesus."

Chapter 61

$\mathcal{M}$ary lifted a corner of her apron to wipe her brow while she surveyed the broken pots and mounds of soil and wilted flowers.

She and Michael had been asleep when the earthquake tossed them off their bed. He had pulled her to his chest and yanked the thick pallet off their bed and drew it over their bodies. They crawled to the center of the room and huddled while the house shuddered.

After the shaking eased, he helped her stand. "Are you alright?" he asked.

She nodded. "We must check on the others."

Father Nicodemus' forehead was cut from a broken amphora thrown across the room. Mary left Michael holding a folded cloth to his father's head, while she ran to the kitchen area.

She found Ruth with Elisheba. The elderly servant was standing in the center of the room, dispensing orders like a general on the battlefield.

"Jeremiah, get a basket and start cleaning the dining room. You, Esther, go to the family courtyard and see if there is damage. Nahum, you are bleeding. Sit here and let me clean it. Mistress Ruth, would you please hand me a clean cloth and the amphora of water?"

When she saw Mary, she gave a quick greeting and listened to her request. "It does not sound like a serious wound. Here," she said, piling a basket with cloths, a jar of ointment, and an amphora of water. "Clean the wound and apply some of this ointment to it. Then tie a cloth around his head. It would be best if Rabbi Nicodemus would lie down; head wounds bleed freely. However, I do not expect he will do that. As my grandmother—may her memory be blessed—used to say, 'Children and men never do what is best for them.'"

Elisheba proved right. After she tended his wound, Father

Nicodemus refused his bed. "I have a house full of people and I must check on them."

"Father," Michael said, "I will check on them."

"Of course you will, Son. With two of us, the task will be easier. As it is written in the Holy Word, *"Two are better than one, because they have a good return for their work."* Now Daughter," he turned towards her, "you look weary. Perhaps you should rest."

"Father is right, Beloved," Michael said. "You should go back to our room and lie down."

She shook her head. "I cannot. I am mistress of this house and it is my responsibility to oversee everything."

Mary worked through the night, tending to the injured, overseeing the clean-up, and helping Elisheba prepare food and drink for the household. As the sun rose the next morning, while the servants carried out baskets of debris, she went to the last place needing attention: Mother Hannah's garden.

She walked through the room, righting containers that had been overturned; stepping around those that had been broken, inspecting the plants. Several containers had fallen into the ornamental pool, leaving the water murky. Most of the clay containers had cracks, but it appeared the plants had suffered minor harm. It would take a while to know which plants would survive. The roses Michael had given her had lost several branches, but appeared to not sustain serious damage.

The pot with the jacinth seed had overturned, scattering some of its soil on the floor. Setting it upright, she saw that the container had not sustained any damage, but there was still no sign of the jacinth.

Is it dead, she smoothed a hand on her abdomen, *like our baby? Our baby,* her throat constricted as she blinked back tears. *Why did I survive, yet our baby died?*

"Mistress?"

She brushed away the tears before turning. Jemima was standing at the door of the room. The servant was disheveled; all in the house had worked through the night. Mary stretched her mouth into a thin smile. "Yes, Jemima? What is it?"

"A message arrived from your cousin, Rebeca." She extended a scroll.

"My cousin?" Mary frowned as she took the rolled parchment from the servant. Rebeca could neither read nor write. Her father—*Never again will I acknowledge him as my kin*—had proclaimed he would not waste coin on teaching a *woman* those skills. "Thank you, Jemima. When you have finished your work, please go to your bed and rest."

"Thank you, mistress," she bowed her head and left.

Mary walked to the far side of the room where the sunlight was streaming through the window and unrolled the scroll. The handwriting was bold, not at all what she would expect from a woman. She read:

Greetings Cousin. I hope that you and your household did not suffer during last night's earthquake.

Forgive the lie; I told the messenger to say it was from my sister as I knew you would refuse anything from me.

I arrived home last night. Please come to our house. I wish to see you, to speak with you. I have news you would wish to hear.

Abel ben Joktan

"See me?" Mary crushed the scroll and threw it down. "Well, I do *not* want to *see* him! There is nothing he could say that I want to hear." She stomped on the scroll. "He and his father were part of those who *crucified* the Lord Jesus." She twisted her foot, ripping the parchment. "He *stoned* Stephen ben Chariton." She kicked the shredded document into the pond. It floated for a moment before sinking beneath the murky waters. "His father *stoned* me and *killed my baby!*"

Wrapping her arms across her chest, she wailed, rocking back and forth. *My baby! My sweet, innocent baby! I will never hold my baby. Never watch my baby grow. Never hear that sweet laughter.*

She heard a sigh as wind blew in from the window. It set the leaves and petals of the plants dancing.

"Mary." The voice echoed softly around her.

Mary gasped. She *knew* that Voice. It was *Him.*

"Lord Jesus," she whispered.

"Mary, why are you weeping?"

"Lord, You know."

"Forgive them. Forgive Abel. Forgive Joktan."

Mary's eyes widened. *Forgive them?* She shook her head. "Lord, I cannot forgive *them*."

"Mary…there is no life in unforgiveness."

"He killed," her throat tightened, "my baby." She dissolved into tears.

"Mary."

A thrill shot through Mary. She knew the loving voice of her friend and Lord, and she was coming to know the comforting voice of the Holy Spirit. But this…this *Voice*…the room was filled with the weight of *Holy*.

Dropping to her knees, she touched her forehead to the floor. "Yahweh… Father."

"Speak what is in your heart."

"Yahweh," she filled her lungs, "Father. Why? Why did I lose my baby?"

"What I give is never lost." The wind blew across her prostrate body. *"Look."*

Straightening, Mary looked up…into the eyes of Jesus.

He was in the room, but He was on the cross.

She was remembering that day, but it was happening before her.

His face was covered in blood and bruises, His beard torn out by handfuls, His hair a bloodied mat from the crown of thorns forced over his brow.

He was looking at her, as He had on *that* day.

In His gaze, she saw pain and sadness, but she also saw the same *love* He had when he told her that she was worth so much more. When He told her that she was beloved of Yahweh. When He had told her that what she had done for him—anointing His feet with the spikenard from her alabastron—was *beautiful*.

"Mary," the voice of Yahweh spoke, *"what I give is never lost. What I use is never wasted."*

As the face of the Lord Jesus faded, the wind whispered, *"Trust Me."*

Chapter 62

*M*ichael was exhausted. The earthquake had sent a shock of energy pulsing through his body. That had been useful when he worked alongside his family and servants to restore their house. Now, he was spent. He had seen that his father was resting in his bed chamber and was wandering through the house searching for his wife. After looking in the *mikvahs,* their bed chamber, and the family courtyards, he walked down the corridor to the garden room.

The sun was glinting through the window, bathing everything with gold. Including his wife's prostrate body.

He smiled. *She has fallen asleep.* Although he had been concerned with her wishing to work last night—she was so frail—it encouraged him to see her supervising the clean up or tending to someone's wounds. *She was as she had been before…*he refused to finish that thought.

Stepping quietly to her, he knelt and laid a gentle hand on her shoulder. "Beloved," he whispered.

She straightened, and looked at him. There was no shadow of sleep or hint of fatigue in her countenance. She smiled at him; a joyous, peaceful smile.

"Michael, something *wonderful* just happened."

"Beloved, please tell me."

"I will," she took his hand and stood, "but later. Now we must change our garments and go."

"Go now?" He lifted an eyebrow. He was not about to deny *that smile* anything, but he could not imagine where she would want to go *now*.

"Yes, now." She patted the dirt and leaves off her garments and smoothed her hair. "We must go to my Aunt Naomi's house; to see my cousin Abel."

Chapter 63

"*I* had seen the Lord Jesus' face for so long," Abel said, "in my dreams, then on the faces of those who followed Him. I always thought He was angry at me, for not believing His teachings, and for my part in His…*crucifixion*. I thought that He…," he sighed, "hated me and wished me harm. I was afraid and did not want to see His face. I wanted to either run or to…*drive* the vision away."

He looked at his cousin, Mary, and her husband Michael ben Nicodemus. He had wondered whether she would come to his home, and would not have blamed her if she had refused. When he opened the door to their knock, he greeted them and added, "Cousin, I am sorry…for *all*—," when Mary stopped his words by throwing her arms around him.

"Abel, I forgive you, as the *Lord Jesus* forgave me."

He escorted them into the main room, where his mother and sister had food and drink prepared. While they ate, he told them about what had happened.

"Then, yesterday, on the slopes of Golgotha, when He appeared, I was too weary to resist any longer, even if it meant I would die. I looked into His face.

"The vision was the same as before, but what was different was *me*. I had no strength for hate or fear or fight. This time, I saw," he shrugged, shaking his head in wonder, "acceptance. I saw kindness. I saw," he smiled, "*love*. I realized I had never understood love, had never truly," his smile faded a bit, "experienced it." He filled his lungs, "But what I saw, that *love*, filled me with a freshness, as fresh as spring, as fresh as in the Garden where Yahweh walked with Adam and Eve."

"That is wonderful!" Mary looked from Abel, to her aunt and

Rebeca, and back to Abel. "It is what I had wished for, what I had prayed for. That you would know the love of the Lord Jesus. What about," she faltered and then lifted her chin, "my uncle? Have you told him?"

"I did," Abel's mouth turned down. "I went to the Valley of Hinnom the moment I left the slopes of Golgotha. I told him about the Lord Jesus and pleaded with him to believe. He was… furious…and demanded I renounce the Lord Jesus." He shook his head. "I refused. Nothing will make me renounce the Lord Jesus. *Nothing!*" He reached over and took his mother's hand. "We will continue praying for my father. Perhaps, one day…"

"Perhaps one day," Naomi and Rebeca repeated.

"Amen," Mary said.

The room was silent; then Michael spoke.

"And you say that Saul Paulus is now a believer?"

"Yes!" Abel smiled. He shared the story of what happened on the road to Damascus, of what happened three days later when the man Ananias came to the inn where they were staying. The scales falling away from Saul's eyes and the face of the Lord Jesus appearing over his face.

"The last thing I heard Saul Paulus say was, 'The Lord Jesus loves you!' And he was right!" Abel laughed. "He does love me! I hope you do not grow tired of me, Cousin, Michael. I wish to spend lots of time with you, hearing the stories of the Lord Jesus and learning about Him."

Mary laughed and laid a hand on Abel's arm. "We will never get tired of telling you about the Lord Jesus." She looked at her husband. "He has done so much for us."

"Amen," Michael smiled and looked at him. "Abel, what will you do now?"

He shrugged, spreading his hands wide. "I do not know. I cannot go back to finish my training at the Temple. Rabbi Gamaliel was kind to me, and I understand that he was responsible for sending money to Mother and Rebeca," he arched an eyebrow at Mary and Michael, "even though I have *no* idea why."

Mary looked away, while Michael grinned.

"Thank you," Abel smiled. "To go back to your question, I do not know what I will do. Being a priest at the Temple was what Father wanted and, because of him, what I wanted. I will have to learn a trade. In the meantime, there is, however, one thing I want to do," he filled his lungs. "I want to convince those who follow the Lord Jesus that I am one of them and they have nothing to fear from me. Will you help me?"

"Yes, of course we will," Michael smiled. "I will speak to Father. We will reach out to everyone and let them know."

"Thank you. Also," he paused, "I am not certain how to ask. Would you help me *pray* to the Lord Jesus and ask His guidance on what to do with my life and wisdom on how best I can serve Him?"

Chapter 64

"It was wonderful receiving letters from both Lazarus and Martha," Mary finished braiding her hair. "The courier found them quicker than I expected. They are pleased about our cousin."

Michael sat on the edge of their bed and removed his sandals. "I am surprised they believed Abel was now a follower of the Lord Jesus."

"To speak truth, I did not know if they would believe me when I wrote the letter." She picked up a cream linen night tunic and slipped it over her head. "Nor would I have blamed them if they did not. Since the day we met the Lord Jesus, my cousin," she paused, "and my uncle did not like Him, and questioned all of His words."

"Now, all Abel wishes to do is listen to all the Lord Jesus said and did." Michael pulled back the linens on their bed. "I am thankful John Mark ben Gershom wrote down the Apostle Peter's memories of the Lord. It makes it easier to share."

"I would love to have our own copy of Peter's memories," Mary plumped her pillow.

"That is a wonderful idea, Beloved," Michael slipped into the bed. "I will speak to Father about hiring a scribe to make a copy."

After Michael offered up prayers, she kissed him and settled her head in the hollow of his shoulder. "Mmmm…this is my favorite position to sleep."

He pulled her closer, "I agree, my Beloved. I missed having you in my embrace."

"I did as well, my Beloved. I will always grieve over the loss of our baby," she lifted her hand to wipe her eyes, "but I am thankful for the Lord's healing of my heart. For now, we must trust the Lord Jesus' promise that one day we will see our baby again."

She smiled and snuggled closer, slipping off to sleep.

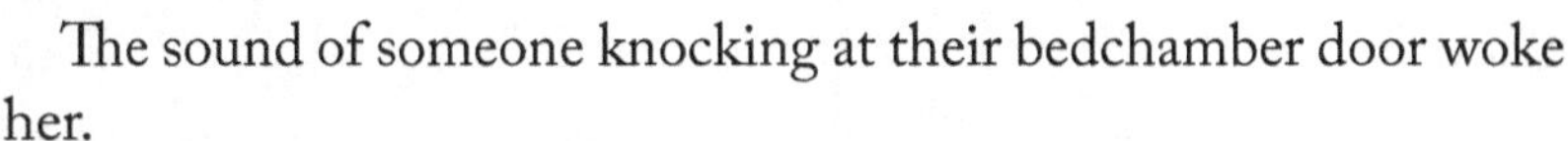

The sound of someone knocking at their bedchamber door woke her.

"Michael, Mary, wake up."

Michael sat up. "Father?" He swung out of bed and crossed the room.

Mary pulled on a robe and ran to open the shutters. The night sky was growing lighter.

Michael opened the door. "Father, what is it?"

She hurried to join her husband as her father-in-law stepped into the room.

Although it was not yet dawn, he was fully dressed. A frown creased his brow. "My children, I have news of concern."

"News?" she laid a hand on Michael's arm. "Father Nicodemus, what is it?"

"You must get dressed; both of you."

Michael looked at her and then at his father. "Father, what has happened?"

"A message arrived from Naomi bat Simeon."

"My aunt?" Mary rushed to get her clothes. "Is anyone ill?"

"No," he shook his head. "It is Abel." He filled his lungs. "Two Temple Guards arrived at your aunt's house. Abel has been summoned by the High Priest."

She froze in mid-stride.

"Caiaphas?" Michael gaped. "What does he want with Abel at this hour?"

"I do not know," Father Nicodemus frowned. "But any summons by Caiaphas ben Joseph after the sun has set never portends anything good."

"I will go to my aunt's house," Mary said.

"There is no need," her father-in-law said. "I sent Daniel to bring your aunt and Rebeca here. Daughter, you and Ruth will act as hostesses. After what happened the night the Lord Jesus was arrested, it is best to lean towards caution. Even Caiaphas would not harm anyone under the shelter of our roof."

"I will go with you to the Temple." Michael strode across the room to pull on his clothes.

"*I* will go to the Temple," Mary's father-in-law said. "*You* will go to Caiaphas' house. If Abel is not there, go to the house of Annas ben Seth. From what Naomi bat Penuel said, the Temple Guard did not indicate where they were taking Abel. It will be best if we take all precautions."

Chapter 65

*T*he clouds bled pale morning light as Abel and the two Temple Guards reached the house of the High Priest. It seemed surreal to him that, the other time he had been here, was the night the Lord Jesus had been arrested.

Located in the Essene Quarter, it was more palace than mere residence. A fortified dwelling, there were turreted sentry watch-towers on the outer wall, and barracks for the guards who protected the High Priest.

They passed the small garden where Abel and his father had met with the High Priest. He noted the oleander and cascading roses were flowering as they had been on the night Caiaphas had instructed them what to say during their *testimony* of the Lord Jesus.

It had been a mock trial, he thought. *All the witnesses—including Father and me—had spoken lies.*

The Guards led him past courtyards, public rooms, gardens, and ceremonial *mikvahs* for the officers, attendants, and tax collectors of the High Priest. Walking down a corridor, they turned into a room.

"Stop. Wait here," one of the Guards said. "I will inform Rabbi Caiaphas of our arrival." He nodded to the other Guard, who moved to stand in the doorway, his hand on the hilt of a sword.

Abel tried to ignore the Guard and turned to look around the room. Smaller than the Chamber of Hewn Stones, the walls were bare and there were no rugs on the floor. A single stone bench and table was placed beneath the far window. Two lamps on stands were placed on either side of the room. While the chamber was not designed for the comfort of guests and dignitaries, Abel breathed a prayer of thanksgiving that he was meeting the High Priest here and not in one of the underground interrogation chambers or in a cell for prisoners.

Although I might end up there.

He had no doubt about the purpose of this *meeting*. He had known it was only a matter of time before word got back to the High Priest that Saul Paulus had abandoned the commission to seek the followers of the Lord Jesus. Abel had no illusions about *his own* importance to Caiaphas, but he was the one connection to the Tarsuian Jew.

As the time passed and he had not heard from the Temple, he had begun to think perhaps the High Priest had turned his attention to other matters. Abel had relaxed and learned to enjoy life. He spent time with Rabbi Nicodemus and Michael, learning more about the Lord Jesus. His cousin Lazarus had sent him a letter, giving praise to Yahweh for Abel following the Lord Jesus and offered him the position of working at their warehouse. For the first time in his life, he was able to support his family on money he had *earned*.

Ironically, it also allowed him to care for his father. Shortly after that day when he had told his father about following the Lord Jesus, the man Itamar had showed up at his house. He handed him a note from his father, demanding Abel renounce the Lord Jesus. It also said his scribe would come for his daily provisions and the money they needed.

Abel had smiled wryly as he handed the man the provisions. *Father refuses to have anything to do with me, yet he still wants my coin.*

Since then, this man or his son had showed up each day, to leave letters filled with his father's blistering condemnation and demands and to take a basket filled with food, clothing, and other supplies.

From the first, he had thought it a waste of coin for his father to have a courier; now he saw some value in having a personal messenger. As it was, when the Temple Guard demanded he accompany them, Abel had hugged his mother and sister, assuring them he would be alright and whispering to get word to Rabbi Nicodemus and tell him what had happened.

The sounds of sandals on stone drew him out of his thoughts. Turning, he watched as the Guard stepped aside and bowed his head as the High Priest entered the room. His father-in-law, Annas ben Seth, was at his side, and a dozen other men dressed in priestly garments followed them. One man carried a roll of parchment and the tools of a scribe.

Caiaphas and Annas were considered the most powerful men among the Jewish people, yet it was obvious who held greater power. When they crossed the floor to the stone bench, the older man sat, nodding his head to where his son-in-law should stand.

While the other priests positioned themselves on either side of the stone bench, and the scribe prepared his implements, the High Priest and his father-in-law studied him beneath lowered brows.

There had been a time when Abel would have not even met the eyes of these two men; but he found he was no longer afraid of them. Lifting his chin, he calmly returned their gaze. Yet, he knew this summons was not a matter to take lightly. *Lord Jesus, be with me. Let me know what to say.*

Caiaphas opened his mouth, but Annas spoke first. "Abel ben Joktan, you are back in Jerusalem and yet you have not reported to us. Why?"

"I…uh…have nothing to report, sir."

"Where is Saul Paulus?"

"Sir, I do not know. The last I saw him was in Damascus."

"Why are you not with him?"

"Sir, I felt it best to…ah…part ways with him."

Annas *harrumphed.*

The High Priest finally spoke. "I gave you and Saul Paulus a commission that had two parts. First; you were to arrest the *racha* people who are members of The Way. From the number of prisoners you and Saul sent back to Jerusalem, it appeared you did that task.

"Yet, we," he gestured to his father-in-law, "were more concerned with the second part; to find where these people had hidden the body of the Nazarene criminal, Jesus ben Joseph. Did you do that?"

Abel smiled. *There is no body because You, Lord Jesus, are alive.* "No."

His vision exploded from the slap of the Temple Guard nearest him.

"You will speak with respect to Rabbi Caiaphas!"

Abel wiped blood from his mouth. "No, sir. We did not find the body of the Nazarene."

"Yet you returned to Jerusalem. Again I ask; why?"

Lord Jesus, help me choose my words. "Sir, I returned to my home, to care for my mother and sister."

"And your father? I understand you have been providing food and clothing for your father."

Abel lowered his brows, looking between the High Priest and his father-in-law. *How would he know that?* "Yes, sir," He stretched out the word. "I have."

"Caring for your parent, even one who is afflicted with leprosy, shows honor and respect for the Law of Yahweh." Caiaphas spread his lips in a thin smile. "As does *obeying* one's parents, would you agree?"

Abel nodded; his mouth dry.

"Then, perhaps you will understand our," he glanced at his father-in-law again, "*concern* to receive this letter." He reached into his girdle and pulled out a scroll. He unrolled it slowly. "The man who delivered it was strange. He was obviously crippled, yet he claimed he was employed as a *scribe* to," he looked at Abel, "your *father.*"

Abel fought to keep his expression blank. "My father sent a message to you, sir?"

Caiaphas nodded. "He did. He was quite concerned over you, as a good father would be. I must confess, after reading it, I can understand his concern."

Abel swallowed. "What was my father's concern?"

Caiaphas scanned the parchment. "Hear his message:

'To Caiaphas ben Simon, High Priest of the Holy Temple of Yahweh, from Joktan ben Philemon.

Sir, My son has fallen away from my training and from the teachings of the Holy Scriptures. He has become a follower of the Nazarene, Jesus ben Joseph.

A gasp rippled through the room. A few of the priests took a step away from Abel, as if in the presence of a leper. Caiaphas continued reading:

When I learned of it, I demanded he renounce this man and plead with Yahweh for forgiveness for his blasphemy. He refused and continues in his sinful ways.

Rabbi Caiaphas, I am demanding my right according to the Law of Moses. The Law allows a father of a rebellious son to bring him before the elders of the town. I cannot come into the city, but I am demanding you summon him to appear before you. If he does not repent, then I demand that the Law be followed, and my son be stoned.'

Abel's heart beat wildly. *Father, what have you done?*

Caiaphas rolled the scroll up and handed it to the scribe. "Abel ben Joktan, is your father speaking truth? Are you a follower of The Way?"

Abel nodded. "I am."

"After all you did to see that this man, this Nazarene, was arrested and crucified, you *follow* him?"

"Abel lifted his head, "I do."

"Why?"

"Because," Abel smiled, "the Lord Jesus is the *Messiah*, the Son of Yahweh.

"You," he pointed at the High Priest, "and you," he pointed at Annas, "and you," he pointed towards the other men in the room, "hated the Lord Jesus."

The room was silent as he continued. "You conspired to kill Him. You," he pointed towards Caiaphas, "gave Judas Iscariot thirty pieces of silver to betray the Lord Jesus. I was in the garden the night He was arrested, when He *healed* your servant. You put Him on trial, bringing in false witnesses, including my father," he swallowed, "and me. You had the Roman governor flog Him and demanded that He be crucified.

"I was there," he pointed towards the outer wall, "on Golgotha. I was there that whole day, from the time the Roman soldiers," he swallowed, "drove *nails* into His hands and feet. I was there while He hung on that cross, while people—including my father—insulted Him and laughed at His suffering.

"I was there for those long hours until He…*died*. I know He was buried in Rabbi Joseph bar Neriah's tomb. But," he smiled, "He did not stay in the grave. Three days later, He rose from the dead! For the next forty days, He was seen by hundreds of people, before He ascended into Heaven. That is why you cannot find the Lord Jesus' body."

Abel lifted his hands, looking upward. "He is *alive* and seated on the right hand of His Father Yahweh."

Abel drew a deep breath, smiling. He felt as if the warmth of the sun was racing through his veins. He heard a still, small voice whisper in his ear, *"Well done."*

"Blasphemy."

Abel lowered his gaze.

Annas was standing, his arms rigid, his fists balled. "Blasphemy!" He screamed. "You *dare* to name this *man* as the Son of Yahweh?" He lifted a hand to point at him. "Think carefully, Abel ben Joktan, before you respond. Your own words have the power of your life or your death. Obey your father and renounce this blasphemy. Are you willing to *die* for this man? Think carefully."

Die for Him? For the Man Who transformed my mother and sister from cowering mice into strong, peace-filled women? The One Who took away my fear and gave me peace? The One Who showed me that I am loved?

All of this passed through his mind in the time it took Abel to shake his head. "No."

He drew his lips into a thin line. "There is nothing to *think* about. Neither my words—nor anyone's words—have the power of life and death over me. Only Yahweh and His beloved Son, the Lord Jesus." He filled his lungs. "I will not renounce Him! I will *die* for Him! He died for me, because He loves me! He loves me!"

Annas lifted his hands to grasp the neckline of his tunic. "Blasphemy!" He pulled, ripping the fabric and exposing his chest. "By his own words he had confessed to blasphemy!" He turned to his son-in-law and those in the room. "What say you?"

As one, the High Priest and the other men ripped their garments, screaming, "Blasphemy!"

Turning to the Temple Guards, Caiaphas said, "Take the blasphemer to the Kidron Valley," he looked at Abel, "to be stoned."

Chapter 66

"*H*urry, Daniel! We must reach the Kidron Valley before that," Michael spit, "*racha* High Priest has Abel stoned."

"Yes, sir." The servant slapped the reins over the horses' rumps.

Michael held on to the seat as the carriage bounced and careened through the streets of Jerusalem. He ignored the startled, angry faces of the people jumping out of the way of the thundering hoofs. "Yahweh, Lord Jesus; be with Abel," he prayed.

After Michael had seen his father off in one of their other carriages, he had waited until Daniel returned with Mary's aunt and cousin. Helping the two women down, he handed them over to Mary before climbing up next to the driver. "Pray," he said to the women. "I will send word when I can."

Their home was in the Upper City, where most homes of the wealthy were located. It was not far from the Essene Quarter. Soon, he was stepping down in front of the home of the High Priest.

He was not surprised to see Temple Guard standing on either side of the main door. Michael controlled his impulse to demand they tell him whether Abel was there, remembering something Elisheba had always told him, "When the kettle boils over, it overflows on its own sides." *It will not help Abel if I am arrested for trying to force my way into the house of the High Priest.*

He approached the Guard and nodded. "Greetings. I am Michael ben Nicodemus."

Normally he was hesitant to flaunt his family's position and power; yet there were times when mentioning his father's name carried weight. This was one of those times. The two Guards glanced at each other. "Greetings," the one on the right side of the door said. "We know of your honored father."

"I am looking for my wife's kinsman, Abel ben Joktan. I was told he might be here."

The guards looked at each other, the respect in their gaze dimming. "He was here," the second Guard said.

"*Was* here?" Michael looked from one man to the other. "He has left?"

"He did indeed," the first Guard spoke. "He left with a group of priests."

"A group of priests?" Michael asked. *That does not portend good news.* "Do you know where they have gone?"

The two Guards exchanged glances again before looking at him. They grinned. "To the Kidron Valley."

Michael's eyes widened. Turning, he ran up the path, the guards' laughter chasing him. He leapt into the carriage. "Go!" He told Daniel. "To the Kidron Valley."

"Please, Lord Jesus, no!" he prayed. "Save Abel! Help us get there soon! Protect Abel!" With each bump of the carriage on the road, he continued praying. "Save Abel! Get us there! Help Abel!" As he called out to the Lord, he fought back the memories of that horrible day at the Kidron Valley. *Surely the Lord would not let this happen again.*

Yet, as the carriage shot through the Water Gate, the echo of shrieks reached them. *No! Lord, not again! Help Abel!*

Arriving on the edge of the ravine, the nightmare before him was the same. Directed by Caiaphas and Annas, the priests screamed like blood-thirsty hyenas as they scurried to find rocks, ran to the edge, and threw it at a man in the valley.

At Abel. His wife's kinsman. His new brother in the Lord Jesus. His friend.

"No!" Michael jumped from the moving carriage, grunting as he hit the ground. Rolling over, he pushed himself up and ran to the nearest man and knocked the rock from his hand. "No!" He turned and slammed his shoulder into another man. "Stop!" Reaching the edge of the valley, Michael felt as if someone had punched him in the stomach.

There was Abel, covered in blood, bones protruding through rents in his clothing. He moaned as each stone slammed into his body.

"Stop!" Caiaphas ben Simon walked to the edge of the ravine. "Abel ben Joktan, do you renounce the blasphemer, Jesus ben Joseph?"

Abel winched as he drew breath. "No," he wheezed through bruised lips and broken teeth. "I do not. I will *never* renounce the Lord Jesus."

"Stone him!" a voice screamed from behind Michael. He whirled around to see a man—dressed in rags, his face covered—standing at the far back of the crowd. He held a large stone. "He is stubborn and refuses to obey me! You must stone him; it is my right! Stone him and purge the evil from among us! Stone the blasphemer!"

The crowd scattered screaming, "Leper!" as Joktan ran to the edge of the ravine.

"Stone him!" he threw the stone, hitting Abel squarely in the face.

Blood spurted from his nose and mouth. He groaned as he righted himself. Lifting a hand to wipe the blood from his eyes, he looked up at Joktan. "Father," he groaned, "I forgive you." Looking at the people gathered on the edge of the ravine, he called out, "Lord Jesus, do not hold this against these people." Then he looked at Michael. And smiled.

Michael gulped back tears as he looked at Abel; just as he had looked at Stephen. While he stared, Abel's face faded and was replaced by the countenance of Jesus, covered in blood, wearing a crown of thorns. After a moment, the vision faded, to be replaced by the bloody face of Abel. Heart pounding, Michael clinched his fists and, filling his lungs, smiled at his brother and friend.

Abel nodded. Grimacing, he shifted his body to lift his broken hands towards the sky. "Lord Jesus, receive my spirit!" and slumped to the ground. His cry echoed around the Kidron Valley and then faded away on a soft breeze.

Laughter erupted.

Michael turned to see Joktan clapping his hands.

"Abel, where is your Jesus now?" The leper began dancing around the edge of the ravine, his filthy rags swaying. "You cried out to the blasphemer, but Jesus could not help you." He twirled, "Because he is dead! Dead!" He picked up one last rock and threw it at the body of Abel. "Just like you are dead!" Turning, he ran away from the ravine.

Michael watched as Joktan ran up to the city wall and turn southward; towards the Hinnom Valley. As he ran, he laughed and screamed. "He's dead! The blasphemer is dead!"

Rage raced through Michael's veins. He clinched his hands, imagining how *good* it would feel to smash Joktan's pompous face. The man who had been responsible for the death of the Lord Jesus, who had killed Abel. The *racha man* who had stoned his beloved Mary and killed their baby.

Kill him! He ground his teeth.

"Sir?"

Michael turned to see Daniel.

The servant looked at the priests—who were gathered in small groups, talking and pointing at the leper—and stepped closer. He lowered his voice. "Sir, what do you want to do?"

Michael looked at the body of his friend. He turned and grasped his servant's arm. "Daniel, go and find my father. Tell him what has happened. Help him bury Abel's body."

"Sir, where are you going?"

Michael looked at the receding figure of Joktan and then at his servant. "Avenger of blood," he growled.

It was an old practice, from the days when the Jewish people first received the Law Yahweh gave to Moses. *"If a man schemes and kills another man deliberately, take him away from My altar and put him to death."* It allowed for a kinsman to avenge the death of a family member. Another law stated if a man hit a pregnant woman and she gave birth prematurely, the offender would be fined whatever the woman's husband demanded. *"...you are to take life for life..."* It was an old practice, but Michael knew no one would deny his right to kill Joktan. And he wanted to *kill* Joktan.

He ran up the hill towards the city walls and turned south, following the leper.

He knew Joktan dwelt among the lepers in the Valley of Hinnom, but he did not know exactly *where*. He was *not* going to lose him.

"'Take him away from My altar and put him to death,'" he panted, jumping over a rock. "'Life for life.'"

Joktan glanced back as he reached the corner of the city walls. His eyes widened when he saw Michael. He turned and ran.

Michael picked up speed, the thirst for vengeance pumping through his body. He turned the corner of the city walls—cutting his hands, arms, and legs—as he slid down the steep ravine, following the murderous leper into the Valley of Hinnom.

He had heard about the horrors of the valley, but rage pushed away revulsion and compassion. He ran past the poor and lepers, dodging the burning mountains of refuse, kicked feral cats or wild dogs out of his way, all the while keeping his eyes on Joktan. With each step, he remembered seeing Daniel carrying his beloved Mary in, bloodied and near death. He recalled the heart-wrenching pain of learning she had been with child and, because of that murdering *racha*, had lost their baby. "'Life for life.'" Pausing to pick up a thick branch, Michael took aim and threw it, hitting Joktan between his shoulders. The leper stumbled and fell.

Joktan grabbed the branch and scrambled to stand. He turned, holding the limb as a weapon.

Michael ran up and knocked it out of the leper's hands. He kicked Joktan's knees.

The leper fell with a scream.

Michael picked up the cudgel.

"Stop!" Joktan cried. "Abel was my son. He disobeyed me. You cannot do this!"

"I have the right! You attacked my wife. You killed our unborn baby. I am the Avenger of Blood." He raised the club over his head.

"What would your *Lord Jesus* say?"

Michael froze. "What?"

"Abel told me he was supposed to forgive as the Nazarene would." Joktan coughed. "Are you not also to forgive as *he* did?"

Michael's gaze turned inward. He was standing beneath a cross. He had spent hours listening to people lie about the Lord Jesus, watched the Roman soldiers flog Him, heard Pontius Pilate pronounce the sentence of crucifixion. He had followed as the Lord

Jesus dragged that rough cross through the streets of Jerusalem to Golgotha, where the soldiers drove nails through the His hands and feet and left Him to die between two brigands. Michael, along with Mary and others, had stood at the foot of the cross. Joktan had mocked him and the soldiers had gambled for His clothing.

After speaking comfort and the promise of paradise to one of the brigands dying next to Him, the Lord Jesus had turned and looked at Michael.

His throat tightened, fighting tears, as he remembered looking at the Lord Jesus. He remembered the sadness and the pain he saw in His face, but there was something more. He saw *acceptance*. He saw *acceptance*, he saw *strength*, he saw *determination*, he saw *trust*. Michael remembered committing to follow the Lord Jesus' teaching. Before He died, the Lord Jesus had asked Yahweh to forgive those who were crucifying Him. Stephen had asked the same, as had Abel not an hour before.

Michael's gaze focused on the leper cowering before him. *"Are you not also to forgive?"* he had asked.

Michael lowered his arms. "Yes," he dropped the club, "I am also to forgive as the Lord Jesus forgave. Joktan ben Philemon, I forgive you for what you did to my wife and," he swallowed, "to our baby." He turned to walk away. He had not gone more than a dozen cubits when he heard laughter. He turned.

"You are *racha*," Joktan laughed, using the club to push himself upright. "Just like that *racha* son of mine. Just like *all* the *racha* blasphemers who follow the Nazarene." He dropped the club and bent down to scoop up several stones. He threw one. "You cannot do anything!" He threw another. "You have to *forgive* me, just like the," he laughs, pitching his voice high, "the *Lord Jesus* would!"

Michael watched Joktan bend over, rocking and laughing, and straightening to point at him.

"Just as the Lord Jesus—*ahhh!*" the leper gasped as he stepped back onto the club. Arms waving to regain his balance, he stepped on a stone, twisted his foot, and stumbled beside a burning mound of refuse. A spark flickered against his dry-rotted rags, smoldered, then burst forth into a brilliant flame. Joktan stared, a look of curious amusement crossing his face, before being replaced with stark terror. "*AAAAAiiiiiii! Help me!*"

"Joktan!" Michael sped back. He circled the fire, reaching in and dodging the flames several times before grabbing the edge of Joktan's garment. He pulled, but fell backwards as the fabric gave away. He scrabbled up, but it was too late.

Michael's mouth fell open in horror as he watched the flames race up Joktan's old rags, hungrily consuming them before feasting on his flesh. The leper opened his mouth, but no sound escaped. First the tufts of his beard ignited, then what was left of his hair became a torch, embers bursting into the sky above his head, before Joktan ben Philemon collapsed into a burning mound.

The sun was climbing in the sky when the flames died down, black flakes carried away on the wind.

Michael looked around, disoriented from shock. He knew he had come from the east and the—he swallowed—the Kidron Valley. He turned towards the other direction, where home—where *Mary*—waited.

He stepped carefully, giving wide berth to the heaps of burning refuse. He stopped when he heard howls and squawks of feral dogs and carrion eaters. Unwrapping his girdle, he stooped to pick up several large rocks and tied them into the center of the fabric. He continued walking, swinging the weighted cloth in front of him as a weapon. He had reached the slope of the ravine when a different sound froze his steps.

A baby crying.

"No!" he shook his head. "I cannot be hearing things as Mary did. I cannot be losing my mind." He took another step and heard it again. Closer. He stopped and turned slowly, straining to listen.

A wail.

He turned his head. *There.* A large rock several cubits away. *The sound came from there.* Lifting his weapon, he placed his feet quietly as he crossed to the rock. Leaning over, he glanced beyond the rock to see…

…a baby.

Michael gaped.

Naked, eyes shut against the sunlight, the infant girl cried, waving her tiny arms and legs.

Dropping to his knees, he slipped his hands beneath the babe. "Shhhhhh," he cooed, picking her up. He glanced over the baby's body; he could see nothing wrong with her. He had heard stories of Roman soldiers leaving their malformed children to die exposed to the elements and predators. He frowned; this baby had not been abandoned because of any defect or deformity, but because she was female. *She would have died if I had not followed Joktan to the Valley of Hinnom*, his eyes widened, *to kill him. Lord Jesus, what just happened?*

The babe whimpered.

"Shhhh, little one," Michael whispered. "Do not worry." Lifting her to his chest, he wrapped his robe around her tiny body. He caught his breath when she reached a tiny hand out and grasped his hand.

"I have you." He rocked her gently, humming wordlessly, until her cries stilled.

Chapter 67

*M*ary softly closed the door to the guest chamber. Her heart was heavy with Father Nicodemus' news of Abel's death. *Welcome my cousin into Your Presence, Lord Jesus.* She sat with her aunt and Rebeca, holding them while they wept, praying with them, urging them to partake of the food Elisheba had prepared. Although it was after midday, they had been awake since the previous night and had finally succumbed to exhaustion. She covered them with a linen sheet and walked silently out of their room. Michael had not yet returned. *He must be helping Father Nicodemus and Daniel to bury Abel.*

She walked through the corridors, pausing to speak to the servants busily cleaning. She had grown up desiring a rich house with many servants. Now that she had that, she realized the responsibility, not for the possessions; but for the people.

People. When all else was gone, it was the people who mattered most. Friends. Family. Her husband.

A sad smile hovered around her mouth at the thought of Michael. His love and care for her, especially since that day in the Valley of Hinnom. His gentle urging that she eat, never chiding her for her constant sorrow, for spending hours sleeping, and not taking up her responsibilities as mistress of the house. He never blamed her for her actions that led to the loss of their babe.

Her eyes misted as she smoothed the fabric over her flattened stomach. *May your memory be blessed, my little one. One day I will see you again.* She would never forget that she had been a mother, yet the overwhelming sorrow was gone.

Passing a window, she noticed the gloom had lifted, and the flecks of golden sunshine mingled with the few wispy clouds in the sky. Adar was her favorite month of the year, when the winter was over and the branches on the trees turned that special green only seen in spring. That was why she loved tending the garden in her family's home in Capernaum and now in Mother Hannah's garden; she loved watching for the signs of rebirth.

In fact, that is just what I need right now.

Turning down a corridor, she passed several rooms to the courtyard garden.

This room held many memories for her. As children, she and Ruth had played in here. On the night the Lord Jesus was crucified, she had come here, as had the Lord's mother. It was here she had held the older woman, listening as she poured out her grief over the loss of her son. After her marriage to Michael, caring for the plants in this room had become her respite.

The room had been restored from the earthquake; the ornamental pond had been cleaned and new containers awaited soil and seed. Moving among the surviving containers, she noted most of the plants were bare stalks; it was too early for many of them to awaken from their winter's sleep.

The wind blew in through the window, filling the room with a soft fragrance. Mary lifted her head and sniffed, trying to identify its source. She knew it was not the lilies; she had just passed them. *Rose?* She crossed to the containers that held her roses. There were swellings on the stalks, where leaves would form, but they held no blossoms. She lifted her nose and sniffed again. It was a heavy, sweet fragrance. *It smells like…* Her eyes widened. Lifting the hem of her tunic, she hurried down the row of roses to the container covered by a tall fern. Lifting the frond, she gasped.

In the center of a container, long, narrow leaves curved gracefully away from tall spires of clustered purple-blue blossoms.

"My jacinth!" She laughed, clapping her hands. Bending over, she buried her nose in the heady, sweet fragrance. She touched the blossoms, marveling at their softness.

Suddenly, a sound froze her hand.

The wail of a baby.

She shook her head, her heart pounding. *It cannot be. The nightmares are gone. Lord Jesus, please!*

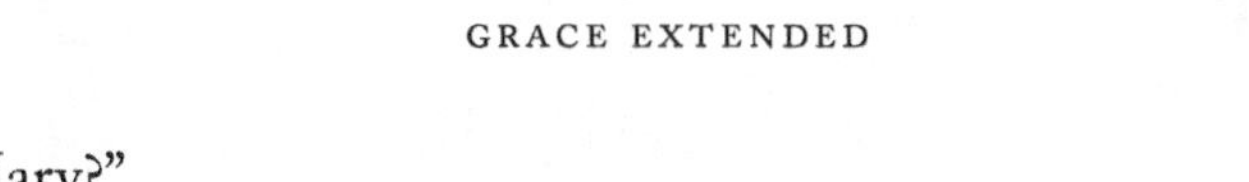

"Mary?"

Spinning, she saw Michael in the doorway. He was dirty, and there were dark spots on his garments. He held his arm against his chest, his robe covering it.

"Michael, are you alright?"

He nodded, his eyes wide. "I am."

She took a step towards him. "Michael, I heard…" she swallowed, "a baby crying."

"I know." He moved his robe. Lying in the crook of his arm was a babe. She squirmed and whined.

Mary crossed to her husband and took the babe, lifting the child against her shoulder. She felt the baby nuzzle the base of her neck. "Shhhhhh….it is alright." The infant smelled of dirt and smoke. "Michael, whose child is this?"

"She is ours."

"Ours?" She frowned. "What do you mean?"

"I found her—in the Valley of Hinnom."

She listened wide-eyed as Michael told her what happened between himself and her uncle. "I followed Joktan to the Valley of Hinnom, intent on death; but Yahweh," he lifted a finger to stroke the baby's cheek, "intended I find…life."

"You mean, she is truly," she blinked back tears, "ours?"

Michael nodded, the muscles in his throat working. "What shall we name her?"

Mary looked at the babe in her arms, and then at her husband. "Hannah."

Postscript

Capernaum, Four years later

"Hannah bat Michael, do not go into the lake!"

The young girl turned to wave, her long dusky curls blowing in the wind. "Yes, Mother!" She skipped along the edge of the water.

Jemima shook her head. "That child should have been born a fish!"

"You speak truth!" Mary laughed. "But I cannot blame her. I loved playing in the lake when I was her age."

The servant lifted her eyebrows. "You played in the Lake of Galilee when you were four years old?"

Mary nodded her head. "I did indeed. Every summer when my mother and father brought us here, I spent as much time as I could in the lake or in my mother's garden." She looked around, shaking her head. "Even after all these years, I still cannot believe what Michael did."

"Did I hear my name?"

Mary turned to see her husband step onto verandah. "You did," she smiled.

"Good morning, sir," Jemima bowed her head. "Mistress Mary, I must check on the bread."

"Thank you, Jemima."

"I hope you are also preparing some oat and honey cakes," Michael grinned

"I am making them now, sir." She nodded her head again and went into the house.

Crossing the blue-tiled floor, Michael bent over to kiss Mary. "How are you feeling, Beloved?"

"Better, thank you."

He laid a hand on the gold linen tunic covering her swelling abdomen. "Has the nausea settled?"

"Somewhat," she cupped her hand over his. "Jemima and I planted more mint, just in case."

"That is wise." He laughed and sat down on the bench next to her. Closing his eyes, he filled his lungs. "Ahhh…. I will never grow tired of this!"

"I agree. I was just telling Jemima I still cannot believe that you bought the house from Lazarus as a gift for me."

He smiled. "I knew how much you love this house."

"But I love our home in Jerusalem, with Father Nicodemus."

"But this house holds happy memories of your family, your parents. Speaking of family, it was wonderful to get letters from both Lazarus and Martha."

She nodded. "It was thoughtful of Rabbi Joseph ben Neriah to bring their letters when he returned to Jerusalem. While I am pleased Martha and Simon are happy and sharing the message of the Lord Jesus, I am sad they decided to stay in Gaul. I would love to see them and their children."

"Perhaps we can travel to Gaul someday to visit them." Michael lifted an amphora to pour milk into two cups. He handed one to Mary. "Or we could go to Cyprus and see Lazarus and Abigail and their family.

"Thank you." She took a sip. "I would love to go," she patted her stomach, "later. I was surprised to hear that Lazarus is leader of the believers there." She laughed. "Imagine, my brother, a priest!"

"I agree!" He grinned. "And Martha's news of your cousin's betrothal was a surprise."

"It was!" She smiled. "Who would have thought timid little Rebeca would marry? I am so happy for her. And for my Aunt Naomi. How kind of Simon and Martha to invite my aunt and cousin to live with them. Even as followers of the Lord Jesus, my aunt and cousin had so many unhappy memories in Jerusalem."

"Mother! Father!"

She looked up to see Hannah running up the path, her hands cupped. "What do you have?"

Hannah jumped across the marble floors and opened her hands. "Look! Shells!"

"They are beautiful," Mary hugged her daughter. *My daughter!* "Just as you are."

"Mother!" the child huffed. "I am not a shell!"

"No, but they are like you because they were—"

"—created and loved by Yahweh!" Hannah finished. "You say that all the time!"

"Because it is true!" Mary smiled.

"Mistress," Jemima walked through the door of the house, a small boy in her arms. "He woke up."

"Here," Michael extended his arms, "let me take my son. Come here, Abel."

"Fodder, Muffer," the little boy said. "I thirsty."

"Oh, poor baby." Mary poured milk into another cup and held it against her son's lips. "Here, drink this."

The boy drank the milk and then laid his curly black hair against his father's chest. Sticking a finger into his mouth, he closed his eyes.

Michael kissed the top of the toddler's head. He filled his lungs and looked at Mary. "This. This is life. We are blessed."

Mary's eyes misted. "You speak truth." She looked from her daughter, to her husband, to the child in his lap, "The Lord Jesus has indeed blessed us." Her eyes misted. "I do not understand all that has happened to us, to our family and friends. I do not know what the future holds for us. But I do know the Lord Jesus will be with us, and He will make everything beautiful."

Author's Notes

 hen I read stories in the Bible, I wonder about how or why the people said or did certain things. How did Noah gather the animals into the ark? Why would Rebekah and Isaac favor one son over the other? Why did Balak not run screaming in terror when the donkey spoke to him? What did Peter think when he was walking on the water? Who could afford perfume that cost a year's wages? What was it like to see Lazarus walk out of his tomb or watch Jesus ascend into the clouds?

Perhaps because of their "moment in time" nature, the people in these Bible stories are often viewed as iconic figures on a stained-glass window. David was a courageous young boy. Solomon was the wisest of all. Peter was brash and impulsive. Judas was a traitor. Martha fretted over a meal while Mary sat peacefully at Jesus' feet. People misunderstood Who Jesus of Nazareth truly was.

But these people were more than a boy with five stones; a man with a floating zoo; parents who played favorites; a disciple who acted before thinking; a woman with an expensive bottle of cologne; or people following Jesus the Messiah. They had flaws and strengths, likes and dislikes, favorite foods, hopes and fears, pride and insecurities.

Just like us.

One reason I am drawn to writing biblical novels is that, for me, when I view these people as simple humans, when I research their time period and culture, the Bible stories come alive and I glimpse possible answers to some of my questions.

My original plan was to finish the *Sisters of Lazarus* series with *Glory Revealed*. After all, the characters watched Jesus ascend into the clouds. After the book released, I continued to hear from people wanting to know what happened to the characters or asking about certain story lines. That is when I realized I had not tied up all the loose ends, and the idea for *Grace Extended: Sisters of Lazarus, Book Three* was born.

The third—and final—book in the *Sisters of Lazarus* series begins on the Day of Pentecost, taking the characters through the events mentioned in the first nine chapters of the Book of Acts. All the characters you loved—and those that you hated—from *Beauty Unveiled* and *Glory Revealed* are in it, as well as a few new characters, including a foreign-born Jewish believer named Stephen.

Beyond the biblical stories, the *Sisters of Lazarus* books had underlying messages of our value being found in the fact that we are created and loved by God, or how we deal with our spontaneous acts of worship. *Grace Extended* examines the power of forgiveness and grace and the millennia—old question of why bad things happen to people who are trying to live good lives.

Part of the inspiration for this story came from a book, *The Way Back; How Christians Blew Our Credibility and How We Get it Back*, written by Phil Cooke and Jonathan Bock.

> *"Why did the Early Church succeed where we are failing? How did they transform the Western World in such a relatively short time? They did things that baffled the Romans. The Early Church didn't picket, they didn't boycott, and they didn't gripe about what was going on in their culture. They just did things that astonished the Romans. They took in abandoned babies. They helped the sick and wounded. They restored dignity to the slaves. They were willing to die for what they believed. After a while, their actions so softened the hearts of the Romans that the Romans wanted to know more about who these Christians were and who was the God they represented.*
>
> *The question is—what could our Christian community do today that would so astonished nonbelievers that they would be forced to reexamine what we believe and why we believe it?"*

Lovers of grammar will notice that, in some parts of this book,

I used the divine pronoun, while in other parts I did not. This was intentional. For those who do not know what I mean, the divine pronoun is any pronoun associated with God, Jesus, or the Holy Spirit. The AP Stylebook does not capitalize any divine pronouns; the Chicago Manual of Style does. In my personal writing I typically capitalize all divine pronouns. In this book, I took a different approach. If the person speaking was not a believer—Abel, Joktan, the High Priest, etc.—I did not capitalize the divine pronoun. If the person speaking was a believer—Mary, Martha, Michael, Nicodemus, the Disciples, etc.—I did capitalize the divine pronoun. It was a small way of expressing the believers' reverence for the Lord Jesus.

If you would like to learn more about the research I used for different aspects of this book, visit my website: www.paulakparker.com. Under the "Autographed Copies" menu, there is page for "Sisters of Lazarus Glossary, Useful Information, and Research."

Finally (and this is a big request), if you liked this story, would you consider leaving a review wherever you bought this book, or on your favorite social media platform? I love this story and want as many readers as possible to discover it, and your voice can help do that. Leave a review and tell a friend! Word-of-mouth is the best way to introduce this story to other readers.

Thank you, dear reader, for giving your time to read this book. Stories need an audience. It means a lot that you trusted me to entertain, and hopefully excite, you with this story.

Acknowledgements

I have a confession. I have read books and closed the cover without reading the author's acknowledgements. I didn't know the people and didn't care that they had any part in the creation of the book.

Now that I have been on the other side of the book creation process, I realize a book is one child that takes a village. The conception of the story might take place in the author's imagination, but it takes a team of behind-the-scene people to carry it through to the published state. Not to mention the author's family, who selflessly sacrificed so that he or she could craft their story.

Therefore, please take a moment to allow me to publicly acknowledge and thank these people.

Thank you to everyone who read *Sisters of Lazarus: Beauty Unveiled* and *Glory Revealed*, and then encouraged me to write the series' final book. Your enthusiasm, your kind comments, and readers' reviews were a blessing and balm to my heart. I wish I could list each of you by name, but alas, there is not sufficient space.

Thank you, Malcolm Down. Even though we no longer work together professionally, your belief in my writing and your comments made me realize that it was possible to finish the story that began with that first book.

Thank you, Rick Larson, for sharing information from your research about the *Star of Bethlehem* and the *Christ Quake*.

Thank you to those in my prayer group. Your encouraging words, prayers, and suggestions carried me through the valleys and hills of writing this novel.

Thank you, David and Dee Warren, for your friendship, your immense talent, and generous nature. My new head shot is amazing, and the book cover is simply breathtaking.

To my mother, Helen Jones, thank you for always believing in me and my ability, and for being one of my biggest fans. To Jean Parker, thank for your encouragement and for being the best mother-in-law ever.

To my children: Rachael, Anna, Joshua, Bethany and Mary; my three sons-in-law; Nathan, Billy, and John; and my grandchildren: Isabella, Penelope, Aubrey, Harrison, William, Charlotte, and Eleanor. You are everything I've ever prayed for and one of the reasons that I do what I do.

To Mike, my best friend, the father of my children, the best husband a woman could ever have, and now my publisher. Thank you for the love, support, encouragement, and courage to pursue our dreams and chart a course into untested waters.

Of course, I cannot end an acknowledgment page without thanking the One who loves me more than anyone in the world, Who sacrificed everything for me, Who daily reminds me that I am worth so much more, and Who holds my life in His hands; my Lord and Savior, Jesus Christ.

About the Author

*E*arly training in music and theater led Paula K. Parker to a life-long love for the arts. This passion eventually brought her to Nashville, Tennessee, where she—along with her writer husband, Mike—helped establish local community theaters, Carpenter's Playhouse and Springhouse Theatre Company.

Paula co-authored *YHWH: The Flood, The Fish & The Giant* and *YESHUA: The King, The Demon & The Traitor* with New York Times Best-selling novelist, GP Taylor, before penning her own bestselling novel, *Sisters of Lazarus: Beauty Unveiled*, and its sequel, *Glory Revealed: Sisters of Lazarus Book 2*.

An internationally acclaimed playwright, Paula has written numerous short sketches, one-acts and full-length plays, including *The Sam Jones Story*, a historical play commissioned by Nashville's Summer Lights Foundation, and her popular adaptations of several of Jane Austen's classic novels, including; *Jane Austen's Pride & Prejudice*, *Jane Austen's Sense & Sensibility* and *Jane Austen's EMMA*. To learn more about Paula and her writing, visit her online at www.PaulaKParker.com

Also available from

WordCrafts Press

Maggie's Song
  by Marcia Ware-Wilder

In Search of the Beloved
  by Marian Rizzo

Until Then
  by Gail Kittleson

The Mirror Lies
  by Sandy Brownlee

You've Got It, Baby!
  by Mike Carmichael

www.WordCrafts.net